Praise for *In Twilight's Shadow*

"Nonstop action, magic-laced suspense, and some sizzling sexual chemistry fuel *In Twilight's Shadow,* Patti O'Shea's best inventive paranormal romance."

—*Chicago Tribune*

"*In Twilight's Shadow* is a fresh and dark paranormal romance that should not be missed."

—*Romance Reviews Today*

"*In Twilight's Shadow* is a terrific new story from Patti O'Shea. She bats them out of the park, one after the other. This one will keep you on the edge of your seat and reading well into the night."

—*FreshFiction*

Praise for *In the Midnight Hour*

"Patti O'Shea is a voice and talent to be reckoned with. *In the Midnight Hour* is gripping and wonderful, everything paranormal should be."

—*Sherrilyn Kenyon*

Tor Books by Patti O'Shea

In the Midnight Hour
In Twilight's Shadow
Edge of Dawn

Edge of Dawn

Patti O'Shea

TOR®

paranormal romance

A TOM DOHERTY ASSOCIATES BOOK
NEW YORK

This is a work of fiction. All of the characters, organizations, and events portrayed in this novel are either products of the author's imagination or are used fictitiously.

EDGE OF DAWN

A Tor Book
Published by Tom Doherty Associates, LLC
175 Fifth Avenue
New York, NY 10010

www.tor-forge.com

Tor® is a registered trademark of Tom Doherty Associates, LLC.

ISBN 978-0-7653-6169-1

First Edition: July 2009

Printed in the United States of America

0 9 8 7 6 5 4 3 2 1

For my writing buddy, Melissa Lynn Copeland, who kept me sane and went above and beyond. Again. I couldn't do it without you. Also, thanks to my fabulous and supportive agent, Lucienne Diver; to Theresa Monsey for getting me on track; and to my parents for always being there for me.

I'd also like to express my appreciation to all the readers who've taken a chance on my stories. Thank you for letting me share them with you. If you'd like more information on my books or to sign up for my sporadic newsletter, please visit www.pattioshea.com

Edge of
Dawn

1

CHAPTER

Every step Logan took on the path eased his tension. Up here he didn't have to deal with his sisters; he didn't have to guard himself against a city full of humans and the press of their energy against his mind's protective barrier; and since his brother wasn't here, he didn't have to worry about Kel either.

There was still his job. Logan touched the cell phone at his waist. No troubleshooter could be out of touch without getting it cleared by the council, and because he wasn't sure what kind of service he'd have as he hiked up this mountain trail, he'd warned them. If they couldn't reach him normally, they'd use telepathy, but he was hoping for a quiet day.

Nature was cooperating. It was a perfect June afternoon. The sun was shining, the temperature hovered in the mid-seventies, and the most dangerous thing he'd run into was a grouse. Logan figured the bears and cougars should give him a wide berth, and if they didn't, he'd use his magic to transport them somewhere else.

If only it were that easy to get rid of the people out here with him. He'd passed a few groups earlier and the fact that they were behind him kept him from completely relaxing.

Sometimes Logan wondered if wariness of humans was hardwired into the Gineal. It wasn't as if he didn't understand that there were good and bad people, and he'd never had any kind of run-in that would account for his distrust, but it was there anyway.

The narrow trail took him up the slope, past wildflowers and fallen trees bleached ash gray by the sun. Logan breathed deeply, soaking in the clean air, but he didn't stop walking—not until he rounded the bend. Through a break in the pines, he could see mountains tumbling off into the distance beneath an electric blue sky.

Reaching for his water, he absorbed the beauty of the panorama laid out before him. This trail was rated as difficult, but coming here had been worth it. He uncapped the bottle and drank. Even after he stowed it away again, he didn't move, not immediately.

Muscles that had been tight for months slackened and a soul-deep peace spread through him. With a last glance, Logan continued on. From everything he'd read, there were better views farther up the track and he wanted to reach the summit before the humans caught up with him.

The path was clogged with vegetation and trees again, but as he hit another switchback, the incline leveled out. He picked up his speed, eager to reach the top where he could look out and see forever—or at least into Canada.

An arm went around his neck from behind, taking him by surprise.

He'd relaxed too much, damn it.

Logan forced his fingers between his throat and his attacker's arm, broke free from the hold, and turned, expecting to take on a human who thought he'd found an easy mark.

One glance had him scrambling to adjust his mindset.

Bouda. Not a demon, but nearly as dangerous. Adrenaline surged as Logan sized up the creature—well over seven feet tall, heavily muscled steel-blue skin covered with thick scales, and razor-sharp talons at the ends of long fingers. Its mouth was deep and large, filled with teeth that were designed not only to hold its prey, but also to tear chunks of flesh from the victim. The clothing it wore—brown leather trousers, knee-high boots, and a sleeveless leather jerkin—were intended to shield it from injury during an attack.

Logan blocked the first strike, and began to silently intone spells. The first was to protect himself, the second to keep humans away from the area, and the third to get rid of the pack he had on. He couldn't afford to be weighed down.

His brain raced through the facts he had about the monster—fast, strong, and with incredible stamina. It also had a guard against magic that was as solid as the physical defense it had around its body. The usual strategies weren't going to cut it.

He stopped the second blow with his forearm. Pain shot to his shoulder and he grunted.

Shifting out of the way of another swing, Logan ran through potential weapons and tactics. There weren't a lot of options. The bouda's scales were bulletproof, resistant to everything including armor-piercing ammunition. A memory from his training surfaced—it would take magic wielded simultaneously with a physical weapon to win.

But why the hell was it attacking him? They weren't stupid creatures and going after a Gineal troubleshooter was a bad bet. Logan ducked to avoid a hammer fist to his head.

He backed away, buying a few seconds, and it dawned on him that the bouda probably didn't know he was Gineal. It didn't have the ability to scan energy like demons could. This type of dark-force being liked to eat attractive humans and it believed that it had found its next meal. His lips curved. Fat chance.

One strike. That's all he'd get before the creature discovered he wasn't human. Logan needed to make it count.

He jumped away from a swipe, stumbled over a rock, and lurched to regain his balance. Two-inch talons narrowly missed ripping open his left biceps.

Putting his hands behind his back, Logan called forward a pair of double-bladed katars. If the weapon could puncture the armor of medieval knights, it might pierce the bouda's scales. The double-edged blades were positioned over his knuckles, allowing him to punch his strikes.

The monster snarled at him, its lips drawn back.

Logan tightened his fingers around the hand grips, gathered his magic, and charged.

At point-blank range, he hurled a lightning ball into the bouda's belly. The katar blades followed a split second behind. The knives slid across the scales without penetrating.

He leaped out of range of the claws, but not quite fast enough. The talons ripped into his shirt and the creature clenched them into a fist, dragging Logan closer. Its eyes had no iris, no color, and as he stared, the black seemed endless, eternal.

It was the smell of fetid breath that freed Logan from his trance. Fighting the need to gag, he struggled against the hold, but it took magic to break loose.

The bouda roared in displeasure and a gale force wind burst from its maw. The turbulence slammed into Logan, almost knocking him over.

He leapt above the air stream and levitated until it died down. Drawing a deep breath, Logan girded himself for a protracted battle. Going in low, he shot another bolt of lightning and positioned the katars to strike. But before he could get within range, the bouda reached out with its long arms and grabbed him.

Instead of pulling him closer, it threw him, sending Logan sailing down the side of the mountain.

He hit the slope hard enough to drive the air from his lungs and he slid. Rocks, brush, branches, and plants tore at his clothes, at his flesh. Logan couldn't stop, not until he intoned a short spell.

For an instant, he didn't move, taking stock of his condition. He felt abraded, his cuts stinging, but his protection spell had prevented any real injury.

Looking up, he measured the distance to the trail. He'd fallen a long way. Slowly, Logan pushed to his feet and began the climb. He didn't get far before the bouda appeared above him and tossed a boulder over the side.

Quick reflexes and a stand of evergreens protected Logan.

There was an endless supply of ammunition and he was a sitting duck down here. Opening a transit, he crossed from the mountainside to the path behind his adversary.

Without hesitation, Logan rushed forward, throwing a rope of fire as he tried to drive the katars into his enemy's back.

He still couldn't ram the knives home, damn it.

The monster whirled and hit Logan with a backhand that sent him flying up the mountain slope. This landing was harder and the shield around him gave, the impact driving the air from his lungs. His eyes watered, his chest hurt, but he staggered to his feet.

Logan knew he didn't have time to catch his breath; the bouda would be coming for him. He raised the wind, making it strong enough to push the creature over, then he rasped in oxygen while he had the chance.

The minute he was able to breathe, he barreled back toward the trail. If he could get to the creature while it was down. . . .

His adversary stood before Logan made it halfway, and throwing back its head, the bouda roared. Great, all he'd done was piss it off. Grimacing, Logan reinforced his protection spell. He was running through his magic fast. Too fast.

A cracking noise made him whirl and he barely managed to spin out of the way of a falling pine. He had his back to the bouda, but before Logan could turn, he took a blow at the knee.

He landed in the dirt. Immediately, he sprang to his feet and found his enemy brandishing a tree trunk.

Clutching the katars tightly, he cast a spell to increase his velocity and dove toward the creature.

Logan crashed into the bouda, going in low to avoid the tree it held. Grabbing it around the calves, he brought it to the ground. They both grunted from the impact, but he didn't hesitate. He pinned the monster with his weight as well as his magic, and slashed at the exposed scales, hoping to slice away a patch and drive the knife home.

Something that sounded like sizzling bacon made Logan stop and turn his head. Rock slide. It picked up intensity, swelling from sizzle to thunder in a heartbeat.

Small stones pelted him and the bouda took advantage of his distraction. Its teeth sank in deeply.

The protection spell saved him from having a chunk of flesh ripped out of his biceps, but it still hurt like hell. Logan stabbed the katars against the creature's head over and over. It didn't cause any damage, but it did get the bouda to release him.

Larger rocks were striking him now and Logan abandoned his position. Casting another levitation spell, he hovered above the stones and boulders rolling down the mountainside.

The bouda seemed untroubled by the hits it took, opening its arms as if welcoming the strikes.

How the hell was he going to beat this thing?

From the air, he shot a rope of flame at the top of its head, but the monster was shielded there, too. Logan dodged hard left, barely avoiding the burst of wind directed at him. Just the edge of it was enough to send him sailing back about ten feet.

The instant the rockslide slowed, Logan landed. Before he could attack, though, the bouda raised its hand to the sky and a medieval battle-axe appeared. Damn. Fighting against a bladed extension weapon was one of his least favorite things.

His opponent whooshed the axe through the air in intricate patterns, displaying just how adept it was at handling the thing. The demonstration was purely meant to intimidate and Logan wished he could pull a gun like Indiana Jones and just shoot it.

The quick spell he chanted to get rid of the weapon didn't work. Next he tried to heat the metal axe head enough to melt it. That didn't do a thing.

It had to mean the bouda's magic was stronger than he'd realized.

Keeping a wary eye on the show the creature was still putting on, Logan debated trading in his knives for a sword. He couldn't match the bouda weapon for weapon since he'd never learned to wield an axe—clearly an oversight in enforcer training—but the sword was another bladed extension weapon.

Except a sword might break if it took a hit from the axe.

He decided to stay with the knives. His protection spell should hold for a while longer, and if he could get inside the reach of the axe, he'd have more maneuverability.

Two-pronged attack. He'd been trying to fire magic and hit with the weapon at the same time. What if he focused on magic and worked to weaken the bouda's shield first? Logan jettisoned the katar on his left hand and let loose with a barrage of fire.

The monster walked through it like it wasn't even there.

Logan jumped, avoiding the first swing of the axe, and backed away. He called up a sandstorm, surrounding his enemy with the fine grains. They might be small enough to penetrate the minuscule gaps between scales and maybe widen them slightly. At the very least, it could cause the bouda some discomfort.

As he worked to keep the intensity of the sand strong, Logan cast an incantation to protect his ears, and then he began intoning another proclamation. In his left hand, he formed a ball of pressurized air, ramping up the magnitude as high as he could. When the creature fought its way free of the sand, Logan closed the spell and threw the orb.

Despite putting a buffer on his hearing, Logan heard the roar as the sphere exploded. The bouda dropped the axe and grabbed its head.

In the blink of an eye, Logan was on it. He released blast after blast of fire and lightning as he punched the katar against the area he was magically striking. The monster tried to push him away, but it was weakened and reeling from the explosion.

He was still unable to breach the scales, damn it. Logan chanted another spell, one that would form ice over the bouda's body.

Its growl sounded confused.

Logan's lips curved and he backed farther away. When he reached a safe distance, he brought down a cloud of steam.

The ice on his adversary went from freezing to blistering in a heartbeat and the bouda cried out. It tried to escape the vapor, but it staggered and fell. Logan released the incantation and launched himself across the distance.

This time the lightning bolt affected the monster. Its body spasmed and the black eyes rolled back into its head.

With a shout of satisfaction, Logan drove the remaining katar into the creature's belly. It sank in.

As soon as it penetrated to the hilt, he activated the mechanism that scissored the blades. His opponent screamed as the knife opened, tearing through its abdomen.

With pleading eyes, the bouda gazed up at him.

"No mercy," Logan snarled. He pulled the knife out, not bothering to close it until he had it free, then he drove it into the bouda's heart and opened the blades again.

The creature's last noise was unintelligible.

Logan stopped opening and shutting the knife and released the weapon. Panting, he rolled to the side, and closing his eyes, he laid there, sucking in oxygen.

He hurt. With adrenaline ebbing, he felt each bruise, each cut. They were nothing except nuisance injuries, but he wouldn't be able to heal himself for awhile, not as low on magic as he was. The thought of summoning a healer when he got home made him grimace, but he wasn't willing to spend hours feeling like this when it could be avoided.

Logan forced himself to sit up and take a look around. He had some more work to do before he could lift the spell that kept humans away. First on the list was getting rid of the bouda's body. Resting a hand on the corpse, he quietly chanted the incantation that transformed it into energy and returned it to the universe.

The area was a mess and it took more spells to get rid of the blood, return the rocks to where they belonged, and erase all traces that a battle had taken place.

Cleaning up lowered his power level further than he liked and Logan scowled. He'd been in fights that had lasted a lot longer than this one, but the shields surrounding the bouda had required he put more magic than usual into each strike. This was damn inconvenient, and when he reported to the council, he'd have to let them know just how bad off he was. A healer could repair him physically, but he'd need time to recharge his powers.

The sound of voices drifted up the trail, reminding him that he couldn't sit here all morning. Logan whispered the spell to open a transit and pushed slowly to his feet. Blood rushed away from his head and he swayed before catching his balance.

What the hell?

He took a step forward, but as he looked into the mirror-like glow of the gate, it began to spin. Images kaleidoscoped by at light speed. Logan staggered closer, his vision narrowing with each step.

Lift the spell.

Yeah, he had to open the area to humans again. It took two tries before he felt the incantation disappear.

Instead of walking across the transit, he fell through it. Shaking his head, he looked around, realized he was in his living room, and relaxed. That was a mistake. Pain seared through his body, dancing along the nerves until he couldn't contain a groan.

Transit. Had to shut the transit.

His attention splintered, shattering into a million pieces and exploding outward. Logan gritted his teeth against the pain, against the split-second flashes of images that he couldn't quite grasp. Humans couldn't be allowed to see the transit. He fought hard for one instant during which he could focus. When he had it, he didn't hesitate. With a wave of his fingers, the portal closed.

That small movement taxed the last of his resources and his hand thumped to the floor. Sweat ran into his eyes, but he couldn't move, couldn't wipe it away.

Tremors coursed through him, and no matter how hard he tried, Logan couldn't stop them. It scared him. Not just the spasms, but the loss of control. He always had his self-command. Always.

The shaking became more violent, frustrating him even as it made his stomach twist. What had the bouda done to him?

His thoughts started to feel fuzzy and Logan fought harder. Bright lights spun across his vision, blinding him to his location. They started out white, turned to yellow, and then he had a rainbow of colors swirling faster than a tilt-a-whirl. Nausea welled. Reaction to the lights or another symptom?

Images returned. Place upon place upon place, all superimposed over each other until he didn't know what anything was, didn't know if he'd ever been to these locations. Until he didn't know what was real and what was imaginary. Logan closed his eyes, trying to make it stop. Wishing it would stop.

It didn't.

He attempted to push himself onto his hands and knees, but his shaking was too violent now. His awareness dimmed further, his thoughts as sluggish as wading through sludge.

That's when he felt it. Them. Him. One presence or many, he couldn't tell. Logan tried to shake his head, to back away.

Fetid. Repulsive. Evil.

The tilt-a-whirl picked up speed. Impressions came and went, and no matter how hard he worked to see them, hear them, sense them, he couldn't sort anything out. Couldn't slow anything down. His brain hurt as badly as if someone were stabbing him with a pitchfork.

Pain seared through his body even more intensely.

Logan didn't know when or where it would come, only that it consumed him when it happened. Random. The randomness made it worse, made it more agonizing. They/he/it knew that. Counted on it. Used it as a weapon.

He'd killed the bouda. This couldn't be happening. He'd won.

Needed help. Logan tried to call out, but he couldn't make his tongue move. It felt thick, swollen, and that added to his fear.

Blinding white light surrounded him before his vision tunneled, went to black, but Logan was sure he wasn't alone. And when the next jolt of agony shot through his abdomen, he knew he was right; the other was here. He fought then, trying to find the enemy, trying to hurt him/it/them as much as he was hurting, but no matter how hard he punched out, his tormenters were beyond his reach.

The roar of outrage became a cry of anguish.

And then it was as if someone flipped a switch in his head—Logan felt it happen—and . . . nothing.

2
CHAPTER

The phone rang. Logan groaned quietly and reached for a pillow to muffle the sound. He couldn't find one and the shrill peal came again. He raised his hands to cover his ears, and then he remembered.

Damn, it had happened again after his call-out last night. Fear clawed at his belly, but he squashed it before it could mushroom. After six weeks of these seizures, he should be used to them, but he wasn't.

Another ring. Reluctantly, Logan sat up, stifling a moan as his body protested a night spent on the floor. As much as he wished otherwise, ignoring the phone wasn't an option, and he stood, swaying until his head cleared.

A fourth ring. One more and voice mail would pick up. He staggered forward, his aches intensifying, and grabbed the receiver. "Yeah?" he growled, his voice rasping.

Logan nearly cursed when he recognized the caller as one of the council's aides. An assignment—just what he needed first thing on a Monday morning when he felt like this. As he listened, though, he changed his mind—a job would be better than being summoned to face the ceannards. The aide didn't give him a chance to ask more than a few questions—none of which were answered—before she ended the call. Slowly, he hung up the phone, dread seeping into every cell of his body.

The council must have discovered his seizures; that's why they were bringing him in to talk. He blew out a long breath in an attempt to get rid of his sudden tension.

He'd come to the conclusion that he couldn't blame the bouda for what he was dealing with—those creatures didn't have magic strong enough to last a month and a half—but he was damned if he could pinpoint what had triggered his problem. All he knew was if he used too much power, he paid the price, and that amount seemed to grow smaller each time he had one of these episodes.

It was easy to guess the council would pull him from his position and that was the last thing he wanted. Hell, it was why he hadn't told anyone about the convulsions to begin with. They'd replace him and Logan loved Seattle. He loved it enough to buy his own home, foregoing a Gineal-owned residence, and he had his garage set up exactly how he wanted it for his projects.

If he eventually received another placement—and that was a big *if* since the ceannards would always wonder about his stability—he'd most likely end up in a sparsely populated, low-stress area. The idea of being assigned to somewhere like Whitehorse in the Yukon made him grimace. It might be a great place to visit, but Logan didn't want to live there.

The air conditioner kicked on, jolting him out of his thoughts. He had less than half an hour before he had to face the Gineal leaders and he better use it wisely. Logan ran a hand over his chin. At the very least, he needed to shave.

Staring at his reflection in the bathroom mirror made him groan. His eyes were bloodshot, his hair standing up and shooting out in about twenty different directions, and with the stubble, he looked like someone coming off a three-day bender.

Great.

A little magic cured the redness of his eyes and Logan turned the shower on, letting the water heat up while he brushed his teeth. He stripped out of his clothes, leaving them where they landed, and stepped in the marble-tiled stall. Standing under the stream, he let the water soothe him.

He felt better after the shower—looked better, too. Maybe even good enough to convince the council there was nothing wrong with him. He reached for his razor.

After he finished shaving, he gave himself one last, critical assessment. He was still pale and drawn, but only someone paying very close attention would see that. Of course, if the ceannards knew about his seizures, they *would* be studying him that carefully. With one towel wrapped around his hips, he used a second to dry his hair and walked into his bedroom.

From the closet, he grabbed a pair of jeans, but changed his mind and opted for khakis instead. He tossed them on his bed, pulled out the rest of his clothes, and dressed. After threading a belt through the loops of his pants, he dug out his best tennis shoes and saw they were dusty. Logan began to rub them off on his thigh, realized that wasn't the best idea, and grabbed his damp towel off the floor to use instead. Ready with minutes to spare, he squared his shoulders and opened the transit.

The small room outside the council chambers was empty. He prowled the circumference, but didn't pick up voices or any other sounds. Not that he'd expected to, but it would be nice to know the mood of the ceannards before facing them. With a frown, Logan settled into a chair and waited.

Headquarters wasn't the Bat Cave. Their society might have gone underground centuries ago, but they were hiding in plain sight. The Gineal Company was a multi-national conglomerate that employed hundreds of thousands of people worldwide—many of them human—and the council acted as the board of directors. Normally, the corporate camouflage struck his sense of humor, but not today.

Logan was brooding, staring at a particularly uninspired

print of the Golden Gate Bridge, when someone entered. Immediately, he straightened in his seat.

The aide, Jess, gave him a polite smile and said, "The ceannards are ready to see you."

Her tone didn't tell him anything and Logan hated flying blind. Despite that, he didn't hesitate to enter the council chamber when she gestured for him to do so.

The door closed behind him with a final-sounding *thunk.* His heart rate sped up, and surreptitiously, Logan wiped his palms on his pants. He hadn't been this nervous about entering the room since he'd been an apprentice.

All nine ceannards were present. If this had been something minor, he'd be dealing with only a few of them. Their table was arranged to form an obtuse angle, and Nessia, the council leader, sat behind the point. Logan moved toward them, stopping a respectful distance away, and studied their faces. Their blank expressions told him nothing.

He bowed his head. "Ceannards."

"Logan," Nessia greeted him in return.

Most of his tension eased and he struggled to hide a relieved grin. If he were about to be disciplined, the council leader would have called him *laoch solas,* the title that belonged to the troubleshooters. It was an even more promising sign that she'd used his first name rather than his surname.

The fact that he wasn't in trouble hardly had a chance to sink in before Nessia continued speaking. "We have an assignment for you."

Logan straightened abruptly and his muscles went taut again. He'd never before been given a mission by the entire council—anything that serious was nearly always handled by a roving enforcer. "What—?"

Nessia held up a hand, stopping his words. "We'll brief you first, then if you have questions, you may ask them."

It wasn't a suggestion, but he nodded anyway.

"A monitor picked up the presence of a Tàireil male in the Seattle area."

That explained a lot. It was his territory, and while a Tàireil was critical enough to warrant the presence of all the councilors, he didn't necessarily require a rover. The darksiders had the same range of power as the Gineal did and any troubleshooter should be able to handle the situation. It was unusual, though, that one had crossed over into their dimension; the two societies tried to avoid the other's home turf.

"Why's he here, Ceannard?" Logan asked. Nessia's frown reminded him that she wanted him to wait with his questions.

"We believe," she said with the slightest hint of frost in her tone, "that he's come for revenge. Last month, one of our rovers killed a Tàireil to save three human women that had been attacked. Now this new male has appeared and he was sensed in the vicinity of the rover's sister. Your job is to protect her."

There was a lot of information in what the council leader said as well as what she'd implied, and Logan ran through it. One, troubleshooters rarely were assigned to protect family members because emotion was dangerous in battle and it made sense that the mission fell to him. Two, power was genetic, so even though the sister wasn't strong enough to be an enforcer herself, she'd still be able to help him if the need arose. That would make keeping her safe easier, and considering his current situation, that was definitely a bonus.

"Ahh, Logan, the job is not as simple as you think."

Logan was only a little disconcerted by how easily Nessia had read him. After all, the council was made up of retired troubleshooters and they understood how he'd been trained to weigh data. "What don't I know, Ceannard?"

Nessia's lips tilted slightly, the closest thing to a smile that he'd seen from her today. "Your charge is a dormant, completely oblivious to the existence of the Gineal and her own heritage. It must remain that way. You are expressly forbidden from telling her anything about us or about magic. Do you understand?"

"Yes, Council Leader." And because he knew she was going to ask for his word, he added, "You have my vow to remain silent."

The secrecy didn't surprise him. What did catch him off guard was the fact that a troubleshooter had a sister who was a dormant. "How?" Logan asked after a short hesitation.

There was a moment of silence and he suspected the council was telepathically debating how much to tell him.

"Nearly thirty years ago," Nessia said at last, "the council faced a situation that required them to mete out a harsh punishment. The couple had their powers stripped, their memories replaced, and they were set up in a new life without their son. It was after this that they had a second child."

"What—"

"That's all you need to know, laoch solas."

Logan nodded. Maybe it was because of their ability to communicate with thoughts, but privacy was something revered by his people, and without a compelling reason for him to be told more, the council would stonewall him. "What can you tell me about the dormant?" he asked instead.

Nessia waved a hand and a life-sized, three-dimensional projection of the woman appeared off to his right. The image wasn't completely solid, but it was close enough to give him a clear picture, and Logan studied her intently.

She was tall; he estimated her height at close to six feet and guessed she was in her mid-twenties. Her hair was dark and long, falling past her breasts, her eyes were a deep brown, and her lips were full and moist.

He looked closer. She was fine-boned, and that gave her a delicate appearance despite her height. For some reason, that raised a protective urge, but that wasn't all he felt. Logan recognized the beginning buzz of arousal and worked to tamp it down. This was a mission and she was a dormant.

"What's her name?" he asked, tone neutral.

"Shona Blackwood."

That had the same effect as dumping a bucket of ice water

over him. Of all the rovers, Creed Blackwood was the one Logan least wanted to tangle with, and as protective as the man was said to be with his extended family, Logan imagined he'd be much worse with his younger sister. It didn't matter that they hadn't grown up together.

A thought occurred to Logan that made dread pool in the pit of his stomach. If he lost it and hallucinated while defending Shona—or made some other mistake that got her hurt—he'd be facing an enraged Creed Blackwood.

The Yukon was starting to look pretty damn good after all.

Shona stared out at the sea of people and frowned. Normally, she enjoyed going to clubs, especially this one. She loved being surrounded by the energy, the excitement, and the crowds. It never took long before her cells started humming and her creativity bubbled. But not tonight.

Tonight the place was too hot, too loud, too packed. Her long-sleeved, royal blue shirt had seemed sensible when she'd heard the temperature would be in the fifties, but inside the bar, it was nearly unbearable. It didn't help that strangers had invaded the banquette she sat on, pushing her over until she clung to a tiny strip of seat. Shona wanted to find somewhere quieter, but she couldn't leave her spot. She and Farran had agreed to meet here, and her friend would never locate her in this crush if Shona moved.

The padded bench had no arm and she sat facing the side, looking into the club. That was the only reason she didn't end up on the floor when a newcomer rushed over to the group behind her and tried to make a place for herself among them. Bracing her feet on the floor, Shona pushed back into the jostling women, fighting for her few inches of seat.

Damn it, why did Farran always have to be late? This night out had been *her* idea to begin with, something she'd talked Shona into doing, and now she was stuck here alone, waiting.

Okay, so Farran was right—if Shona had stayed home, she would have done nothing except sit around. So what? No one lost a piece of their soul and got over it in a couple of months. But coming to the club wasn't helping, at least not yet. Maybe if she could dance with some of the guys who'd asked, she'd be having a good time by now—it wasn't like she'd have to come up with much to say with the music blasting—but until her friend arrived, Shona was stuck.

The group behind her finally left and she immediately scooted back, reclaiming her fair share of the banquette before anyone else sat down.

As she made herself comfortable, Shona felt her cell vibrate and pulled it out of the pink phone wallet she wore at her waist. The text message was from Farran. *Sorry. Car died. Waiting 4 tow. CU tomorrow.*

Shona tapped back a quick reply and put her phone away. She didn't need to hang around here any longer; she could mingle, dance, have fun, maybe find that groove she usually hit when she was surrounded by people.

Or she could go home.

That last option was the most appealing. As she debated, another group settled on the banquette, bumping her, and Shona made up her mind. She was out of here.

It took time and patience to thread her way through the hordes of people to reach the exit. Shona pushed through the door as if she were escaping, and maybe in a way, she was. The cool air was a relief, and for the first time in a while, she felt as if she could breathe.

Her comfort was short-lived. It took a minute, but the quiet finally penetrated. Where was everyone? There were always crowds in front of the club on a Friday night—people waiting to get inside, people chatting and laughing—but tonight the sidewalk was deserted. Even the bouncer who manned the door was missing. The bar was near Pioneer Square and the area had hotels, restaurants, parking—someone had to be around. Shona looked farther down the street, but she didn't see a single soul.

It creeped her out. A stray memory surfaced of a movie she'd seen on late night television when she'd been a teenager. In it, a comet had passed by Earth and released some substance that killed everyone except those protected by metal. The heroine had been one of the few left alive.

There wasn't even the sound of traffic. The absence of people was eerie, as if something horrible had happened that she didn't know about. Yet.

Shona changed direction. She'd return to the club, and when others left, she'd go with them and walk to her car.

A feeling of dread washed over her and it was strong enough to freeze her in her tracks. Something, some sixth sense maybe, told her not to go back inside. She didn't understand it, but Shona trusted her instincts.

Still she hesitated, torn between her gut and her logic. Shaking her head, she tugged her purse strap higher on her shoulder and forced her feet to move. The longer she stayed here, the more she'd freak herself out, and besides, standing around didn't get her to her car. As Shona walked and nothing happened—no zombies jumping out at her, no serial killers wearing hockey masks—she relaxed. This must just be one of those weird happenings where everyone was doing something inside.

She made it a couple of blocks when a man turned the corner in front of her and headed her direction. The sight of another human being eased her nerves—she wasn't the only person left in the world.

Her giddiness didn't last long. Something about him made her uneasy. Without giving herself a chance to second guess, Shona pivoted, and started hurrying back to the club.

He was on her before she made it a full block.

Shona screamed, brought her elbow back into her attacker's belly, and ran. It was pure instinct.

In less than two steps, he caught up with her. His hands

went around her throat. Terror flooded her, mixing with adrenaline until she worried she'd pass out. No way.

She tried to scream again, but nothing except a squeak emerged. Not because of his grip. Fear had seized her vocal cords. Shona grabbed his hands with hers, and somehow, broke his clasp. She turned to confront him head on.

For a moment that seemed to last forever, they stared at each other. With her height, she rarely had to look up to meet a man's eyes, but this guy was at least half a foot taller and heavily muscled. Stringy blond hair escaped a knit cap, his goatee needed to be trimmed, and his hooded sweatshirt was stained.

As he lunged for her, time resumed its normal pace. Shona managed another weak squeal and slapped at him.

If the guy wanted her damn purse, she'd hand it to him. If he wanted her phone wallet, she'd give that to him, too. But he wasn't trying to grab either of those things, he was trying to grab *her.* She wasn't going to be raped and murdered without fighting. She would not be a statistic.

Anger lifted some of her anxiety and her chest felt less constricted. Shona let loose with a loud, long scream.

The guy swore at her, but she barely heard him over the pounding of her heart. He grabbed her wrist tightly and Shona brought her other arm back, aiming for his nose. The heel of her hand connected with his eye.

She heard him suck in a sharp breath, but it didn't break his hold. Instead, he drew her inexorably closer. She leaned away from him, pulling back with all her strength. Somehow that was enough to keep the distance between them.

Almost against her will, she looked into his eyes, and the coldness there had fear rushing back. Shona punched at him with her free hand. He grimaced each time she connected, but he didn't release her. Shona thought about kicking at him, but that would throw her off balance. Maybe even enough for him to pin her against his body. She couldn't risk it and she felt safer with both feet planted on the sidewalk.

Why weren't there any people around? She needed help.

The thought alone seemed to weaken her and her assailant tugged her closer. Shona screamed one last time and prayed for a miracle.

3
CHAPTER

Shona twisted, continuing to struggle. The outcome might be inevitable, but she wouldn't surrender.

He restrained both her wrists with one hand, and with the other, grasped the neck of her shirt. Shona whimpered. *Oh, God, please—*

"Hey!" someone shouted behind her.

For an instant, her heart stopped, then it skittered, racing even faster. Would this new man help her? If he didn't want to get involved, would he at least call 9-1-1?

Her attacker released her and Shona watched him run away, amazed that someone that big could move so quickly. The second man raced past her, giving chase, but the other guy had already disappeared from view. Her rescuer gave up after about a dozen yards and stopped, but he hesitated, maybe debating whether or not to continue the pursuit.

Shona kept her eyes on this second guy, trying to take his measure. His dark hair was neatly cut and that relaxed her enough to draw in a deep, shaky breath. It was stupid—short hair didn't mean he was safe—but it made her *feel* more secure.

The guy turned and walked toward her, coming to a halt far enough away that she didn't feel threatened. Shona raised her gaze, read compassion and understanding on his face, and knew he'd kept his distance deliberately.

Instead of speaking, she took another few seconds to study him. He was only about two or three inches taller than she was, so he didn't loom over her and he wasn't freakishly muscled like the 'roid user who'd grabbed her, but he made her feel delicate anyway. That was a rare experience for Shona.

His eyes grabbed her attention. They were cobalt, the color of the deepest ocean, and held absolute calmness. Something inside her lurched. She'd love to replicate that shade in her studio, to create a piece that represented his serenity. Her brain raced, tried to figure out exactly what imagery would work best. The answer seemed tantalizingly close, but before Shona could grasp it, the buzz drained away and that heavy emptiness she'd lived with for the last two months returned.

He held out his hands, palms up, and said, "I'm not going to hurt you."

That simple gesture made blood roar in her ears and her body ignited with fine tremors. He said something else, she saw his lips move, but she couldn't hear the words, and Shona swallowed hard, hoping that would lessen the internal thunder.

"Are you okay?" This time, his tone was sharp enough to penetrate.

"Yes, fine." Her voice came out weak, raspy, and she wasn't surprised when he looked skeptical.

"Are you sure?"

She nodded. Shona fought back tears and willed him to leave before she lost the battle and embarrassed herself. All she wanted to do was go home and cry where no one would see her, but he didn't seem to be in a hurry to go anywhere. Digging deep, she found enough strength to sound normal. "Yes, absolutely. Thank you for the rescue."

He considered her for a moment, then in a heartbeat, his eyes changed from peaceful ocean to hurricane-whipped seas. "Good, then you can tell me what the hell you were doing walking alone at night."

Shona went from weepy to angry. "This area is safe!"

He looked skyward, muttered something in a language that she didn't recognize, and then pinned her with his turbulent gaze. "It wasn't safe tonight."

"Nine times out of ten—"

"Statistics don't count for much when you're number ten."

Tears pooled in her eyes and Shona blinked hard to make them go away. She wasn't fast enough, she knew it when she saw his expression change.

"Sorry," he apologized with a short grimace. "You don't need to listen to a lecture from me after what happened. I just get tired of people making questionable decisions and putting themselves at risk."

Nausea swamped her. If her parents had been in town, they would have insisted that she meet Farran at home and the two of them go together to the club. Maybe they were right to stress caution. Look what happened when she took a very slight, calculated risk. She wrapped one arm around herself to hold back the queasiness and to try to stop her sudden shivering. Raising her other arm, she rested her hand on the center of her chest, her palm covering the stone of the necklace beneath her shirt. It had become a habit to touch it whenever she needed comfort and right now was one of those times.

He reached under his jacket and Shona forgot all about being cold. Her muscles went rigid. The guy slowed his movements and lifted the bottom of the jacket to allow her to watch him go for his phone. As he pulled it from its clip, she swallowed a laugh, afraid it would sound hysterical.

Her rescuer held up his phone. "My cell," he said, pitching his voice like she did when she soothed a frightened animal.

"Wh—," Shona began, then cleared her throat. "Who are you calling?"

"The police."

"No!"

That stopped him cold. "What do you mean, no?"

"There's no reason to bother the police. Nothing happened. It's not a big deal. Really."

For a moment, he simply stared at her, his face unreadable, then he lowered his arm. "You're wrong. Not only did something happen, but it was serious. You have to report this."

Shona breathed deeply, trying to dampen the panic. He had to listen to her. She took a step toward him, hand outstretched, and stopped. "They're busy; we don't need to bother them about this, not when you showed up in time, and they have real crimes to worry about." She paused, and then confessed, "It's . . . embarrassing. They'll think the same thing you did—that walking alone at night makes me too stupid to live."

His grin was slow and sexy and hit Shona like a blast from her furnace at full fire. She'd noticed parts of him tonight— his hair, his eyes—but this was the first time she'd really looked at *him*. A lick of flame ignited inside her and she wondered at it. Her emotions had been all over the map tonight, but the last thing she'd expected was attraction.

"I don't think you're stupid," he said, "but I don't believe you used your best judgment."

The lack of inflection in his voice drove Shona to a precipice. She teetered there for a moment, torn between anger and tears. Anger won. "Listen, mister—"

Someone honked their horn, interrupting her. Shona looked around. People! There were cars driving on the street and men and women strolling along the sidewalk. She wasn't sure when they'd reappeared, but things were normal again! Her legs gave out as relief poured through her and she had to lock her knees to keep from going down.

"Are you okay? Do you need me to call an ambulance?"

He was raising his cell phone as he asked and Shona quickly said, "I'm fine! Don't call anyone."

Without saying a word, he stared at her, and his gaze made Shona's skin feel warm, but it didn't melt the ice that had formed deep inside after her near-miss. Instead, as hot and cold met, goose bumps popped up and the shivers started again, this time more persistent and more violent than before. His eyebrows drew together.

"I'm sorry," she apologized, teeth chattering. "I don't know why I'm so cold."

"You're crashing off the adrenaline." He hooked his phone back on its clip, unzipped his jacket, and shrugged out of it. "Here, put this on." He held it open for her.

"I can't take that." Her purse slipped from her hand and she watched it hit the ground, but was trembling too hard to retrieve it.

"You need it more than I do."

He was right and his thoughtfulness brought on a second wave of tears. She lowered her head to hide them and slipped into the jacket. As soon as she had it on, he released it and stepped back. The fleece was warm from his body, and when she bent to zip it up, Shona caught a trace of his after-shave. Something about his scent calmed her and her shaking slowed.

When she raised her head, he held out her purse. "Thank you again," she said, taking the bag from him.

"You doing better now?"

She nodded.

"Okay," he said, tucking his fingers into the front pockets of his jeans, "let's talk about calling the police then."

Shona clenched her hands around her purse. "Really—"

"Let me throw out a scenario for you." He did a quick scan of the area before meeting her gaze again. "We don't call the cops, they don't know to watch out for your attacker, and miss an opportunity to arrest him. This guy goes out hunting another woman. She's not as lucky as you are—maybe no one is around when she screams, maybe she doesn't manage to scream at all—either way, this time he succeeds."

Shona felt the sick feeling in the pit of her stomach expand and she trembled again as the incident replayed in her head. She huddled deeper into the fleece, searching for comfort, but what she really wanted to do was cover her ears with both hands and pretend she couldn't hear what her rescuer said.

He didn't stop. Looking intently at her, he asked, "If someone else is raped and murdered, will you be able to live with yourself?"

The answer was simple—no. "Call them," she capitulated.

Without giving her an opportunity to change her mind, he pulled the cell free and phoned it in. From his side of the conversation, Shona learned two things. First, she was going to have a bit of a wait since the police were busy, and second, her rescuer's name was Logan Andrews.

"You heard?" he asked when he disconnected the call.

"About the wait? Yes. Did they say how long it would be?"

"Not really, but I'd guess fifteen or twenty minutes." Logan put his cell away. "This isn't an emergency any more."

Shona nodded. "Well, I suppose I just stay here till they come." She thought about shaking hands with him, but decided that was too formal. "Thanks again for your help. I hope this didn't disrupt your plans too much."

His lips curved slightly. "I'm sorry that I'm making you so uneasy that you can't wait to get rid of me."

That wasn't completely true. He did make her uncomfortable, but it had more to do with her reaction to him and her embarrassment that she'd needed to be rescued than with any huge concern that Logan would hurt her. No, she didn't quite trust him, and yes, she was leery, but uneasy? Not the way he meant. She started to deny it, but he shook his head, cutting her off.

"I can't leave you standing alone."

"I'm not alone; there are other people all around here." There were—now—but she had this fear that they would disappear like they had earlier. But what really made her jittery was that she didn't know what she could talk about with him for twenty minutes. It was up to her to carry a conversation with this good-looking stranger. Her stomach went on a downward plunge at the thought. When she went out dancing, the noise, the music, and the crowd acted as a buffer with the men she met, but now she had nothing.

If Farran were here, she'd be doing the chatting and Shona could stand and listen, only needing to say something if she were asked a question. She'd always let other people lead the talking even as a kid. Her parents had been happy to step into the gap for her and she'd been happy to let them.

"And," Logan continued, "I'm a witness; the officer who responds will need to talk to me, too."

Shona didn't have an argument for that. With a quiet sigh, she resigned herself to his presence and searched for something—anything—to say. "Nice evening."

He grinned. "*Nice* isn't the word I'd use."

"I'm glad you find it funny," she snapped, "but I'm trying to make conversation."

That sobered him. "I'm sorry. I wasn't laughing at you, more at the situation. It doesn't feel as if we just met after what happened tonight, but that is the truth. Why don't we try to start out as if it were a normal night?"

She wasn't sure what that meant, but Shona nodded. Anything had to be better than her trying to come up with something to say.

Holding out his hand, he said, "I'm Logan Andrews."

"Shona." Reluctantly, she put her palm against his, but the handshake was quick and businesslike.

"You don't trust me with your last name, huh?" he asked with a tilt to his lips that she took as amusement.

Flash fire shot through her cheeks and she couldn't meet his gaze. It left her feeling vaguely embarrassed and guilty, but her parents had warned her over and over her entire life to be careful. It was a hard habit to break, even if he probably thought she was paranoid.

"Too bad you weren't this cautious earlier," he added.

She hated being out of control, but she couldn't stop the plunge into anger. "What are you? Some kind of expert?"

"I work in the security division of the Gineal Company."

"Oh." That deflated her. "You're a guard?"

"Something like that."

His bland tone suggested he was more, but Shona didn't have the energy to worry about it. "Tell me something. How long does this emotional roller coaster last?"

Logan shrugged. "It depends on the person. Unless you're an adrenaline junkie, you probably won't feel normal until you've had time to sleep."

"If I ever sleep again," she muttered.

"Yeah, there is that. Believe it or not, you'll get through this and— I think this is our squad car coming now." He walked over to the curb and signaled to the police officer.

That hadn't taken twenty minutes and Shona suddenly wanted that time. She wasn't ready to talk about what happened. Hugging her purse to her chest, she tried to make herself believe that getting it over with was a good thing. Really. But her stomach still took another dive when Logan and the officer stopped talking and headed toward her.

Her heart started racing nearly as fast as it had while she'd been fighting her attacker. She let Logan handle things and focused on trying to breathe. On trying not to vomit.

"Ma'am, could I get your name?" the officer asked.

"Shona Blackwood."

It was only when she saw Logan smother a smile that she realized what she'd done. Shona swallowed hard. She'd better pray that he was as nice as he seemed because she'd just given him enough information to track her down.

* * *

Shona sat with the black fleece jacket in her lap and stroked her fingers over the soft fabric. It was stupid, a schoolgirl thing to do, but it comforted her. She wasn't sure why she needed to be soothed—she was secure inside her own home, the late afternoon sunshine streamed through the windows, and everything was peaceful—but she'd been jumpy for three days.

It wasn't difficult to figure out why his jacket calmed her. Logan had shown up when she was scared, vulnerable, and he'd made her feel safer. Because he wasn't here now, she'd transferred that association to an article of his clothing. Simple.

That was probably the same reason why she couldn't stop thinking about him and feeling a stab of attraction.

Adrenaline, he'd said, but the real crash had happened after she'd locked her front door, washed up, and changed into her pajamas. Shona hadn't realized how tightly she'd been hanging on until that moment. The tears had seemed unending, she'd shaken for hours, and in the middle of her jag, she'd nearly called her mom and dad. Only the knowledge that they'd be on the first plane out of Heathrow had stopped her.

She'd needed comfort and clasping her necklace hadn't helped. Neither had roaming the house and she'd been too keyed up to sit through the guided meditation she'd borrowed from her mom's collection. It wasn't until she'd picked up his jacket and wrapped it around her that her agitation had eased. Only then had Shona been able to curl up in bed and actually sleep.

Her fingers caressed the fleece. Logan couldn't be as good-looking or as sweet and kind as she remembered. She was building him up in her mind because he'd rescued her. But it was tempting to discover just how much of her perception was real.

Shona made herself put down the jacket. She was being silly. If he wanted anything to do with her, he had an excuse, but he hadn't called or stopped by to retrieve it.

It wasn't because he couldn't find her. Not only did he have her full name, but he'd been within earshot when she'd given the police officer her address and phone number. Maybe she should be more concerned about that than she was, but it was hard to worry when she was safe at home, and besides, Logan had done everything he could to make her feel secure. Would he have gone to the effort if he wasn't a good guy?

Thank God her parents hadn't called until after she'd regained control. They were so overprotective and it didn't matter to them that she was twenty-six. If they'd had the slightest inkling that she was upset, one or both of them would have been on her doorstep as fast as they could get here. They'd always done that, swooped in and taken care of things before she had the opportunity to do it herself, and she'd always let them.

Be careful. Shona had heard that at least a million times. It was as if her parents feared that if they didn't watch over her every second of every day, they'd lose her. It wasn't until Friday night that she understood how deeply their caution had seeped into her behavior.

They wouldn't trust Logan. They'd remind her that he was a stranger and just because he helped her didn't mean he was honorable. All her life, her mom and dad had discouraged her from trying anything they thought might hold even a small risk. Calling a man she didn't know fell into that category.

She stood, walked over to the table, and picked up the business card lying next to the phone. Logan's. She'd found a packet of them in one of the zippered pockets of his jacket. *Special Vice President—Security.* It embarrassed her that she'd assumed he was a guard.

Did she call him to return the jacket or didn't she? For three days now, she'd been debating what to do. It had been easier over the weekend—she could tell herself he wouldn't be at the number on the card anyway—but today was Monday and that excuse was no longer valid. Although if she dithered long enough it would be after office hours and she'd have another reprieve.

Shona stared at the card. The truth was she wanted to phone him. *Be brave. He can't think you're any more hopeless than he already does.* She reached for the receiver.

The doorbell pealed and she jerked her hand back. Part of her—the foolish dreamy part—wanted to believe it was Logan, but the pragmatist knew it wasn't—he'd have gone to the main residence and she lived in the garage apartment behind her parents' home. Despite that realization, her heart thumped in double time and her palms had gone clammy. She slipped his card into the back pocket of her jeans and went to answer the door.

Even knowing it couldn't be him, it was still a letdown when she looked out the window and saw Farran standing there. Forcing aside the irrational disappointment, Shona opened the door and smiled. "I didn't expect to see you today. I thought you had to work."

"I got off early and decided to stop by. After standing you up on Friday and canceling our Saturday plans, I didn't want you to think I was blowing you off." Farran held up a Wendy's bag. "I brought a peace offering—Frosties. The large size," she added as if the extra temptation was necessary.

Standing aside, Shona gestured for Farran to enter. Her friend headed straight for the kitchen, and Shona trailed behind her, feeling gauche. As always, Farran was polished—there wasn't a strand of caramel hair out of place in her chin-length bob, her white blouse was free of wrinkles, and her black trousers had sharp creases. In comparison, Shona's jeans with the hole in the knee, faded red T-shirt, and bare feet looked sloppy.

The kicker, though, was that Farran was dainty and only slightly above average height. It made Shona feel like an awkward, hulking giant and her step hitched as she tried to walk more gracefully. Farran didn't seem to notice Shona's lack of coordination. Her friend gave her a smile as she put the bag down on the bistro table and opened it.

After the cups were distributed, Farran hopped up to sit on the red barstool and said, "This isn't all I brought." She unzipped her purse and pulled out a magazine folded to an article. Handing it across she said, "Look, *Seattle* previewed that art show you're going to this weekend. As soon as I saw it, I knew you'd be interested."

Shona forgot about her Frosty and scanned the first page, before flipping through quickly to look at the pictures.

"The work is really impressive," Farran commented.

"He's the master of art glass and his vision is awe-inspiring." Shona put the magazine aside and sat on her own stool. "I practiced for years, but I still can't make my pieces feel as realistically fluid as this." She tapped a picture of an undersea scene and slid her Frosty back in front of her.

"I've seen your work and that's not true. You're a brilliant artist in your own right."

Her stomach twisted and Shona curled the hand resting atop the table into a fist. "Past tense."

"Maybe not." Farran reached over and squeezed her hand briefly. "Maybe a year from now you'll be looking back at this and it'll be nothing except a distant memory."

In her dreams, but she didn't say anything because she didn't want Farran to think she was throwing the support back in her face. Instead, Shona changed the subject. "So what happened this weekend? Your messages didn't say a lot."

"I left work Friday night, got into the car, but it wouldn't start. Do you know how long I had to wait for a tow truck?"

Shona shook her head.

"More than an hour!" Farran took napkins from the sack and put them at the center of the table. "I had it brought to a service center, but of course no one was there that late."

"It was the start of the weekend," Shona said.

"Yeah. I thought I'd make lunch on Saturday, but it took the mechanic hours to discover what was wrong, and by that time, all the loaner cars were gone. I still don't understand what the problem was, but I do know it was expensive and it took hours to fix. I probably read every magazine in their waiting area."

"You should have called; I would have gotten you."

"I didn't think of it, but I wasn't in a good mood by then anyway and there was no sense inflicting that on you."

Shona opened her Frosty. She'd eaten a few spoonfuls before Farran broke the silence and asked, "Forgiven?"

"There's nothing to forgive. You can't help that your car died. What kind of friends did you have before we met anyway?"

"Obviously not ones as understanding as you." Farran paused. "Does this mean you don't want your Frosty?"

"Not a chance." Shona wrapped her hand around the cup and pulled it closer. "I deserve this after what happened."

"You mean my standing you up?"

"No," Shona said, the lightness leaving her in a rush. "Some guy grabbed me and I think he meant to rape me."

"What?" Farran's voice shot up about three octaves on the word, her face went white, and the plastic spoon fell out of her hand, splattering chocolate Frosty all over the glass tabletop.

Her friend's reaction seemed extreme, especially when Farran was usually so poised and in control. Maybe she thought Shona *had been* raped. "I was lucky," she added quickly, wanting to relieve any worry. "Someone heard me scream and scared him off."

"That isn't possible."

"What do you mean?"

Farran's head jerked as if she were breaking out of a trance. "It isn't possible that someone tried to hurt you."

"I thought the same thing until it happened." Shona picked up Farran's spoon, handed it to her, and used a couple of napkins to wipe up the mess. She was only delaying the inevitable, but she tossed the wadded-up napkins away anyhow before she began an abbreviated recap. That sick feeling returned to the pit of her stomach as she shared and Shona talked faster. She finished with, "Somehow, don't ask me how since the guy was hugely muscular, I managed to hold my own with him long enough for someone to come running."

"Adrenaline can give people superhuman strength," Farran said. "You've heard stories of mothers lifting cars off their children to save them."

"True." But Shona had a hard time believing it in her case. Deciding she'd had enough of reliving the attack, she moved on to the more interesting part of the night. "The man who rescued me . . ." She let her voice trail off.

"What about him?"

Shona hesitated, but didn't having a best girlfriend mean you could share anything and not feel stupid? "He was cute," she said in a breathless rush. Had she really used *cute*? That made her sound like a teenager oohing over the latest hottie while she paged through *Tiger Beat* magazine. "I mean gorgeous."

Farran smiled, but it was cheerful, not mocking. "I'm thinking this could be a great romance story to share with the grandkids one day. Did you give him your number?"

"Kinda, but he hasn't called."

"What about you? Did you get his name and number?"

Reaching into her back pocket, Shona pulled out Logan's business card and tapped it against the table. "I've been debating whether or not I should contact him. I forgot to return his jacket Friday night and that would be a good excuse."

"Go for it," Farran encouraged.

"What if I sound stupid, or worse yet, desperate?"

"Women call men all the time; it's not a big deal and he's not going to think you're desperate. As for getting flustered, you can write out what you want to say before you call and just follow the script."

"I don't know."

"Just invite him to meet for coffee or something and end the call. It's not like you have to talk to him for an hour, you know." She gestured toward Shona's hand. "Is that his business card?"

With a nod, Shona passed it across the table to her friend.

Farran glanced down at the card, froze for an instant, and when she raised her gaze again, she appeared concerned. "Are you sure you want to get in touch with this man?"

"What?" Shona didn't understand what had Farran uptight. "That's a quick turnaround. Why the sudden change in attitude? Do you know him or something?"

"No, but vice president of a major corporation?" Farran tossed the card back on the table. "He's too old for you."

Shona relaxed. "You don't have to worry about that; he's around my age."

"I don't have to worry? Really?" Her friend shook her head. "There's only one way to reach that level so quickly— sheer ruthlessness. You'd be no match for someone like that. You need someone more your speed."

Logan hadn't come across as ruthless. He'd remained patient with her mood swings and had been incredibly sweet. "I could return the jacket and decide whether or not he's my speed."

"I don't think that's a good idea."

"Why not?" Shona had wanted her friend to talk her into calling Logan, not discourage her.

"How about that you don't know him? Maybe he saved you, but that doesn't mean you can trust him."

Shona knew her parents would agree with that. "But—"

"You're probably building him up in your mind, making him more than he was because of the situation. Do you want to chance disappointment if you meet him and he's not all you remembered?"

"I know it's a risk, but whenever I think about him, I feel things I've never felt before."

"Hero worship."

Shona stayed silent.

"Look, sure, you think this guy is your Prince Charming—who wouldn't after you met him like you did—but you have to be sensible. There are so many reasons not to contact him." Her friend must have noticed the way her jaw tensed because she changed tacks. "Look, you said he hasn't called—have you considered that he might already be married or maybe seriously involved with someone?"

"No," Shona admitted in a small voice, the starch leaving her spine. It was a possibility. Most single men weren't as good with women in emotional situations as Logan had been with her. Then there was his relaxed confidence, his good looks, his sweetness—yeah, he probably had a lover, someone who'd smoothed off his rough edges.

"Here." Farran returned the card. "You can mail that jacket back; you have his address."

"Sure," Shona said, returning it to her pocket.

With a smile, her friend dragged her cup back in front of her and dug out a spoonful of ice cream. "You're making the smart decision. Besides, how embarrassing would it be to call him and have his wife answer and ask who the hell you are?"

"Humiliating," she agreed, but it was Logan's business number. If she called, she'd either get him or his secretary, and if he was involved, she wouldn't be causing any waves in his relationship. She could just tell him she had his jacket and ask if he wanted to pick it up somewhere. If he asked her to send it, she'd know. And if he did meet her, said thanks, and left, she'd know then, too. There was nothing to be embarrassed about even if she was a geek when it came to men.

She knew better than to say anything to Farran. For some reason Shona didn't get, her friend didn't want her to contact Logan. Her arguments were valid, but it was such a turn-around from the woman who was always encouraging her to take a risk.

Absently, Shona answered questions about the police investigation, but she didn't know much.

"Shona, you're brooding."

"Sorry, I was thinking about the attack." It was kind of true. "The police don't have much chance of catching the guy and I think they realize it."

"There's alwa—" Farran's cell rang and she grabbed her purse, pulling the phone out of a little pocket on the side. The call wasn't long. "That was my father. Family meeting. I have to go. Sorry." Her friend was agitated as she tossed her cell back into her bag.

"I understand." Shona didn't ask if something was wrong because Farran always became edgy when her father contacted her. It worried her, but Shona had been firmly rebuffed when she'd asked if Farran was abused. She hadn't found a way to bring it up again, but she would. She had to. It wasn't normal for a twenty-five-year-old woman to get this rattled.

Shona was pensive after Farran left, but there was nothing she could do to help right now. As she cleaned off the table, she ran through different scenarios, ways she could bring up her friend's family situation, but she'd done this a dozen times before in the two months since they met and had never come up with a good answer.

Instead, she started thinking about Logan. One call. It was after five, so she'd likely get voice mail anyway. She could just leave a message and the ball would be in his court. His response or lack thereof would tell her a lot.

Wouldn't it?

She walked into the living room, pulled his card out of her pocket, and stared at the phone. All the reasons Farran had given her were spot on. She knew it, but something inside her felt almost compelled to make the call. How stupid could she sound if she just said who she was and that she wanted to thank him again, and oh yeah, she had his jacket? Simple.

But what if—

Before she could talk herself out of it, Shona picked up the phone and dialed.

4

CHAPTER

Logan pulled up short to avoid plowing into the two human women who came to an abrupt stop on the sidewalk in front of him. One gave him a quick apology and he smiled before detouring around them. The sun was shining and the temperature was warm, but the weather wasn't why he was in a good mood. Things had taken a turn for the better yesterday when Shona had called him.

He'd been royally reamed by the council when he'd reported the attack. They'd demanded to know why he hadn't been at her side, preventing something like that from happening, and Logan had needed to remind them that there were laws against stalking.

That had blunted their comments. Seeing the ceannards at a loss for words wasn't something that happened often, but what could they say? An invisibility spell would zap almost all his magic, leaving him unable to defend Shona, and if a stranger trailed her everywhere she went, she'd call the police. Or at least she should.

The pedestrian light was red and he stopped at the corner, waiting to cross the street. He'd done the best he could to keep her safe, staying close enough to read the energy of the beings around her, but not close enough for her to spot him. No way was a darksider set on revenge going to shoot her from a distance and be done with it. Nope, he'd want to see Shona suffer, to enjoy his vengeance to the fullest, and that would give Logan plenty of time to get there and intercede.

At least that had been the plan. He frowned. The human who'd grabbed her had been a surprise. According to everything he'd been taught, Tàireil didn't work with them, but Logan had felt darksider magic as he'd run through the barrier that had been cast to isolate Shona.

The signal turned and he crossed the street. Nothing seemed to fit what he knew and the council had been as confused by the turn of events as he was. There'd been a brief debate, but it hadn't taken long before they decided to assign him solely to protecting Shona and let someone else cover his territory.

Logan wasn't sure how he felt about them choosing Kel for the job. It had only been in the past few weeks that his brother had begun to lose the haunted look in his eyes, but the improvement was minor, something only someone who knew Kel as well as Logan did would notice. Would covering two territories eradicate that incremental recovery?

He grimaced. Kel had already told him to butt out and focus on his own job, and that *was* what Logan needed to do. What had started out as a simple assignment had become complex and he had questions without answers. Had the man who attacked Shona been compelled by the darksider or was he a willing accomplice?

Tàireil were next to magicless during daylight hours and Logan had been standing watch over Shona from sundown to sunrise. He slept in the morning and he spent the afternoon combing the city, trying to find the darksider. If the human had been bespelled then Shona remained safe when the sun was up. If he was an ally rather than a stooge, the danger increased and Logan needed a reason to stick by her 24/7.

Why had the man been involved at all? In their dimension, humans were serfs and the Tàireil considered themselves far superior. That fact had Logan leaning toward the human being controlled by magic—he just couldn't come up with a single reason why the darksider male hadn't launched his own assault.

There were a few pieces of the puzzle missing and that put Shona at greater risk. He'd been trying to come up with a new plan to protect her, one that kept him closer at hand, when she'd called. By the time he'd disconnected, Logan had known what to do. Date her.

He was making some assumptions—like the fact that Shona would agree to go out with him—but she had phoned and made plans to meet him to return his jacket when she could have mailed it. His address was on his business cards. Logan grinned as he recalled how flustered she'd sounded. If she wasn't interested, why the nerves? It had to be a man–woman thing.

His smile faded. While dating her would give him a reason to hang close, there were drawbacks and the biggest was his attraction to her. Friday night he'd been distracted and had needed to remind himself to scan for threats. Not good. Then there'd been how protective he felt toward her. He'd expected some of that, but not the overwhelming—

Logan spotted Shona up ahead and his thoughts derailed.

Friday night her hair had been straight, tamed; today it tumbled in waves to just above the small of her back. Her sky-blue T-shirt was tight and short, baring her midriff and accentuating her full breasts. Her jeans were pale yellow and fit her every bit as closely as the pair she'd worn last Friday. For someone tall and lanky, Shona was nicely curved and Logan felt an unwelcome surge of warmth return. He swallowed hard.

She hadn't seen him yet, not with all the people between them, and he took the opportunity to stop and stare. He was too far away to really see her face, but he remembered—the high cheekbones; the elfin chin; the rich, chocolate-brown eyes now hidden behind dark lenses; and her full lips. Just the memory of her sexy mouth was enough to intensify the heat inside him.

Someone jostled Logan as they walked by and it brought him back to his senses. He closed the remaining distance.

As he neared the coffeehouse, Shona caught sight of him and pushed her sunglasses to the top of her head. Her lips curved and that small, tentative smile was enough to knock him off balance. With a deep breath, Logan reminded himself that he was a Gineal troubleshooter; he was trained to control his emotions, not let emotion control him, but damn, she hit him hard.

"Hi," she said.

"Hey, Shona." He kept his tone easy because she looked anxious. "I hope I didn't keep you waiting."

"I was early."

Her hands tightened around the white, plastic bag she held hard enough to make it rustle. "Is that my jacket?"

"What? Oh! Yes, here." Shona thrust the bag at him and Logan had to make a lunge for it to keep it from hitting the ground. "Sorry," she said, her face flushed.

"Don't worry about it. Want to grab a cup of coffee?" Logan gestured toward the building behind her.

"I was going to invite you to show my appreciation for your help." Her eyes widened. "Not that a cup of coffee comes close to repaying my debt, but I don't know if anything could."

"You don't owe me anything." She tried to interrupt him, but he held up a hand. "I know you're grateful I came along when I did, but that doesn't incur a debt on your part. I look at it as doing what's right, kind of like racking up good karma points with the universe." He smiled at her. "And I have three sisters; I'd like to think someone would help them if they found themselves in a similar situation."

Which was unlikely. If someone was stupid enough to grab one of them, any of his sisters would blast him with a spell before anyone needed to come to their aid.

"Paying it forward," Shona murmured.

"Something like that." Logan took her elbow, steered her

toward the entrance to the coffeehouse, and held the door for her. The place was crowded and there was only a single open table. "Why don't you grab that," he pointed to the one available spot, "and I'll get the coffee? What do you want?"

"No. You take the table and I'll get the coffee. My treat, remember?"

He wanted to argue, but there was something in her demeanor that suggested she wasn't going to allow him to buy. Logan silently capitulated. "A large coffee. No cream, no sugar, none of that other frou-frou stuff. Just black, okay?"

"Got it."

Reluctantly, he left her and grabbed the table. It was in the middle of the room, and without a wall at his back, Logan felt exposed. An itch began between his shoulder blades and he shrugged, trying to get rid of it. He loathed sitting in the open and it didn't matter that everyone was more interested in their conversations than in him.

Wanting his hands free, he almost tossed the bag onto the floor at his feet, but stopped and took a glance inside. His jacket was neatly folded, and because of that, Logan put it down carefully. He'd been surrounded by women long enough to learn they got bent out of shape about the strangest things and he didn't want her mad.

Shona was about three back in line yet and Logan tapped his heel against the floor, not quite able to quell the antsiness. He eyed the people sitting along the walls, but no one looked close to leaving yet. Taking a deep breath, he tried to focus on something else.

Logan was almost positive now that she was interested in him. She was cute when she was flustered. Attraction would account for her tension today, although how a woman who looked like Shona Blackwood could possibly be nervous was beyond him. Males had probably lined up to ask her out from the time they were old enough to realize the difference between boys and girls.

Shona reached the counter, pushed her hair behind her shoulder, and adjusted the wallet-on-a-string thing she wore crossed over her body. There was an earnest expression on her face as she talked to the clerk and Logan's lips curved. She intrigued him, maybe because she was different from the Gineal women he spent time with.

He was admiring the tight fit of her jeans when there was a tingle on his nape. This time he didn't dismiss it as a product of being exposed, not when the sense was insistent. Logan used his magic to scan the room.

Losassi at three o'clock.

The demon wore jeans, a T-shirt, and beat-up Nikes, blending in easily with the humans around him as he sat, reading the newspaper. Logan blew out a silent breath and debated. The losassi tended to be playful rather than dangerous, but sometimes their tricks got out of hand. Was it worth confronting him?

Shona turned from the counter, caught his gaze, and smiled. It was there and gone in a flash, but it was enough to make him stupid for a moment, then Logan remembered the losassi. He'd keep an eye on the demon, he decided, and step in only if there was no other choice.

She put a cup down in front of him. "Black, no frou-frou."

"Thanks." Logan grinned at her teasing. He waited until she sat and took a sip of her coffee before asking, "How have you been?"

"Fine."

"No nightmares?"

She looked away from him, one hand coming up to rest over the center of her chest and the other curling into a fist on top of the table. "A few. Nothing I can't handle."

He brushed his fingers lightly over her clenched fist and said, "Sorry. It's just that I've been worried about you."

"I'm the one who's sorry." Shona curled her hand around her coffee cup. "It's natural you'd be curious."

"Not curiosity, concern." He rubbed his fingers over the thigh of his olive khakis, trying to erase the tingling sensation and the memory of her soft skin.

"Sor—"

"Don't apologize again, there's no need." He took a swallow from his cup. "Why don't we talk about something else?"

She nodded.

Logan waited for her to pick a subject, but she didn't say a word. It caught him flatfooted. With four women in his family, he'd learned two things: one, it was easier to step back and follow their conversational lead, and two, they liked it when men listened. Why wasn't she saying anything? Their gazes met for a millisecond and he read her discomfort. Was Shona shy?

"You must have a pretty flexible job to get away like this. What do you do?" he asked.

The relief that crossed her face told Logan he'd nailed it—Shona Blackwood, a woman beautiful enough to be a supermodel, wasn't at ease in social situations. Who'd have thought? He sprawled back in his seat, hoping his relaxed pose would help.

"I'm an artist."

She didn't embellish and what Logan knew about art would fit on a small-size Post-it note with space remaining. He searched for something to say. "Uh, painting or sculpture?"

"Glass."

Damn, she was killing him. Why didn't she give details instead of short answers that tossed the onus back on him? He racked his brain for everything he knew on the subject and remembered his mom's purchase of art glass. "You make vases?"

Shona shook her head. "Not really, I mostly focus on glass sculpture." He must have looked as lost as he felt. "I do representations of nature in glass, like plants or the ocean."

"I don't suppose you have any pictures."

"Not with me." She leaned back, unzipped her purse, and brought out a pen. After writing something on a napkin, she slid it across the table to him. "This is the Web site of the gallery where I had my last show. They have images up there of my pieces—if you're interested."

"Definitely interested," he assured her, and carefully folding the napkin, he tucked it in his front pocket. A quick check to his right showed the losassi was still engrossed in the newspaper and Logan focused on Shona again. "Tell me more about how you create your art."

Her expression went blank. "I don't want to talk about my glass; let's find another subject."

What had he said to shut her down? He didn't know much, but Logan had no doubt that art was an avocation someone had to be avid about in order to pursue and people always liked to talk about their passions. Usually. "Pick a topic," he said.

She took a sip of her coffee—he pegged it as a nervous gesture—then blurted, "Where are you from? Originally, I mean."

"What makes you think I'm not from Seattle?"

Her fingers tightened around her cup before she put both hands in her lap. "You have an accent. Not much of one," Shona said, sounding apologetic, "but I can hear it."

"You have a good ear; most people don't pick it up." Logan grinned. "I grew up in Naperville—it's a suburb of Chicago."

"How'd you end up here?"

"Job transfer." Logan glanced over again, but this time the losassi met his gaze and nodded. Great. Demons had the ability to sense what kind of being someone was the same as the Gineal, so it wasn't a surprise that he'd been detected, but what concerned him was the devilment dancing in the male's eyes. Logan shrugged. "I'd never even been to Seattle before being assigned here, but I discovered it's home."

The silence lasted a couple of seconds too long before Shona asked, "Is your family still in Chicago?"

Logan hid a smile, afraid she'd think he was laughing at her if she saw it. It wasn't amusement. He felt oddly proud that she was pressing on despite how nervous she was. And Shona was on edge around him; that was obvious. In some ways, it required more courage to overcome shyness than it took to fight a demon. "My parents and my two youngest sisters are there, but the rest of us are scattered."

"How big is your family anyway?"

The incredulousness of her tone did make him laugh. "I'm one of five. Let me guess. You come from a small family."

"I'm an only child. And I didn't mean to sound . . . I knew you had three sisters, but . . ." Her voice trailed off and she waved a hand as if she were at a loss for words.

"Don't worry so much. The way I phrased things might have made it sound like there were dozens of us." Or maybe for someone who'd grown up without any siblings around, five was as good as dozens.

After a quick check on the losassi, Logan launched into some amusing stories about his brother and sisters. He didn't spare himself either and it didn't take long before Shona was smiling, and then chuckling at some of the trouble he and Kel had gotten into. Her laughter, the soft glow on her face, the fact that she was finally almost at ease encouraged him to keep going.

"I think we were about eight, maybe nine, when Kel and I decided to put on a mini-circus with grasshoppers as the performers. We spent a couple of days collecting them and we must have had a hundred, maybe more, in a container in our bedroom."

"Uh-oh."

Logan finished his coffee, took another look at the demon, and pushed the cup aside. "Yeah, uh-oh. One of us—Kel insists it was me, I say it was him—bumped the collection on our way out to catch more. Neither of us had an inkling something was wrong until we arrived home, opened our bedroom door, and were greeted with the insect equivalent of chaos." He grinned. "We knew we'd be in trouble if our parents saw this, so we were rushing around, trying to recapture the bugs and doing pretty good."

"Until?" Shona prompted.

"Until Iona, my middle sister, got up from her nap and toddled over to see what we were doing. Damn," he said with affection, "that girl could scream. And scream and scream."

"So what happened?"

"Grounded. Two weeks. Insects, rodents, and reptiles were forbidden in the house and this wasn't the first time we'd violated that rule." It hadn't occurred to either him or Kel to use magic to get rid of the grasshoppers, although that was the first thing his dad did when he saw what had Io in hysterics. But then they'd been told over and over not to waste their power and they'd already been in trouble—no point in digging the hole any deeper. "My mom loves nature, but she loves it *outdoors*."

"I'm jealous."

"If you want grasshoppers that bad, I can get you some. I think I still remember how to catch them."

Shona laughed. "I was talking about your relationship with your family. I always wished I had a sister or brother."

The wistful note in her voice took Logan off guard and made him feel guilty. She did have a brother, she just wasn't aware of it. "Yeah, it has its moments, but then there were the times when I would have given anything to watch whatever I wanted on TV without having to fight for the remote first and I had to share the bathroom with three girls."

"You don't have to sound so horrified. It couldn't have been that bad—you lived to tell the tale."

"Only because I was out of the house before they started dating." This was getting close to quicksand territory—how did he explain leaving home at twelve for troubleshooter training?—and Logan changed the subject. "Did you ever get in trouble as a kid?"

"Oh, yeah. Who hasn't?"

Logan glanced over at the demon, but he'd gone back to his paper. "Then tell me one of your stories."

Shona settled back in her chair and looked thoughtful for a moment before she said, "I had a book on art from the library and one of the chapters was on mosaics—you know where they take pieces of pottery or glass and inlay them to create a picture."

"I saw plenty of mosaics when I was in Italy."

"Sorry." Logan thought he'd kept his voice even, but her face went red again. "It's just that you didn't seem to know much about art and—"

"Don't worry; I'm not offended. I wanted you to realize that I'm not a complete philistine—just a partial one."

She smiled and some of her tension went away. "Okay, so you're familiar with mosaics. Do you also know that art books suggest finding old pottery, glass, or tiles, putting them in a bag, and taking a hammer to them?"

Logan shook his head, and taking a peek over at the demon, discovered he was pouring sugar onto a napkin. Logan's eyes narrowed and he tried to unobtrusively glare at the losassi.

"My parents were out and I wanted to try my hand at making one. I sketched a pattern, decided to use my old tea party table as a base, found grout, adhesive, and the other supplies. All I needed was something to break and use as tiles."

"I think I know where this is going."

"Yes. My mom had this bowl with great colors that she never used and I thought that it was because she didn't like it."

"Which made it perfect for you to smash up."

"Absolutely. I was laying out my design when my folks came home. It took them a moment to work out what I'd hammered into a thousand pieces, but once they did, you probably heard my mom shriek all the way in Chicago." Shona smiled faintly. "I learned that not only did she love that bowl more than any other, but that it was also worth a small fortune."

Now the demon was emptying the salt shaker. "How long did you get grounded for?"

"One long month."

Logan watched the losassi put the sugar into the salt shaker and nearly groaned. Talk about lame pranks.

"Hey, am I boring you?"

"What?" Her question wasn't as assertive as it sounded; Logan heard the thread of self-doubt and the hurt beneath the bravado. "Of course not," he assured her. "Why would you think that?"

"You keep looking away, that's why."

"Sorry. Occupational hazard." Logan shrugged. "I saw someone who set off alarm bells and I've been keeping an eye on him."

"Really?" She leaned forward and lowered her voice. "Who?"

"The guy who's pouring salt into the sugar dispenser."

"Ooh, yeah. That's one dangerous character."

The comment took him by surprise and he grinned. "I know. What can I say? I have an overdeveloped sense of who's up to something."

"Way overdeveloped." Shona sat back. "What exactly does a Special Vice President of Security do anyway?"

That question got his full attention. "Why do you ask?" He was buying time, trying to figure out what he was going to say.

She was quiet, studying him intently, before she said, "One, you're not wearing a suit and it's Tuesday, not casual Friday. Two, you're not worried about the time or about getting back to the office. You don't even have a watch on. Three, you're too young to be a vice president of a corporation as large as the Gineal Company. You can't be much more than thirty."

"Twenty-eight," he corrected.

Raising both her eyebrows, Shona asked, "What gives?"

It would have been easy for her to back down since he wasn't being forthcoming, but she showed a tenacity that he liked—and respected. Logan met her gaze and said, "My job isn't corporate, I'm more of a troubleshooter."

Her eyes got big. "Like some kind of enforcer who goes around breaking kneecaps?"

Logan choked, but he couldn't contain his laughter. What made Shona's comment even funnier was that troubleshooters were referred to by the Gineal as the council's enforcers; the two terms were interchangeable. Damn, she was a dichotomy—sophisticated in some ways, yet naive in others; shy, but persistent—and so far, she'd kept him on his toes.

When he saw storm clouds gathering in her eyes, Logan forced himself to sober. "Sorry, I wasn't laughing at you." She didn't look as if she believed him. Smart lady. "It was the mental image of my boss as Don Corleone that got me. Although, now that I think about it, Nessia does give orders I can't refuse."

Shona hesitated long enough that Logan feared he'd really blown it, but before he could come up with something to make things right again, she said, "I think you have to say that last line like Marlon Brando for it to have any impact."

"If I attempted to do an impersonation, you'd be cringing and that's not the kind of response a guy's hoping for when he's out with a gorgeous woman." A gentle blush tinted her cheeks. "And before you think I'm evading your question, I can tell you with a hundred percent honesty that I've never deliberately harmed a human being in my life—although if I'd gotten a hold of the man who grabbed you, I wouldn't be able to say that."

The losassi stood, gave Logan a small salute, blew a kiss at Shona, and then sauntered out the door.

"Cheeky devil, isn't he?"

"He's got a style all his own," Logan agreed. But then most demons from that branch did have a certain flair.

Shona cleared her throat, drawing his attention back to her. "Back to my original question. Since you're not a thug, what does your job entail?"

"When our auditors find an irregularity, I follow it to the source and do what it takes to set things right." That wasn't a lie—exactly. Monitors audited the energy fields in their assigned areas and looked for dark-force creatures who were irregularities, abominations, and when he defeated them, things were right again.

"You're an accountant then?"

Logan winced. "Do I look like an accountant?" He didn't wait for an answer. "*Troubleshooter* fits best because I deal with a wide range of problems. I've learned to be flexible since I'm never sure what I'll be handling."

That killed the conversation, and from the way her gaze was skittering around the room, it looked like Shona was nervous again. Grimly, Logan lowered the odds of his plan working. If he made her this anxious, there was no chance she'd accept an invitation to go out and put herself through more stress.

He wasn't used to this reaction—Kel was the one who made people uncomfortable, not him. Logan thought about sending his brother a telepathic request for some advice, but decided there was no point in that. Kel never tried to put others at ease.

"I'm sorry that I make you jumpy," he apologized.

"It's not you, not directly." Shona's lips twisted. "This isn't easy for me and I'm trying to work up my courage."

"To keep talking to me? I'm not scary. If I were, my sisters would stop bugging me all the time, but no matter how many times I snarl at them, they keep coming back. I haven't even shown you the scowl that has zero effect on them."

Shona chuckled, but she didn't lose the panic. "I wanted to ask you a question, that's why I'm psyching myself up."

"Something that has you more nervous than asking if I break kneecaps for a living?"

He heard her swallow. "Are you involved with anyone?"

The words came so fast, Logan had to mentally replay them before he understood what she'd said. *That* question had her stressed out? "No, I'm not involved."

"Do you have plans for Friday night?"

"Are you asking me out?"

She nodded, her head jerking like a bobblehead doll, and if anything, Shona looked more scared than she had a moment earlier. "I have to go to a party. It's an art thing and getting an invitation is a pretty big deal, but I've been dreading attending by myself. But if you can't go, don't worry. I was planning to attend alone anyway, so it's not a big deal. Really. I shouldn't have expected you to be interested anyway."

Her fingers were mutilating the napkin on the table in front of her and Logan reached out and put his palm over her hands. "I'd love to go, Shona."

"You would?" He nodded. "Wow. I mean, great!"

"Is this the first time you've asked a man out?"

"It showed, huh?"

"Just a little," Logan said gently. "It's okay, though, because it makes it easier for me to ask if you have plans for tonight, and if not, how do you feel about going out to dinner?"

Her fingers spasmed under his, but her shoulders went back, and she met his eyes squarely when she said, "I'd love to."

5

CHAPTER

Farran turned off her car's engine and stared up at the neon sign over the doorway. It was barely dusk, but the name blazed in the twilight—*ucky's Bar*. The *L* was burnt out, but she hoped they didn't get it fixed. Ucky. That was truth in advertising.

She swung out of the sedan and threaded her way through the bikers and hoods loitering in the parking lot. There were catcalls and leers, but these men didn't scare her. Her magic might be weak by her family's standards, but she had more than enough to take care of any human foolish enough to try something.

Maybe her attitude made them think twice. Or maybe no one wanted to expend energy on a lazy summer evening, but Farran walked into the bar without having to level anyone.

The dive was more appalling inside than it was outside. Every wall was covered in graffiti, some of it was names or words, and there were drawings of oversized penises and symbols that Farran was unable to identify. Also on the walls, scattered, were lighted beer signs and suspended over the pink fluorescent tubes.

The odor was nearly overwhelming. Mixed with the scent of spilled beer was the stench of unwashed bodies and the hint of urine. She walked farther from the door and saw that some of the decor consisted of bras and panties—autographed. Wrinkling her nose, Farran searched the neon signs for a particular brand of beer and the man who'd be sitting beneath it.

Someone bumped into her, nearly spilling his drink all over her. "Watch where you're going, bitch," he growled.

Instead of replying verbally, she unobtrusively shot the man with enough energy to make him sway as he stumbled off. He made it about twenty feet before he staggered into another man who shoved the guy hard enough to send him to the floor. A few women screamed and the area grew quiet for a moment, but then the conversations resumed. The man didn't get up again. "I don't like to be called *bitch,*" she muttered under her breath before continuing on her search mission.

Farran felt the weight of his stare before she spotted the correct sign. She took her time crossing the room, letting him wait. It was the least she planned to do to him tonight.

"Beat it," the guy told the man sitting at the table with him. Scooping up his bottle of beer, the biker stood, cast one fast glance at her, and melted into the crowd. "You're late," her thug accused.

"Sue me." Farran took the vacated seat and stared hard at the man across from her. The lighting was dim, but she could see the stains on his brown T-shirt and blue Seahawks baseball cap. His unkempt goatee had a few crumbs in it and his long blond hair was so stringy, she had to believe he hadn't washed it since the last time they'd met more than a week ago. Shaggy. That was his name, but Filthy or Dirty would be more accurate.

"You owe me money."

"I owe you nothing," Farran disagreed.

"We had a deal."

"We did and the key element was that you wouldn't hurt her."

"I didn't."

Farran clenched her fists. "You tried to rape her!"

Shaggy looked surprised before anger suffused his face. "The hell I did."

"She told me—"

"I don't give a fuck what she told you, she's wrong."

Narrowing her gaze, Farran gathered the energy for a truth spell. It was complicated and it took more magic than she cared to use, but she had to know what this mercenary was capable of. She closed the incantation. "Did you try to rape her?"

"Hell, no! I already told you that."

She let out a slow breath and relaxed slightly. "Why did she say that then?" Shaggy shrugged and Farran said, "Tell me what happened in detail. Don't omit anything."

When he finished, she ran through things and concluded that it was the way he'd grabbed Shona's shirt that had made her believe that rape was imminent. It made sense, but luckily it wasn't true. Farran needed Shaggy and now she could continue to use him. She lifted the spell.

The man shook his head, and with a small furrow between his brows, said, "Let's get back to business. I want the rest of my money."

"Our arrangement was half up front and half when the job's finished. The job isn't finished."

"Bullshit," Shaggy disagreed sharply, "I did everything you said; it ain't my fault that dude showed up. You told me no one would be around."

Farran shrugged. The barrier she'd created hadn't been designed to keep out one of the Gineal, but she hadn't sensed any in the vicinity. Chalk it up to her bad luck that he was a troubleshooter. He would have felt the magic she'd used and now he knew of her presence in this dimension.

"That doesn't mean our deal has changed. You want more money, you finish what I hired you to do."

Shaggy leaned forward, trying to intimidate her with his size, but Farran wasn't backing down, she couldn't. Too much hung in the balance and finding another lowlife who could be semi-trusted would take more time than she had.

He growled, and when he realized she wasn't frightened, grabbed his beer bottle. After taking a swig, he slammed it down down with a thunk. "It ain't fair."

This time she leaned toward him. "It's exactly fair," she told him. "We agreed to very specific terms and you haven't met them yet. Do your job and you'll see how fair I can be."

"How about half of the half you owe me?" he tried cajoling.

"No. Or is your rep as a man of his word wrong?"

His face immediately went red. "Don't you inpew my rep."

Inpew? Whatever. "I won't impugn your honor as long as you hold true to your end of our bargain." She stood, rested both hands on the table and got in his face. "The next time you ask for the money, you better have finished what I hired you to do or you'll rue your impudence." He frowned. "Go to dictionary dot com and look it up."

Straightening, Farran pivoted and strode out of the bar.

Shona let the gentle motion of the ship lull her as she waited for Logan to return from the bar. The last thing she'd expected was a dinner cruise, and this was a five-star restaurant on an enormous yacht complete with candles and fine linens. As soon as the meal had ended, the wait staff had cleared the tables and disappeared, only to reappear as the band. While that left the guests to fend for themselves at the two bars set up on either side of the dining room, the music was wonderful.

The entire night had been great so far. Not only had the food been fabulous, but the service had been attentive, though not intrusive, and the crowd was light enough that she and Logan were able to have a table for four to themselves next to the large windows. Best of all, though, he'd kept the conversation going until she'd felt comfortable enough for her mind to unfreeze.

She'd learned a few new things about Logan tonight. For one, he liked to have a wall at his back and he'd claimed a spot in the corner. The seating was arranged with the short sides of the rectangular tables against the windows, but if she sat facing the bulkhead, she'd have her view cut short because of the way the ship was designed. Sitting next to him, though, allowed her to see the bay, and so she'd settled in with the windows on her right and Logan on her left.

He also had a habit of regularly scanning the room. When they'd been at the coffeehouse, Logan had told her it was something he did automatically, and while Shona had mostly believed him, part of her had wondered if maybe she *had* been boring him. But over the course of the evening, she'd discovered that it was a reflex with him. He did it unobtrusively, but it was as if she could feel his focus on her lessen, then intensify again as he finished his perusal of everything around them.

Logan was talking to a man next to him in line and Shona envied him the easy ability to chat with strangers. For her, it was torture. She was okay only if someone else took the lead and asked her questions about her art. Her stomach would still be all knotted up from stress, but at least she could answer.

Shona watched Logan laugh and sighed. As good as he'd looked in jeans or khakis, the man was devastating in a suit and tie. But even in corporate attire, he didn't come across like a VP of anything. Instead, it seemed to underline his dangerous streak. It was well hidden, but it was there and the idea of his letting it loose with her—in bed—took her breath away.

Think about something else. She'd debated what to wear tonight, leaning toward pants since he'd appeared to like casual clothing, but she was relieved that she'd gone with a simple coral-pink dress. The style was plain—sleeveless with a crew neck and it fit closely to her body before flaring out at her hips—but Shona had slipped three chunky gold bangle bracelets on her right wrist and that made the outfit formal enough for the ship. The only other jewelry she had on was her necklace. It was beneath her clothing as it always was, but Shona wanted the warmth of the stone near her heart.

Logan glanced over and caught her staring. She felt her cheeks warm, but she didn't look away. He didn't either, not for a long moment. The heat intensified and she curled her toes, trying to keep from going up in flames from his gaze alone. Before she could do something more embarrassing, the bartender addressed him and he turned to reply.

Shona shifted her attention to the couples on the dance floor and wondered why it took so little for Logan to rev up her hormones. It left her confused. Why him? It wasn't gratitude. If it was, she'd be over it by now, but every time she saw him, her desire grew stronger.

She liked Logan. A lot. More than liked him, but she'd been interested in other guys at other times in her life and they'd never made her ache the way this man did. It threw her off balance and left her tongue-tied at odd moments— usually when he asked her a question while she was wondering what it would be like to kiss him or have him touch her. She had it bad and it was only getting worse.

When she saw him leave the bar, Shona took a moment to enjoy the graceful, powerful way he moved before shifting her gaze. The last thing she wanted was him catching her gawking again and guessing what he did to her.

"Bellini martini," Logan said, placing her glass on the table.

"Thanks."

He put down his own glass and settled in the seat beside her. As close as he was, it wasn't near enough, and Shona reached for her drink to keep from leaning into him. She took a sip and asked, "What are you having?"

"Mineral water."

"I would have put my money on an imported ale."

Logan smiled and her heart sped up. "You'd have lost. I don't drink."

"Ever?" Shona wasn't much of a drinker either, but she couldn't imagine not having a glass of red wine with pasta and marinara sauce or the occasional martini if she went out.

"Never," he confirmed.

"Why not?" Shona blushed as it dawned on her what she'd asked. She really was a hopeless idiot in social situations. "I'm sorry. Asking a question that personal was rude. Forget I said it, okay?"

"It's not too personal," he said, and Shona thought he was curbing his amusement. "I have an allergic reaction to alcohol, not a drinking problem."

"Oh." She raised her glass to her lips, buying time while she tried to come up with something else to say. Her mind remained stubbornly blank even after she returned her drink to the table. Why wasn't Logan rescuing her?

But he was frowning and pulling the cell phone off the clip at his belt. She hadn't heard it ring, but likely he'd had it set on vibrate. He checked caller ID. "Sorry, I have to answer this."

"Your job?" He'd told her he was always on call.

"No, it's my parents' number." Logan flipped open the cell. "Hello?" His scowl deepened. "Keavy, I can't talk right now."

Shona relaxed. Keavy was his youngest sister—she couldn't forget an unusual name like that. According to Logan, it meant *beautiful* in Gaelic and she thought that was cool.

Logan was already talking softly, but he lowered his voice further when he said, "Because I'm on a date, that's why." A brief pause. "That's none of your business." He put his hand over the bottom of the phone and whispered, "I'm sorry."

"Don't worry about it," she said every bit as quietly, and to give him what privacy she could, Shona did her best to ignore the conversation. She listened to the old standards the band was playing and watched the dancing. This wasn't normally her type of music, but she had to admit there was something very romantic about it. She wondered if Logan danced.

The thought of being held close while they moved on the floor was enough to make her skin tingle. There'd be a respectable distance between them, just like there was between all the other couples, but every now and then, her breasts would brush his chest or their thighs would meet. She'd always had a good imagination—it was as necessary to an artist as air or water—but this time Shona could picture it so vividly, her body physically reacted.

Needing to regain her composure, Shona glanced away from the dance floor toward the windows. Her eyes were already moving on, when she realized that she'd seen something. With a gasp, she jerked her gaze back toward the glass.

"What is it?" Logan asked.

Shona shook her head and peered more intently.

"What's wrong?"

She didn't see anything now. Well, of course not. What she'd thought she'd seen didn't exist. Turning her back to the windows and facing Logan, she said, "Nothing." He was off the phone now, but he continued to hold it. "It was a trick of the light, I guess." He didn't say anything, just waited and Shona sighed. "I thought I saw the Loch Ness Monster out there."

He didn't laugh at her or suggest that maybe she give up drinking if half a martini could incite hallucinations. Instead, he looked thoughtful as he put his cell back on its clip. "There shouldn't be anything like that in the bay."

That surprised a laugh from her before she realized he wasn't joking. "Of course there isn't," she said.

"I meant," Logan said, "there aren't any legends that I know of about unidentified creatures in these waters. Nothing that could be mistaken for a sea monster, that's for certain."

His correction didn't make complete sense to her, but she was too grateful that he wasn't patting her on the head to ask for clarification. Most men would have humored her or said something patronizing, but Logan hadn't. "It's pretty dark out there. It must have been some kind of shadow created by the moon or something." Embarrassed, Shona changed the subject. "Is your sister okay?"

Logan grimaced. "Yeah, Keavy is just fine. Sorry about the interruption. It's the same old story—our parents told her no and she wanted to enlist me to battle them on her behalf." His frown faded. "I wonder how much longer it's going to take her to realize that all I do is play mediator when things get heated. My other two sisters caught on faster than this."

"Do they still ask for your help?"

"Rarely. They're both old enough now that when they come to me it's usually for advice or to vent instead of expecting me to fix things for them." His grin returned. "Hell, Tris might kick my butt if I so much as thought about stepping into her fight."

"Someday you'll be saying the same thing about Keavy."

"I hope so." But Logan didn't sound convinced. He shrugged. "Let's not talk about my sisters anymore. You probably know more about them than you ever wanted to."

"I've enjoyed hearing about them." She had. It allowed her to experience vicariously what it was like to have a sibling and she'd gotten to know him in a way she might not have if he hadn't shared those stories. Besides, these conversations were the main reason she'd been able to put aside the caution her parents had instilled in her and trust Logan enough to allow him to pick her up at her house and why she'd let him get her a drink without standing right there next to him at the bar to take possession of it. He might not realize how careful she usually was, but Shona rarely took chances.

Quiet stretched between them and she tensed, trying to come up with something—anything—to say. Her art was out—not only did he not know much about it, but the ball of fear in her belly grew bigger when she thought about it. He didn't want to discuss his family again. She—

"Relax, Shon," Logan said. His hand touched her knee for an instant, then was gone. "We don't have to talk every minute."

Shon? Something inside her went soft. No one, not even her parents, had ever shortened her name and she liked it. She especially liked it in Logan's deep, sexy voice.

The skin on her nape prickled, erasing the warmth and she fought back a shiver. With only the windows and the bay behind her, she was afraid to turn to the right and see what was out there. "Want to dance?" Shona blurted.

"Sure." Logan stood and offered her his hand to help her to her feet. He didn't let go, linking their fingers as he led her to the dance floor. Instead of enjoying the slight abrasion of his calloused palm against hers, Shona fought the need to look over her shoulder. She didn't want to know what was back there, but part of her was compelled to check. To fight temptation, she focused on the man beside her, on the brush of his shoulder against hers, the solid warmth of his hand.

They reached the floor, Logan held up his arms, and she stepped into them. Sensation flooded Shona and her worries about the Loch Ness Monster receded. There was only here, only now.

The music was sultry and slow, the lighting was dreamy and romantic, and Logan was charming and sexy. She picked up the faint scent of his aftershave and leaned in slightly to take a second, deeper breath. He smelled good and Shona wished he would tug her closer.

The other diners became part of the background and she lost herself in the dance, in Logan. They didn't talk and her senses grew hyper-aware. She could see the little navy flecks in his eyes, feel each line of his palm beneath her hand, and hear each breath he took.

Logan moved her into a turn that allowed her to ease nearer to him and Shona took advantage of it before she could talk herself out of it. Now she could discern the beat of his heart, the pulse of his blood through his body and her own slowed to match his rhythm. It was strange, but not frightening, and Shona decided not to worry about it.

One song segued into another and then a third, and still they danced, her gaze locked on his. There was a banked heat at the back of his cobalt eyes that matched the leashed arousal she could sense in him. Shona shivered.

It left her giddy, excited, like the high school geek dancing with the star football player at prom. It was silly, a holdover from when she had been the butt of a million jokes. String bean, Jolly Green Giant, stilts—she'd heard them all and then some—and she should be over it by now, but years of ridicule were hard to leave behind. Logan, though, didn't seem to care that he was only a couple of inches taller than she was, he was interested in her anyway. A rosy glow descended, making the entire evening that much sweeter.

We will watch. We will judge.

At the same instant she heard that strange voice in her head, the music switched to a fast, upbeat song. Shona stumbled, shock stopping her cold. First she was seeing mirages, now she was hearing voices? Fear constricted her lungs, making it difficult to draw a full breath.

Logan tightened his hold, steadying her physically and emotionally. "Are you okay?"

"Yes, fine." She cleared her throat. "The sudden change in tempo took me by surprise."

"Yeah." Logan scowled and drew her closer, getting her out of the way of another couple who were dancing with more zeal than skill. "Is it okay with you if we sit this one out?"

"Of course."

His hand went to the small of her back as he escorted her off the floor, but Shona drew him to a halt before they reached their table. That was where her trouble had started. "Why don't we go up on deck? I'd like to get some fresh air."

With a nod, he adjusted their course. The door they exited through led to the ship's stern and Shona walked to the railing, curling her fingers around it.

It was cooler outside than she'd expected, but the breeze cleared her head and she could finally take a deep breath. Her tension ebbed. Moonlight danced on the water, illuminating the small chop the yacht left in her wake. Shona was aware of Logan standing at her side. He shifted, his shoulder brushing her bare arm, and she shivered.

"Here," he said, shrugging out of his suit coat. "Put this on."

Shona turned to face him and Logan held his jacket until she slipped her arms through the sleeves, then his hands tugged the lapels, crossing them over her collarbone. He didn't release the fabric; instead he stood looking down at her. Something in his eyes made it hard for her to draw air and she parted her lips, trying to get oxygen.

"Oh, hell," he muttered. Logan brushed his mouth over hers, there and gone in a heartbeat.

She nearly groaned when he began to pull away. "Again," Shona ordered, "and this time, don't tease." She surprised herself, but before she could get anxious about saying something that bold, Logan gave her one of his crooked smiles.

There was nothing tentative about their second kiss, but he kept it gentle and easy. She waited for him to loose the fire she'd seen in him, but to her frustration, he didn't take the kiss deeper, and instead of embracing her, he kept his hands on the suit coat.

When he started to ease away, she wrapped her arms around his waist, pulling herself against him, and opened her mouth beneath his. His hesitation lasted just long enough for Shona to feel a stab of panic, then his tongue dipped into her mouth.

Didn't he understand she didn't want him to be a gentleman? Kissing him the way she wanted to be kissed, Shona turned and he moved with her. With his back against the railing, she leaned into him, settling between his legs. She arched her hips, pressing more firmly against him, and his arms went around her, anchoring her against his body.

He took over then, giving her what she'd demanded. But even as he kissed her hungrily, Shona was aware of two things—his hands remained at her waist and Logan still had his self-command. It brought her back to her senses. Shona didn't step away—she didn't want to—but reined in her own desire.

You can make him lose his control.

This voice didn't startle her. It wasn't the same one as earlier, but gentler somehow, feminine. Maybe this inner urging didn't come from outside herself, but from some deep-down part of her that wanted to be a . . . ah . . . a vixen.

Logan took the kiss down a notch, then another, but this time, Shona let things wane. Her lips clung to his for just an instant when he eased back and reluctantly she opened her eyes.

She'd always thought of blue as a cool color, but the inferno she saw in his gaze changed her mind. He was still a gentleman, still taking care of her even when she hadn't wanted him to be cautious. The conflagration, though, hinted at something she'd suspected—if they let this relationship progress to the point where they became lovers, Logan wouldn't be polite in bed. He'd let all that heat free and send her up in flames with him. And he'd want everything from her. Everything. The idea enticed as much as it frightened.

Not wanting to give him a chance to guess what she was thinking, Shona hugged him, putting her cheek against his and looking over his shoulder. She stared into the black water, trying to figure out what to say, what to do.

"Relax," he said, lightly stroking her back through his suit coat. "And look on the bright side—when I take you home tonight, you won't have to worry about our first kiss."

Shona grinned. "There is that."

Her smile faded, though, as she caught movement on the bay. It wasn't another ship or a bird. At the very edge of the light thrown off by their yacht, a head broke the water. A head connected to a long, long neck.

Clutching Logan more tightly, she watched its eyes begin to glow red. Demonic red.

Remember, we're watching.

Then, with what she'd swear was a wink, it disappeared beneath the surface.

6

CHAPTER

Logan clambered over a pile of debris, mostly wood and broken stone, and ignored Kel's quiet cursing. His brother hadn't been happy since he'd realized the Seattle Underground wasn't a collection of trendy boutiques and cafés, but actual subterranean passages beneath the current-day city. His explanation about the town burning in the 1800s and being rebuilt one story higher had gotten him a glare. Kel's mood had soured further when they'd left the area that was part of a tour and ventured farther out.

There were no lights here. Kel had thrown a spell to illuminate the area around them, but it was no brighter than a flashlight and only covered a slightly larger distance. They were scanning with their other senses anyway.

The brick walls of the old buildings were in better condition than Logan had expected. There were a few stones missing here and there and some were chipped, but overall, the workmanship had survived. Green moss covered the walls in spots, metal had oxidized to the point that it was beginning to flake, and cobwebs had accumulated until they were thick enough to be used as rope—which was probably what had Kel in such a foul temper. He hated spiders.

Logan sent out a scan. His brother liked to make periodic sweeps over a long distance, but he preferred to scan more often at a shorter distance. Both methods had their pros and cons, but it was one of many ways that they differed from each other.

Sometimes he wondered if they'd developed their distinctions subconsciously as kids. It wasn't always easy being twins and since others, especially humans, had looked for their similarities, it seemed natural that he and Kel had focused on what made them individuals.

Of course, that didn't mean they'd never played it to their advantage. They couldn't trick any of the Gineal because everyone had a unique energy signature, but humans were another story. They'd switched places in grade school more than once and no one had ever caught on. Logan studied Kel unobtrusively. They wouldn't fool anyone now.

In the past, his brother had always been well-groomed, but now his hair was long enough to fall past his eyes and he was rarely clean shaven. Today Kel had about two days' worth of stubble on his chin and it would probably be another two days before he used a razor. Hell, Logan was used to being the casual one, but Kel had changed, his already intense nature heightening even further.

They came up to a barrier made of spider webs and stopped. "Why the hell did you have to drag me along on your search mission?" Kel griped.

"You're the one who says that brothers stick together. Has that changed?" Logan heard Kel growl and had to fight a smile. "You know," he needled some more, "if I felt like listening to a lot of moaning and groaning, I would have invited Keavy."

Kel rounded on him. "Are you comparing me to a seventeen-year-old girl?"

"If the attitude fits . . . Kidding. Kidding!" He held up both hands in an I-surrender gesture. Kel wasn't going to hit him, but the banked fury was enough to make Logan stop the baiting. Not that long ago, Kel would have given as good as he got, but that was something else that had changed.

Logan began looking around for something to tear down the webs. His phobias didn't involve anything with four, six, or eight legs, but he had no desire to plow through that. Their jeans and T-shirts were already dusty and grimy—hell, Kel's white shirt looked gray—and fighting to the other side of the webs would leave them even dirtier. That was, of course, if he could get his brother to attempt to walk through it.

"This place is a disaster." Kel had his arms crossed over his chest and he was scowling.

"At least it's not falling down around our heads." Logan located a long board and jiggled it out from the pile it was buried under.

Taking another look around, Kel said, "It's hard to imagine wanting to hide out here. Who tipped you off that the Tàireil you're after went underground?"

"No one." Logan stabbed the board through the webs and started moving it around, clearing their path.

From the corner of his eye, Logan saw Kel jerk his gaze from the wall to stare at him. "You scried?"

"No." Logan kept his face and his tone carefully neutral. Once, his ability to remote-see had been phenomenal— almost as good as any of the monitors. Then Kel had gone missing and Logan had short circuited his talent trying to find him.

The silence between them became uncomfortable, something else that was new. "So," Kel said a bit too loudly, "how did you find out the darksider was hiding here?"

With a shrug, Logan lowered the board, studied his handiwork, and decided it was open enough now that even his arachnophobic brother wouldn't balk. "We all know that they like their hidden lairs and this fits the bill."

"Wait a second. You're guessing?"

Incredulity laced Kel's voice and Logan frowned. "It's an educated guess."

"No, it isn't," Kel disagreed. "The so-called hidden lairs of the Tàireil are secret corridors and rooms inside their mansions, not dilapidated underground passages. I can't believe you dragged me here for nothing."

"You don't have to sound disgusted." Logan tossed the slat he'd used back on top of the pile where he'd found it and wiped off his hands on the thighs of his jeans, trying to get rid of some of the dirt. "They don't have palatial estates in our dimension."

"That doesn't mean a darksider is going to choose squalor."

Logan gestured around him. "Look at this place. No one comes here. The tours stay in a three-block area and that's it. He'd remain undisturbed."

"Would you live down here even for a couple of days?"

"Of course not, but—"

"Then why do you think a darksider would?"

"They're different than—"

Kel cut him off. "Did you research after getting this assignment?"

Immediately Logan became wary. His brother didn't go off on tangents and that meant there was something brewing that he probably didn't want to hear. "I didn't need to. We learned about the Tàireil when we were apprentices."

Using both hands, Kel pushed his hair back out of his face and cursed. "Little brother, you need to stop playing with your damn cars and start studying."

Anger bubbled. Logan hated it when Kel called him *little brother*—seven minutes was negligible—but what really had his temper steaming was the accusation of not hitting the books. Maybe he wasn't the student that Kel was, but he'd never shirked his duties as a Gineal enforcer. "I study."

"Obviously not enough. If the ceannards find out, they'll force you to spend time at the tasglann. Do you want to waste hours there every week with some apprentice librarian hovering over you? And would you like to bet that the council will start giving you quizzes the same way they did when you were training? Is this what you're shooting for?"

"I study," Logan ground out between clenched teeth.

"If that was true, we wouldn't be down here." His brother shook his head. "The Tàireil are us."

"They're not like us, that's why it's a big deal when they jump to our dimension."

Kel kicked a pebble with the toe of his sneaker, watching it skitter across the ground, hit the wall, and go still. "I didn't say *like* us, I said they *are* us." Logan was trying to sort out what Kel meant when his brother added, "Yep, uh-huh, you study all the time—that's why you don't have a clue what I'm talking about."

"You know," Logan said conversationally, "no one likes people who are smug. Fill me in instead of acting superior."

His brother finally met his gaze again. "If you've read our history," Kel said with a snideness that irritated Logan further, "you'd know that back when we were being hunted there were two strong factions fighting for control. One wanted us to hide in plain sight and police ourselves so that humans would never know we existed. The other was lobbying for the Gineal to use magic to protect our people and eliminate any threat. Our populace was evenly split, even the men and women who sat on the council at that time were divided. It came down to one vote."

Logan forgot his aggravation with Kel as he began to get an idea where this topic was headed. He'd always been fascinated by multiple dimensions and the Gineal ability to travel among them. Almost all were Earth-like to a degree and the theory held that these alternate realities had broken off the main time line—usually at some crossroads—and developed from there, maybe even splitting off again and again, leaving a nearly infinite number of universes out there.

"You're saying," Logan spoke slowly, "that the decision on how to deal with humans was the fork in the path that separated the Tàireil's world off from ours. That means they're not a separate magical race."

"Or it split us off from them, but yeah, a long time ago they were Gineal, too. Their choices evolved them into what they are today."

Logan narrowed his eyes as he considered this. "How much substantiation was included with the hypothesis?"

"Several hundred pages' worth—which you'd be aware of if you'd done the necessary reading."

He took a step toward Kel, hands clenched. "Look—"

"Sorry, I know, you study." His brother smiled, but it was a shadow of his usual crooked grin. "To be honest with you, I skimmed that stuff; the researchers can go on and on. What I remember it boiling down to was DNA results, commonalities in how we're governed, and histories back in antiquity that seem similar if not shared. Beyond that, you'll need to go through it yourself because I can't recall anything else."

Logan would find the material and scan it at some point, but not right now. He had the basic facts and that's what he needed to protect Shona; details could wait until she was safe. "You know, the darksiders changed over time. Maybe they evolved until they like subterranean tunnels."

"Give it up, would you? We live in normal upper middle-class homes and we wouldn't stay down here. Do you think someone who's spent their entire life in a palace is going to last ten minutes in this filth?"

"No," he was forced to admit, "but I was hoping this was it." Logan crammed his hands into the front pockets of his jeans. He wanted Shona safe ASAP. "Do you know how many damn hotels there are?"

Kel shrugged. "A lot and you couldn't stop there. You'd have to consider rental units or that the darksider decided to just take over someone's home. Killing or imprisoning a family wouldn't faze him."

That wasn't something Logan had thought of, but he should have. Kel was right—the Tàireil took what they wanted from humans without thinking twice. When he factored in all the upper-end homes in Seattle and its suburbs as well as the four and five star hotels, the odds of locating one lone man were daunting. "Hell, finding him will be almost impossible."

"Damn near. Come on, let's get out of here and grab some lunch." Kel headed back the way they'd come in. "Lucky for you, your job isn't to locate him, it's to protect the dormant."

Falling into step beside his brother, Logan pulled his hands from his pockets and said, "Her name's Shona."

Kel shot him a quick glance. "I know—Shona *Blackwood*. If you're smart, you won't forget that second part."

"Believe me, I'm aware that Creed Blackwood will come after me if I let his sister get hurt. I'm going to do my best to make sure nothing happens to her."

"I know that and I'm not worried about you getting beat by some darksider. You'll take care of him."

Logan wished he were that confident about the outcome, but then Kel didn't know about the fits Logan had been having whenever he used too much magic. "If you think I can handle the job, why'd you bring up Blackwood anyway?"

"Because if you don't keep your pants zipped around his little sister, the man is going to annihilate you."

For a moment, Logan was unable to respond. Kel had done it again. "How do you do that? There's no way you could have known I'm interested in her from what I said and yet you nailed it."

"Must be our special twin bond."

Logan snorted. His psychic abilities were no stronger with Kel than they were with any other Gineal. "Some day, man, I'm going to figure out your secret."

"Good luck with— Oh, hell."

"What?"

"Scan to our four o'clock position."

He didn't ask for a distance, automatically adjusting to use his brother's preferred range. At the outside edge, he sensed what Kel had picked up. Koznain.

The creatures were a kind of short, monstrous vampire, but instead of going after blood, they sucked bone marrow. Maybe the Tàireil didn't want to stay beneath Seattle, but their henchmen, the koznain, lived underground and would have gravitated toward this choice burrow. "I'm reading six of them," Logan said.

"I had five, but they're likely clustered together. Koznain stay in packs unless they're hunting. Do you need me to brief you on them?"

Logan saw red, but he took a long, deep breath before he asked, "Is there some reason why you're trying to get me mad enough to fight you before we go into battle? 'Cause I have to tell you, I prefer to have my self-command in these situations."

"No, I—" Kel appeared startled. "Sorry. I wasn't thinking."

He gave a nod to let Kel know his apology was accepted and ran another scan. "I'm not picking up any darksiders around."

"I think the creatures are meant to be a distraction. The Tàireil had to realize you sensed him when you rescued Shona and he'd want you too busy to zero in on him. Why not call over a gang of koznain and set them loose in the city? Imagine all the trouble they could cause."

"A lot," Logan agreed, "but the darksider couldn't count on me leaving Shona on her own. It's routine for the council to send another troubleshooter in to help if the need arises."

"Yeah, but as far as he knows, you just came across Shona accidentally. He'd figure that since this was your territory, you'd be assigned to track down each koznain, leaving him free to do whatever he wanted. Perfect diversion." Kel hooked his thumbs in the waistband of his jeans. "As luck would have it, though, we came here looking for a darksider and found his minions instead."

"My ignorance pays off." Logan grinned, but it was short-lived. "I'm going to cast a spell to contain them in the section they're in right now, then we can work out a strategy."

Kel shook his head. "You'll use up too much magic trying to cast something strong enough to hold them. It's better if we merge our powers to create the field."

"Yeah," Logan said unenthusiastically. It wasn't the effort it would take, although it would be considerable. No, what had him worried was what Kel would discover if Logan was open enough to meld energies. It didn't matter how close they were, if he learned Logan had episodes, his brother would be honor bound to tell the council about them.

"You know I'm right," Kel insisted. "Now let's get it in gear before the koznain sense our presence."

Surrendering, Logan lowered his primary mental barrier. It wasn't something any of their people did without careful consideration. Members in a society of telepaths learned to shield their minds early and only send the thoughts they wanted others to have. It was a far cry from allowing someone—even a brother—to have wide-ranging access.

The link was a struggle and the amount of time it was taking worried him. They couldn't allow the koznain to roam loose. Just before he was about to call it off, they finally managed the merge and Logan allowed the energy to flow through him. In some ways, this felt natural, as if they'd done it a billion times, but something inside him still rebelled and he needed to subdue it before they could complete the union.

Logan didn't try to snoop when they had the connection made. As curious as he was about what had happened to Kel, he'd never abuse his brother's trust, but he was very aware that part of Kel's mind had a fortress around it. Of course, Logan had bulwarks in place as well to protect his own secrets.

With their powers joined, they intoned the incantation to barricade the koznain. "And so it is," they said in unison, closing the proclamation. The instant the spell was in place, they severed the bond and Logan had a sense that Kel was as relieved as he was that it was done.

"Between the two of us, do we have enough magic to send the dirty half-dozen back home?"

Kel looked thoughtful for a moment before shaking his head. "Against their will? We might manage one or two if they're not shielded, but five or six? There's not much chance of that."

"If the darksider I'm after brought them over, those koznain are protected."

"That's what I think, too."

With a grimace, Logan ran through other possible strategies. The most obvious was that he and Kel penned the koznain between them and fired away, but it was too easy to accidently hit each other in the thick of battle. He was assessing a second idea, looking for pitfalls, when something occurred to him. "Overkill. Bringing the koznain here to distract one enforcer is overkill."

"How do you figure that? He wants Shona and he knows that you're standing in his way."

"Yeah, but because of the density of the koznains' bodies it takes a hell of a lot of magic to jump them between dimensions, especially a group of them. It was probably enough to drain the darksider for about forty-eight hours or a little longer. Why risk it? He's already at a disadvantage without powers during the day, but none at all? He'd have to hope I didn't track him down until after he recovered. If he bided his time, he'd probably find an opening to reach Shona at some point anyway—it's impossible to protect her completely at all times, so why didn't he wait and watch? The logic is off."

"You're right," Kel said slowly. "Without getting her to stay inside your house for the duration, there probably would be an opportunity to get at her. So yeah, this doesn't make sense unless there's more happening here than we know. You need to have a talk with the council."

"I did that after that human attacked Shona and I think they're as mystified by what's going on as I am." He shrugged. "Right now, though, the whys don't matter. We need to take care of the koznain before worrying about anything else."

"They're not going to be easy to bring down. Suffocation is out—they're anaerobic—and that also takes care of trying to drown them or bury them alive. All they'd have to do is wait for our containment spell to degrade and then dig their way out. Even blasting away at them will be hard."

"I know. They have too much damn protection." And it was too early for the darksider's shielding spell to begin to deteriorate. Logan tested a few more scenarios before he admitted, "I can't think of anything besides hammering at them."

Kel scowled. "I can't either, but I'm not sure the Gineal have fought enough koznain to come up with a better method."

"Then that's what we do. We for damn sure can't stand here and discuss it endlessly."

"No, we can't." After a short hesitation, Kel said, "Logan." He took a step nearer. "When we get in there, you watch your back. They like to feed from the spinal column and they'll likely attack that spot again and again in an attempt to break through your body's protection spell in that area."

Anger reared, but Logan tamped it down. Kel wasn't being a know-it-all, he was mentioning this because he wasn't sure how familiar Logan was with the koznain. "If we can't keep them in front of us, we'll fight back to back. That way we can defend each other."

Kel nodded, and after they reinforced their shields, he opened a transit big enough for both of them to cross. The instant they were on the other side, his brother waved a hand, closing the glowing portal behind them. They had just entered a cage match with a group of amoral killers.

Logan threw light into the space immediately. He had a fraction of a second to record countless details: the layout of the Underground section they were in, what kind of debris he had to contend with, and the position of the koznain.

There were *eight* of them and they had already encircled the chamber, anticipating his and Kel's arrival. Damn.

Without pausing, Logan moved so that his back met Kel's and he began blasting away. His lightning bolts and Kel's ropes of fire lit up the Underground.

And had no effect. The creatures didn't move, didn't fight back, hell, they never even flinched.

Logan continued to shoot. He'd never seen a koznain in the flesh before, and he sized them up, looking for a weakness. They were about five feet tall with stocky, solid bodies, and gray, wrinkled skin. He took in the long pointed ears, sharp teeth at least as long as a sabertooth tiger's fangs, and eyes that glowed a strange pinkish-red color. It took a few seconds before he realized they didn't have noses. Anaerobic.

A long tongue-like thing shot out of one of the creature's mouths and Logan fired at it, beating it back. They could extend it with enough velocity to penetrate muscle and burrow into bone. That creeped him out, but he forced it out of his mind.

He fought off another strike from a second koznain. Because shooting at all the monsters he faced was doing nothing, Logan concentrated on a single individual, hoping that by focusing his firepower, he'd be able to take it down.

Bolt after bolt ricocheted off his target and hit buildings, sending shards of brick flying. It didn't dent the koznain's shield.

Kel's shoulders bumped into his and Logan twisted around to see what was happening. His brother had two creatures moving toward him, but he was handling them fine.

A sharp sting on Logan's forearm jerked his attention back to his own side of the sealed-off tunnel. Three of the creatures were barely more than an arm's length away and he fired repeatedly with full strength.

He managed to drive them back about two feet. Barely.

The koznain didn't seem concerned. With their tongues darting out now and then, they looked like frogs lazily waiting on their lily pads for a fly to wander too close and he and Kel were the insects.

It was bizarre—he'd never shot at any dark-force being who didn't fight back. It made sense, though. If he and Kel weren't causing any damage, why not wait till they ran out of magic and kill them when there was no risk involved?

They don't care that we're hitting them, Logan sent to Kel. *I know the Gineal have beaten the koznain before.*

Yeah, but there must be some trick to killing them.

And they didn't know what it was.

He was burning through too much magic. His stomach knotted and Logan had to remind himself to breathe.

When he'd fought before, he only worried about draining himself; now he had to be concerned about when he would trigger the seizures. If those started, he and Kel were both dead. He knew his brother and he'd never leave Logan behind even if it cost him his own life.

Logan slowed his firing and weakened his shots to minimize his use of power. All he wanted was to keep the koznain at a distance until he figured out a way to bring them down.

Think, damn it, think.

The answer couldn't be hard. Battle wasn't good for deep thought and if other troubleshooters had come up with the solution, he should be able to do it, too.

Okay, they couldn't asphyxiate the koznain, couldn't drown them, and couldn't bury them alive. They had enough protection around them to prevent damage from lightning and fireballs and that meant a bladed weapon or gun would be useless as well.

Warm blood trickled down his forearm. If a koznain had been able to cause that much damage through his protective shield, Logan didn't want to know what it could do when that barrier fell. How much longer did he have before his magic weakened enough that he wouldn't be able to reinforce it?

And how much time did he have before he went into convulsions?

He took a second to wipe the blood off his arm and on to the leg of his jeans, but he wasn't quick enough. One of the koznain whipped its tongue out farther than Logan thought possible, catching him just above the right knee. It ripped through denim and bit into his flesh. He bit back a curse.

Calling on his magic, Logan unloaded until the creature withdrew its appendage.

It was only after he was clear that Logan realized he'd fallen for it. They wanted him to use up his store of power more quickly and he'd obliged. Moron.

Kel cursed, but this time Logan didn't check out the problem. He couldn't. As soon as his attention was diverted, there'd be another attack, and while his shield was still holding, the koznain were causing physical damage.

You okay? Logan asked.

Yeah, but their damn tongues are dangerous.

I know. The blood hadn't stopped flowing from his arm yet and he'd probably have a red stain near the knee of his jeans. He could feel the warmth there and—

Warmth. Hadn't he read that the bodies of koznains ran extremely hot and that they needed to continually cool their blood through the pores of their skin? What if they couldn't do that heat exchange? What happened then?

Logan grimaced. He wasn't sure, and even if he had paid attention in biology class, the same rules might not apply to monsters. But blocking their pores might cause damage.

Hell, it was worth a try.

But would anything contain them? Or would that damn protection spell thwart this idea, too?

Keeping up a weak stream of shots, Logan ran through possibilities, what he knew of the Tàireil, and shielding incantations. Realization struck.

If the darksiders had split off at the time the Gineal had gone to ground, they would have had no reason to develop technologically. Not when humans were held as serfs and the Tàireil had magic. Since protection spells were created to meet the needs of the world the creator knew, there was no reason to include things that didn't exist in their dimension. Like plastics.

Without words, he sent Kel a quick impression of what he was planning to try.

Conjuring a liquid polymer while keeping up cover fire wasn't easy. He slipped a few times and Logan had four more tongue slashes before he was able to complete the spell.

He started with the four koznain he could see, coating every centimeter of their bodies with molten blue plastic. They didn't react, but Logan wasn't surprised they were protected from this. Burning oil would be something the Tàireil had in their world.

He continued to flow the liquid over them, but now he brought up an arctic breeze, hardening the plastic.

One of the creatures grunted, but it sounded confused, not angry. Logan lessened the wind, brought more of the polymer down and then hit it with the cold again. He wanted that covering thick enough that the koznain wouldn't break through it.

This was costing him a lot of power. More than he should be using, but Logan didn't have much choice. He wanted to get himself and his brother out of this alive and Seattle was his territory.

Fear was never far away when he had to use magic—not any longer—and it reared up now, almost choking him. Logan ignored the nausea, ignored the cold sweat beading across his forehead, and he tried to ignore the shaky feeling that warned him he was getting too damn close to a seizure.

The plastic, though, stayed in place and he took that to mean he'd guessed right—the koznain had no defense against it because it wasn't a substance the Tàireil had in their world.

Logan heard something that sounded like a squeal behind him. "What are you doing?" he asked.

"Same thing you are." When Logan didn't comment, Kel added, "What? Did you think I was going to let you have all the fun?"

"We don't know if this is going to work."

"It's working, at least it is on my side. Not only is the plastic holding their heat in, but they're absorbing the toxins in the material. A double shot."

He stopped dripping polymer and firing lightning and waited. There were no more little flicks that sliced his skin and none of them moved. Maybe it was working. Logan leaned forward, attempting to get a closer look, but he couldn't see anything through the thick, colored plastic.

It was risky, but he chanced a couple of steps forward. The fine tremors in his quads were another warning sign, but Logan had time yet. He walked up to the koznain without a response from any of the creatures. They had to be out of commission.

Still, he backed away before turning to check out what was happening on the other side of the chamber. His brother, Logan noticed, had used clear plastic, that was why Kel had been certain the covering had worked. Through the translucent coating, their skin appeared to be the color of a plum. "They died faster than I expected."

"They're not human," Kel said. His brother's hair was wet from sweat and there was a six-inch splotch of blood on the chest of his T-shirt.

"How banged up are you?"

"Not bad. Looks like you got hit about triple the number of times that I did."

Logan looked down. Blood flowed easily from all his cuts. "Damn anticoagulants." Because of them, he was going to have to use more magic to heal himself and that was the last thing he wanted to do. Scowling, Logan ran his fingers over the slices on his arms, leg, and chest.

"That was good thinking on the plastic." Kel punched him lightly on the shoulder. "Guess you do use your brain now and then."

"Thanks," he drawled sarcastically, but he wasn't angry. Kel was teasing and Logan was too relieved to see it to care that it was at his expense. In other circumstances, he would have done some baiting of his own, but he couldn't hang around much longer. He was keeping the shaking hidden now by sheer will. "Let's take care of these guys," he gestured over his shoulder with his right thumb, "and bug out of here."

Transmuting the bodies and sending the energy out into the universe was easy enough to do—usually—but it was enough to push Logan to the edge. He had to leave. Now.

Opening a transit, he said, "Thanks for hunting with me today. I'm going to head home."

"What about your Jeep?"

Logan clenched all his muscles, trying to hide the shaking a few seconds longer. "We can't walk on the street looking like this. I'll head back and pick up the SUV later."

Kel nodded and Logan didn't wait for more conversation. He crossed the transit as fast as he could and closed it behind him. His knees buckled and the best he could do was make sure he didn't hit his head on the coffee table as he collapsed.

The first wave of convulsions jolted through him before he was prone on the floor.

7

CHAPTER

Shona sat on a stool pulled up to her workbench, rubbing the roughly faceted stone of her necklace with her thumb. She stared down at a blank page of the sketchbook resting in front of her and tried to visualize herself drawing something, anything.

Nothing came to her.

With a sigh, Shona slumped back. She'd never been more than adequate with a pencil and paper, but before working with her glass, she'd always sketched out a rough version of the piece she saw in her mind's eye. Everything she used to draw was on the table in front of her—pencils of all kinds, pens, charcoal, crayons, and erasers—but nothing called to her.

She hadn't been to the studio in more than a week, but life had gone on without her. Gary had started a new series of photos, Montana had nearly finished a watercolor of Elliot Bay, and Rafe was experimenting with a new medium— clay. No one had cared that she hadn't been here recently and no one had stayed long before wandering off to create something. Once, she'd appreciated that because it allowed her to get to her own work, but not today.

The collective was just about the perfect place to have a studio—reasonable rent, access to furnaces, and other creative people to talk to. She shared the space with two other glass artists, several sculptors, a bunch of painters, and one photographer. And despite the egos, Shona managed to get along with everyone. Usually.

Right now, she wasn't feeling too charitable toward any of them. For two months she hadn't been able to work—two endless, agonizing months—and not one of them had been supportive of her. At best, she'd gotten a pat on the head. At worst, barely concealed glee.

Maybe it was to be expected. There'd been some jealousy when she'd gotten her first significant exhibition. She'd been paired with an extremely successful artist and that had garnered her more attention than if she'd soloed or had showed with a less established painter. She'd pulled down some good reviews and the gallery owner had been excited about the response Shona had received. Things had been going her way and she'd been elated.

Then the bottom had dropped out.

Circling her thumb over the stone, Shona waited for fear or panic or dread. Something. All she felt was numb. And sad.

Her art was her heart, her soul, her passion and it was gone. Why didn't she care more? Why wasn't she wailing or throwing things or screaming? There should be something more than apathy. Something more than this sense of sorrow.

No one got it. Her parents had suggested that she needed a break and she'd work again when she was ready; her not-so-generous acquaintances had told her oh, well, those things happened; and her nicer friends had said it was fear of success.

They were wrong.

Scooting off the stool, Shona walked to the window. In the distance to her right, she could see Gary shifting position to get a different camera angle. The sun was shining, giving the day a happy feel and that was wrong. It should be raining, nature crying the tears that Shona couldn't.

She *wanted* to cry, wanted to release the heaviness around her heart, but something prevented that. It was as if that thing which had sucked away her artistic energy had also taken her ability to mourn her loss.

With another deep sigh, she wandered over to her shelves and stared at the supplies. They took up most of the small cubby she called her room, but the bulk of her work was done out in the area with the furnace, the annealer, the powder booth, and most of the rest of the equipment she shared with the other glass artists.

She reached for one of the blue rods, studied it, and returned it to its niche. Shona really did want to try to replicate the gorgeous cobalt color of Logan's eyes, but even that wasn't enough to motivate her to work.

Thoughts of Logan did inspire something else, though.

Shona tightened her hand around the stone she was still rubbing. She wanted to throw out a lifetime of being cautious and jump the man. It scared her just how close she was to actually doing it. Like last night when he'd brought her home from their dinner cruise—he'd kissed her good night and she'd thought about grabbing hold of his maroon tie and dragging him into her bedroom. The only reason why she hadn't was that the idea had shocked her enough to hesitate and Logan had ended the kiss.

Tugging the top of her T-shirt away from her body, Shona dropped her necklace back between her breasts. Her nipples were hard. Damn it, just thinking about Logan aroused her and that was mortifying. If he ever figured out what he did to her . . . Her lips curved and her pulse sped up. If Logan ever figured out what he did to her, she'd be having the hottest sex in the history of mankind. And if she'd known him longer, she wouldn't be agonizing about it at all.

Be careful. That wasn't the only warning her parents had repeated like a mantra. *Be a lady.* Her mom had started cautioning her about boys before Shona understood what she was being told. Maybe that had been the idea—get her while she was young and it would be indelibly imprinted in her brain.

She returned to her workbench, sat down, and made herself pick up a pencil. Across the room was a glass pumpkin that she hadn't been entirely happy with, but it was something she could sketch. Shona drew a curved line on the pad.

At first, she found herself easily distracted. It seemed as if she could hear every small noise, pick up a whiff of every scent—clay, turpentine, oil-based paint—but Shona refused to give herself permission to stop. She was going to do this because if she didn't, it was the same as admitting defeat.

As she worked, she found herself sinking into the process of drawing. Flipping the page, she kept going, losing herself in the moment, in the act of creating even if it wasn't her glass. Maybe *because* it wasn't her glass. Shona became so engrossed, that she jumped some time later when the door to her studio opened.

"I didn't think it poured like this in Seattle," Farran said as she shut the door. "I'm soaked!"

Shona looked up and blinked. "It's raining?"

Farran laughed. "More than raining. You must have been really deep if you didn't hear it coming down."

The last time she'd checked, it had been a sunny day with hardly a cloud in the sky. Strange. "It wasn't supposed to rain today."

"That's why I didn't grab my umbrella when I left the house. I know, I know—no one in Seattle uses an umbrella. Call me a wimp, but I don't like to be wet." Farran pinched the material of her green blouse between her fingers and shook it gently. She made a face when the fabric settled back against her skin.

"A little sprinkle never hurt anyone."

Farran grimaced. "Even you would concede that this is more than a light mist. Take a look."

Turning her head, Shona glanced outside and saw the

skies had opened up, but she teased her friend anyway. "It's not that bad. Another year and we'll have you converted."

"It will take longer than that. But enough about the weather and onto the big question—are you able to work again?"

"Um—"

"Is that your next project?" Farran headed across the room.

Shona glanced down at the sketchbook and her eyes widened. Instead of drawing a second version of the pumpkin, she'd drawn Logan and she'd done a more-than-decent job. A shiver went down her spine. How could she be oblivious to what she'd been sketching?

She didn't have time to close the book and hide it. The space was too small and Farran moved quickly.

"Ooh, yum, who's that?" she asked, dropping her purse on the worktable. It fell onto its side, but Farran left it like that.

Shona's face scalded. "Logan."

"That guy who rescued you? You have an incredible memory to draw him from one meeting."

She bit her lip, but she couldn't lie. "We went out last night. Dinner and dancing."

Farran's face paled. "What? I thought you said you weren't going to see him. That's what we agreed on."

The tone put Shona's back up. "I changed my mind. What does it matter to you anyway?"

"It matters," Farran said, "because you're the best friend I've ever had and I don't want to pay a trip to the morgue to identify your body."

That made Shona feel petty about her irritation. "That's not going to happen," she said. "Logan is sweet."

Her friend shook her head. "Don't all the people who know serial killers always say something similar when the man is finally arrested?"

"He's not going to hurt me, I know it."

For a moment, Farran didn't say anything, then her jaw firmed and Shona tensed. "I don't want to make you angry, but

I care about you so I have to say this. You live in the garage apartment behind your parents' home, they paid for your college, they pay for your studio rental as well as your supplies, and they pay for the clothes you wear and the food you eat. Frankly, Shona, you've been sheltered your entire life and you've never really had to learn any street smarts."

"I'm taking care of both houses while my parents are living in London." Shona's eyes burned, but she beat back the tears by sheer dint of will. She was used to taking grief from other people about having everything handed to her, but she hadn't thought Farran would be one of them.

Her friend made a growling noise and circled the room a couple of times before stopping in front of the workbench. "I did offend you, and I'm sorry for that, but letting the housecleaning service in once a week and making sure nothing burns to the ground while they live abroad isn't the same as being out in the world. Experience is a hard teacher and the lessons aren't pretty—believe me, I know."

"Logan," she said, her voice so thick it rasped, "isn't going to kill me. I might be sheltered, but my instincts aren't nonexistent."

Reaching across the table, Farran covered Shona's hand with hers. "He doesn't have to kill you in order to hurt you, he doesn't even have to do anything violent or malevolent. It's a sure bet he's more worldly than you are. What if you get your heart broken when he moves on?"

Shona had to admit that Farran had a point. She dropped her gaze to the sketch in front of her. This wasn't some flat representation done by an artist sketching a subject. Instead, she'd rendered Logan's image with emotion, it was there, obvious in every stroke of the pencil—after going out with him once. What would happen if she kept dating him? What would happen if they became lovers and he lost interest in her? What would happen if she fell for him and he left?

She raised her head and met Farran's gaze. Her eyes, her face were intense and there was no mistaking her concern. "I like him," Shona said and almost winced at the pleading note. She was an adult, she didn't need permission, but her friend was saying the same things aloud that Shona had been telling herself.

Farran squeezed her hand, released her grip, and came around the table. "I know you do and he's probably a good guy just like you say, but breakups happen every day. It hurts, and if you fall in love with him, the pain won't go away quickly. You'll feel stabs of it at odd moments months—even years—later. Do you want that?"

Swiveling her stool, Shona turned to face her. "No, of course not, but what if he falls for *me* and I break *his* heart?"

"How likely do you think that is? Honestly?"

Shona wanted to insist that it could go either way, but that would be a blatant lie. She might be twenty-six, only two years younger than he was, but Logan was more confident than she was and a lot more sophisticated. "Not very," she admitted.

"Like I told you before, you need someone more your speed." Farran's face lit up. "The guy who lives next door to me would be perfect for you. Honestly. His grandmother raised him, and when she fell ill, he took care of her until she died. He's truly nice and hasn't dated much either."

Farran kept talking, but Shona stopped listening. She didn't want to go out with some nice man who'd tended to his ailing grandmother—she wanted Logan.

Seeing him did mean risking her heart, but she'd rather take her chances with a man who heated her blood, who made her forget that they'd only known each other a few days, than waste time with someone who'd never be more than a friend. Logan made her laugh, he put her at ease when other men made her anxious, he made her feel petite, and since she was just shy of six feet, that was incredible. Most of all, though, she enjoyed talking with him, being with him.

"Who are you calling?" Shona asked, jerking her attention back to her friend.

"Ernie. I bet he'll be eager to meet you."

"No!"

Lowering the cell phone a few inches, Farran said, "Don't be nervous; he'll love you."

She started to raise the phone again and Shona reached out and caught her arm. "I don't want you to call him. I'm not interested in some blind date."

Slowly, her friend broke Shona's hold, flipped the cell shut, and returned it to her purse. "Okay, if you're sure. I do think you have the right idea about dating. It gets you out of the house and keeps you from brooding about your art. Although, if you're at your studio and sketching again, maybe you're on the verge of breaking through the block."

"Don't I wish." Shona slumped back in her seat again. "Nothing's changed."

"It could happen without you having any inkling it's coming. I mean, you did tell me that it went away without any warning, so why wouldn't it return the same way?"

Shona looked down at her hands. She'd used her fingertips to smudge the pencil and they were a deep gray. It wasn't something she was used to because the sketches for her glass pieces weren't this detailed, but even with the extra care she'd taken, even with emotion guiding her hand, her rendering was merely adequate. Glass had been the only thing she didn't have to struggle with. The only thing that felt natural.

Raising her gaze again, she said, "I don't think my creativity is coming back." The admission increased the weight resting on her heart and Shona drew in a shaky breath, trying to ease the pressure.

"It's too soon to know that." Shona shook her head. "It is!" Farran insisted.

She ignored that. "I . . ." Swallowing hard, Shona tried again. "I'm not very good with people, especially people my own age. Too many years dreaming, I guess, or maybe too much time spent around my parents and their friends."

"That happens with only children, or so I've heard."

Shona appreciated Farran's immediate support, but she

didn't stop to say that. "I'm not a great athlete, I don't really cook, I'm not quick with a quip, I was a straight B student in school and I didn't improve on that in college."

With a deep, shuddery breath, Shona shook off her friend's attempt to interrupt. "The exception was my art classes. From the first time I picked up a crayon, something clicked. I might not be good enough to draw professionally or paint, but I was better than most of the other kids, and when I tried glass, the world opened up. It didn't matter that I was a six-foot geek who towered over the rest of her seventh-grade class. I knew then what I was meant to do. Who I was supposed to be."

It took a great deal of control to fight off the tears. "If I'm not an artist, Farran, I don't have an identity. That's what scares me. Not only losing the art, but losing *me*."

"You're more than your glass."

"No, I'm no—"

"The hell you aren't." Farran clasped both her hands. "Art is only one of the hundreds of facets that make up Shona Blackwood. You simply haven't taken time to delve into them because you found your talent early."

"Do you really think so?"

"Of course." Farran squeezed her hands and then released her. "I still think you're writing off the art too quickly, but while you're blocked, why don't you explore some other interests? You could do some reading to find out what grabs your attention, or borrow your mom's meditation CDs and ask for guidance."

Shona mulled that over for a moment. Perhaps she should consider this a chance to discover more about herself, to stretch her wings, and spending time with Logan might be the perfect way to do that. After all, he did incite feelings inside her that were way out of her comfort zone. "You could be right," she said slowly. "Maybe I've only focused on one dimension of myself for too long."

"That's the spirit! And when your feel like working on

your glass again, you'll be even better because you've explored other avenues."

Her friend's enthusiasm made Shona smile, and in that moment, she realized the pressure had eased up around her heart. "Thanks for caring," Shona said. "It means a lot to me."

"That's what friends do, they care about each other, worry for each other, and do what they can to help each other." She returned the smile. "And I haven't had anyone like that in my life before you, so I hope you appreciate how special you are."

Shona didn't know what to say, and before the words came to her, the moment was lost.

"It stopped raining," Farran announced and walked to the window. "I think there might be a faint rainbow over there." She pointed, but Shona didn't leave her chair.

Farran wandered back and set her purse upright on the worktable. It was only then that Shona saw the red and white bull's-eye painted on the side of the brown bag. The symbol looked . . . tacky, but from past experience shopping with her friend, Shona didn't doubt for a moment that the thing had cost at least a few hundred dollars.

"You have a unique sense of style," Shona said, deadpan.

"I know and not everyone could carry it off with the panache that I do." Farran grinned, looked around, and pulled over a second stool to the short side of the table to Shona's right. At just about average height, she needed to hop up to sit. "Why don't we go shopping tonight? We can get you this purse in the leopard-print style."

Shona looked away for a moment, drew a deep breath, and squared her shoulders. "I have plans for tonight."

Suspicion replaced Farran's smile. "Oh? What are you doing?"

"I'm not sure." Shona hesitated. "Logan didn't say."

"You know, you don't have to tell him in person that you're not going out with him anymore. You can call and do it."

"I'm not going to say that to him." Shona raised her voice

to talk over Farran's protests. "You won't find me in the morgue and you know it."

"But—"

"If I get my heart broken, you can say *I told you so,* but I'm not arguing with you about this. I plan to keep seeing Logan."

8

CHAPTER

Shona felt butterflies skittering around and took a hand off the steering wheel to rest it over her stomach. Farran's insistence that Shona didn't know Logan well enough to trust him kept haunting her. Why had she agreed to drive over to his house and spend the evening watching movies? She hadn't even bothered to tell anyone where she was going.

In all honesty, she didn't expect Logan to harm her in any way, but it was easier to worry about that than what was really on her mind—wondering if he had plans to talk her into his bed. The thrill that went through her said clearer than words what her body thought about that idea, but it was her head that was waving the caution flag.

Logan hadn't sounded like someone who was under the weather when he'd phoned to tell her he'd gotten a migraine-type headache and couldn't tolerate going out. Disappointment had winged through her when she'd thought he wanted to cancel, and then resignation had set in. He wasn't the first guy she'd bored to death—her dating history was filled with men who said they'd call her and then never had—but she hadn't thought Logan would lose interest, not the way he'd kissed her good night.

Shona returned her hand to the wheel as she braked for a stop sign. Because the rain had stopped a couple of hours ago, the roads had dried out, and she appreciated that when she was driving in unfamiliar territory.

Maybe she'd been compelled to agree to spend the evening at his house out of relief that he wasn't blowing her off. And even if he was looking for sex, she could always say no.

She hadn't dressed for seduction—mostly. Her hair was pulled back in a french braid, a look she hoped was demure, and her clothes were casual. She'd put on black jeans and a white T-shirt with diagonal stripes across the stomach as her way of saying, *let's just hang out,* but underneath she wore her raciest lingerie.

She reached for the directions Logan had given her over the phone, scanned the final few entries, and accelerated through the intersection. Watching for street names kept her mind occupied and Shona welcomed the distraction. She'd been mentally going around in circles for hours and hadn't reached any conclusions.

Her stomach knotted tighter when she made the turn into Logan's driveway. Farran was right, he was out of her league and not just when it came to experience. He lived on a wooded estate, for crying out loud.

The house itself came into view and Shona stopped. Mansion. It was a damn mansion with a fountain bubbling in the middle of a circular driveway. She nearly put the car in reverse, but she feared she'd run onto his lawn if she tried to back up the entire distance to the street.

Maybe he was house-sitting.

That thought gave Shona the courage to drive the rest of the way and turn off the engine. For a moment longer, she stared. The exterior was brick and stone, and had a European flavor to it that made her think of an English country manor. It wasn't the type of home she'd imagined Logan owning, not by a long shot.

She had to psyche herself up to get out of the car and ring

his doorbell, but she clutched her purse tightly and did it. And was left standing on the front portico.

Did she ring again or make a run for it?

Before she reached a decision, the door opened. Logan was pale, his face drawn, and the sparkle that was usually glinting in his eyes was missing. "You look terrible!" Oh, geez, had she really said that?

"I probably look worse than I feel."

This was her chance to escape. Turning slightly, she gestured over her shoulder toward her car. "Maybe I should leave and let you rest."

"I want to spend time with you, Shon—if I didn't, I would have canceled instead of asking you to come here."

She hesitated as a tug of war went on inside her. His words melted her and she wanted to spend time with him, too, but the out-of-her-league part wouldn't go away. "Are you sure?"

"Positive." He opened the door wider in invitation.

Shona studied him for a moment longer, then stepped inside the house. Her eyes nearly bugged out. The large foyer had a marble floor, a crystal chandelier, and white wainscoting on the walls. Her parents had a fair amount of money, but they couldn't afford anything like this.

"Um, are you house-sitting?" Please let him be house sitting, she pleaded silently.

Logan shut the front door and moved beside her. "No, this is mine. Why?"

"You're only a little older than me and people our age don't live in homes like this." Not without family money— unless they were drug runners or hit men.

He must have read her mind because a ghost of a smile crossed his face. "No, I don't have anything to do with smuggling and I swear to you—again—that I've never deliberately hurt a human being in my life." Logan rested a hand on the small of her back and urged her more deeply inside. "I thought we'd order a pizza. Does that sound okay to you?"

"Fine." But now she had another room to gape at.

"What do you like?"

"Everything except anchovies, peppers, and onions."

Logan left her to go to an end table and grab a cordless phone, but Shona was afraid to move. What if she knocked something over? She raised her purse to her chest, wrapped her arms around it, and watched him call in their order.

Something occurred to her as he talked and it relaxed her. Shona lowered her arms, took a couple of steps to lay her bag on the coffee table, and smiled. Maybe the house was unexpected, but she was still with Logan.

"What's funny?" he asked when he hung up the phone.

"You have the pizza place on speed dial."

He returned the smile. "You're thinking I'm helpless in the kitchen, right?" She made a noncommittal sound. "Sorry, not true. My mom made sure my brother and I can cook and that my sisters know how to change a flat and add oil. That doesn't mean I don't order out."

"A lot," she tacked on for him.

"A lot," he agreed. "We have about half an hour until it arrives; did you want to start watching a movie?"

"Actually, if you don't mind, I'd like a tour. I've never been in a mansion before."

Logan snorted. "It's not a mansion, but it is a hell of a lot bigger than I need."

Shona nodded. "Why'd you buy it then?"

"Two reasons. First, it sits on five acres of wooded lake front not that far out of Seattle."

"And second?" she prompted when he didn't say more.

"I'll explain when we reach that part of the tour. You saw the entry. This is the great room and over there is my own personal English pub."

"For a man who doesn't drink." Shona wandered over to the pub area and admired the rich wood. "It's beautiful."

"It's stuffy," he disagreed. "If you go through there," he gestured to her left, "you'll be in the dining room."

She did as he said and stopped short just inside the doorway.

The room had a tray ceiling, a round wooden table with six heavily upholstered chairs, and a built-in china hutch. "Wow, you must have some pretty fancy dinners."

"I've never used it."

"Why not?"

"Too damn fussy."

Shona looked around and nodded slowly. "It is ornate for your personality. Why'd you hire an interior designer who didn't match your taste?"

"The builder decorated it for some luxury home and garden tour. I bought it furniture and all."

She walked over to him. "Why don't you change it?"

"Because I don't care." He put his arm around her waist and steered her back to the great room.

"This is another area you don't use." Considering the tingles that started coursing through her when Logan had touched her, Shona was proud she sounded normal.

"Too fussy," he repeated. "Let's keep going or the pizza will be here before we're done."

He breezed her through a sunroom, a protected back porch, and in through another set of doors that brought them into a kitchen—a gourmet kitchen with two center islands. "This looks slightly more lived in."

"I told you I cooked." Logan nodded and tugged her along without letting her look at the room off the eating area. When they passed a closed door that he didn't explain, Shona stopped, drawing him to a halt. "What's behind here?"

"The basement and sorry, but it's not included on the tour."

Shona nodded and didn't argue. It might not be finished or it could be loaded with boxes or other junk. They went past another closed door. "What about this one?"

"Pantry. Not very interesting and mostly empty." He smiled, but there still was no sparkle in his eyes. Logan opened the third closed door. "Office."

Again, this room was heavy on the wood and the only thing that seemed to belong to him was the computer on the desk. She didn't look long. The idea had been to learn more about Logan from his house, but nothing she'd seen yet was him.

He led her through a utility area with a mud room, laundry room, and half bath before opening yet another door. "This," Logan said, "is the second reason why I bought the house."

"The garage?"

"Yes." He hit the switch to turn on all the lights. "Go down the steps and I'll show you."

Shona paused, then descended into the garage. It was a big space, but her view was blocked by his Jeep Cherokee. "Well?"

"It has four stalls and there was room to add on a fifth." Logan took her hand and led her around the SUV. "This is a 1968 Ford Mustang Fastback. I finished restoring her about a week before we met."

He went on and on about engine size and finding parts, and though Shona tried to pay attention, she had zero interest in cars. She stopped listening to the words and let herself enjoy the passion in Logan's voice. Something close to his usual liveliness was back in his expression, and she watched his face, loving how enthusiastic he'd become. When it was appropriate, she murmured little noises that made it sound as if she were following him and that seemed good enough.

The next car was blue and that was all Shona needed to know, but he ran through the same kind of detail he had on the first one. They went through this again on the third and final old car. She perked up briefly when he said Ferrari, but it didn't last long. After about forever, Logan wound down.

Shona tugged loose, went to the passenger window, and peered into the car. "You did a nice job."

"Thanks."

She straightened. "You shouldn't leave your keys in the ignition. Someone could steal it."

"I've got security," he said and something about his expression made Shona wonder just what kind of system he had.

She didn't ask because that was none of her business. "Can we finish the house tour now?"

"I know you're bored, but indulge me for one last stop and then we'll go inside."

At her nod, he led the way over to the far wall. He opened a door, turned on the lights, and gestured for her to precede him. Shona crossed the threshold and looked around another garage. This one wasn't for parking cars, though, it was for working on them. There was a bench with all kinds of tools, other equipment she couldn't identify, and it even had a hoist.

She'd learned he was passionate about his hobby, but this space showed her just how much, and it touched her that he was sharing it with her. Shona made a slow circuit of the shop before coming back to stand in front of him. "What's your next project going to be?"

Logan grinned, almost looking like his usual self. "I've got a lead on a 1966 Shelby 427 Cobra convertible, and thanks for asking; I know you're not interested in my classic cars."

"Not in the putting them back together part, but I wouldn't mind driving them. Would you let me get behind the wheel?"

That wiped the smile off his face. "After I ride with you a few times to get a feel for how you drive, then we'll talk about it—*if* you're a careful, safe driver."

With a laugh, Shona walked past him and out of his workshop. "Which one of your sisters wrecked a car?"

He shut off the lights and closed the door before answering. "It was my brother." Logan caught up with her as she went back into the house. "The paint was barely dry and Kel totaled it."

"Was he hurt?"

"Not a scratch on him, but the Camaro was another story."

"That must have broken your heart."

"Damn near. Kel being okay was more important, of course, but my muscle cars are off limits to him now except in a dire, life-or-death emergency."

When they were back inside the house, he took her up a

set of stairs near the kitchen and held her hand as they walked through the upper level. There were three bedrooms here, a study, another laundry room, and a sitting area. "Holy cow. What do you do with all these bedrooms?"

"Not much, but they come in handy when my family descends on me." He smirked a little. "It always helps keep the harmony when my sisters are on another floor."

"You expect me to believe that?" She squeezed his hand. "I've heard the indulgent note in your voice when you talk about them. You're as soft as they come."

"Not quite," Logan said, but he didn't give her an opportunity to disagree before taking her down a second stairway on the opposite side of the house. Directly in front of them was an open door. "Library. I don't use it much, it's—"

"Too fussy," she said in unison with him.

When he gave her a look, she explained, "That's been your theme for the day."

"I guess it has."

Logan began to turn to their right, but Shona dug in her heels. "What's that direction?" she asked, pointing left.

"My bedroom."

"I don't get to look at it?" This was potentially dangerous territory, but Shona wanted to see his personal space. The garage had been the most intimate part of his house that she'd viewed and it wasn't enough. She wanted to know more about Logan. A lot more.

He grimaced slightly. "I guess you can—if you really want to." A faint blush tinged his cheeks, making him even sexier. "I, um, wasn't expecting to have you back there and it's a little messy."

Shona felt her heart turn over. Logan had been telling the truth when he said he wanted to see her even if he wasn't at a hundred percent. One look at him had told her he really wasn't running at full speed, but she'd still wondered about his motives. Now she knew he hadn't invited her here for sex. "I promise not to grade you, but I am curious."

He gestured toward his bedroom, silently offering an invitation. Shona opened the door and found herself in a mauve-colored sitting room. Not only was it fussy, but it had a feminine feel and it was so *not* Logan that Shona nearly laughed. "You need to get your sisters to redecorate for you."

That earned her another snort. "Tris would deck me for asking and God only knows what Keavy and Iona would come up with. It might be worse than what I already have." He opened a second door. "The bedroom is better."

"Wow," Shona breathed. *Better* was an understatement. The room was beautiful—beyond beautiful. She was mesmerized, and while she was aware of Logan moving around, grabbing clothes and towels off the dove-gray carpet, she couldn't stop gawking.

There were two strips of white crown molding near the ceiling and the walls were a two-tone gray. The black king-size bed faced a large fireplace and Shona could imagine snuggling up with Logan after making love and watching a fire burn. That had her cheeks heating, both with embarrassment and arousal.

"Sorry about the mess," he apologized.

"At least you made the bed."

"Barely," Logan muttered and walked away.

Shona followed him. This room looked like a little breakfast nook with a table and built-in mini-fridge, but she found Logan in the bathroom, jamming his armload of clothes into a hamper. It was another incredible room with a fireplace at the foot of a spa tub with a flat screen television above it. Behind that was an enormous glass-enclosed shower and there were two vanities, one on either side of the room. She easily picked out which one Logan used—the sink with a couple of wadded up towels and a bunch of clutter around it.

She continued on and found a walk-in closet that was so large, it was broken into four segments. Logan's clothes filled about a half of one percent of the space—if that—but then it would be difficult to own enough things to fill it.

There was another door she hadn't tried and when she opened it, she was back in the breakfast area. Logan was sprawled in a chair at the table, eyes closed and he had a furrow grooved between his brows. She realized then that he was worse off than he let on and there was a temptation to go to him, run her fingers through his dark hair to soothe him, and kiss the lines on his forehead. Shona clenched her hands to stop herself from crossing to him and doing just that.

"How bad is your headache?" she asked quietly.

Looking startled, Logan straightened in his seat. In the next instant, he smoothed out his expression, hiding how deeply his pain ran. "I'm on the downward side. In a couple of hours, you'll never know I had one. Promise."

Before she could reply, the doorbell rang, and Logan was on his feet. "That must be dinner," he said on his way out, and she had the sense that he'd catapulted himself from the room to avoid answering any more questions about his head.

Shona hesitated, took one last look around, and slowly followed. She reached the foyer in time to see Logan closing the door, pizza box in one hand. "C'mon, let's eat."

Shona was enjoying the evening a lot more than she'd expected. She liked to go out, liked to be in the energy of a crowd, but she found an odd contentment as she watched the movie while snuggled against Logan's side. He had his arm around her shoulders and every now and then he'd run his fingers over the bare skin beneath the cap sleeve of her T-shirt. She found herself waiting for those moments, eagerly anticipating them, but they didn't seem to happen nearly often enough.

After they'd finished eating, he'd asked her to pick out the movies while he put the leftover pizza away and she'd opted to go with a Keanu Reeves double header—*The Lake House* and *Speed*. They'd kicked things off with the quieter film, and at some point during that picture, Logan had begun to feel better. The weird thing was that he hadn't said anything, she'd just known.

Now they were watching *Speed,* and as many times as Shona had seen the movie, she never got tired of it. Best of all, there wasn't only a great romance, there was a lot of suspense, too. Like the scene on the screen. She knew the bus successfully jumped the gap in the freeway, but she tensed up anyway.

"Shon," Logan said, voice choked. "Do you know where your hand is?"

Less than thrilled to be pulled out of the story, she reluctantly looked away from the screen and down. With a gasp, she jerked her arm away. *Oh, my God!* Her hand had been high on his thigh—another inch and she would have been cupping him. The damn thing was that she was tempted to reach back over and do just that. Her heart rate jumped another couple of notches as she pictured herself with her hand on him, and involuntarily, her eyes went back to his lap. She couldn't be certain in the dimly lit room, but Shona thought he had an erection.

"I'm sorry," she apologized.

"I didn't mind." She had no trouble seeing the intensity of his eyes. "I just couldn't take the teasing any more."

"Teasing?" What had she been doing?

"You were running your fingers up and down the inseam of my jeans." He grinned. "It's a good thing I've seen this movie before because I haven't paid attention to anything except you since the cop jumped on the bus."

Her face burned so hot, she was surprised it didn't light up the room. She'd been completely unaware of what she was doing. What was he thinking? Shona studied him, trying to figure that out, but she couldn't decipher his expression. Damn, she wished she could read his mind.

Images swirled through her head.

She was naked, lying on Logan's great big black bed. Her legs were parted and he knelt between them, his eyes drinking in the sight of her. Shona felt fire everywhere his gaze touched and she lifted her hips, inviting him to put his body over hers. He ignored it and continued to stare.

After an eternity, he moved, hooking his arms under her thighs and pulling her closer to him. At last he covered her and Logan took her mouth in a kiss so carnal that she writhed against him, begging for release.

He rubbed his hard-on against her, and she was wet enough that he was able to slide easily. Every time he bumped the center of her pleasure, shock waves rippled through her. She wanted him inside her, not tormenting her, and she was willing to beg for it. "Please, Logan."

She nearly came as he entered her, her arousal so far off the scale that she could do nothing except moan. Tight. She was so tight around him that the pleasure. . . .

Shona blinked. She was tight around him? Where did that come from? Something else was off. It took her a minute to realize that in the fantasy, not only were the small burn scars on her hands missing, but she wasn't wearing her necklace either. And if this were her daydream, why would she be seeing herself and not—

Her gaze shot to Logan's and she knew. *She knew.* Those were his thoughts, his fantasies, not hers. Alarm ricocheted through her. She didn't tap into other people's thoughts, not ever, but before her fear could shoot out of control, the scene escalated. The dream Logan began to rock his hips, thrusting into her. Shona gasped, both in the fantasy and in real life.

And the here-and-now Logan met her gaze squarely.

Arousal more intense than anything she'd felt before had her squirming again, seeking release. Frustrated, she reached for Logan, tugging his lips to hers.

She kissed him with the same feral heat that he'd used in his imagination. Impatience ate at her and her hands gripped his navy T-shirt, pulling at it until Logan raised his arms and helped her strip it off.

Muscles. She loved a man with muscles. Shona gaped,

appreciating his chest, his shoulders, his arms before exploring him with her hands, her mouth. As hyperaware as she was, she could detect the faint residue of soap that remained from his shower, taste the slight saltiness of his skin.

This time wriggling exacerbated her arousal rather than relieving it. With a growl, Shona shoved Logan down on the couch.

"Shona?" He tried to sit up, but she straddled his hips and pushed him back into the cushions.

His erection pressed into her exactly where she needed it and she rocked. So good. So damn good. She did it again, undulating against him.

Her panties were damp and becoming wetter with every push of her pelvis against his. She wanted to strip them off, wanted Logan naked, too. Shona wanted to feel him deep inside her, but she couldn't wait that long. She couldn't wait that long!

Logan tried to hold her hips and she grabbed his wrists, pinning them at his sides. He cursed, a word she hadn't heard him use before, and arched his hips, driving his hard-on more firmly against her. A keening wail escaped her and she rode him harder. She was close.

As if sensing that, he moved to her rhythm, driving her nearer to the pinnacle. Shona gasped and rocked against him. Her head fell back, her eyes closed and the orgasm roared through her, potent enough to make her start crying.

When Shona became aware of her surroundings again, she discovered she was lying on top of Logan, her face pressed against his throat. He was still hard, but his hands were gentle as they stroked up and down her back. She was fully clothed and the only thing he had off was his shirt.

Heaven help her, she'd jumped the man, and when he'd tried to slow her down, she'd overpowered him.

That couldn't be right.

Shona pursed her lips. Logan was six-two, and with his muscles, had to be at least two hundred pounds, there was no way she could overpower him. He must have let her have control. She squirmed, but this time it was in mortification.

His hands grasped her hips. "Hold still," he ordered in a rasp. "I haven't come in my jeans since I was fifteen and I'd like to keep it that way."

She groaned, beyond humiliated now. Shona wanted to leap to her feet, grab her purse, and race out of here so fast, her tires would leave skid marks on Logan's driveway as she squealed away. Too bad her legs were trembling enough that she didn't think she could stand, let alone tear out of here.

"Honey, you don't have to run from me—there's nothing to be embarrassed about."

"Easy for you to say." Knowing she had to face him some time, Shona pushed up onto her elbows, and sucked in a quick breath. It was then she understood how much control he was exerting over himself. Logan's eyes were blazing, and if she said the word, he'd have them both naked in a flash.

The desire she thought had been banked with her orgasm, flared back to life. She was in trouble here.

"I have to leave." Because if she didn't, Shona knew they'd have sex and it wouldn't matter a damn that she'd only met him five days ago.

9
CHAPTER

Logan chose the jazz club because its intimate size made it difficult for a darksider to sneak up on them, but to his surprise, he discovered he liked the music. When this was all over and Shona was safe, he wanted to bring her here again and let himself have a good time. Tonight, he had to remain alert, continually scanning his surroundings.

Shona. He'd known she'd try to back out on their date, so he'd disengaged the voice mail on his cell phone and circumvented her. Logan hadn't been wrong—caller ID showed she'd tried to get a hold of him almost a dozen times. He'd half expected her not to be home when he went to pick her up, but she had better manners than that. They had taken a huge step backward, though—she was quiet and on edge again—and even his best stories hadn't managed to relax her.

He rolled his shoulders, trying to get rid of the twitchy feeling he always had when his back was exposed. Shona was going to try to run on him, Logan didn't doubt it for a minute. The only question was if she'd dump him today or wait until after her art function tomorrow. His money was on tonight, which meant he needed to come up with a preemptive strike before she worked up enough courage to tell him to get lost.

Turning his head, he studied her. The candle on their table bathed her face in a soft glow, highlighting her high cheekbones and full lips. His pulse rate picked up speed. It was more than her beauty that got to him, it was her, who she was.

Logan smiled faintly as he thought about what she had on. Her dress was conservative—sleeveless, but with a neckline that went all the way to her throat—and the color was the blue of the deepest ocean. Shona had her hair loose, but she'd tamed it and it was as prudent as the knee-length hem of the skirt. Her bare legs were the only deviation from the hands-off message she'd wanted to project, but he'd never seen her wear nylons.

Somehow he'd have to convince her there was nothing to be frightened of—a pretty neat trick when what they had was so strong, it scared him, too.

Shona must have felt his gaze. Their eyes met for a moment, then she hurriedly looked back to the stage. With a silent sigh, Logan did as well. He wasn't going to have much more time to come up with a way to calm her down. If his guess was correct, the show wouldn't last much longer.

Nothing was more urgent than making sure Shona didn't close him out, but Logan had a list of problems that was growing by the minute and none of them seemed to have an answer. It still bothered him that a Tàireil had included a human in his scheme—that flew in the face of everything he knew about them—and he didn't like the koznain's involvement either. Kel's explanation was logical enough, but it had holes.

The biggest was, why had a darksider wasted magic to transport dark-force creatures from his dimension to theirs? It wasn't as if the Gineal world wasn't loaded with them and there were plenty that were as powerful as the koznain.

No, something else was going on, but Logan was damned

if he had any idea what that could be. There were pieces of the puzzle missing and he didn't like it.

Add his seizures to the list of difficulties and that the aftereffects were getting worse. Logan was used to the pain and the intense headaches that followed a bout, but for the first time he'd been physically weakened as well. Shona had been able to pin him, for God's sake. And he thought it might have taken longer for his powers to fully recharge than in the past.

Without magic, he'd been all but helpless last night, and if Shona hadn't agreed to come to his house, Logan would have been forced to ask for assistance to watch over her. That would have revealed his secret and someone else would be assigned to protect her. The idea of another troubleshooter spending time with her made him tighten up and he forced himself to relax his clenched fists and take a deep breath.

The attraction they felt for each other was another complication he didn't need. Want it or not, though, it was there, and after watching her ride him until she came, Logan had reached a decision—he was done fighting what she did to him.

Reminding himself that the council wanted her to remain ignorant of the Gineal hadn't dissuaded him from his choice. Neither had thoughts of facing an enraged Creed Blackwood if he ever found out Logan had slept with the man's little sister. The consequences were in the future, though, and Shona was now.

As if all this weren't enough, last night the universe had thrown a curve ball—she'd read his mind. There was no question about what had happened. Shona had picked up on his sexual fantasy and echoed it back to him with a few adjustments. Logan fought a grin. Her impatience had played itself out in the images she'd returned and he'd loved the hell out of that.

Of course, she shouldn't have had a clue what he was thinking. That sobered him.

His mind shield had been firmly in place and he hadn't

projected to her, not even unconsciously. Some dormants were able to access small magical talents, but if another Gineal couldn't bypass his mental protection, she shouldn't be able to do it. There were also a couple of instances where Logan suspected he'd read her mind as clearly as if she'd sent the thoughts to him.

Shona probably hadn't brooded over that part—she was too upset about how close they'd come to having sex—but when it did dawn on her, odds were good she'd be freaked. Especially if it happened again, and since Logan had no idea why she'd been able to do it at all, he doubted he'd be able to prevent a repeat.

Applause jerked him from his thoughts and he joined in. Damn. At most, all he had left were a couple of encores, then the show would be finished and he'd be alone with Shona. The only way he knew to deal with her embarrassment about what had happened was to talk it over, but imagining her reaction to the conversation was enough to make him wish the set went on forever.

Long before he was ready, the music ended and the house lights came up. Logan held Shona's chair while she stood and rested his hand at the small of her back to escort her from the club. He ignored the way she stiffened at his touch.

Once they were in the Jeep, Logan loosened his tie and unfastened the button at his throat before starting the SUV and pulling out of the parking lot. He'd worn a suit more times since he'd met Shona than he had in the previous year, and in other circumstances, he might have said something to her and made a joke, but not now.

"I've never listened to jazz before, but I thought the music was great."

Shona made a little humming sound that could mean anything.

"The club was nice, too," Logan said, hoping some casual conversation would relax her. "The way they arranged the seating really fostered the sense of intimacy with the performers."

No response.

He gave up on reducing her edginess and debated. Maybe driving along in the dark would be the best way to have this conversation. Shona's gaze had been skittering away from his all night and it might be easier for her when she knew he couldn't take his eyes off the road. "Okay, Shon, let's talk."

From his peripheral vision, Logan saw her muscles go rigid. "We have nothing to talk about."

Oh, yeah, he recognized that tone—no man who'd grown up with four females could miss it. Proceed at your own peril. Well, no guts, no glory. "I know you're upset about what happened at my house. It's made things uncomfortable between us tonight, and unless we resolve it, it'll be just as bad tomorrow night at your party."

"About that—"

Logan cut her off. "You have nothing to be embarrassed about, you know."

"What makes you think I'm embarrassed?"

"Maybe the way you fled last night or the expression I saw on your face before you jumped off me and ran out the door. Then there's the fact that you've hardly said ten words to me tonight and you haven't met my eyes for more than a few seconds before looking somewhere else. It's too dark in here to see you, but I'd be willing to bet your face is scarlet right now. You really don't have to feel awkward with me, though, I was just as aroused as you were."

Shona clasped the filmy fabric of her skirt and rubbed it between her thumb and forefinger. "You're a guy; you don't understand."

"I understand more than you give me credit for. You're either embarrassed because A—you were the aggressor. B—it was our second date. C—I watched you come. Or D—the attraction we share went from simmering to boiling over in a split second and you don't like the loss of self-command."

"Try option E."

"E?"

"All of the above."

Logan knew better than to downplay her emotions or to compare her to other women, but he wasn't sure what he should say. He switched lanes, giving himself a few seconds to collect his thoughts. "The heat goes both ways, you know. I was as out of control as you were."

"That's a load of manure," Shona shot back. "You did stay in control."

"Barely. I was hanging on to it with both hands. If you'd come a few seconds later, you would have seen how little restraint I really did have and then we'd both be embarrassed." One side of his mouth quirked up. "Nothing like a big wet spot on the front of my jeans to show how smooth I am."

"I don't know whether to laugh or hide my face. Are you always so blunt?"

Reaching over, he took the hand that was pleating her skirt and linked their fingers. "No, but I thought it might make you feel better if I told the unvarnished truth. Does it?"

Shona smiled. It was reluctant, but Logan caught it in the split second he had his eyes off the road. "A little."

He released the breath he'd been holding; she easily could have been offended. On to the next item. "As for you taking charge—damn, that was hot." She tried to pull her hand free, but Logan didn't release her. "No, seriously. I think it must be every guy's fantasy to have a gorgeous, sexy woman let him know how much she wants him."

She tried to tug loose again, and this time, he let her. "I've never done anything like that before."

Logan sucked in a sharp breath. He'd suspected, but . . . "Damn, that makes it even hotter." He heard the thickness in his voice and cleared his throat. "Since you know how much I liked it, you don't have to worry about that any more, right?"

"I wouldn't be concerned about any of this if I'd known you longer," Shona said in a rush.

So that was the crux of the situation. Logan extended his arm and held it palm up, inviting Shona to put her hand back in his. It took a minute, but she finally accepted the offer and he considered that a good sign. "That's funny because even though we just met, I feel as comfortable with you as if we've known each other for years."

For a long moment, she was quiet, but he didn't prod. If she needed time to think, he'd give that to her. At last Shona said softly, "Me, too. Most of the time, at least."

"Then let's take things as they come without worrying about shoulds and shouldn'ts," Logan suggested. Reluctantly, he released Shona's hand to use his turn signal.

Her sigh was loud in the confines of his SUV. "That's easy for you to say. Your mom didn't spend your formative years lecturing you about behaving like a lady."

Logan laughed. "Nope, definitely not, but I did get lectured on how to *treat* a lady, so you don't have to be scared that I'll push you. You set the pace on how fast things progress between us and I'll respect your boundaries."

She was still mulling that over when he turned into her driveway and drove past the main house to the garage apartment behind it. In case Shona planned to say goodnight in the Jeep, he had the engine off and was around to help her down before she had an opportunity to tell him not to bother.

He was ready for her protest, but it didn't come and Logan offered her a hand. "Thank you," she said and this time she was the one who laced their fingers as they walked to the door.

"Invite me in; we need to finish this conversation." She frowned and Logan added, "Please?"

"Okay, but that's all we're going to do—talk."

"Like I said in the Jeep, we go at your speed."

Shona stared at him suspiciously for a moment, then freed her hand. Opening her clutch, she searched through it and Logan had to hide a smile. Tiny bag like that and she couldn't find her house key without digging through it.

When she finally located it, he took it from her, his fingers brushing lightly over hers. Even that small, inadvertent caress was enough to send shockwaves through him and he thought Shona felt them, too. Before she could think better of letting him inside, he unlocked the door and opened it, gesturing for her to precede him.

Taking the key from him, she returned it to her purse and then entered. Logan followed, looking around curiously when she turned on the lights. The space was small, but he'd expected that. It was the bright colors that took him by surprise.

The walls were stark white, but the paintings hanging there were all riots of color. Over the bland oatmeal carpet, she'd laid down an area rug with two shades of purple and green, some blue, yellow, pink, and red patches as well. Her furniture was arranged on top of it. Logan searched his memory for the names his sisters had used for the colors—dark seafoam for the sofa; one of the chairs was aqua; and the other was Caribbean blue.

He thought about it and then smiled.

This boldness was the real Shona Blackwood, the woman he'd only seen glimpses of so far.

"Do I get a tour?"

"You mean you want to waste the five seconds it would take to go through the apartment?" She didn't give him time to reply. "This is the entryway. Two strides and we're in the living room." Shona took those steps and Logan followed, closing the front door behind them. "To the right is the kitchen and to the left is my bedroom and the only bath."

"I like this." And he did because it was a home, not a showplace.

"So do I," she said and smiled. "Even if the entire thing can fit inside your kitchen." Shona put her purse down on the table next to her phone. "I'll get us something to drink. Is orange juice okay?"

"That would be fine," he said gently. If she needed a few minutes to regroup, he could be patient.

"Have a seat; I'll be right back."

Logan nodded, but didn't sit. Instead, he looked around the

room again and this time he noticed what was missing—Shona didn't have any of her glass work displayed. He watched her walk through the swinging door that led to her kitchen and wondered if the absence meant anything.

A choked-off scream had him running, heart in his throat.

Damn, he was a moron. Why the hell hadn't he scanned her home? In the second it took to reach the door, he picked up human energy only.

He burst into the kitchen, afraid of what he'd find, but the only injury belonged to the intruder. Shona had bloodied his nose and she continued to struggle with him.

In a blink, Logan took in the scraggly goatee and the long greasy hair. The man saw him and pushed Shona in his direction before racing out the backdoor. Logan steadied her and did a second scan. No darksiders around. He ran after the human.

His brief hesitation had cost him, but Logan didn't allow the head start to discourage him. He wouldn't be able to pursue for long—not with Shona alone and vulnerable—but he wanted this guy and he wanted answers.

This was the same bastard who had attacked Shona six nights ago.

10
CHAPTER

"You fool," Farran snarled into her cell phone: "I told you to coordinate all your actions through me."

She'd managed to sound enraged, but she was fortunate she was alone in her apartment. One glance was all it would take for Shaggy—or anyone else—to realize she was scared to the toes of her Amalfi pumps.

"What the hell were you thinking?" she demanded.

Money. He wanted the other half of the money and he'd been too impatient to wait. It was bad enough that Shaggy had failed again, but to make it all so much worse, the troubleshooter had been there. Farran was under no illusions. The Gineal would have identified Shaggy as the same man who'd previously attacked Shona, and even though he would have sensed no Tàireil màgic, Andrews would assume the thug was there at the behest of her people.

She rubbed her forehead and fought off tears. This made everything harder. Everything!

Shona might have chalked up the first attack to bad luck, but no matter how sheltered she was, the second must have made her suspicious. She'd be cautious from now on and alert to potential threats.

Shaggy might not realize it yet, but he had created another problem for himself. There was little doubt that after last night the police had moved capturing him up on their priority list. The only thing that might slow that down was the fact that two different jurisdictions were involved.

Farran walked to the patio doors and leaned against the jamb. One of the lawn maintenance men trimmed the hedges, the other mowed the commons area, and for a brief moment, she wished her life were as simple and uncomplicated as theirs must be.

Time was running short. She rested her forehead against the glass and blinked rapidly. There were mere days until her deadline and the consequences for missing it. . . .

Her thug-for-hire continued to justify his actions and that allowed Farran to compose herself. She couldn't afford to lament what had happened or even berate the human for his stupidity, she needed a plan, some way to pull victory from this latest defeat.

"I don't want to hear any more excuses," she interrupted. "You sit tight and don't do anything else until you hear from me. No. I give the orders. You wait until I tell you what to do—no more improvisation."

Farran disconnected the call, closed the phone, and slipped it into the pocket of her skirt. Her hands were shaking, but she crossed her arms over her chest and took deep breaths until the emotion passed. It was Friday. Shaggy should be able to squeeze in one last attempt before her time was up.

All she needed now was a foolproof plan, because if she failed, Roderick would take over. Heaven help Shona then, because there would be nothing Farran could do to stop him.

Shona stood in front of the full-length mirror in her bedroom and carefully checked her appearance. The dress was too revealing—she should change into something else—but she'd bought it weeks ago specifically for tonight's party and she loved the berry-colored cocktail gown with its asymmetrical hem and feminine spaghetti straps. Maybe it was more modest than she thought.

It wasn't too daring in front, Shona decided. The bodice barely showed the top swell of her breasts, and while the satin fit closely, it was shirred, offering a sense of concealment.

The problem started with the empire waist. From that point until past her hips, the garment was form-fitting. Shona frowned. It was lined, though; that took away some of the sexiness factor, right?

Reluctantly, she pivoted. This was what had her worried. Shona didn't want to tease Logan or send the wrong message and she was afraid the back did exactly that. It plunged, leaving her shoulder blades completely exposed and she'd be bare to the small of her back except for two twists of fabric offering about an inch of cover each. A bra—even a strapless one—was out of the question.

Turning again, Shona took in the whole picture and frowned. As much as she hated to wear something else, the dress was too much; she had to change.

She hurried to her closet, threw open the door, and started flipping through the hangers. The blue dress—no, she'd worn that last night, the coral dress had been Tuesday night, the white dress with the red circles was too casual, the—

The doorbell rang. With a gasp, Shona straightened and looked at the clock. He was five minutes early, damn it.

Maybe she could still—

He knocked and Shona scowled. He wasn't going to wait on her doorstep while she picked another dress. Unless it was someone else at her door. She crossed to the window and peeked from behind the curtain. The front stoop was out of view, but she recognized the car. Logan had brought the white Ferrari.

Another knock.

"Just a second," she hollered. Oh, yeah, she bet all his dates were classy enough to shout at him through closed windows.

Shona cast one last look at the closet, then conceded. She'd wanted to wear this dress anyway, now it seemed she was going to.

Walking to her dresser, she slipped two thin silver bangles on her left wrist and put in silver hoop earrings. The gold chain of her necklace fell beneath her bodice, and she knew she should take it off. She reached for the clasp, but the stone pulsed between her breasts and Shona couldn't remove it. Mixing metals was in, wasn't it? And if it wasn't, she was an artist. People would just shrug and talk about her quirkiness.

She grabbed the silver evening bag and forced herself to stroll to the door rather than hurry. Logan's expression was a combination of irritation and concern, but it disappeared as soon as he caught sight of her. A dumbstruck look replaced it and Shona smiled. It was bad of her, but seeing him gape shot a little thrill through her. That was only fair since the sight of him in a dark suit with a crisp, white shirt and a conservative tie made her pulse trip.

"I'm ready," she said, taking a step forward. It was only then that she realized her silver open-toe pumps brought her to within a fraction of Logan's height. "Oops, I'll go change into some flats."

He shook his head. "Don't bother on my account. I don't have a problem with it."

Shona bit her bottom lip. She'd actually forgotten how tall she was and that was nearly unbelievable after the mockery she'd received when she'd towered over all the boys in junior high. "Are you sure?"

"Positive. Do you need a jacket or something?"

"You're kidding, right?"

Logan grinned and shook his head. "Why did I even ask? I know better than that—it would ruin the look."

"Absolutely." Shona had her key on the foyer table and she grabbed it before stepping outside. As she turned to lock the house, Logan made a wheezing sound. Concerned, she glanced over her shoulder and lost her breath. She'd never seen that particular look on a man's face before, but she knew what it meant. If she opened the door and moved back inside, he'd take her up on the invitation and have her in bed in less than a minute. Temptation tugged at her and an ache developed, but she locked up, putting distance between them.

"I—" He cleared his throat. "I probably should have driven the Jeep. As low-slung as the Ferrari is, you're going to have a hard time getting in and out of it."

"With a little help, I'm sure I can manage. Besides, it's a Ferrari—I've never ridden in one before." She started to walk past Logan, but he put an arm around her waist, stopping her. "What? Did I forget something?"

"No, I did. Shon, I just want to say that you look amazing. You're going to have me sweating all night." He gave her a smile before he brushed a soft kiss over her lips.

"Thanks." She couldn't think of anything else to say, but before she could get anxious about that, she remembered who she was with. Logan never judged her on her social skills.

He did have to assist her into the car, but Shona wasn't about to complain. She was going to a party that any artist would kill to attend and arriving in a classic car with the hottest guy in Seattle at her side. It was like Cinderella, but without the wicked stepsisters thing.

Maybe life was compensating her for taking away her ability to work with glass. It wasn't only meeting Logan, she'd had a lot of other cool stuff happen in the last two months—her glass had still been showing and she'd gotten some nice accolades and sales; she'd met Farran, a friend who was as close as any sister could be; and around the same time, she'd stumbled across her pendant while killing a half hour at a thrift store. And hey, she'd discovered the dress that had made Logan's jaw drop. Now that was really something.

"You're quiet," Logan said, breaking into her thoughts. "Did you get any sleep after I left last night?"

Shona's breath hitched. She didn't want to talk about this, but she knew Logan was concerned about her. "Not much, but once the sun came up, it was easier to relax."

"You should have let me sack out in your living room like I wanted; you would have slept better."

"Then we'd both be tired. You're too tall to be comfortable on that couch." And he never would have stayed out there the entire night. Shona would have caved, would have asked him to lay beside her and hold her and it wouldn't have stopped there. "I appreciated the offer, though."

"It's the least I could do since I wasn't able to grab the guy. These dress shoes slowed me down." Logan scowled. "But I probably wouldn't have caught him anyway. He had a head start and he's faster than me."

"You did what you could."

"Which was a damn sight more than the police."

Shona's mellow mood was evaporating fast. "I don't want to talk about this any more."

"I still can't believe how lightly they took the whole thing even after we told them it was the same attacker."

He was tense now, too, she noticed and Shona reached over and put her hand on his leg. "I'd guess the cops that answered the call last night don't deal with much serious crime. They probably didn't know how to handle it."

"Then they should ask for help from the Seattle PD."

His voice was tight enough to stun Shona for a minute—no one except her parents and Farran had ever been this concerned about her. But Logan, she realized, had protected her—and not just physically—from the moment they'd met.

Her heart twisted before it did a free fall.

The reception was in a large, prestigious Seattle gallery and it kicked off a show for one of the premier glass artists in the world. Shona was awed to stand in the same building as the man and to be invited to this? It took her breath away.

She knew what it meant—she was considered an up-and-comer in the field—but she felt like a fraud. It had been two months since she'd had the urge to work and about six weeks since she'd stopped trying to force it. And as she walked among glass pieces so beautiful she couldn't stop staring, Shona felt a stab of envy sharp enough to make her physically hurt. It didn't last long before the bleak numbness returned and she hated that.

As if sensing her sadness, Logan slid his arm around her waist and tugged her to his side. Another emotion roared through her so fast and hard that it knocked the despondency right out of her. Lust, desire, need—all those words fit.

Of course, wanting Logan hadn't been far from her thoughts at any point tonight. It was as if she were in heat. She continually pressed her body to his, rubbed against him as unobtrusively as possible. And she was wet. So wet that she didn't dare sit down.

Last night she'd planned to tell Logan she couldn't see him again, and here she was tonight, distracted because she couldn't stop thinking about jumping him. Part of her—the part that could still manage to think—was speechless with disbelief. This wasn't her, she didn't act this way. Yet it was her, the person she became when she was with this one man.

It would be nice to blame it on alcohol, but she hadn't had anything to drink tonight, not even a soda. She couldn't even accuse Logan of priming her—he'd been a perfect gentleman—she'd been the instigator.

The thought made her realize she was pressing her breasts against his chest and swaying. That stopped her cold, her gaze darting around the room. Thankfully, no one seemed interested in them, but she couldn't keep teasing Logan—or herself—this way. Somehow she'd become attuned to him and could tell his level of arousal. Right now, it was running about medium, but it wouldn't take much to drive it higher.

For a moment, she hesitated, not wanting him to see her fever, but Shona needed to gaze into Logan's eyes. She looked up and nearly gasped at the intensity shining there. "I was counting on you," she said, "to maintain control for both of us."

"Don't." His voice was thick and deeper than usual.

Swallowing hard, Shona nodded, and squeezed her thighs together, trying to ease the ache. Desperately, she searched for a distraction and spotted one of the more diminutive works on display—a pearl resting on a bed of blue, waving seaweed. Shona pointed discreetly and said, "Why don't we take a closer look."

He nodded and his hand went from her waist to the small of her back. Her heels sounded inordinately loud as she walked on the hardwood floor, the conversations, the laughter in the room, seemed high in decibels, and she could pick out the beat of Logan's heart even though the room was filled with people. Shona checked it out, but the loft-style ceiling didn't have any acoustic panels, only track lighting to illuminate the art. She didn't understand why her senses were so heightened tonight, but she was picking up nuances easily—scent, sound, sight, everything.

The piece sat on a pedestal that put it at waist height. Nothing protected it, no Plexiglas, no velvet rope, and Shona had to link her fingers together in front of her to resist the urge to touch. The texture of the seaweed was exquisite and it curved and waved as if it really were a plant held captive to the ebb and flow of the ocean.

Her vision sharpened and Shona could see each gentle rise in the glass. The colors seemed deeper, more vibrant than they had a moment earlier, but no matter how outstanding the blue seaweed appeared, it didn't compare to Logan's eyes.

"Is this the kind of work you do?" he asked.

Their bodies brushed and Shona turned into his side again, unable to stop herself—unable to care that she couldn't stop herself. "Mostly, although I've done a bit of everything and I'll use whatever technique I need to get the look I want." She focused on the work once more. "Wow, see how that pearl shines and reflects the seaweed?"

"Why do you do that? Change the subject whenever I ask about your art?"

"Maybe because I don't want to talk about it." Stubbornness settled on his face and she knew he was ready to push. "Not tonight and not here. Tonight's about just being, okay?"

Logan frowned, then nodded. "Soon," he warned.

"Soon." She could trust him with her deepest pain, the fear juxtaposed in some odd way with numbness. He might not understand—Shona didn't think anyone who hadn't been through it themselves could get it—but she'd share it with him.

The gallery was crowded tonight—men and women with whom she should be networking—but the idea of approaching strangers and inserting herself into their conversations seemed impossible. Besides, despite how crowded it was, everyone else had receded and it was as if she and Logan were the only two people present.

Someone jostled her from behind and Logan wrapped both arms around her waist to steady her. Shona's whole body rested against his and she inhaled harshly. She scented his arousal as easily as she picked up the citrus tang of his aftershave and it drove her own need higher. Hanging on to him, she fought the instinct to grind her pelvis into his, but sweet heaven she wanted to so badly that she ached.

"Don't look at me like that," Logan warned.

"Like what?" she asked in a whisper.

He put his mouth next to her ear. "Like you wouldn't care if I shoved that pearl thing to the floor, bent you over the pedestal, and took you in front of everyone in this room."

Shona moaned quietly and his arms tightened. She could see it, almost feel him inside her, pushing into her from behind.

Her last shred of restraint went up in smoke.

For an endless moment, she met his gaze, then she made a decision. It was crazy, it was stupid, and she didn't care, not even a little.

Breaking his hold, Shona took his hand and tugged. That was all the impetus Logan needed to follow her through the crush. Her heart pounded, her breath came in shallow gasps, and her head whispered dire warnings of public humiliation, but she was driven by something more basic. Something primal.

There wasn't a gallery in Seattle that was unfamiliar to her and she knew this one had two sets of restrooms—one on each floor. The party was held on the first level and she was betting the second was empty.

They passed no one as they wended their way through the displays on the dimly lit second floor and Shona didn't know herself if she was hoping for her theory to be proved or disproved. Logan remained quiet, not asking any questions and that made it all that much easier to ignore her common sense.

The light in the alcove between the restrooms was on. Every cell in her body was smoking hot as she opened the door and drew him inside.

They were rushing across the lounge when Shona stopped short. Logan bumped into her and she felt his arousal. "Wha—"

"Condom!" she said and grabbed one out of the bowl on the counter in the lounge. Thank heavens for gallery owners who advocated safe sex. He had her inside the handicapped stall with the door locked before she could draw another breath.

"This is insane," he muttered, pushing her against the tile wall and taking her mouth.

She grabbed him, her purse hitting the floor, but she didn't let go of the condom. He had one hand at her nape, holding her in place, the other grabbed the back of her skirt and started pulling it up. Logan growled with frustration, tugged her away from the wall, and yanked her skirt up the rest of the way.

She moaned softly as his hand clasped the bare cheek of her bottom. He caressed her, his fingers tracing down her rear and between her legs. Shona gasped.

Logan groaned low in his throat. "Damn, Shon, you're soa—"

Before he could finish his comment on how wet she was, Shona tugged his mouth back to hers. She knew, damn it.

Her butt met cold tile as he pushed her into the wall, but his erection pressed into her belly and she didn't care about anything except how hard he was.

Logan stepped away, grabbed the hem of her dress, and pulled up the front, too. Her knees nearly buckled as he stared at her skimpy panties. "Keep your skirt up," he ordered thickly.

With his hands free, Logan unbuttoned his suit coat and unbuckled his belt. She did some staring herself as he dropped his pants and briefs to mid-thigh. The sight of his naked erection made her forget to breathe.

Everything. She wanted to do everything with this man and she wasn't sure where to start.

She shifted fabric so she could keep her dress up with one hand and reached for him. Her fingers barely grazed his shaft before he moved out of range. "Next time," he promised and snagged the condom from her grasp.

His hands shook as he rolled it on, then he was back. He cupped her, his fingers stroking her lightly through the silky material of the thong, but that didn't last long. Tugging the fabric aside, Logan touched bare skin. Shona's gasp changed to a moan when his thumb circled the center of her pleasure, and the sound cut off abruptly when he slipped a finger inside her.

The second finger nearly made her come.

Cool air replaced his hand and Shona opened her eyes in time to see Logan dip down. As he began to enter her, her head fell back against the wall and she savored the sensations rocketing through her.

Slowly, he straightened, grabbing her hips and moving deeper inside her. Shona fought to keep her eyes open, to watch his face.

His hands and the wall kept her steady, but the feelings going through her were so intense, she was afraid she'd sink to the floor.

"Lift your leg."

She obeyed immediately, and Logan's hand slipped under her thigh, hooking her leg around his hip and staying there, helping her hold the position.

"Tilt your hips up a little. Yeah, yeah, Shon, just like that."

Logan rocked into her and she couldn't keep her eyes open a second longer. Every time he pressed forward, he hit her sweet spot and she knew she wouldn't last long. She held on to him tighter, needing him to bring her off.

He stopped cold. Shona started to protest, but Logan kissed her, cutting her off. Then she heard voices and froze, too. He lifted his head.

Oh, my God! Shona felt a stab of panic. If they looked under the stall door they'd see two sets of feet. Or at least a pair of man's shoes and one of her shoes. Before she could stop herself, she tightened the leg she had around Logan's hip, drawing him in farther.

"Can you believe that Ashley had the nerve to show up tonight?" The woman sounded contemptuous.

"I doubt she had an invitation," the second said. "The owners knew Walter would bring his wife."

"She always was a brazen little slut."

Someone ran the water, drowning out the response, but Shona didn't care. She didn't know who these people were, and even if she did, she was on the edge of coming. Unable to stop herself, she tensed her inner muscles, squeezing Logan. His jaw went so tight, she could see a muscle begin jumping in his cheek. She did it again.

It was a mistake.

He couldn't move as firmly as he had before, but he was pressing rhythmically into her again. Shona had to bite her lip to hold back a moan.

One of the adjacent stall doors closed. She held on to Logan for all she was worth and struggled to restrain her impending orgasm. There was no way she'd stay quiet once she started coming. No way.

The conversation going on around her was nothing but an annoying buzz. *Get out, get out, get out,* Shona silently chanted, but neither woman seemed to be in a hurry.

Logan thrust harder and Shona buried her face against his throat, trying to muffle her gasp.

"Are you okay?" the woman in the stall asked.

Oh, God! "Fine," Shona managed, her voice almost sounding normal even though Logan was still moving. Should she offer some explanation? "Cramps."

"TMI," the woman said and Shona heard the toilet flush.

The water ran again and the conversation resumed. Weren't they ever going to leave? Logan had her on the brink and she grabbed his hips, trying to force him to remain motionless. She shook her head, warning him silently how close she was.

Shona was ready to cry in frustration by the time the voices grew distant. The instant she heard the outer door close, she arched into Logan's next thrust.

She was more than ready, and on the following rock of his hips, the pleasure came crashing down on her. Shona arched hard, and a soft keen escaped as she rode out her orgasm. The intensity started to lessen, but then Logan came, and he pushed her back up again. Her knee gave out, and only his body pinning her to the wall kept her upright.

When the haze lifted, Shona had both feet on the floor and Logan had his cheek against hers. He was panting, but so was she and her heart was racing as if she'd just sprinted for a mile.

"Do you know how close we came to getting caught?" he asked.

Too close. She shivered. "I know."

"It turned you on."

Shona would have stiffened, but all her muscles were soft and languid. "It did not."

Logan lifted his head. "Honey, I felt you tighten around me. Most women would cool down under the circumstances."

She didn't like him comparing her to other women. "If that's the case, then it turned you on, too. Wouldn't most men lose their erection in the face of imminent discovery?"

"Guess we're both pervs. Can you stand on your own?"

"I think so."

He stepped back and Shona immediately missed his heat. His hands stayed at her hips until he was confident she was steady, then he released her and disposed of the condom.

Unable to move, she stayed where he'd left her, skirt still hiked up around her waist, panties pulled to one side. His eyes dipped in that direction as he pulled up his briefs and trousers. "We can't do this again," Logan said, zipping his pants. "Once was a big enough chance, especially when there are people downstairs who can help or hurt your career."

"I know."

He fastened the button on his suit coat. "Shon," he bent and kissed her, lingering at her mouth. "Please drop the skirt before you get me hard again."

"I can't," she said, cheeks heating. "I might stain the dress." She gestured helplessly with one hand.

It was even more embarrassing when she saw realization dawn. "Hang on," he told her and unlocked the stall door. He returned with a moist paper towel. Shona tried to take it from him, but he evaded her, and crouching down, gently ran it over her inner thighs and between her legs. When he finished, Logan kissed her *there* before tugging her panties back into place and standing once more. "You should be safe now," he said thickly. "But I messed up your hair and makeup. You're going to need to make some repairs."

Shona carefully lowered her dress and straightened away from the wall. "I guessed that."

"Are you okay?"

"Yes, why?"

"You're trembling." He bent down, picked her purse up

from the floor, and handed it to her. "I can't stay here much longer, but I don't want to leave you like this."

"I'm fine." She was. "And you do need to get out of here before someone else comes in."

"Yeah." He kissed her again. "I'm going to duck into the men's room. I'll meet you at the foot of the stairs, okay?"

She nodded, but he didn't leave. "What?" she prompted.

He frowned and she could almost see him arguing with himself. Finally, Logan shook his head and said, "What happened? It was special. It meant something. Don't start second guessing it and tearing it apart. Please."

Another kiss, then he ducked out of the stall. Shona didn't move until she heard him leave the restroom.

11
CHAPTER

Farran's heart sank as she turned in the driveway to Shona's house. She'd learned the other woman's habits and Shona only did things like wash her own car when she was upset. That didn't bode well for someone who planned to ask for a favor.

Shona stopped spraying off the coupe when Farran pulled up and turned off her engine. Cautiously, she opened the door and called, "Is it safe to come out or are you still mad at me?"

"You're safe." Shona dropped the hose and walked over to shut off the spigot.

After tucking her keys into her purse, Farran swung out of her sedan and reached for the bag of sandwiches. Another peace offering—she hadn't been sure of her reception after they'd argued about the Gineal troubleshooter. For a moment, she stared at the multi-colored stone hanging around Shona's neck. Farran felt the pull of the gem and her palms tingled with the urge to hold it, to take it and wear it herself. She fought to suppress the reaction.

"I think you're as wet as the car," Farran said, taking in

the damp hair and the water dripping from Shona's camouflage cutoffs and green tank top.

"I had a little issue with the spray nozzle," Shona said with a frown. "You're on your way to work?"

"I have to be there at one, but I thought we could have lunch first." Farran held up the bag. "I haven't seen or heard from you much this week and I was worried you were angry at me."

Shona reached for her pendant, gave the stone a caress, and dropped it behind her top. "I'm not mad." She grimaced slightly. "I am sorry, though. I hate women who ditch their friends when a guy comes along, but I did that to you."

Closing the distance between them, Farran took Shona's hand, squeezed it, and stepped back. "Not really. We didn't have any plans that you canceled, but I have missed talking with you and I thought we could have lunch together today." She hesitated, then decided she better come clean up front or it would raise questions later. "And I have a favor to ask."

"What kind of favor?"

There was curiosity on Shona's face, but no wariness and Farran took that as a good sign. "I'd hoped to soften you up with food and then lead into it gradually, but I guess I blew that." She drew a deep breath. "Tomorrow is the anniversary of my mother's death."

"I'm—"

Farran stopped Shona before she could express her sympathy; she hated using her mother's memory in this way, but she had to ensure her friend's compliance. "My dad wanted to have the memorial on the actual anniversary, but there was a last-minute conflict at the church and he rescheduled it for today. I called everyone and no one can fill in for me at the store."

"Did you contact Marge?" Shona asked. "She's usually willing to come in if something happens."

"I did call her—she's in Napa Valley with her husband this weekend. This is where the favor comes in. You used to work at the gallery, would you close for me tonight? It would only take a couple of hours."

"I haven't worked there in months."

"I know. When I talked to Marge, I asked her if she'd have a problem with it and she said no, that you were her model employee." Farran decided a slightly pleading look might help her cause and donned one. "I wouldn't ask you to help out if it wasn't my mother. Please, Shona?"

"A couple of hours, you said?"

"I'd need to leave by 4:30, and you know the drill—by the time you close up, it would be almost 6:30 before you got out of there." Farran relaxed. It was a done deal now, she knew it.

"That should be okay. Marge really didn't have a problem with it?"

"None." Farran had spellcast to make sure the owner would agree. "We could call her if you need verification."

"Not necessary; I trust you, and maybe working at the gallery again will give me a creative boost. I made some of my best pieces while I was there."

"Thanks, I really appreciate this! And it would make me feel a lot better about asking if it did benefit you."

With a shrug, Shona changed the subject. "Do you mind if we eat out here? I can't go inside until I dry off."

"Why not? It's a shame to be indoors on such a beautiful day." And Farran didn't care where they sat now that she'd convinced the other woman to go along with her scheme.

It didn't take long for Shona to raise the umbrella on her parents' patio table or to dig out cushions from the storage box, and while she did that, Farran ran over to the apartment and grabbed a couple of cans of soda, and then laid out the food.

"So," she said after they'd had a chance to take a few bites of their subs, "who has you upset enough to wash your car?"

"I'm not upset, not exactly."

"What word would you use then? Worried? Bothered?"

"Bothered, I guess." Shona reached for her soda and took a sip from the can, but she wasn't looking at Farran.

"Let me guess—man trouble."

"I wouldn't say trouble, not exactly."

Farran took another bite from her sandwich and chewed slowly as she considered Shona's responses. "You keep saying *not exactly,* but it's sounding more like an evasion than a need to be accurate. Did something happen? Do you want to talk?"

"No."

That one word brooked no argument, but Farran didn't have a doubt in her mind that Shona needed to confide in someone. She didn't dare press, though. Shona wasn't the type of person to go back on her promise to work at the gallery, but Farran simply couldn't take the chance. "Okay," she agreed. "Just remember I'm here if you need me."

"You're such a good friend." Shona's eyes filled with tears and she blinked them away, but her hands clenched around the sub until a chunk of roast beef fell to the wrapper beneath it. "Thank you."

"I feel the same way," Farran said. Her own fingers tightened and she made herself relax before she mutilated her sandwich. Time to change the subject. "My favor didn't mess things up for you, did it? Did you have plans for tonight?"

"I don't know. Logan didn't say anything yesterday or call today." Shona shrugged, her gaze fixed firmly on the table.

"That's why you're bothered."

"It isn't, not exactly." Shona grimaced. "I said it again, but it's true, that isn't *exactly* right, although I guess it's a part of it." More meat slipped from her sandwich. "After our first date when I wasn't sure what to wear, he's always told me what he's had planned, only I don't even know if he intends to show up tonight."

Shona put down her sub and grabbed a napkin to wipe her fingers. Her movements were agitated and abrupt, and that had Farran lowering her own sandwich. "What happened?"

"Nothing."

That was such an obvious lie that Farran didn't bother to call her on it. It was also apparent that Shona wanted to share what had occurred or she wouldn't have said as much as she had. "How do you expect me to help if you don't talk to me?"

There was absolute silence, but Farran had a sense of water building up behind an earthen dam. She waited quietly. It only took a moment before it burst.

"I had sex with Logan last night," Shona blurted in a rush.

It was a good thing she'd put down her sub, Farran thought with a strange detachment, because if she hadn't, Shona's announcement would have made her drop it. Two separate things left her stunned. The first was her friend having sex. In the two months since Farran had met her, Shona had always kept men at arm's length. She didn't think Shona had even had a date during the time she'd known her.

The second thing that left Farran amazed was the Gineal. Troubleshooters were taught to maintain control from the time they began their training and many had parents who instilled self-command in them even before they left home to apprentice at the ripe old age of twelve. She had no doubt that from the moment Logan had sensed Tàireil magic, he'd taken Shona on as an assignment. For all she knew, he'd reported the situation to his rulers and *they'd* charged him to protect Shona. For an enforcer to forget himself to such a degree was significant. Farran just didn't know what it meant.

And then it dawned on her—Andrews had seen the dracontias!

She nearly gasped, but stifled it in the nick of time. His spotting the stone had only been of moderate worry before this because Shona always kept it against her skin and her friend was such a prude when it came to sex, that Farran didn't think he'd get Shona out of her shirt any time soon. She'd been wrong and now the consequences were too terrible to contemplate. Her father, Roderick—

When she realized Shona was looking even more miserable, Farran forced herself to stop thinking about what would happen in the future and concentrate on her friend. "And that's why you think he hasn't made specific plans," Farran said slowly. "Because he got what he wanted and he's moving on?"

Shona nodded and her eyes filled again. "I've known him one week," she said so softly that Farran had to strain to hear her. "If you don't count when we met for coffee, it was our fourth date." Shona's cheeks blazed red. "I dragged him into the ladies' room at the Covington Gallery last night."

"You did him in the bathroom?" Farran's voice shot up an octave on the question. It wasn't until Shona went from red to ashen that she realized what she'd said. "I'm sorry, I wasn't judging. That was sheer amazement. You're fairly reserved."

"I know, that behavior isn't me." Shona studiously avoided Farran's gaze. "And I would have asked him to spend the night with me if I hadn't been so—um, tired."

Farran felt hope rise inside her. How likely was it that Andrews had stripped Shona when they were taking a chance just having sex in the bathroom? "Weren't you worried about being found naked in public?"

Shona frowned. "We, um, kept our clothes on."

With a shaky exhale, Farran watched Shona twist the napkin she held until it broke into two pieces. There was a good chance then that the Gineal hadn't seen the dracontias. There was still time for her to act.

"He must think I'm a total slut," Shona whispered thickly.

This was her chance to drive a wedge between Shona and Andrews, she realized—everything would be easier if the Gineal wasn't standing guard—but Farran couldn't do it. She was a weakling, a soft-hearted fool, and her father would call her worse, but she couldn't hurt her friend. Besides, if all went well, everything should be wrapped up this evening and the enforcer's presence around Shona wouldn't matter any longer. And if it didn't go well, he might be the only one who could protect Shona from—

Reaching out, Farran closed her hand around both of Shona's. "I don't believe Logan's moved on. Did you ever stop to think that he was thrown off balance by what happened last night, too?"

"He's a guy."

"So? Maybe you helped him live out a fantasy, but that doesn't mean he took it in stride." A Gineal troubleshooter losing control to such a degree? The man had probably been reeling once his actions had sunk in, but of course, Shona knew nothing of what he really was or how much out of character his behavior must have been.

Shona shrugged. "I guess this is where you say *I told you so.* You were right. I'm so far out of my depth with him, it's laughable. He played me perfectly."

"Before you write him off, why don't you give the guy a chance? At least give him a few more hours to get his head on straight and call you."

"Why are you defending him? You've never even met him." Shona finally looked her in the eyes. "And you're the one who tried to warn me away from him."

"I did, and no, I haven't met him, but obviously there's something important between the two of you. Don't shake your head at me, you know I'm right. You never would have been intimate with him if there wasn't." Farran tightened her grip on Shona's hands. "You know what I think? I think you were carried away last night and that scared you so much that you're looking for reasons to run from what you have with Logan."

"I'm not running." Shona pulled her hands free.

"No? You shared your body with the man, which was a big step for you, but you're smart enough to know that if you keep seeing him, you're going to have to share yourself emotionally, too. That's what I think has you frightened."

"It's not true."

"Isn't it?" Farran hesitated, then dove in headfirst. "You're afraid that if he gets to know you—the real you—that he won't like you, aren't you? Well, you know what? You're wrong. It's time for you to believe in yourself. You're a special person and you deserve a man who'll love you heart and soul. Maybe Logan isn't the one, but heaven knows you won't find out if you run from him now."

For an instant, Shona looked taken aback by the speech and Farran didn't blame her—she wasn't sure where that had come from herself—but her friend *was* special. That's what had her so torn the past couple of months because the only way Farran could protect Shona was to betray her.

Calling Marge's shop a gallery was pushing it, but that's how the woman referred to it and Shona had always thought of it that way. Certainly, nothing was set up with the attention to detail that the Covington Gallery had shown, but this cluttered store with different types of artwork hanging and shelved everywhere was where Shona had gotten her start.

The people who came in here were tourists or locals looking to decorate their apartments and homes without spending a lot of money. Some of the pieces were done by amateurs who considered it a hobby, but there were also some very talented undiscovered artists represented. Marge had always had a good eye and it had been her efforts that had gotten Shona noticed.

The Menagerie was how she'd met Farran, too. Her friend had gotten a job here, and since Shona dropped in often, they'd started talking and had ended up hanging out together.

To keep herself occupied, Shona straightened items on one of the shelves, arranging the miniature wood carvings so that they were presented better. It was nearly time to lock up and then she'd shut things down for the night and head home—where she'd probably sit watching reruns and feeling sick about Logan.

He hadn't called.

She'd kept her phone turned on all day even though Marge had a strict rule against that. Shona didn't work here any longer, and besides, the last hour on Saturday was usually dead anyway. It hadn't mattered, her cell hadn't rung even once.

Stupidly, she'd even dressed up, putting on a white dress covered in black polka dots, a white, cropped blazer, and black cowboy boots with white paisleys all over them. She'd been so certain he'd call and that he could pick her up here. What an idiot. His silence spoke volumes and Farran had only been trying to be nice when she'd offered excuses for Logan.

The shop's phone rang and her heart sped up even though she realized there was no way Logan knew she was here. She darted back behind the counter anyway. "The Menagerie. How may I help you?" She listened briefly. "I'm sorry, we close in five minutes. We open at noon on Sundays. You're welcome."

Shona hung up the phone and leaned against the stool near the register. She was busy feeling sorry for herself when she caught motion from the corner of her eye. Her head jerked around, but no one was there. "Hello?" she called.

No response. The back door was locked and the front had a buzzer on it—no one could get in without her knowing about it.

In her peripheral vision, she caught more movement and thought she heard the sounds of scurrying. She whirled, but still saw nothing. The hair on her nape stood on end as she sensed the presence of . . . something, and she retreated until her back touched the shelves behind her. She didn't want anything sneaking up on her.

Something like giggling danced through her mind, but her ears didn't hear anything. For nearly ten minutes, she stood frozen, continuing to catch activity from the corners of her eyes, and yet every time she turned to look straight on, there was nothing there. It was freaky and Shona didn't like it.

The front door buzzed and she jerked her gaze in that direction.

"See? I told you they were open," the woman said to the man following her.

Whatever it was Shona sensed left as the couple came into the store and she'd never been so grateful in her life to see last-minute shoppers. "Can I help you find something?" she asked, surrendering her position against the wall.

"We're just browsing," the man said.

Shona nodded and rested her shaking hands on the top of the glass display case that doubled as the counter. What had happened here? Overactive imagination?

While the couple wandered around the store, Shona breathed deeply until she was able to calm down. She walked to the door and flipped the sign to CLOSED to prevent anyone else from coming in and she began to take some of the jewelry off the counter and lock it in the drawer under the display case.

She was able to finish everything except taking care of the register, but the last-minute shoppers were still checking things out. Relief gave way to impatience.

Farran would have hurried them along without offending them, but Shona couldn't do that and so she waited. And waited. It wasn't the least bit surprising that they left without buying anything, but they'd managed to waste nearly forty-five minutes. Heaving a sigh, she locked the door behind them.

Shona took the cash drawer to the office, counted the money, set up the drawer for the next day, filled in the deposit slip, and locked everything in the floor safe. Duty done, she grabbed her purse and left the office.

Halfway through the stockroom, an arm went around her throat. Her scream was weak. No one heard it, no one was coming to help, not even Logan.

Bringing her hands up, she jammed her fingers between the arm and her throat, and pulled with all her strength. She couldn't get free, but she bought herself a breath. This was three times. In the last eight days, she'd been attacked three times and she was damn tired of it.

Anger replaced fear, and calling on all her strength, she

brought her elbow back, ramming her attacker's side. His hold slackened for only an instant, but that was all Shona needed to break loose.

Pivoting, she faced down the man who'd restrained her. It didn't surprise her at all to see the dirty blond hair or the slightly swollen nose. He looked mad, but she was furious. Without giving herself time to think, Shona went after him.

She didn't know thing one about fighting, but she figured he'd be in some serious pain if she hit his nose again. He must have guessed she'd think of that because he blocked her strike.

The toe of her cowboy boot connected with his shin hard enough to make him wince and swear at her.

He dodged her second kick, moving out of her range. The boxes he bumped into crashed to the floor and Shona heard something break. Taking hold of her purse strap, she wound up and hit him with the bag over and over until he grabbed it and tossed it to the side.

Snarling at her, he closed the distance between them. Shona refused to give ground and kicked at him again. He leaned down, trying to grab her leg. Improvising, she bent it, bringing her knee up hard. She managed to drive the air from his lungs.

The man lunged at her and Shona jumped back, twisting away from his attempt to grab her. Her elbow banged into a shelving unit and the thing wobbled, sending some small boxes to the floor.

She caught her balance, but her attacker was too close and there was no way around him. Shona braced her feet and curled her hand into a fist. Space was tight, but she brought her arm back as far as she could and let fly.

The blow landed in the center of his chest and sent him staggering. For a moment, she was too surprised to react, then Shona ran for the door, wanting to reach the street and have a chance of finding help or at least scaring the man away. He grabbed her hair, jerking her to a stop.

Shona gasped at the pain, but quickly rounded on her attacker. He wasn't going to hurt her, she wasn't going to let him.

She wasn't going to let him!

A ball of heat formed in the center of her chest and spread outward until every cell in her body seemed to burn. Anger, she thought. Anger made her stronger, more powerful.

The man's eyes went wide and he backed up.

Shona followed and a sound that was half growl, half snarl escaped her. She took another swing, and this time when she connected, she dropped him to the floor.

His nose bled again and Shona smiled. She'd hit what she was aiming for.

Skittering backward on his butt, the man scrambled to his feet. He looked white in the fluorescent lighting of the storeroom.

Another lunge, but something had given his plan away to Shona and she was prepared. She hit him again, and this time when he went down, she kicked him in his side with all her strength. She thought she heard his ribs cracking, but that was farfetched.

"Leave me the hell alone," he said, rolling to his feet. He clutched his side and moved away from her.

"*You* leave *me* the hell alone," she snarled in return.

He backed away from her and Shona followed. She couldn't trust him, had to keep what little advantage she had. The man bumped into the wall and started feeling around behind him.

When he located the doorknob, he turned it and ran.

Shona started to chase after him, but stopped. She didn't have to run. Her consciousness left her body and went winging out after the man who'd attacked her. She saw when he stumbled, and saw the strange looks he received as he sprinted down the sidewalk. When he reached a car, he fumbled with the handle and got inside.

It was old, beat up, and rusted. Logan would be able to

name the model, but all she knew was that it was brown and it had the Chevy logo on it.

He started the car, and put it in gear. But before he drove away, Shona thought to gaze down and look at the license plate. She memorized it before he turned the corner and she returned to her body.

Whoa.

She shook her head. That wasn't her imagination, she knew it wasn't. She'd just had an out-of-body experience.

Why wasn't she freaking out?

At the very least she should be shaking now that the attack was over, but she wasn't reacting to that either.

Maybe it was numbness or maybe self-preservation.

She shrugged. It didn't matter, not right now; she was calm and in control. Shona headed back to the office to call the police. Somehow, before they arrived, she'd think of a story that would plausibly explain how she had her attacker's license plate information.

12
CHAPTER

Logan sat on Shona's front steps and stared at the deep purple settling on the horizon. Time was running short. If she didn't show up in another few minutes, he'd have to contact a monitor to seek her out, and that meant he'd get another reaming from the council for not watching over her carefully enough.

This time he deserved it.

Even though he knew Shona had a human after her, he'd dismissed that as insignificant. All he'd really been concerned with was the Tàireil, and since they were powerless until sundown, Logan hadn't spent many daylight hours with her.

What a moron. If anything happened . . . He didn't want to think about that.

He straightened as headlights came up the drive and stood when he recognized Shona's car. Logan wanted to rush over to her, make sure she was okay, and then chew her out for worrying him, but he took a couple of deep breaths and fought the urge. If he did that, she'd become furious and they'd have an argument. That was the last thing he wanted, especially after last night. He knew her well enough to guess she'd be running scared over how fast things had moved between them and he wouldn't give her any more reasons to push him away.

Shona didn't appear to be in a hurry—he could tell she was trying to stall—but she finally got out of the car and headed for the house. She seemed tired and Logan watched her as closely as he could in the deep twilight.

It was second nature to scan. He stiffened as he picked up a trace of Tàireil magic and probed more deeply. The spell wasn't on Shona, but on something in her purse, he realized— an energy flux that seemed without purpose. Why?

The bigger and more important question was when had the darksider put an incantation on something of Shona's? Or when had Shona picked up an item that was already carrying a spell? His bet was last night at the gallery since the magic he was reading was weak.

The showing had been crowded, but not enough that he'd worried about missing a darksider. He must have slipped, though, must have let his senses get too fogged with arousal. He should have been more vigilant. He shouldn't have let her distract him until he didn't know or care about anything except her. He should have—Logan stopped berating himself as Shona drew close.

"What are you doing here?" she asked coolly when she reached the stoop.

Taking another deep breath, he came down the steps and stood in front of her. Her dress and jacket made her seem impossibly fragile and Logan had to curl his hands into fists to keep from pulling her against him. "Worrying about you."

"Sure you were. That's why I didn't hear from you all day." A little toss of her hair conveyed her skepticism as well as her words did.

Brushing past him, she went up to her front door and started digging through her purse for the keys. It was dark enough that she was unlikely to find them quickly; that gave him time to unclench his jaw and remind himself that she was looking to pick a fight. When he had control back, Logan followed her onto the porch. "Shon," he said evenly, "I must have called you twenty times today. All I got was your voice mail."

"That's a bunch of crap!" She rounded on him. "I had my phone on and it didn't ring once!"

"I called," he gritted out. "Did you play voice mail?"

"I didn't need to."

"Well, check now. I left a message every damn time I phoned and you should have quite a collection to listen to."

She glared up at him and Logan jammed his hands into the front pockets of his jeans to stop himself from reaching for her. He wanted to draw her to him and kiss her until it sank in that last night had meant something, but that wouldn't help.

"Fine," Shona said. "I'll show you."

"You do that," Logan drawled. He didn't understand why she believed he'd lie when it could be easily disproved, but she was hurt enough not to be thinking clearly.

She whipped her phone out of her purse, and in a flash, Logan figured out what the darksider's incantation had been aimed at. It acted like a barrier around her phone—that's why Shona hadn't gotten any of his calls. He quickly threw his own spell, draining the power out of her battery. It was the easiest way to stop any questions before they started.

Shona pressed a button on the phone. Nothing happened. Shona pressed again.

"Looks like the battery's dead."

"That's impossible, I checked it over and over today and it was working." She frowned and shoved the cell against his chest. He pulled his hands out of his pockets and took it. "Let me open the door and turn on the porch light."

Logan nodded and stayed quiet. He felt oddly satisfied that his call meant that much to her, but he hated lying and making her battery go dead *was* dishonest. She rummaged through her purse again and thrust a few more things at him before she located her house key. Shona opened the door, flipped on the light, and closed the door once more. The message was clear—he wasn't being invited inside.

Shona took her things back, returned them to her purse, and then held out her hand for her cell. Her righteous indignation quickly turned to sheepishness. "I don't understand— I swear I checked that phone dozens of times and it wasn't dead."

"Maybe there was a problem with the tower." Another untruth and he didn't know if it was a plausible reason or not, but he couldn't tell her the real cause. Logan hesitated, then added, "Or maybe you had other things on your mind and thought you were seeing it on."

Her cheeks went red almost instantly and he had to suppress a smile. There was a pause. "I'm sorry," she said with obvious reluctance.

Logan edged closer, afraid he'd spook her. Reaching up, he ran a hand through her hair, pushing it from her face, and leaned down to brush a kiss on her lips. "Did you think I wouldn't call you today? Honestly."

"Why would you? You nailed me."

His temper ignited, but he reined it back in. "Have I ever," he said with a growl to his voice that he couldn't contain, "done anything that gave you the impression that all I wanted to do was *nail* you?"

"No, but—"

"But nothing. Things happened fast between us—faster than you're comfortable with, I get that—but I never, not even for a split second, thought of you as some notch for my belt." She dropped her gaze, but Logan put his fingers under her chin and gently tipped her face up to his. "Don't insult either one of us by thinking about yourself that way."

Shona grimaced. "I'll try, but . . ."

"But what?"

She didn't answer, but Logan caressed her chin with his thumb and gave her time—they were getting into some serious conversational territory here. Shona didn't pull her face away, but her eyelids dipped before she said, "I'm such a geek; why would you be interested in me?"

"You're not a geek. Why do you believe you are?"

One side of her mouth tilted up. "I'm too tall, too clumsy, and socially awkward."

It angered him that she thought of herself that way, but Logan kept his voice calm. "You're not too tall—you're just the right height for me. If you were shorter, we'd never have managed sex in the restroom last night." Her gaze jumped back to his and he winked. Her face went scarlet again. "I've never seen you do anything clumsy and the socially awkward part? Yeah, in the beginning you were reticent, but once you got comfortable with me, that went away."

"I made you work awfully hard."

"It's okay—you're worth it."

Her chin wobbled under his fingers and he watched her struggle against the tears. He gathered her against him and rubbed slow circles on her back with his hand. She held him tightly and he felt her take shuddering breaths.

"I'm sorry," Shona apologized, her face against his shoulder. "It's been an awful day."

"Because you thought I didn't call?"

She shook her head. "A little, but mostly because my stalker turned up again this evening."

"What?" And he hadn't been there. Damn it, he knew better, or at least he should have known better. "What the hell happened?"

The story came out haltingly, but she was coherent and added explanations when he required them without Logan having to ask too many questions. As Shona talked, she gained strength and the weepiness went away. He kept stroking her back anyhow—it made him feel better even if she didn't need the comfort any more.

When she finished, he stayed quiet. Shona was safe and holding on to him as tightly as he was hanging on to her, but things could have ended up being much different. That bastard could have harmed her, or killed her, or grabbed her and turned her over to the darksider, and it would have been Logan's fault. "I hope you hurt him bad."

Shona pushed away from him far enough to see his eyes. For a moment, she only stared. "I kicked him while he was down."

"And you think that's unfair?" She shrugged. "The guy is huge, probably double your weight, and much stronger. Do you think he cared about fair when he attacked you?"

Her mouth opened, closed, and realization dawned. "I didn't think of it that way."

"That's the thing, when you're in a situation like that, you can't be nice. He's not going to fight according to the rule book, so you can't either. Your objective is to get away and if you have to gouge his eyes or kick him while he's down, you do it."

"You think he's going to keep coming after me, don't you? That's why you're giving advice."

"Three times in eight days—he hasn't given up yet." Logan didn't like the persistence and the human was the tip of the iceberg. The darksider was still out there and he could call on other dark-force creatures—things that Shona wouldn't be able to fight off. There was only one sure way to keep her out of harm's way and that was to put her inside the walls of his house. "I think you should move in with me until this is resolved."

Shona yanked away from him. "What?"

Uh-oh. He recognized that tone, but he couldn't back off—it was too important to keep the Tàireil and his minions away from her. "You'll be safer there. I have a security system."

"I'm not moving in with you." Shona frowned at him and went as far from him as she could get on her small front porch. "And you know what else? We're not having sex again."

"Ever?"

"No. Yes. I don't know. It depends."

Logan fought off another smile. "I told you that you set the pace between us—that hasn't changed—and if you want to back up and take things slower, that's what we'll do. Just remember I have three extra bedrooms that you can choose from—you don't have to sleep on the same floor as me."

For a moment, she stared at him and this time he couldn't read her expression. Then her muscles relaxed and she walked back toward him. "You really did offer up your house out of concern, not to get me back in bed, didn't you?"

"I've never actually had you in a bed." Her face went red once more and Logan grinned. "But yes, I am concerned. I don't want you getting hurt and my house is secure."

"I'm still not staying with you."

"Okay," he said easily, but her decision made things harder for him. "So did the police seem to take things more seriously this time?"

She shrugged. "I guess." Shona paused and Logan had to curb his impatience. It paid off. "This shouldn't last much longer. I gave them the guy's license plate number, so they'll find out his name and where he lives, and go arrest him."

"If he didn't steal the car or swap plates with another vehicle." Crossing his arms over his chest, Logan leaned a shoulder against the front of her house and thought over what she'd told him about the fight. One thing didn't make sense—he couldn't picture her attempting to chase down her attacker. "You know, I'm not completely clear on what happened after he ran out of the gallery. Did you go after him?"

Shona looked uneasy. "How else would I see his car?"

Warning bells started ringing. That was the same kind of evasion he'd pull to hide his use of magic and it made him suspicious. Shona didn't have access to her power, but something was going on. "I don't know; you tell me. How did you see his license plate?"

Her hand came up and covered her chest—Logan was starting to recognize that as one of the signs she was anxious.

For a long moment, she measured him, then Shona shrugged, grimaced, and said, "You're going to think I'm crazy."

"I doubt it."

She didn't appear convinced, but she went ahead anyway. "It was strange, Logan. It was like my mind left my body and flew after him." Shona blushed again, but doggedly continued, "I saw him run to this beat-up old car, I thought to look at the license plate, and when he drove away, I was back in my body." Shona smiled weakly. "Crazy, right?"

Hardly. It was a type of remote viewing and monitors and trackers had that talent. Hell, he'd been able to do it himself sometimes when he scried. "Not crazy," Logan assured her. "Interesting. Have you ever done anything like that before? Maybe when you were half asleep?"

Shona shook her head and that perplexed him. If a dormant had access to a part of her talent, it would be a lifelong thing, not something that suddenly manifested out of the blue. Maybe she didn't remember or had chalked up those occurrences as dreams.

He was still thinking about it when she said, "Something else strange happened today."

"What was that?" Logan braced himself, half afraid of what he was going to hear next.

"I kept seeing motion from the corner of my eyes. When I looked, nothing was there, yet I could clearly sense a couple of presences."

Hell, this was all he needed. What was after her now and were they tied to the Tàireil? "What kind of presences?" Shona looked at him blankly. "I mean, how did they feel—evil? Negative?"

"Nothing like that," she said and leaned her hips against the railing. "Playful, I guess, or maybe mischievous." Frowning slightly, Shona tipped her head back. "There was giggling, but it was an odd laugh, like maybe they weren't human. And I almost had this sense of immaturity, like these were children playing."

The description relieved him—dormants were sensitive

enough to see through a facade and pick up a dark-force creature's malevolence—but he wished there was a way to narrow down what had been drawn to Shona. It had to be tied to the darksider—if things were routinely attracted to her bright aura, she wouldn't have referred to this event as strange. "You've never felt anything around you before, have you?"

"No. You're not humoring me or looking at me like I'm nuts." She looked thoughtful. "And when I thought I'd seen the Loch Ness Monster on that dinner cruise, you took that in stride, too. Maybe you're the weird one."

Logan's lips curved. "If by weird you mean I believe in what can't necessarily be seen or scientifically proved, then yep, I'm as odd as they come."

Shona pushed away from the railing and crossed to him. When she was less than a foot away, she said, "I never would have guessed—you look so normal."

"I'm not sure how to take that."

"As a positive. I'm an artist, I have quirks, but if you're cool with the unusual, I don't have to worry about how you'll react to me."

Oh, hell. Every time she revealed her heart, Shona wound herself deeper under his skin. Logan hadn't been lying when he'd said he was looking for more than fun with her, but he'd never intended things to go as far as they seemed to be headed. "Damn, Shon, you're killing me."

Uncrossing his arms, Logan reached for her. He threaded his fingers through her hair, cupped the back of her head in his hand, and kissed her. He meant to keep things gentle and easy, but Shona pressed her body into his. She fit against him exactly right. Not too tall—perfect.

She tested his control further when she opened her mouth beneath his. Logan managed to resist for a heartbeat before he succumbed. A shiver went through him as he tasted her.

More. He needed more. His free arm went around her waist, holding Shona against him.

Turning, he pressed her against the side of the house and kissed her like he was starving for her. Maybe he was. It seemed to Logan that he'd been waiting for Shona forever. He wanted her. Not standing up in some damn bathroom stall, but in a bed where he could love her the way she deserved. The way he'd been fantasizing about.

Shona moaned softly and Logan felt her arousal, knew it nearly matched his. He started to reach for her leg, planning to hook it around his hip like he'd done last night, but that would push his control to the edge.

Logan broke the kiss. Her dark brown eyes were cloudy with passion, her lips moist from his kisses, and he nearly decided he didn't care if he got her into bed this time—there was always the next.

And then he remembered.

No sex. Logan rested his forehead against hers and fought for self-command. Shona wanted time and he'd give that to her.

"Logan?"

He lifted his head, saw her question. "I promised that you could set the pace. You wanted to back up and take things slower."

For a moment, he hoped she'd change her mind, but then Logan realized even if she did, it would be heat of the moment and Shona would probably regret it later. He didn't want that. Reluctantly, he stepped back from her.

As the blaze between them cooled, the regret he saw in her eyes turned to relief and Logan knew he'd made the right decision. His body would stop protesting sooner or later.

Shona swallowed a sigh. There had to be a million better ways to spend a Sunday than sitting in Logan's garage, watching him fix her car. He'd told her she could stay inside and do whatever she liked, but she'd wanted to be with him. The experience hadn't lived up to her daydream, the one where she competently handed him tools and he talked to her while he worked. She shifted impatiently in the lawn chair he'd found for her at the beginning of this whole adventure, but she'd stick this out as long as she had to—it was her car after all.

She wasn't sure how the topic of vehicle maintenance had come up last night, but when Logan had discovered she didn't know when she'd had her last oil change, he'd volunteered to do it for her. That had been sweet and she'd agreed, although now Shona wished she'd brought it to a shop.

The problem had started when he'd gotten behind the wheel to pull her car onto the hoist. Shona had wanted to drive it on—how cool would that be?—but he'd nixed it, telling her it had to be lined up correctly with the frame. That had been when a half-hour oil job had expanded to a couple hours' worth of overhauling. Logan hadn't liked the feel of her brakes, and when he'd gotten a look at them, he'd added that to his list of things to do. It had necessitated an immediate trip to the auto supply store and purchasing parts that Shona couldn't name on a bet.

The shopping had been the most interesting part of the day for her so far and that wasn't saying much. She sat near the open garage door, but since the lake was on the other side of the house, she didn't have a great view. Looking out onto the driveway and yard wasn't interesting and the day was gloomy and overcast anyway. She wished the sun would come out, then maybe she could get Logan away from her car and out doing something with her instead.

A muttered curse drew her attention. "Are you okay?"

"Yeah. I just scraped a knuckle." His voice was muffled, but he only sounded mildly aggravated.

"How much longer do you think this is going to take?" Shona tried to sound curious, not bored, because she didn't want him to think she was unappreciative of his efforts.

"Almost done."

At least when Logan had been working on her side of the coupe, she'd had him to stare at. With the car raised on the hoist, he'd been able to do all the work standing up and he'd only had to duck underneath the vehicle briefly. She, however, hadn't competently handed him any tool. Oh, sure, she'd tried, but he'd said it would go faster if he did it himself.

He had a point. Logan had needed to tell her what he was asking for each time and that had lengthened the process. If they kept dating, she'd probably need to learn some mechanic-type stuff. The last thing she wanted was to spend hours alone while he was out here doing car things.

And if she went and learned enough to share his interests, Logan was going to learn about hers, too. Her glass work, and art in general, was a big part of who she was. Shona grinned. First up would be a trip to the Seattle Art Museum and then she'd take him to her studio.

Her smile faded. At least her art had been a big part of her life. Would her creative spark come back? That muted, distant panic rose up, making her heart feel heavy and her throat tight. Maybe there was no need to force Logan to study art. Maybe it would never be a part of her life again. Maybe she'd finished all the pieces she had in her and it was time to move on, to find some other interest.

Maybe she'd have to get a regular, eight-hour-a-day job.

That made her feel sick, but while it was one thing to take advantage of her parents' generosity as she pursued her art career, it was another thing entirely to freeload. Two months without working was already borderline in her mind—how much longer did she let this continue?

A loud noise jerked her from her melancholy. She recognized that sound—Logan had put the wheel back on the car and was tightening the lug nuts—he'd explained that when he'd done it on her side of the car. For a minute, it was quiet, then there was more clattering. The sequence continued until the last lug nut was secure. More quiet, then a different sort of banging.

"What are you doing now?"

"Putting my tools away."

Shona breathed a sigh of relief and perked up. She'd been worried that there were more steps before the brake thing was completed, but this had to mean they'd be out of here and doing something soon.

Logan washed his hands before he lowered the hoist, climbed in her car, and backed it into his driveway. Shona got to her feet, but when he returned to where she stood at the front of the garage, he had something in his hand. "What's that?"

"This," he said, holding it so that she could see the cover, "is the scheduled maintenance guide for your car. It was in your glove box with your owner's manual." Logan opened it, flipped a few pages in, and held it up again. "See this list? This is what you should be doing to keep it running smoothly and at what intervals the work needs to be done."

"Uh-huh." Shona wasn't sure she liked where this was going, but she did know that his exaggerated patience irked her.

"You're thinking this is no big deal, right? The car's running, so everything must be okay. Well, you keep ignoring oil changes and you'll be buying yourself a new engine, maybe a brand new car. That's a pain, but it's better than your brakes." His jaw went tight. "Damn it, Shon, do you have a death wish?"

"Of course not!"

"Your rotors had grooves so deep they couldn't be trued without putting them out of spec. Didn't you notice the shimmy in your steering wheel whenever you wanted to stop?"

"Yes, but—"

"But nothing." The patience was gone and now Logan looked mad. "You don't care about your own life and that's bad enough, but what about the innocent people you could take out with you? I'm not exaggerating." He anticipated her argument before she could say anything. "If you'd tried to brake hard on the expressway, you might not have stopped. How would you feel if you rear-ended a minivan full of kids going to a ball game?"

Shona wanted to tell him she tried to avoid the freeway,

but that wasn't the point. "Was it really that dangerous?" she asked in a small voice.

"Yeah." There was no anger left, just grimness and that told her how serious it was.

"Is everything else okay?"

Logan flipped open the booklet in his hands again. "It will be after we get you caught up on this, but you'll be fine in the short term—I took a look at a few other things and they were okay. I'd offer to do the work for you, but I bring my Jeep in to the service station for these checks."

"Why?"

He shrugged, closed the maintenance guide, and tucked it into the back pocket of his jeans. "I don't have the equipment to test all the computer chips the newer vehicles have, but another reason is how tight everything is on cars nowadays. It's easier and more fun to work on the older ones." Logan hesitated before he added, "If you can't afford to have a service center do the work, I'll do as much as I can without the testers—that'll cut down some on the cost."

Her heart picked up speed and she glanced to her left to look at her car before meeting Logan's eyes again. "You'd do that for me?"

"I want you safe."

A warmth started in the center of her chest and intensified until it nearly ached. This had to mean he cared about her, that he had been telling the truth last night when he'd said he wasn't just in this for fun and games. Shona had mostly believed him, but this pushed it to a hundred percent. "Thanks," she said.

Logan took the two steps needed to put his arms around her waist. "Not a problem. So now that the sun's out, did you want to go out in the canoe?"

Shona blinked at the sudden change in topic, then checked outside, and sure enough, the sun was shining. "Canoeing? You don't have a bigger boat?" She put her arms around Logan's neck.

"Sorry, I never got around to buying one."

She debated. "Maybe if we stay close to shore. I'm not a good swimmer and if we tip over . . ."

"You think I'm going to let you drown? Don't worry, I'll outfit you with a life vest, and if I have to, I'll get you to shore. But honey, we're not going to tip over. Promise."

He lowered his lips to hers and Shona closed her eyes, wanting this kiss. She'd expected gentle and sweet, but Logan didn't give her that. His heat consumed her and her need for him rose up, overtook her until there was nothing in her world except his mouth on hers.

Shona stroked his nape, splayed her fingers through his hair and slowly let the strands slip away. Logan's tongue gave one last flick against hers before he withdrew. She followed him, not ready for this to end, but he only allowed her a moment to explore him before he raised his head. She nuzzled his throat, kissing and biting gently—not marking him, but staking her claim. His arms tightened and then he put her away from him.

For an instant, she saw the fire in his cobalt eyes, the barely leashed desire, then Logan won the battle for self-command. It soothed her ego. She'd been a little hurt last night when he'd agreed so easily to her no-sex pronouncement and she'd wondered how much he really wanted her.

Now she knew and it left her stunned.

13
CHAPTER

The lights from his Jeep cut through the gathering dusk as Logan headed south on the expressway. It had been a long day, and if things were different, he'd have booked them into a hotel on the island rather than make the three and a half hour drive back to Seattle. There probably would be vacancies even in high season on a Monday, but he couldn't let Shona have a room by herself, and since she wasn't about to agree to share one with him, there'd been no choice except to head home.

"You're pretty quiet," he said. "How are you feeling?"

"Tired."

"You're not sore?"

"I have a few muscles I was unaware of announcing their presence, but overall, it's not bad."

Logan scowled. He'd chosen the park because most of the paths were easy, but they'd taken one marked moderate. "I shouldn't have let you talk me into hiking that last trail."

"You're kidding, right? That walk had some of the most spectacular views we saw all day. I'm not that uncomfortable and it was worth it." Shona reached out and rested her hand on his knee. "Is hiking something you do often?"

He paused to savor her touch. It was especially sweet because she'd initiated contact between them. "Not as often as I'd like, but yeah, I go out fairly regularly."

Shona's fingers tensed against his leg. "I wouldn't mind doing this again."

One side of Logan's mouth crooked up. This was still a big step for her—suggesting they do something together. Sure, she'd invited him for coffee and to her art show, but mostly she waited for him to do the asking. It was another sign she was becoming comfortable with him and he liked it. A lot.

"I'm glad," Logan said, "because there are more places I'd love to show you." It was too damn bad, though, that she was a dormant. If she were Gineal, they could travel via a transit and not waste time driving to and from the trails. That thought spoiled his good mood. If she were Gineal, a lot of other things would be easier, too—including dating her after his assignment was finished. The ceannards— Logan decided to worry about the council's reaction later. "There are even a couple of trails in Seattle that are worth the time."

Shona relaxed her hold on his leg. "I'd like that. Maybe we could go shopping and you could help me pick out some boots. I want to make sure I get the right kind."

Logan's lips twitched, but he controlled the smile. He hated to shop, but the suggestion was the third sign in a matter of minutes that she was at ease with him. "Why don't we take a few more hikes before you invest in boots. One day isn't enough to know for sure if it's something you'll enjoy."

She was quiet for a minute. "But you enjoy it."

"I do. I'll make a deal with you. If we do this a couple more times and you still like it, I'll do the shopping thing— just for boots, though." If Shona was anything like his sisters, he'd end up on a major expedition if he didn't qualify it.

"Only for the boots," she promised.

He didn't believe that, but he didn't call her on it. Besides, how bad could it be to schlep bags around for her anyway?

"You know," Shona said slowly, "this makes two days in a row now that we've done something you like—yesterday, it was the car and today, hiking. I think it's time you try one of my interests."

The repair work was to keep her safe and her car's engine running, but that was something else he opted not to mention. "What do you have in mind?"

"The Seattle Art Museum."

Logan gave a mock groan as he switched lanes to pass a slower moving vehicle. "First you want to make me shop, now this? You're a cruel woman."

"Somehow I think you're tough enough to take it."

He didn't bother to stop this smile. "I guess I can suffer for you. When do you want to go? Tomorrow?"

From the corner of his eye, he saw Shona shake her head. "No, tomorrow I plan to do nothing except veg out."

Which meant her home, the most obvious place for that human to find her. "Want to do that at my house? You can stake out the patio or the sunroom or the family room if you want to watch television and I can do more work on your car."

She straightened in her seat. "I thought you wanted me to bring it to a service center."

"Did you make an appointment?"

"No." Shona's voice had gone cautious and he knew she was afraid he was going to lecture her again.

"Then I might as well get started."

"It's not like you gave me much time to find somewhere."

"I wasn't criticizing, just volunteering."

Her sigh was loud in the confines of his SUV. "Sorry. As adamant as you were yesterday, I thought . . . Well, you know what I thought."

Logan dropped a hand from the steering wheel, put it over

hers where it rested on his knee, and gave her a gentle squeeze. "Yeah, I know. So now that you understand I wasn't ragging on you, do you want to do that?"

"Let me think about it."

"Okay," he said easily enough, but Logan wasn't thrilled. How many things were there to do that would keep her with him all day and deep into the evening? Simply finding places to take her that would make scanning for a darksider relatively easy had reached a point where it stretched his imagination. "When are you thinking of expanding my horizons and dragging me to the museum?"

"Wednesday? Or do you have to work?"

"I'm free." Logan put his hand back on the wheel.

After a moment's silence, Shona said, "You know, you seem to have a lot of down time."

He grinned. Protecting her was his job, and while he loved spending his days and evenings with her, his mission was to keep Shona safe. "Not as much as you think." Before she could question him, Logan said, "Like I told you, my hours have always been sporadic. I might be off for a week, even two, and then work every day for a month. It just depends what's going on."

"Do you like that?"

Logan shrugged. "I'm used to it. How about you? Your art is as much a career as my job, but you seem to have a lot of down time, too." Shona's fingers tightened on his leg, before she withdrew her hand. He missed her warmth, but it was time to push on this topic. "You ready to talk?"

The absolute silence told him the answer was no, but he wasn't going to concede defeat, not yet anyway. This was a good time and place—the inside of his Jeep was dimly lit and Shona shouldn't feel exposed. That had to make it easier, it would for him if things were reversed. "I know there's some problem—there has to be the way you've avoided the subject every time I've asked. Do you think I can't understand because I'm not an artist?"

"It's not you." Shona slumped back in the seat. "No one gets it, not even other artists."

Her tone was a mixture of bewilderment, frustration, hurt, and anguish and this time Logan was the one who reached out and put his hand on her leg. "Talk to me anyway—if nothing else, I can offer some sympathy."

Shona didn't say anything, but this was a different type of quiet and Logan was content to wait until she sorted it out. They'd gone a good ten miles before she said, "I can't work." Her voice was hushed, nearly choked. "For two months, the part of me that I tapped into for inspiration has been missing. Maybe that's not the right way to describe it. It's not that I'm creating bland or boring pieces, it's that I have no desire to attempt to make anything at all."

Logan wasn't sure what to say to that. Taking his hand from her knee, he reached for hers and laced their fingers together. Shona hung onto him tightly.

"I tried forcing it, thinking if I worked for a while, I'd find that energy again, but it never happened—it was a waste of time and materials. Then I thought if I took a break, didn't work for a while, that the fire would return. It hasn't, but you know what's the strangest thing of all?"

"What's that, hon?"

"Glass was my life and it's gone—shouldn't I be freaking out? I'm not, though, and that's what terrifies me the most, that I just can't seem to make myself care that much."

"You feel numb?"

"That's the way I describe it—mostly numb."

"You ever think that's your way of coping with the loss? You said this was your life." Logan caught her nod in his peripheral vision. "It seems natural to me that you'd shut down emotionally to deal with its absence, otherwise it would tear you apart."

"I'd agree with that theory except for one thing—there never was any strong emotion. I'd think that I'd have at least a day or two or even three of panic and terror before I went numb, but I didn't."

He waited for Shona to say more, but she stayed quiet. Logan tried a different angle. "You can pinpoint when this happened pretty concretely—did something happen two months ago?"

"Yeah," Shona said and there was an edge to her voice he couldn't quite label. "I had my first significant showing."

Logan thought about that for a moment. "That's why the other artists don't understand," he guessed. "They're attributing your block to this show—fear of failure or fear of success—and that's not the cause, right?"

She clutched him before her grip relaxed. "Right. I was still able to work for nearly three weeks afterward and it wasn't like I'd gotten some scathing review at that time or even a glowing one. It just happened. One day everything was great, and the next, I had nothing."

Something about the suddenness bothered him. Wouldn't it be more likely to happen gradually? "There weren't any signs beforehand? Like maybe a loss of focus or procrastination?"

He half expected her to try to yank away from him, but she didn't. "No. I've thought about it and played it out dozens of times in my mind and there was no warning. I know it's hard to believe, but it really was as if someone flipped a switch."

And that's what he didn't like. It was two weeks ago today that the council had told him a Tàireil was after Shona. He'd guess that the monitor had picked up the energy a matter of hours before Logan had been summoned, but the darksider had been lying low since then and no one had detected him again.

What were the odds that the man Logan was after had been in this dimension for a while before he'd been spotted? What if he'd put a spell on Shona to steal her creativity?

It was ludicrous. Insane. It didn't make sense. Why would the Tàireil bother to take her talent? Why would he hang around a couple of months after doing it? Why hadn't he attacked her? But then Logan was still trying to figure out why the man had enlisted a human rather than going after Shona himself. Nothing about this mission made sense and he hated that. If Logan didn't understand what was happening, it made it more likely he'd miscalculate, make a mistake, and leave her vulnerable.

"You're awfully quiet," Shona said.

"I was trying to come up with reasons why this happened to you, but nothing I thought of is worth sharing."

"I don't expect you to have answers when I don't have any myself, but I appreciate the effort."

Logan raised Shona's hand to his lips and pressed a kiss on the back. "I'm sorry you're going through this. If there was something I could do to fix it for you, I would."

"Thanks. You'd fix it, my parents would fix it, Farran wants to fix it, but no one can—even I can't fix it."

They were nearing Seattle and traffic was heavier now. Regretfully, Logan freed his hand and returned it to the steering wheel. He ran the name Shona had mentioned through his memory, got a hit, and asked, "Farran's your girlfriend, right?"

"My best friend," she confirmed.

"You don't mention her much."

"We've had a lot of other stuff to talk about. And it's not as if you've ever brought up your best friend. Do you even have one?"

"Sure, I do; my brother, Kel. We do things together all the time. At least we used to." Logan frowned as the concern roared back, but he pushed it aside. "He's the one who got me hooked on hiking, by the way."

Shona didn't go for the feint. "You said you used to do things together all the time. What changed?"

He debated briefly, but he was the one who'd raised the subject, and maybe he did want to discuss it. It wasn't as if he could bring up this topic with his family, not when everyone was worried about Kel as it was. "I'm not sure," Logan finally said. "Kel dropped off the map for a few weeks, no one could find him, and when he reappeared, he was different."

Logan tightened his grip on the steering wheel. He'd

searched everywhere for Kel, called on every talent he possessed and he'd been as helpless as the rest of the Gineal. There should have been some way to get to his brother sooner, before—

Shona touched his forearm, bringing him back to the present. "How was he different?"

After a moment to collect his thoughts, Logan said, "Kel was always the more reserved of the two of us and he was pricklier. It's why people considered me the 'good twin' even though the reason Kel's walls were thicker was because he was a lot more sensitive and empathetic than I am." He shrugged. "That reticence didn't extend to the family—at least not much—and was almost nonexistent with me. Until whatever it was occurred."

Her hand stroked him, running from his wrist to his elbow and back again. Shona didn't prod him to speak, simply offered him comfort and he absorbed it.

"We knew everything about each other. Maybe we didn't talk about it, but we didn't have to. I can't say that about him any longer. He avoids me, and when I've tried to push him to discuss what happened, he closes down even more." Logan swallowed hard. "I'm afraid to press him too hard, frightened that if he shuts down any further, I'll never get him to open up again—not to me, not to anyone. I'm scared we're losing him, Shon. He's put so much distance between himself and everyone else."

Shona's hand stopped midway on his forearm and clasped him briefly. "How long has it been?"

"A little over six months, but it feels like forever."

"Any chance of getting him into counseling?"

"I doubt it." Logan exited the freeway. "I'd be surprised if he'd even consider it."

Not that the Gineal had the kind of counselors that humans did, but there were a few healers who were venturing in that direction, and if his mom was named successor to the current head of the healing temple, that would expand in the years to come. But Kel wouldn't ask for help—at least Logan didn't think he would—and he wondered if his brother was hiding things from everyone, including Logan, to prevent the council from learning of them. In the last six weeks, ever since the seizures started, he'd been guilty of that himself.

"We spent the afternoon together a few days ago. There were moments where I thought things might be improving, but then he'd be deliberately antagonistic. I don't know. I can't fix things for Kel or for you and I hate feeling helpless."

She gave his arm another squeeze. "No one expects you to be able to wave your hand and make everything better. Sometimes, it's enough that you're willing to listen and be there. I'm sure your brother knows that he has your support and that's worth a lot."

There was the rub—he was used to solving problems by waving his hand, shooting a little lightning, and kicking some butt. Logan pulled to a stop at a traffic light. "Kel would absolutely hate it if he knew I'd talked to you about this."

"I'm not going to tell him."

Logan had to fight another smile. She sounded so earnest—and sweet. "I know that, and if I didn't trust you, I wouldn't have said anything."

Shona settled back in her seat and folded her hands in her lap, but he had a sense that she was pleased. That left him feeling satisfied, and although he hadn't been able to go into detail about Kel, it *had* helped him to voice his concerns.

And she was doing it again, damn it—digging herself deeper under his skin—and he couldn't seem to prevent it. Hell, he wasn't sure he wanted to stop it, not when he liked how it felt. The light turned green and Logan took his foot from the brake. He wasn't going to worry about this, too; he couldn't, not when there were bigger things on his list.

It was another fifteen minutes before they reached her

house. The conversation had been light, sometimes silly, and Logan was feeling content when he pulled in her driveway. He scanned the area before he turned the engine off, but didn't sense anyone in the vicinity. Good.

He got out, pocketed the keys, and went to help Shona. She grimaced as she stood. "Still want to go hiking again?" he asked.

"Yes." She turned to retrieve her small backpack from the floorboards of the Jeep before adding, "I'll be fine once I get my mountain-climbing muscles in shape."

Logan smiled and shook his head—the trail hadn't been that bad, certainly easier than the one he'd taken the last time he'd gone hiking. The memory wiped away some of his good mood. That was the day he'd been attacked by the bouda and had his first seizure. Shutting the door, he put his arm around Shona's waist and slowly walked her toward the front door.

They were halfway to her front steps when Shona grabbed his arm. "Something's wrong."

He immediately went on alert, but kept his body relaxed. The scan of her house and the immediate vicinity, though, was still clear. "What is it?" he asked, voice low.

"There are a couple of people nearby and they don't feel right." She looked confused. "I can't explain why."

Nothing. He wasn't getting a damn thing, so why the hell was she? "Where?"

She started to point and Logan wrapped his arms around her to keep her from tipping off whoever was out there. Putting his mouth to her ear, he said, "Just tell me where."

"One is beside the bush on the east side of my parents' house. The other is behind the evergreen midway between my porch and the neighbor's yard."

With his arms still around her, Logan pretended to dance Shona around, and as he moved, he silently chanted two spells—one to protect himself and one for Shona. When he'd narrowed the shooting angles from both locations as much as he could, he stopped. It wasn't perfect. Because the two positions were about twenty yards apart, it wasn't possible for him eliminate the threat to her completely.

Now that he had her as safe as he could manage, Logan directed hard probes at the places Shona had mentioned. This time, he didn't come up empty. Tàireil. A pair of them when there was only supposed to be one.

The fact that they hadn't fired reinforced his belief that they wanted to take her alive and torture her before they killed her. Everything else he knew about this assignment might be wrong, but that fit. It was also clear they'd expected him—why else would they waste the magic it took to hide their energy signatures?

"Okay, here's what we're going to do. We're going to go slowly toward your house. I'm going to keep my body between you and them as much as I can, so make sure you stay even with me. Can you sense any more of them or is it still just the two?"

"Just the two," she whispered after a pause.

"Okay. I'll walk you to your front door as if we're saying goodnight. As soon as you're inside, lock up and go hide in your closet with the door closed. Don't come out until I tell you it's clear."

"What if something happens to you?"

Logan nuzzled her temple, trying to keep up the pose that they were sharing a romantic moment. "I'll give you my cell phone. Kel's number is programmed in; call him, tell him who you are, and give him a summary. He'll take care of you."

"He can't get here quickly enough to do any good."

"You'll be surprised at how fast he arrives." Shocked would be more like it, but if it came to that, he'd let Kel deal with that little problem.

"The police—"

"Aren't going to be too concerned about a couple of trespassers." Great, *now* she wanted to bring in the police. Ten days ago when she'd been grabbed on the street, he'd practically had to force her to call the cops.

"I guess."

"Can you get your keys out without a ten-minute search first?"

Shona frowned at him, but nodded.

"Do it. When you have them out, leave your pack open and I'll drop my cell in, then you can zip it up again."

"Got it."

She followed orders exactly, but Logan didn't know how successful they'd been at camouflaging her actions. He'd thought the Tàireil would attack by now, but they might be betting that he wouldn't be around long to protect her. Minimum fuss and effort for them. Or maybe they were on recon, getting the lay of the land for a future assault. Either way, it didn't matter—he wasn't letting anyone get to Shona.

"Remember—keep my body between you and them." At her nod, he turned and escorted her to the door. They made it without incident. So far, so good.

"Unlock the door, I'll kiss you briefly. Then you go inside and barricade yourself in the closet like I told you."

"But—"

"Don't argue with me." She looked militant and Logan added a magical prod to make her follow his orders. "Do it now."

For a second, he wondered if he'd need to add a second push, but she turned and used her key, then she looked up at him, her lips in a tight line. Logan kissed her anyway. He closed his eyes, but he kept his senses tuned in on the darksiders. They stayed put. Good.

"Go," he whispered against her lips.

As soon as Shona was inside, he cast a spell so that any human who happened to glance over at the Blackwood property would see a quiet house and yard, but nothing more. Whistling, Logan went down the stairs, just a guy who'd come to the end of a date. If there had been more cover, he'd have played it differently, but sneaking up on either one of them was an impossibility.

He headed for his Jeep and focused on drawing power. They thought they'd remained undetected and he wanted to strike hard while he had the element of surprise.

When he was behind his SUV, Logan shot lightning bolts from each hand, trying to take out both darksiders at the same time. They had their own protection in place, damn it, and his shots didn't dent them.

He ducked behind his SUV just in time. Ropes of fire came at him from each hiding place.

They didn't drop their cloaking spell and that bothered him. Why were they wasting magic? And it meant he had to expend more energy to keep tabs on them.

Logan allowed himself to feel the stab of fear—to deny it gave it power—but only for a moment. He couldn't fight if he was worried about using too much magic and he wasn't about to risk Shona.

The fire eased enough for him to straighten and shoot another burst of lightning. Crouching, he made his way to the back end of the Jeep. Not that the shift was going to do much—the darksiders knew where he was—but a little change was better than standing in one place.

Bringing up the wind, Logan directed bursts at the enemy. It immediately died.

Hell. He'd hoped that neither of them was that strong.

As they let loose with more fire, Logan decided to show a talent of his own. He doused their flames, making them peter out before they'd traveled ten feet. It would cost him too much to do it again, but it gave them something to think about.

The darksider closest to Shona's home began to move, and Logan ignored the other to focus on this one. He let loose with a barrage of lightning.

Fear. He hadn't expected that, but he was scared the darksider would get to her. Logan wanted her at his side. Now.

She was safer in her house—the rational part of his brain understood that. Out here, Shona could get hit by a stray shot or the Tàireil could concentrate on her, leaving him scrambling to defend her. No, the only advantage to her being with him was that he could keep an eye on her and be sure she was okay.

Logan cast a quick spell to extinguish the droplets of fire raining down on him. His protection held, but he was worried they'd ignite the house or grass.

What if there were more darksiders out there?

The thought made his arm jerk mid-fire. He hadn't sensed anyone until Shona had pointed them out and he'd taken her word that there were no others present, but she didn't have access to her magic. She didn't even know what a darksider was. What if it was sheer, dumb luck that she'd discerned the two she had and there was another making his way to her?

He waited for the cloud of fire they'd surrounded him with to burn itself out and tried to beat back the terror. If anything happened to her. . . .

Images flashed through his head, possible scenarios where she was captured or injured or killed. His gut twisted and sweat trickled down his spine. Logan fought for breath. It wasn't the burning cloud around him; anxiety had constricted his lungs.

And the dark forces chose that moment to begin whispering enticements.

He could keep Shona safe if he embraced them. He'd be more powerful, more formidable than his opponents. He would be invincible. Unstoppable.

Logan fought off the thrall. It wasn't easy. The dark forces hadn't distracted him in battle since he'd been a young apprentice and that made it harder to block them.

The cloud dissipated at last, but it had cost him a lot of his shield. Logan reinforced it and checked his magic level. He was still okay, but he hadn't won yet. Getting to his knees, he tossed a couple of fireballs around the back of his SUV.

Emotional control. That was why the dark forces had gotten through his defenses. Under normal circumstances, he was cool in battle, but tonight, fear had taken over and opened a crack for them to come streaming in. They started their siren song in his mind again and Logan worked to quash the terror that had settled in the pit of his stomach. He wouldn't let anything defeat him—not when Shona was involved.

Back in command, Logan considered the situation. The Tàireil were constrained by the same lack of cover that he had to deal with, but there were two of them. Why weren't they trying to use this to their advantage?

If he was in their place, he'd pull a flanking maneuver. Either one would have a limited amount of time in the open before he was able to reach the house or the garage and use that as a shield. Their magical protection would last at least that long. So why the hell were they staying put and shooting it out?

What didn't he know?

The one nearest Shona tried to move again. Logan wasn't about to allow that. He created a wall of lightning and surrounded the darksider with it. A short shriek told him that the man had touched the field.

His satisfaction was short-lived and the incantation had taken more power than he'd wanted to use. With one enemy contained at least for the moment, Logan focused on the other one.

His shield couldn't take many more direct hits before he lost it. He threw a lightning bolt and measured the distance between where he stood and the bush beside the main house. Could the darksider get off the half dozen shots it would take to drop Logan's protection before he reached him? Not impossible, but difficult.

To increase his odds, he lobbed a lightning ball toward that Tàireil, and keeping to the shadows as much as possible, made a run for the man's position. The ball would dance around, sparking out mini-bolts for about forty-five seconds' worth of distraction. He shouldn't need more than that.

A ball of fire connected, lighting up the protection he had around him, but Logan didn't stop moving.

His lightning ball disintegrated about the same time he reached the darksider. Logan leaped, launching himself at the man. He had no protection in place against a physical blow and Logan took him to the ground and got in a solid punch before his enemy rectified the situation.

It didn't matter. Logan pinned him, kneeling on the man's wrists.

His prisoner tried to fight his way loose, but Logan subdued him easily. That had him taking a closer look. The darksider had defiance burning in his eyes—and he was maybe twenty years old. "Go home, little boy," Logan sneered. "This is the Gineal's dimension."

The kid erupted with a string of profanity that was as inventive as it was colorful.

"Does your mama know you talk like that?"

Logan shut up the second stream of cursing with a lightning bolt to the heart. It didn't penetrate the kid's shield, but it did jolt him enough to quiet him.

A rope of fire had Logan ducking. The other Tàireil was free now and it was two against one again. "You bring your daddy with you to fight your battles, little boy? Or is that your mommy?"

He easily blocked the fire the kid tried to shoot at him. It was a clumsy effort on the darksider's part and Logan suspected that he'd never learned to fight without using his hands. Given what Logan knew of the Tàireil world, maybe he'd never needed that skill.

This one wasn't going to be much of a problem, Logan decided, but the other might be a different story. Flipping the kid over, Logan conjured a piece of rope and tied his hands between his back. With the kid secure, Logan leaned him against the bush and called on the plant to grow and wrap strong branches around the bonds. He added a containment spell for good measure, but he didn't put enough behind it to make it stick for long.

Satisfied that his prisoner was going nowhere, Logan turned to find the other one—and was just in time to dive out of the way of the most enormous fireball he'd ever seen.

The kid laughed, but he was a moron. Battle wasn't about who looked the coolest or the toughest.

Battle was about walking away alive at the end.

Scanning along the trajectory of the missile, he located the darksider. He was out in the open, but then so was Logan and that meant it came down to whose protection could last the longest and who had the stronger magic.

Logan returned the shot, took stock of how much he had left, and grimaced. He was okay on the amount of magic—at least right now—but he was nearing the danger zone for triggering one of his damn episodes.

His heart accelerated and his breathing became shallow. Logan fought for control, but it was hard. The dark forces were singing their siren song to him again, and damn it, they seemed reasonable. Logical.

He managed to deflect a rope of fire off to his side.

With a deep breath, he took his fear and visualized jamming it in a box. He turned a key, locking it inside, and tossed it into the deepest recesses of his mind.

That shut up the dark forces.

The shot that hit him from the back told him the baby darksider had gotten loose. Great. With fire coming from both sides, Logan knew it was only a matter of time before his protection faltered. But he wasn't losing. He couldn't.

Lightning hadn't done much against these two, but what about the opposite? Logan conjured up two large balls of ice. He hated expending that much power, but he had to try it. Once they were ready, he flung one in each direction.

As they touched the magical shields around the Tàireil, they exploded, sending shards of ice out like shrapnel.

They penetrated, caused damage.

The darksider in front of him opened a transit and Logan saw blood on his face in the soft glow from the gate. This one was close to his own age and not an inexperienced kid. The man's eyes challenged him, but Logan didn't fire. He wasn't going to be able to kill him before he ducked through the transit and there was no point in draining more magic on a farewell shot.

Logan watched the darksider disappear and turned to watch the young one give him the bird before crossing his own transit. Either that symbol was universal, or the boy had spent enough time in the Gineal world to pick it up.

He added the relatively quick retreat to the list of things that were bothering him, but he didn't waste time mulling it over now. Instead, Logan took in his surroundings. With a wave of his fingers, he fixed the damage to the lawn and shrubbery. Another flick took care of the burn mark on the side of the main house. Swaying, he made one last scan, decided he'd better fix the blistered paint on his SUV, and then lifted the spell he had around the area.

His first step was nearly a stagger, but Logan regrouped and walked to the house. He didn't have to check his magic level to verify he'd gone too far—he could feel it—the white morass was headed for him. At least he hadn't reached the point where it was roaring down on him like a fighter jet on takeoff. He needed the extra couple of minutes he had to take care of a few things.

Her front door was locked, but it took only a tiny burst of magic to gain entrance. Carefully, he closed the door behind him, locked it, and threw a spell around her entire house. It wasn't strong enough to keep out the Tàireil, but it would slow them down enough that there'd be a warning.

"Shona?"

"Logan?" He heard scrambling, then she burst into the room. "Are you all right?"

"They're gone," he said instead of answering the question.

She studied him, but aside from him being disheveled, she shouldn't be able to see any other hint of the fight. "Is everything okay in here?"

"Yes. What's wrong? And don't tell me *nothing*—your pupils are dilated and your focus looks off."

Hell, he hadn't realized there were outward signs. "Here's the thing, Shon," Logan said, keeping his voice calm and relaxed. "I have seizures and I've got one coming on now."

"I'll call an ambulance." She was halfway to the phone before he managed to stop her.

"Don't! There's nothing the EMTs can do and it's taking them away from people who might really need them."

"But—"

"I promise, it looks scarier than it really is." And the sensations were closing in now. Logan curled his hands, trying to hide the way they'd started to shake. "I'm really sorry about putting you through this, but I'm not going to make it home."

"Do you think I care about me?" Shona crossed to where he stood and reached out for him. "What can I do?"

"Make sure I don't hit any of the furniture." He tried to smile, but Shona paled anyway.

"You can lie down on the couch or my bed."

Logan shook his head and immediately regretted it. "No, I'll fall. I'm just going to stake out a piece of the floor. Keep your distance once it starts; I don't want to hurt you."

His legs nearly gave out as he lowered himself and Shona had to grab on to him. As soon as he was on the floor she hurried around, moving the coffee table and the chairs away from him. "Are you sure you don't need me to call someone? Maybe your brother?"

"No! No," he repeated more calmly. Then he reconsidered. "Don't call him for me, but if you sense any more of those strange people that you felt when we got home, you call him then and ask for help. Tell him I'm out for the count."

Logan laid down on the rug before he toppled over. The

blinding light was *that* close to consuming him. He heard Shona's voice, but the words were unintelligible.

He couldn't hold it off any more. The white swallowed him.

14
CHAPTER

"Logan!"

Shona rushed toward him, but stopped short when he started convulsing. Oh, God, what should she do? *What should she do?*

When she realized she was standing there actually wringing her hands, Shona fought to calm down. She couldn't help him if she was a wreck. Think. Think! He'd told her to make sure he didn't hit anything. She'd moved the furniture, now she made a visual sweep, looking for smaller things that might be too close. Everything seemed to be out of range.

Logan's entire body shook and Shona felt a dull ache begin at the center of her chest. She brought her hand up to cover her heart, then slid it lower until her palm was over the stone of her necklace. It took a few deep breaths to ease the constriction in her throat.

Get his cell phone. She'd left it in the closet, but she might need it. If she had to call for an ambulance, his family would want to know about it.

Shona hesitated. She didn't want to leave him, not even for the thirty seconds it would take to retrieve his phone.

Shifting from foot to foot, she studied him. There was no

change. Maybe she could chance it, but oh, how she wished she had that cell in the room with her right now. Why hadn't she grabbed it when she'd heard him come in the house?

She shook her head. There was no point berating herself for that. She'd be quick. He'd be okay for the short trip to her closet and back. He had to be.

Shona turned to race for her bedroom and kicked something, sending it tumbling over the carpet. With a frown, she stared at it, not quite comprehending what it was. Then it sank in and she gasped. How the hell had his phone gotten in here? She *knew* she'd left it behind.

Slowly, she walked over and bent to pick it up. Shona held it at arm's length and frowned. Before she could solve the puzzle of the phone's appearance, Logan groaned and she shoved it in her back pocket.

He'd gone from convulsing to thrashing and that ripped apart her hard-won control. Her eyes burned. Shona raised her fist to her mouth and bit down on the knuckles to fight back the tears. The last thing Logan needed was her falling to pieces and she refused to let him down by giving in to the weakness. He'd always looked after and tended to her—tonight it was her turn to take care of him.

Her first few breaths were shaky, but with each one, Shona felt a little steadier. Logan's agonized groan nearly undid her, but after one shuddery inhale, she regained her poise.

Shona reached for her pendant again, but this time pulled it out from beneath her T-shirt. She was upset enough that she needed to directly touch the warm stone. It seemed to pulse against her palm and the rhythm soothed her further.

Logan's entire body went rigid and spasmed as if he were being electrocuted. Shona gasped and clenched her crystal harder. She wanted to go to him, to wrap her arms around him, and hold him close, but he'd told her to keep her distance. She understood why—he might hit her as he jerked around, and if he did, he'd feel awful when he came out of this.

A person having a seizure can swallow their tongue and

choke to death. The thought froze her. Was that true or an old wives' tale? If she owned a computer, she could go online and check, but she didn't and there was no chance she was leaving Logan alone to go to her parents' house and use theirs.

She'd keep an eye on him. If he choked, then she'd do something. Shona exhaled, her breath hitching on the way out.

Perching on the edge of her couch, she kept watch over him. *It looks worse than it is,* Logan had told her. He'd know, right?

Epilepsy? Except he hadn't said *I'm an epileptic,* he'd said *I have seizures.* He didn't wear a medical alert bracelet or any kind of necklace, and while it was possible that he had a card in his wallet, Shona would bet he didn't.

He screamed, a strangled sound that had her rocking, trying to comfort herself. Brain tumors caused seizures. What if he had an inoperable tumor? What if he had months left to live? Oh, God, he couldn't die, not when she'd just found him. Shona rubbed impatiently at the tears running down her cheeks. Damn it, she wasn't going to cry. She wasn't.

Logan wouldn't have started something with her if he was dying. She knew him and he'd never deliberately hurt her. Besides, if he was terminally ill, he'd spend his last months with his family—there was no question about that.

The tears eased up. Shona pulled his phone from her pocket and went searching through the programmed numbers. She found his parents, the numbers for two of his three sisters, and his brother's number. It was tempting to call him, to ask how to handle the seizures, but she moved her thumb away from the button. Logan had asked her not to contact anyone and she'd honor that unless she had no other choice.

Once again, he thrashed and groaned, drawing her attention. She shut the phone and returned to monitoring his condition. He called out, but the language he spoke in was one

Shona didn't understand. The sofa was too far away, she decided, and she moved closer, sitting cross-legged on the floor just out of Logan's reach. His phone was near her hip, an easy grab if she needed to dial 9-1-1.

He'd been apologetic about having a seizure in front of her. What? Did he think she was shallow? That she would drop him over a medical problem? Before she could build up a head of steam and release some of her fear by getting angry, she realized it had nothing to do with her. Logan had been embarrassed. Since they'd met, he'd always been strong and he'd view this as a weakness in himself, something that he'd hate to show anyone.

It was her turn to be stalwart. Her turn to watch over Logan and keep him safe. She'd allow no one to harm him while he was vulnerable. *No one.*

Fierceness filled her and she welcomed it. He was hers to protect, to defend. To love.

The last thought made her heart freeze for a moment, then pound furiously. It was the truth. Somewhere along the line she'd fallen in love with Logan.

The mix of emotions was interesting. Part of her was able to step back and dispassionately dissect and label them, while another part of her was caught in the maelstrom of feeling. There was elation, terror, contentment, longing, satisfaction, hunger, a sense of relief, and rightness.

Loving Logan simply felt right.

That realization had the two halves of her mind melding together. There no longer was any detachment, only certainty.

Fear clawed at her belly. Logan said he wanted more than sex with her, but he hadn't talked about wanting forever. Maybe it was too early for that. It had only been ten days since he rescued her, one week since they'd met for coffee and had their first real date. The talons raked harder. It *was* too soon. How could anyone fall in love in a week?

Before she could begin to hyperventilate, Logan's body

stiffened and he spoke again. His voice was a rasp, the words so slurred she couldn't understand what he was saying—she didn't even know if he was talking in English—but the tone was clear. He was pleading.

"I'm here, Logan. I'm not going to let anyone or anything hurt you. You have my promise."

He didn't hear her—couldn't hear her, she guessed. And then the screams came once more. They seemed unending and Logan was hoarse before he finally quieted.

Shona put her elbows on her knees and dropped her head into her hands. One sob broke free, but she stifled the rest. It was stupid to tell herself it was too soon. She loved him and if he hurt, she hurt. It might not be comfortable, but it was a fact. She could hide from it or she could deal with it, but it wasn't going away.

Accepting it didn't mean she had to tell him. That helped her unclench her muscles. Her feelings belonged to her, to share or not as she wanted.

It was time to stop running, Shona decided. How stupid was it to tell him *no sex*? If things fell apart and he walked away from her, would the pain be any less if they'd only done it once? The answer to that was easy—no. It would hurt regardless, and in the meantime, she was denying herself as much as him. Why? Because she was afraid? Because she didn't want him to think badly of her? It was silly and he'd never judged her, never treated her with anything except respect.

Lifting her head, she looked at Logan. Her body tightened in a way unrelated to tension as it remembered the feel of him inside her, the way he'd moved—the orgasm she'd had despite the position and the circumstances. She wanted him again, somewhere that she didn't have to worry about being caught. His big black bed immediately came to mind.

The decision to stop fighting her need for him felt right, too, and she found a kind of peace—maybe acceptance was the correct word—that calmed her.

His keening wail sliced through her heart and she clutched her stone again, needing its comfort. How much longer would he convulse like that? Weren't seizures usually over in a couple of minutes? She didn't know what time it was, but surely it should be finished by now.

She checked the clock on his phone, but she didn't know when this had started. The next twenty-three minutes seemed eternal. Shona ached for him, she teared up a few times, and she had to struggle against the need to go to him again and again. The only thing that stopped her was his flailing and how he'd make himself miserable if he accidently bruised her.

And then he went still.

Shona put the phone back on the floor and held her breath, fearful that this was just a temporary respite. It took a few minutes before she finally believed it was over.

Getting to her knees, she crawled over to him. The first things she noticed were that he was covered in sweat and his hair fell into his face. Shona brushed it back off his forehead and used the bottom of her T-shirt to blot the perspiration from his cheeks. Logan's jaw was tight, his brow was furrowed, and his lips were turned down, but the worst was over, she knew it. She ran her fingers down his arm and took his hand in both of hers. Slowly, she leaned over to kiss his palm.

A night spent on the floor was going to increase the soreness he'd probably have from the convulsions, but Logan was too big for her to move. Since getting him into her bed or onto the couch was out, Shona decided she'd have to make him as comfortable as possible where he was.

As she stood, she realized she was stiff and sore herself, but how much of it was from hiking and how much was from sitting on the floor, tensing every time Logan went into a new round of tremors, she couldn't say. For a moment, she hesitated—she really, really didn't want to leave him—but he remained quiet.

When she returned, her arms were filled with bedding. Kneeling at his side, she carefully raised his head and slipped one pillow beneath him and then gently lowered Logan back down. Shona shook out the blanket and spread it over him, making certain he was completely covered.

Satisfied that all was well, she double-checked to ensure the doors were locked, turned on the kitchen light, left the door ajar, and shut off the living room lamp. There was enough glow coming from the kitchen to allow her to see where she was going. When she reached Logan, Shona put the second pillow beside his, kicked off her shoes, and crawled under the blanket with him.

She turned so she could wrap her arm around him and felt the steady beat of his heart beneath her palm. "Sleep well," Shona said, and snuggling nearer, closed her eyes.

Farran drove her car slowly up the illuminated driveway of the waterfront mansion she thought of as command central. It wasn't a shock that she'd been summoned for a family meeting—she'd been waiting for the call since her final plan failed on Saturday evening. No, the surprise was that her father had waited until Monday night to order her here.

Pulling to a stop, she turned off the engine, but didn't move. Instead, Farran focused on calming her nerves. She couldn't give anything away, not by voice, expression, or gesture. The jackals would pounce at any sign of weakness.

By the time she exited her vehicle and strolled up the front walk, Farran was coolly collected. She didn't bother to ring the bell, but went right in. The door wasn't locked. Why would it be? Woe be it to any human foolish enough to trespass on what Hammond Monroe claimed as his. He hadn't earned the moniker "The Hammer" because of his forgiving nature.

The heels of her sling-back pumps seemed to echo for miles as she walked across the marble-tiled foyer. She scanned as she moved, located where everyone was gathered, and proceeded to the family room. Considering the opulence of the room with its imported marble floors, hand-woven area rug, and hand-crafted furniture, calling it a family room was a bit of a mis-nomer. *Great room* might fit better.

Conversation came to a halt as she entered.

Experience had her taking in everyone's position. Her father and Roderick stood together near the brown marble fire-place, Derril was sitting to her right on the gray sofa, Lathan stood by the windows overlooking the sound, and Jal paced. Her youngest brother appeared furious and she couldn't stop her muscles from tensing slightly. As dangerous as the oth-ers could be, it was Jal who scared her most—even more than Roderick.

Roderick, her oldest brother, was much like their father—ruthless, cold-blooded, and always maneuvering to fulfill his own agenda. Neither of them was ever reckless nor did they believe in the adage of an eye for an eye—unless it suited their purposes. They were frightening in their iciness, but they also had exquisite self-command.

Jal was another story. He was the youngest in the family, but he was mean to the core and his impulsiveness often had him acting first and thinking later. His casual cruelty had brought shame on the family several times, but no one ex-cept their father had ever been able to rein him in—not even Roderick, the heir apparent.

Her father stepped away from the fireplace, adjusting how much shirt cuff showed beneath the sleeve of the navy blue suit jacket. "You've disappointed me."

Farran's first inclination was to reach for the ends of her hair and twist them in her fingers, but she resisted. She dropped her gaze enough to appease him, but not enough to anger him. Though he loathed meekness from his children, he demanded deference. "I'm sorry."

He waved the apology aside. "The fault is mine. I never should have entrusted you with this task."

Heat stained her cheeks. There'd been no accusation or intended insult; to his mind her weak powers were a liability and he shouldn't have believed she'd overcome it even with someone whose magic was dormant.

"I nearly succeeded, if I had more time—"

"You've had two months; I'll grant no more."

"But—"

"Farran, be seated."

His tone brooked no disobedience and with a nod, she joined Derril on the sofa. She tugged down the hem of her black skirt, folded her hands in her lap, and waited.

"I would have preferred to acquire the dracontias without any of the Gineal becoming aware that it was lost to them," her father said conversationally, "but you failed. More than failed. Somehow you alerted them that the girl was important and they have a troubleshooter guarding her."

How did he know that? Farran hadn't said anything. If she had, her father would have changed the plan immediately and she hadn't been willing to give up one second of her allotted time. His eyes stayed on her and it took all her self-command not to squirm under his regard. If he discovered that she'd withheld this information from him, the punishment would be unpleasant.

Gathering her courage, she asked, "Sir, do they know she possesses the stone?"

Smoothing a hand over the side of his steel-gray hair, her father considered her with eyes that seemed to see everything. "I believe not," he said at last. "If they were aware, they would have had her perform the spell to end her dormancy and then another to meld her powers irrevocably with the dracontias. As neither has happened, there's still opportunity for the stone to come to the Tàireil dragon mage."

She received another look of disapproval. Before she could cave in and plead for leniency, he turned from her. "Lathan."

"Yes, sir," her brother said, immediately leaving his position by the window to join the rest of the family.

"Update everyone on your reconnaissance mission tonight."

Farran didn't move, but she went on alert. Things had obviously gone forward without her knowledge and she didn't like that. And as she listened to Lathan talk about checking out Shona's home and the surrounding area, she liked it even less.

"We would have withdrawn as instructed as soon as it was clear, but the Gineal knew we were there," Lathan continued. "We had cloaked our energy, he shouldn't have had an inkling we were present and yet he focused directly on us."

"Was he that strong or you that careless?" Roderick asked.

Jal rounded on Roderick. "We were not careless."

The venom in his voice was enough to make Farran hold her breath, but her oldest brother showed no fear of the youngest. "It wouldn't be the first time, would it, Jaladi?"

"We weren't imprudent," Lathan said calmly before Jal could do more than take a step toward Roderick. "My vow on it."

"Does it make a difference why they were seen?" Derril asked from beside her. "The damage is done."

"It makes a great deal of difference," her father said. "If they took care and were still seen, the Gineal's power is beyond that of most. If they were incautious, then his magic isn't something with which we need concern ourselves."

"The Gineal is as good as dead," Jal said with a snarl.

Farran wanted to know what had happened to make Jal so angry, but she wasn't about to call attention to herself with an inquiry. Roderick had no such concerns. "How badly were you beaten by the troubleshooter?" he asked with the barest hint of sarcasm.

Jal actually raised his hand to fire at Roderick, but one word from their father had him lowering his arm and dropping his gaze. It was a wise move, not only because no one disobeyed their father without paying the consequences, but because of Roderick. Jal might have meanness on his side, but her oldest brother was the one she'd bet on in a fight. His magical power and his coolness under fire would win, she was sure of that.

"Tell what happened next," her father ordered Lathan.

"He shot lightning at us and we returned fire for a while, then we opened transits and returned here."

Her father raised his eyebrows at the abridged version of events, but didn't ask for more detail. Instead, he crossed the floor and took the oversized chair at the head of the seating area. "You were unable to open the transit immediately upon being attacked?"

There was a momentary silence, and then Lathan said, "The attack was unprovoked."

"That wasn't the question I asked. Was there some reason why you were unable to open the transit and leave at once?"

"No, sir," Lathan admitted, so softly his voice was nearly a whisper.

Steepling his fingers, her father stared hard at Lathan and then at Jal. "Let me make certain I have things clear. I assigned the two of you a simple job—reconnoiter the environs of our target, and if something should go amiss, retreat as soon as possible. You both assured me you understood what was to be done, and yet now you tell me that instead of following instructions, you decided to battle a Gineal troubleshooter in a residential neighborhood?"

"Humans are of no consequence," Jal said with a dismissive shrug.

"In our world, no, but in this one? The Gineal take their protection duty seriously. They also work hard at hiding the use of magic and the existence of creatures humans label as mythical. I didn't want to add the complication of one troubleshooter, let alone an entire platoon, to acquiring the dracontias."

"I'm not frightened of any troubleshooter."

Her father lowered his hands almost in slow motion. "Are you saying I'm craven, Jaladi?"

For an instant, Farran thought he was going to shoot off his mouth, but Jal managed to find control. "No, sir," he said firmly. "I'm merely stating that I'll handle any obstacle that arises on my assignments."

After a measuring stare, her father moved on. "Did the two of you manage to complete your task before engaging in needless battle?"

Neither of her brothers met her father's gaze.

"Can I assume that if I give you the same job a second time that you'll be able to successfully carry it out?" He didn't listen to their assurances long before she became the focus of his attention once more. "So, Farran, did you know this girl was involved with a Gineal troubleshooter?"

All eyes turned to her. Gathering calm around her like a shield, she said, "I knew Shona had started to see someone about a week ago, but I never met him, sir."

While she'd been evasive, everything she had said was the truth and the short time frame made a valid reason why Farran hadn't been introduced to the man her supposedly good friend was dating. Her stomach clenched and twisted as the silence dragged on. He had to believe her, had to.

And then he turned to Roderick and Farran could breathe again. "Have you had any word from the koznain?"

"No, Father, and their continued silence worries me."

"Me as well. Derril"—her brother sat up straighter—"after we adjourn tonight, locate the koznain. If they've become lost in their own pursuits, remind them of their position as guard to the dragon mage. We'll need them as soon as we take the dracontias."

"Yes, sir."

Farran suppressed a grimace. She hated the idea of the creatures running loose here, feasting on unsuspecting humans, especially when their presence was unnecessary. The instant her family had the stone, the melding spell would be done, and they'd return to their own dimension. She'd worked up the courage to suggest they leave the koznain back home when the topic had first arisen, but her father had been adamant—when they returned to their world, the honor guard would be in place.

The argument that bringing them here wasted magic had fallen on deaf ears, and it wasn't a factor on their return— once the incantation for the dracontias was completed, the koznain would be able to cross a transit as easily as she did. This was all about appearances and starting from a position of power with the other Tàireil, but Farran wanted no part of the game playing. She'd abdicate it to her father and brothers.

"It's unfortunate our covert strategy failed, but even the simplest plans can become snarled beyond salvage if the wrong person is entrusted with them," her father said calmly.

Farran dropped her gaze slightly, and mindful not to display any sign of tension, clenched her toes inside her shoes. It was another black mark, one more thing to hold against her. As if it were her fault she was magically weak. That came down to genetics and bad luck, and since everyone on her mother's side of the family tree was incredibly strong, the blame—if there was any to be assigned—fell to her father. Not that she was foolish enough to say that, but she wondered if that thought ever entered into how he treated her.

"I can get the dracontias, sir," Jal said with a gleam in his eye that had Farran's stomach doing a barrel roll.

"You will do a second reconnaissance with your brother and you will follow my orders. Do not incur my displeasure again," he warned. When Jal looked away, her father continued. "I want a thorough study of the area, but that's of secondary importance now. I've chosen an alternate location to take the stone—outside a place called Club Red. This is what we'll do."

Farran felt sick as he outlined his scheme and the part that she would be expected to play. There was no way to bow out, nothing she could do to shield Shona from her family, and her friend did need protection because this latest plot wasn't merely overt—it also showed a complete disregard for Shona's life.

15
CHAPTER

Logan opened his eyes and found himself looking at familiar gray stripes between two pieces of white crown molding. For an instant, he couldn't figure out how he'd ended up in his bedroom, and then he remembered—this was the second time he'd regained consciousness. The first had been when he'd woken with Shona in his arms and a pillow under his head to cushion it from the floor.

A vague recollection of asking her to drive him home drifted through his mind. At least he'd been thinking clearly enough to get her somewhere safe—if she'd remained with him.

Knowing her, though, she was around somewhere. Shona wouldn't abandon him while he was down—even if he probably had freaked her out. He scanned his home and located her energy signature. Sunroom, he decided. There was a door from his bedroom to the solarium and he turned his head to check it out. It didn't surprise Logan to find it cracked open a few inches.

With a yawn, he assessed his condition. He'd slept long enough to lose the headache that always followed one of these episodes. He was sore, but that would fade once he moved around, and magically he put his status at about seventy percent. All in all, not too bad. Things could have been a lot worse.

Logan scowled, but a shiver went down his spine. If the Tàireil had continued to fight, he would have had the seizure in front of them and Shona would be either dead or captured.

Since he couldn't waste time or energy worrying about might-haves, Logan sat up and swung his legs off the bed. He'd been lying on top of the bedspread and that was a good thing, considering he still had on the clothes he'd worn hiking. A shower—he ran a hand over his chin—and a shave. That would make him feel better.

Logan stripped when he got to the bathroom, left his jeans and T-shirt on the floor, and then thought about it and dropped them in the hamper. If Shona came in here, he didn't want her to realize he was a slob—just in case she hadn't figured that out from her first visit.

The hot water made his aches and pains fade and being clean improved his mood. Logan dried off, tied the towel around his waist, and shaved. Now he looked better as well as felt better. He'd get dressed, go find Shona, and apologize for the seizure. She was going to want answers and he hoped he could come up with a good enough story to allay her fears.

He stopped short when he walked out of the bathroom and into the adjoining breakfast area. Shona had pulled a chair out from the table and was sitting, waiting for him, but she stood when he entered.

She'd apparently showered and changed clothes before they'd left her home, but he had no memory of that. For a minute, he appreciated the view—she was wearing jean shorts and a pale green tank top short enough to reveal her navel—and while the outfit was plenty modest, it was still Shona he was looking at. The kick he felt should scare him, but— Oh, hell, she wasn't wearing a bra. The way her nipples peaked, she either found the room too cold or she was getting hot for him.

Logan was becoming a little warm himself and he had to be careful. All he had on was a towel and there was nowhere to hide if he started to get hard. He cleared his throat. "I'm sorry about last night," he apologized. "I didn't want you to see me in that condition."

"I guessed that," she said, but she wasn't looking at his face as she spoke. "How are you feeling?"

"Almost normal."

Shona nodded. "I've done some thinking and you didn't have a migraine the other night when you wanted me to come over here, did you? That was the aftermath of a seizure, too."

"Yeah," Logan admitted reluctantly. "The headache, though, was real. They last for a few hours afterward."

For a moment she was quiet, then she asked, "How often do you get these things?"

"Sporadically. This week was worse than usual." He needed something more substantial than a towel between them, damn it. The way she was staring, it wasn't going to take much more to push him past the point where he could control his body. "I'll go put on some clothes. I'm sure you have more questions."

She followed him into the bedroom. He expected her to keep going, either through the door to the sitting room or the one into the sunroom, but she stopped a few feet away from him.

Maybe she didn't understand. "Hon, I plan to get dressed in here, not the bathroom."

"I know."

That left him confused; they'd agreed to back up and slow down. "I can drop trou—or in this case towel—in front of you and still keep my word, but you better know if you see me naked, I'll get a hard-on. My self-command is only so good."

"I hope so," Shona said and reached for the knot keeping up the towel.

"Whoa, there." He took hold of her hand and only then did he learn she was trembling. Logan looked more closely and realized Shona was nervous. This wasn't some game. "Am I reading you right?"

"I hope so," she repeated.

"What's changed?" He had an awful thought. "You're not doing this because you feel sorry for me, are you? Because I'll tell you right now, I don't want you to sleep with me out of pity."

"I don't pity you." Shona curled her hand around his. "You're taking care of me again and I appreciate that, but I don't need to be protected from you—or from myself."

"Why now?" He needed that answered.

"One of the things that occurred to me last night was that you had a brain tumor and only months to live. You don't, right?"

"No, I'm not dying and no, the seizures aren't caused by a brain tumor." Whatever the hell brought them on was tied to his powers, not his physical body, but Logan was damned if he knew what the problem was. "If that's why you changed your mind—"

"It's not." Shona clasped his hand. "I pretty much ruled out that idea as soon as I came up with it, but it did get me thinking about how short life was and I realized that I'd regret it if my only time with you was in the ladies' room." Her gentle squeeze became a tight grasp. "I decided to stop fighting myself and what we want. So we haven't dated for months; people click sometimes and it doesn't take long for things to feel right. Are you going to turn me down?" Her lips trembled, but she firmed them immediately.

Logan had one last question. "Are you sure?" Shona nodded. "Then hell, no, I'm not turning you down."

He released her and put his hands at her hips, drawing her to him for a kiss. Reaching for his towel might have been a bold gesture, but he knew his Shona and that hadn't been easy for her. Logan wanted her to relax and enjoy everything they did together, not be nervous, thinking she had to take charge.

Their first time had been hurried, their clothing shoved out of the way, but not removed. Logan hadn't been able to see her, to touch her, to love her the way he'd wanted, and today he planned to make up for that.

Drawing her upper lip between his, Logan nibbled gently. He lingered, then pressed a kiss to the corner of her mouth before teasing her bottom lip. A quick nip, then his tongue soothed the sting. Shona tried to deepen the kiss, but he pulled back and looked into her face.

"You have the sexiest damn mouth," Logan said. "I can't look at you without wanting to do this." He nipped at her bottom lip again. When he lifted his head, she looked slightly dazed.

Logan cupped her face with his left hand and ran his thumb over a cheekbone. "You're beautiful. So beautiful, I sometimes forget to breathe, but then you smile and I realize you're real, not some untouchable goddess."

Color tinted her cheeks and she wrapped her fingers around his wrist. She dropped her gaze and said, "I'm not."

"Trust me, you are beautiful. Your shyness probably made other men think you were aloof and they were too scared to approach—that was my good luck."

"You're talking too much."

"No doubt." One side of his mouth quirked up. "But I'm not done yet. There's more to you than your looks and that's what gets to me. You're smart and you're sweet, but every now and then you surprise me, and I love the way you shake me up." Logan tipped her face to his and as their eyes locked, he said, "And so there's no mistake this time—this isn't just sex."

Logan kissed her again before he said something stupid or embarrassed her further. He wasn't sure himself what had prompted the speech except that he wanted her to understand how special she was.

Her mouth opened under his and this time Logan didn't hesitate to deepen the kiss. He traced her upper lip with his tongue before dipping in. As he withdrew, she followed and he gently sucked before releasing her. Shona's arms went around his neck, holding him close.

Urgency overrode his intention to take things slowly. Logan returned his hands to her hips and pulled her tightly against him. Shona swayed, caressing his erection with each undulation.

Needing a minute, he moved his mouth to her throat, nipping her pulse point and kissing his way to her ear. He traced the outer edge with his tongue, then nuzzled her. She turned her head, giving him greater access, and Logan nibbled her earlobe. She gasped and clutched him and he did it again.

Perfect. She was perfect. Soft and warm and meeting his passion with her own. He ran his fingers through the length of her dark hair, and as the last strand slipped free, he put his hand on her back, stroking down to her hip.

He could do this forever—addicted to her taste, her passion, the way Shona returned his kisses. Addicted to her.

Her hands weren't still. She caressed his nape, his shoulders, his back. Her gentle touch against his bare skin pushed him higher and Logan guessed forever was going to be defined in minutes. So much for his control, but he didn't much care. If he didn't hang on to it this time, there was always the next.

Shona protested when he pulled back, but he had no plans to talk. Logan brushed her long hair behind her shoulders and traced his index finger over her collarbone, pushing a spaghetti strap off her shoulder. Leaning in, he pressed his mouth there, using his tongue to continue what his finger had started.

Logan kissed, licked, and nibbled his way to the other shoulder. He pushed that strap down too, but the tank stayed up, keeping her breasts covered.

He reached for the hem to get it out of his way when a

thought occurred to him. Logan closed his eyes briefly and muttered a curse.

"What?"

Her pupils were dilated with arousal and that distracted him for a moment. He shook it off. "I don't have any condoms."

"Oh. I do." And she put both hands in her pockets and pulled some out—not just one or two, but at least a dozen. "I took a few extra at the gallery last Friday."

Logan choked back a laugh, afraid he'd hurt her feelings. That was more than a few, but he didn't say that. Shona put both hands together and held them out, palm up. He took the condoms, walked over to the nightstand to put them within easy reach, and then returned to Shona. "I'm glad you brought those. I think it might have killed me to run to the store."

Her tentative smile reached in and twisted his heart. He framed her face with both hands and kissed her, not trying to hide anything. It wasn't enough. No kiss, no matter how hot, was going to satisfy. He reached for her breast, teasing her nipple through the soft knit of the top.

It didn't take long for her to step away from him and Logan groaned. "My turn," she told him. Shona put both her palms flat against his chest. For a moment, she stood still, then she swept her hands outward toward his shoulders and back again. She traced each ridge of muscle, and by the time she reached his belly, Logan had his hands clenched at his sides, fighting to let her explore him as much as she wanted.

At first, he did okay hanging on, but when she slipped a finger underneath his towel, her time ran out.

Taking hold of both her hands, he moved them to her sides. "Logan!"

He ignored her protest, bent down, put his shoulder against her middle, and lifted her in a fireman's carry. Logan didn't go far, but then he didn't need to—the bed was only feet away. Yanking back the covers, he set her down, and crawled up after her.

Her waistband had two buttons. Logan opened them, his

fingers brushing the warm skin of her stomach, and then lowered her zipper. "Lift for me," he ordered as he started to tug them down. Shona raised her hips and he pulled off her denim shorts, tossing them to the floor.

Her black panties were about as tiny as she could get without wearing a thong and he appreciated every bare millimeter. Logan kissed her between her belly button and the top of her panties. "You have an outie."

"I do not!" Shona propped herself up on her elbows to glare at him. "That's an innie."

"A half-outie, then." Logan grinned. "I can compromise." He lowered his head and rimmed her navel with his tongue. Goose bumps formed on her skin, so he did it again.

The towel began to aggravate him. Logan went up on his knees, undid the knot, and lobbed it after her shorts. Shona gasped and he smiled again when he saw she was staring at his hard-on. "You're good for a man's ego."

Her intentness, though, was rapidly unraveling his control. Lying beside her, Logan went in for another kiss and pushed her tank up with one hand. He could feel her ribs and traced them one by one. Her skin was warm and smooth, her lips pliant beneath his. He'd never get enough of her. Never.

Shona stroked his hip, his thigh, and the back of her hand brushed his hard-on. "Touch me, hon, please."

She did. Shona wrapped her fingers around him and ran them up and down his shaft. He put his hand over hers, tightened her hold and adjusted her speed. When she had it, he released her and ran his palm under the back of her top.

More. Logan needed more. He took her hand off of him, but immediately missed her touch. To compensate, he pressed his erection against her belly and rocked, sliding his heat against her. He wanted her naked, needed her naked.

Back on his knees, he took hold of the tank's hem. Shona sat up, raising her arms up as he pulled it off. There was a gem hanging on the chain between her breasts and something about it gave him pause. Before he could figure out what it was that bothered him, she leaned forward and bit at his pec.

Logan growled his approval and she licked at his nipple. That's what he wanted to be doing, taking her in his mouth. He let her tease him a few more minutes before pressing her back to the mattress. "You don't let me touch you enough."

"Next time," he promised and bent to flick at her with his tongue. "Damn, you're perfect." And she was. Firm and full, she fit his hands exactly right.

She watched him as he ran his thumbs over her breasts and something about that pushed his arousal higher. He kissed her, first one nipple and then the other, before taking her in his mouth and swirling his tongue around her areola. Her fingers dug into his shoulders and she moaned softly. He lightly nibbled before turning to kiss her other breast.

He didn't stop until she writhed and arched against him.

Logan moved lower, kissing and licking back to her navel. He lightly bit the skin just above her panties and then, tucking his fingers beneath the elastic, drew them down her legs and off.

For a minute, he did nothing but stare, then he used his shoulder to make more room between her thighs. She was wet and he ran a finger through her folds, collecting some of her moisture. When her eyes met his, Logan licked his finger, then put it in his mouth. The noise Shona made was somewhere between a gasp and a moan.

With two fingers, he parted her and lowered his head. He kept his tongue soft as he flicked at the center of her pleasure and tried different things until he learned what she liked. Logan took her between his lips and sucked softly before moving down. Teasing her, he thrust his tongue in and out until she moved in rhythm with him, then he returned to where she was most sensitive. Her hands fisted in his hair, holding him in place as if she were afraid he'd stop. He wasn't going to.

She started to come and Logan did what he could to push her higher. He'd wanted to make her scream, but the keening moan was nearly good enough. Next time. Next time he'd get a scream.

As her orgasm began to subside, he gentled his touch. Shona went languid, only an occasional shudder tightening her muscles.

Logan continued to tease her lightly and taste her. He felt when she began to build again and his touch became firmer. When he had her on the brink, he pulled back. Her groan of protest felt like a caress flowing over his body.

Grabbing one of the condoms, he freed it from its package and rolled it on. He settled between her legs, entering her slowly. "Stop tormenting me," she ordered, but he ignored her.

Shona didn't let him get away with that. Her hands went to his butt and she jerked him down as she arched up. They both froze for a heartbeat as he fully penetrated her, then she rolled him over and sat up, undulating against him.

He was happy to have her on top if that's where she wanted to be, but she couldn't find the cadence. Logan took her by the hips, guiding her motion until she had it.

For an instant, he thought her eyes glowed, but then her head fell back and she rocked into him harder. He fought to hang on, fought to make sure she came again. Shona added a little shimmy and he growled his approval.

Her long hair brushed his thighs as she arched farther. Next time he'd have to ask her to trail it over his skin or maybe—

Hell, he hadn't even come yet and he was already thinking about the next time they made love.

He pulled her more firmly against him as his orgasm approached. With a choked cry, Shona found release. Logan urged her to ride him harder.

Almost. Almost. He started coming, his groan ripped from his soul. "Shona!"

She was lying on top of him when Logan regained enough sense to notice the outside world. He gave her rear a squeeze and then stroked her from shoulder blade to bottom and back up again. This had easily been the best sex he'd ever had—Logan couldn't remember ever coming this hard before or having an orgasm that lasted this long—but it didn't surprise him. He'd been with Shona after all.

That should scare him. It didn't.

Her face was pressed to his throat and her breath warmed his skin. Every now and then she'd kiss him and he found himself waiting for those moments, wishing they were more frequent.

As he continued coming down, Logan realized he wasn't going to be able to snuggle with her indefinitely without a quick break first. He shifted her enough to ease out of her. Shona's protest created a warmth in the center of his chest and that made him feel off balance.

"Damn, honey," he teased, "what do you have against the missionary position?"

"Huh?" Shona raised her head just enough to look at him and Logan felt that warmth become a burning sensation. Her hair was wild, her mouth moist and maybe slightly swollen, but what got to him were her eyes. There was something there that made him want to wrap his arms around her and never let go.

"Our first time was standing up; our second, you pushed me over and rolled on top."

"I'm sorry, I didn't realize, I—"

Logan put his thumb over her lips to stop her apology. "No, there's nothing to be sorry for—I loved it." He raised up to give her a fast kiss and moved her off of him and to the side. "I'll be back in a minute," he said and headed for the bathroom.

After disposing of the condom, he cleaned up and rejoined her. Shona had pulled the covers up to her chin while he'd been gone and Logan crawled in beside her, tugging her back into his arms. "Sorry. One of the unromantic elements of making love."

"Oh."

He trailed his fingers up and down her arm, slowly caressing her. Logan couldn't touch her enough—definitely an addiction.

"Do they know what's causing your seizures?"

The question came out of the blue and he couldn't stop himself from stiffening. Damn, he'd thought they were done with this topic. "The cause hasn't been pinpointed. It looks as if it's just one of those things." The answer was deliberately vague, but Logan hoped it was enough to satisfy Shona. It wasn't a complete lie. He had gone through dozens of books, looking for some hint of what was causing his episodes and he'd found nothing helpful at all.

"Are they still running tests?"

"There's no medical reason for them." Again misleading, but true. They were related somehow to his magic, but he'd checked out his physical condition when they'd first started anyway.

His mother was a healer and he'd gotten a dollop of her ability. All Gineal could do healing work—it was a matter of focusing the energy—but only healers could scan the body and find problems that weren't obvious. Logan had been able to run a check on himself and rule out any physical issue. Of course, that didn't eliminate a problem in the auric field surrounding his body, but he didn't have enough healing talent to scan that.

She was quiet for a long while before she asked, "Should you be driving?"

"I still have my license. If a doctor thought I shouldn't be behind the wheel, he'd yank it, right?" She nodded. "I'd never drive if there was a risk of having an accident."

He knew when it was bearing down on him. No magic—no seizure. Not much magic—no seizure. Use too much magic—have a seizure. Simple and easy to predict even if the line kept shifting on him.

Shona didn't look convinced.

"Don't worry so much about me." He was worrying enough for both of them. "These episodes aren't that big a deal." Unless he had one during a battle. Logan changed the subject. "My turn to ask you a question. How did you know those two guys were out there last night?"

She shrugged. "I just . . . I could feel them."

"Have you ever done anything like that before?"

"No. I was completely normal until I met you." Shona pressed a kiss to his shoulder, but Logan barely noticed.

Dormants almost never had any use of their magic, and the few that did usually had one or two small talents show up before they were in their teens. Sensing the presence of two Tàireil was within the ability of someone like Shona, but she should have had experiences like this for years. Was his proximity triggering her access to her powers? It shouldn't work that way.

His kind interacted with dormants as often as they did with humans, and if this Gineal–dormant proximity effect was something that happened, he'd know about it. All his people would know about it. Odds were there'd even be some rules about how much contact they could have with a dormant because the Gineal didn't want to incite their magic.

"Logan."

"What, hon?"

"You never had a chance to tell me what happened with those men. Did you confront them?"

"Yeah." Shooting lightning at them counted as a confrontation. "We had a little tussle and then they cut out."

"You shouldn't have done that," she scolded. "What if they'd been armed? They could have stabbed you or shot you. That's why you wanted me in the closet, wasn't it? To protect me as much as possible in case they started firing."

He propped himself up on his elbow and looked down into her face. Shona's expression was combative. "Yeah, that is a major reason why I wanted you in that closet, but you need to trust me to handle myself."

"Damn it!" She shoved at his shoulder, pushing him onto his back. Her strength surprised him, but before he could puzzle through that, Shona straddled him, and resting her forearms on his chest, got in his face. "Don't you ever do something stupid like that again, do you hear me, Logan Andrews? I want you safe, not running around like some loose cannon."

"I hear you," he said.

That took the wind out of her sails. "Good."

Shona shifted and Logan's attention drifted from her face. Bringing up his hand, he brushed the underside of her breast with his knuckle. He was going for a second graze when he noticed her necklace and recalled that something about it had bothered him. Instead of teasing her some more, he reached for the chain, holding it so he could get a look at the stone.

It had multiple colors—purple, blue, and green. Logan moved it for some better light and it changed, becoming orange, red, and yellow.

"Cool, isn't it?"

"Yeah," he agreed, not taking his eyes off the gem. What was it that was setting off alarm bells? "Where'd you buy it?"

"I stumbled across it in the thrift store, believe it or not." Shona sounded excited and Logan switched his gaze. "I paid three dollars. It didn't even look like it was worth that much when I first saw it. The chain was dirty, and because the stone isn't faceted with sharp cuts, it didn't reflect the light and sparkle." She took the necklace between her thumb and forefinger and he released it. Propping herself up a little higher, she held it out for him. "See how the stone is pitted? It's more like a miniature golf ball than a gem, but I knew right away it was special."

So did Logan, but he couldn't figure out why this necklace was bugging him. All objects were able to hold a person's psychic vibrations, but crystals could contain more and for longer periods of time than most anything else. Maybe one of its previous owners had been messing with something they shouldn't have been and that was what he was picking up.

"Can I see it?"

He meant for Shona to take it off and hand it to him, but that wasn't what she did. Instead, she leaned forward so that he could hold the stone while the chain stayed around her neck.

Curling his hand around the gem, Logan tried to read it. He felt something, but it was muffled. Reluctantly, he lowered his mental shields and opened himself up to the energy. It just about blasted him out of his skin. Holy—

The amount of power in the stone was incredible, absolutely unbelievable. And in a sudden flash, his brain found the information it had been searching for about this crystal.

It was the dracontias. This gem was the damn *dracontias*. The ceannards were going to lose their minds.

Shona Blackwood—a dormant—was the Gineal dragon mage.

16
CHAPTER

"Wait a second," Kel said, closing the refrigerator. "Let me get this straight. You already contacted the council to ask for a meeting and *now* you want my help with some research? Don't you think it would be smarter to have done that first?"

Yeah, a lot smarter, but it had only been after making the call that Logan had started to doubt himself. Enforcers not only spent the seven years of their apprenticeship learning how to fight dark-force creatures, they also had thousands of years of Gineal history and knowledge crammed into their heads. It was no wonder they forgot stuff—or at least he did. And Kel had been mostly right the other day—Logan didn't study enough.

"I know that," he said. "You want to lecture me later? The council could call any minute and tell me to get over there."

Kel sighed and popped the tab on his can of cola. "Fine. What's the subject you're interested in?"

"The dracontias."

"The dragon stone!" Kel lowered the can without drinking. "Shh! Shona's here." They were in the kitchen, a long way from his bedroom, but still . . . "I have a sleep spell on her, but I don't know if it will hold."

Closing his eyes, Kel muttered a curse and then pinned Logan with a hard stare. "Didn't I warn you about having sex with her? Blackwood is going to kick your sorry butt to hell and back."

He wanted to play dumb—there was no reason for Kel to assume Shona was in his bed—but there'd probably been something in Logan's voice as he'd said her name, or maybe in his expression, and his brother knew him well enough to pick up on small signs. "You want to save that lecture for later, too? I'm under the gun here, man, that's why I contacted you. If you're just going to talk, I could get more done without you."

That earned him another long sigh before Kel said, "Okay, what do you need to know about the stone?"

"What it looks like." Logan paused, then admitted, "And I can't remember the legend behind it—just that it involves the darksiders and a dragon."

Kel shook his head and lifted the can to take a drink.

"I know, I know," Logan said, "but even if I'd been as diligent as you think I should be, I probably wouldn't have read up on this. Why would I? The odds of needing the information were minuscule." His brother was still giving him that look. "How much do *you* recall about the dracontias?" Logan challenged.

"More than you."

"Spill."

After taking another swig of pop, Kel drawled, "Once upon a time—or millennia ago—there was an ancient and powerful dragon who was on the verge of dying. Before he passed, he gouged the dracontias from the center of his forehead and channeled all his considerable magic into the gem. He also put a spell on it that makes it appear at the right time for the dragon mage to find it and disappear on the mage's death."

Logan nodded. Now that Kel had mentioned it, that rang a few bells. "The power of the stone can only be controlled by the dragon mage and that person can be either Tàireil or Gineal."

"Close," his brother said. "A mage is born to both societies at about the same time. Whoever finds the dracontias and does the spell to meld their energy to the stone first becomes the one who controls it and its power." Kel looked thoughtful, "I bet this thing with the dragon happened before their world split from ours. That would explain why they have a mage, too."

"Maybe, but that doesn't matter right now. What's important is that the Tàireil are probably here for the dracontias, not revenge." He changed tacks. "Am I right in thinking that only the dragon mage can wear the stone for more than a few minutes?"

"I forgot about that, but yeah, I believe that's right. Why do you need to know more about it, anyhow?"

Logan hesitated. This was something he should tell the ceannards before anyone else, but he and Kel shared a lot and it wasn't like his brother was going to gossip. "Shona's got the dragon stone on. At least I think she has."

"What?" Kel nearly dropped his pop can and quickly put it down on the counter. "You must be wrong; the dragon mage has never been a dormant."

"Are you sure?" Logan asked quietly. "Or maybe the dragon mage wasn't identified at some point in the past *because* he or she was a dormant."

Kel pursed his lips, and after a moment said, "Interesting theory and it's feasible. Why don't we go check your books and see what they have to say? Although knowing you, I figure we'll end up calling titles from the central library." His brother went to the basement door.

"I own books," Logan gritted out. "A lot of them."

Kel ignored that, zapped open the lock, and headed down the stairs. Logan secured it again—just in case.

Sending his mind out, he checked on Shona, but she remained asleep. He didn't know how long it would last, though, not if she was the dragon mage. Logan hoped a while more; he needed the chance to check things out without facing a bunch of questions that he couldn't answer. Great choice—feel guilty for lying or feel guilty about bespelling her. Shaking his head, he followed Kel down the stairs.

While this floor contained his exercise room, another bedroom suite, a media room, and about half a dozen other rooms, most of the square footage was dedicated to his magic. There were bookcases filled with spell and reference books, the tools he used in rituals, and his scrying crystal. This level was as big a part of his life as his cars and he wanted to share it with Shona, too. And maybe after seeing the council, he'd be able to.

By the time he reached the workroom, Kel had already pulled a handful of titles from the shelves and put them down on the table. Logan grabbed a second stool, dragged it over, and started looking through one. Damn, he hated research. The books were invariably handwritten, mostly in the old language of the Gineal, and there weren't indexes or anything else helpful for finding information. No wonder he preferred his car magazines.

"This was all that I could find that might help us," his brother said as he put down a couple more books and took the other stool. "Your library is more comprehensive than I expected, so I guess I owe you an apology."

The words were grudging, but Logan nodded. It had never been easy for Kel to say he was sorry, and despite the tone, Logan knew his brother was sincere. "No problem."

They sat a few feet apart, both quietly paging through texts. It was a while later before Kel said, "I think you're right about why the darksiders are here. This book talks about a pitched battle that happened more than two thousand years ago between the Gineal and Tàireil over possession of the dracontias. They won, by the way, killed our dragon mage, and returned with the crystal to their world."

"Why'd they kill her? Once the darksider melded energies with the dracontias, we couldn't have recaptured and used it anyway."

"Our mage was a him," Kel said, "and it sounds like back then neither side had an incantation that merged them exclusively and irrevocably to the stone. This could have been the event that prompted someone to adjust the spell to make sure the gem couldn't change owners."

Logan shrugged. The only thing he cared about was keeping Shona safe. "You don't suppose a dormant could do that melding proclamation, do you?"

Kel looked at him. "Can a dormant do any spell except the one to become Gineal?"

Muttering a curse, Logan went back to his book. Most of what he came across was a rehash of what Kel had told him, but he did find a list of birth dates for the known dragon mages. He took some time to study them. There'd never been less than a hundred years between them, but there were several gaps of three or even four hundred years. That made him wonder if the mage hadn't been found or if the stone had appeared to the Tàireil at those times.

"I forgot about this," Kel said. "One of the signs that we're coming to Twilight Time is the arrival of the dragon mage."

"You don't believe that, do you?" Kel made a noncommittal sound and Logan snorted. "Look at this list." He held up the book and ran a finger down the columns of names. "These are all dragon mages. If people thought we'd reached the prophesied end times at every appearance, a lot of Gineal worried for nothing."

After staring at the list for a moment, Kel said, "You have a point."

Logan returned to his book, but there wasn't much more left to go through. When he finished it, he put it aside, and reached for the next one. And then the next. He was flipping pretty fast and sailed past the page before the image registered. Backing up, Logan stared down at the drawing of the dracontias and lightly ran his thumb over the paper.

"Here's something interesting," Kel said. Logan didn't reply—he couldn't take his eyes off the picture—but his brother kept talking anyway. "The mage can summon dragons from their dimension to join him in a battle *if* they've measured him and found him worthy of their support. Shortly after the stone is found, two representatives are sent to judge him for all of dragonkind. Can you imagine being able to call on a squad of dragons to fight at your side?"

Something in Kel's voice had Logan lifting his head, but his brother's face was inscrutable. Instead of asking any questions, though, he said, "I was right, Shona is the dragon mage."

"That's the picture? Slide it down here and let me look."

Logan shoved the book over. Kel was quiet for a long moment. "Does it look this incredible in person?"

"More." He paused, remembering. "You should feel the energy it has, that was what was amazing. I had to put my shields back up in a hurry—it was too much for me—but Shona wears it like it's nothing more than some piece of jewelry."

Returning the tome, Kel said, "That shouldn't be a surprise, you said yourself she was the dragon mage."

"True." Logan closed the text and got to his feet.

"Where are you going?"

"We're done. You filled me in on the legend, I found the picture I wanted, and now I don't have to call the aide back and say 'Oops, don't need to see the council after all.'"

That got Logan another one of his brother's looks.

"I know everything I need to," he insisted.

"Yeah? What powers does the mage have?"

That stopped him short. Hell. "Dragon magic," he said.

"Dragon magic." Kel closed his eyes and dropped his head back. "Little brother, don't you think the council is going to expect you to know what she's capable of?"

Probably, Logan conceded, but he hated to let Kel think he was a complete moron. And then something Shona had done came back to him. "The dragon mage can cast her consciousness out of her body and track someone."

"And?"

Logan racked his brain. What else had Shona done that she'd said was weird? "She can sense the energy of others even when they're trying to cloak it." Hell, why hadn't he considered all this earlier? "Last night when I brought Shona home, she picked out two Tàireil hiding behind some bushes. I didn't know they were there and I was sweeping for them. Kel, she's already using some of the dragon's powers, and without her magic, that should be impossible."

For the third time in just over two weeks, Logan stood in front of the entire council, but repetition didn't make it less stressful. Their table was in its V-shape again and they all stared at him. There was something about facing nine stone-faced former troubleshooters that made him sweat.

He had a feeling they knew it, too.

"Well, laoch solas, what was so urgent that you insisted we table our day's agenda in favor of yours?" Nessia asked.

Logan swallowed hard. Maybe he should show some extra deference. "Council Leader," he said, bowing his head, "I think that when you and the other ceannards hear what I've learned, you'll agree that this meeting was necessary."

"What critical information do you have for us?"

Her voice was even cooler now, and Logan decided that he'd better say it straight out rather than leading up to it like he'd planned. "Shona Blackwood wears the dracontias."

The reaction was so subtle that if Logan hadn't been watching closely, he might have missed it. He'd believed the council had been telling him the truth as they'd known it when they'd given him the assignment to protect Shona, but he'd had a sliver of doubt. If the ceannards thought it was in the best interest of the Gineal people, they weren't above twisting the truth or telling an outright lie if it came to that.

"Are you certain?" Nessia asked, the annoyance gone.

"Yes, Ceannard."

The silence led him to believe they were having a tele-pathic exchange on what he'd told them, but even if they weren't, he wasn't about to speak up—not yet.

"Show us an image of the stone," the council leader or-dered.

Logan nodded and closed his eyes, focusing on the crystal he'd seen Shona wearing. He wanted to show it to them in as much detail, as much color as possible, and that included at least an echo of the energy that had emanated from it. When he felt as if the visual was solid in his mind, he did the spell to create a three-dimensional rendering, enlarging it until they could see it plainly.

"Send it along the table so that each of us can view it as closely as we wish, laoch solas," Taber, the eldest councilor, said quietly. "We'll tell you when we're ready for you to move it to the next."

With a short nod, Logan did as instructed, starting with the councilwoman on his far left. Some of the ceannards spent a great deal of time studying it, some even asked him to position the image he was projecting at different heights and angles, allowing them alternate views. When he reached the far end, he stopped and waited.

"You may end the projection," Nessia said quietly. When he complied, she continued, "We'd hoped you were mis-taken, but you are not—that is the dracontias."

He bowed his head briefly and waited.

It was Taber who spoke again. "Do you know how long she's had it in her possession?"

"Approximately two months. Shona told me that she found it in a thrift shop."

There must have been some question in his voice. "You know the stone shows itself to the mage, do you not?" Taber asked.

"I do." Thanks to talking with Kel. "But I'm unclear on

how that's possible. Even with a spell on it, how can it know who the dragon mage is and find that one person among all the Gineal? It's been thousands of years with dozens of different dragon mages—some of them Tàireil—so how can the stone know when it's the right time for a particular one to find it?"

Nessia turned to look at Taber. "We don't teach anything to our troubleshooters about dragons, do we?"

"No," he said and pursed his lips. "I believe it was culled from the lessons about eight hundred years ago. By then, the majority of them had been gone for such a long time that it was clear their return was unlikely, and the few stragglers that remained behind were all dead—largely killed by humans."

"He'd have no reason to study dragons of his own volition for the same reasons."

Taber and several others nodded and Logan swallowed a sigh of relief. It had never occurred to him to research dragons before coming before the council, but it probably should have. Of course, he and Kel had barely finished reading what his books had to say about the dracontias before he'd received word to report to Gineal headquarters, so it wasn't as if he'd had a lot of extra time to squeeze it in.

Tipping her head back, Nessia stared at the ceiling briefly before she met his gaze again. "I asked one of our aides to contact the tasglann and have a librarian send you the best books we have on dragons, the dracontias, and the dragon mage."

"I appreciate that, but it'll be difficult to read that material when I spend the majority of my time protecting Shona."

"You're right, it will." There was a brief pause. "The common misconception is that dragon magic is like ours, only stronger. That's untrue. It's similar, but also very different. We use our powers by drawing on outside energy, sending it through ourselves, and channeling it outward with intent. It's necessary for us to focus on what we're trying to accomplish—that's why we use spells and rituals. Even after years of practice, we recite words for all but the simplest—or most frequently performed—incantations."

Logan nodded. When he was tired or distracted, he still used proclamations for simple spells that he used often and that had to do with concentration and forming the energy.

"Dragons," Nessia continued the lesson, "are one with the energy—it isn't outside them—and because of that, they don't need to memorize any spells. Neither do they have to learn to use magic. It's instinctual to them."

"Are you saying they have instant manifestation? That's a great deal of responsibility," Logan said.

"We don't know; there's very little we can aver to with complete confidence. Dragons are secretive, distrustful of outsiders, and while they were here, waged a disinformation campaign that confused things further."

For a minute, he considered what he'd been told. "So you're saying that we don't know how the dragon managed to imbue the dracontias with the ability to find the mage?"

"Their magic is beyond what we're capable of," Taber answered for the council. "Even the mage is only able to do a fraction of what the great dragons could do."

"But the mage has powers greater than other Gineal, even our troubleshooters, right?"

"Yes and no." Logan must have revealed some of his confusion because Taber added, "Even the mage is limited by the amount of energy he or she can handle at any given time, but the difference between a Gineal and a dragon mage is that our magic is something we're able to compartmentalize. Once the mage finds the dracontias, her power changes. Instead of being merely one piece of her life, it fills her and there is no division."

Logan nodded, his head running through what he'd been told and putting it in context with what he'd seen with Shona. One thing suddenly snapped into place. Two months. She'd found the stone two months ago and she'd developed her artistic block two months ago. There was no reason for her to connect the events—why would she?—but he didn't believe in coincidence.

"Shona is a dormant," Logan said, "and she's an artist. Without magic to tap into, the stone is taking her creative energy instead, isn't it?"

Nessia shook her head. "The dracontias uses everything available. If she were Gineal, it would channel her magic *and* her creative energy."

His stomach sank. He'd thought it would be easy, that once Shona came into her powers, she'd be able to work with her glass again, but if the council leader was right, that wasn't the case. Shon would have to make a choice—her necklace or her art—and Logan suspected the decision wouldn't be easy for her. He'd seen the way she caressed the crystal, the passion in her eyes as she'd talked about it, and he remembered all the times she'd brought her hand up to her chest when she was anxious. Now he knew she'd needed to touch the stone.

"Is she displaying some talent already?" Nessia asked, breaking into his thoughts.

He hesitated. That seemed private, something that belonged solely to Shona, and yet it was information he couldn't withhold from the ceannards. He didn't like feeling torn between loyalty to his people and loyalty to his woman, but it gave him insight into something the council must grapple with frequently. And as Logan accepted what he had to do, he also understood some of their actions in a way he hadn't before this moment.

"Yes," he said, throat tight. "I know of a couple, but there might be more she's done that she's unaware of." Logan swallowed hard and told them what those things were. Several of the councilors shifted in their seats as he recounted the last occurrence.

"Two Tàireil," Nessia said grimly. "I don't like that they're successful in cloaking their energy from us."

Nods from the other ceannards and a silence that Logan didn't dare interrupt. If the Gineal monitors couldn't detect the darksiders when they came to this dimension, that was a problem and something that would need serious discussion. He didn't doubt they were making plans to do that after he left.

Nessia met his gaze again. "Give us a full report on your mission from the time it was assigned until now."

Taking a deep breath, he gave the requested information. He omitted the personal stuff—that was none of their business—but other than that, Logan didn't skim over anything, not even what he'd told them at his earlier update meeting after the first attack on Shona. Today, the context had changed, and while he always tried to be impartial in reporting, he knew his own knowledge and inferences affected the account he gave. He answered a few questions as he spoke, and more when he finished until the ceannards were satisfied.

"A few more things make sense that didn't before," Logan said, "but I still don't understand the human's involvement or the presence of the koznain."

Nessia considered him, her eyes narrowed, and Logan felt his level of discomfort shoot skyward again. "It doesn't explain everything," she said, "but it does help to know that the Tàireil dragon mage doesn't merely gain extra abilities and power from the dracontias. He also becomes emperor of his entire dimension, ruling over everyone and everything."

Uh-oh, should he have known the emperor thing? "So because the stakes are high, unconventional tactics like enlisting a human and the koznain were employed?"

"Possibly that's the answer for the human, but the koznain act as bodyguard to the mage and he needs them. The Tàireil don't particularly care to be ruled by him."

"The koznain weren't that difficult to kill."

"That's in this dimension, in their own, they're nearly indestructible. Any other questions, laoch solas?"

The snap he heard in the council leader's voice made Logan stiffen. She'd been forthcoming with information and he'd taken advantage of that too long. He'd have to research on his own later—or get Kel to do it for him. "No, Ceannard."

"Then retire to the antechamber," Nessia ordered, pointing to the door.

Logan inclined his head and withdrew. He wasn't surprised they wanted to talk about Shona without him present— anything else would have been shocking. It wasn't every day a dormant became Gineal. The only instance in his lifetime was about eighteen months ago, and then the council had faced a done deal.

This time they'd have to consider a number of factors, including how to explain to Shona who and what the Gineal were, how to convince her that magic existed, and more important, to get her to believe that if she did a particular spell, that she would have power, too. Throw in the dracontias and the darksiders and the situation became thornier.

He checked the time on his phone and returned it to its clip. Damn, he'd been here longer than he'd expected and Logan wondered how the sleep spell was holding up. He'd reinforced it before leaving the house, but the dracontias might affect it. The last thing he wanted was Shona waking up alone and thinking again that all he was interested in was getting laid.

He forced his mind off the personal and onto his job. It made the most sense for him to tell her about the magic, but Logan wondered if the council would agree. They might want to do it themselves, but he was the one Shona knew and trusted.

How would he approach the subject with her?

Logan was still playing out various scenarios in his mind when he was recalled to their chamber. Maybe they'd have some suggestions or a plan on how to reveal the truth to Shona because nothing he'd come up with had been too great.

There was a bounce in his step as he walked down the hall. For an instant, he paused, realized it was because he was excited about getting permission to tell Shona about her magic, and took a deep breath to corral the emotion. The ceannards wouldn't like it if he popped into the room like a seven-year-old hitting the toy store, and he'd already earned Nessia's displeasure once today.

He stopped at the place where he'd been standing earlier and quickly ran his gaze over the nine men and women. Their faces were as stony as they'd been when he'd entered before, but something in their demeanor quashed his elation. Logan tensed, then tried to relax. Telling Shona the truth was the only possibility that made sense.

Inclining his head, he said, "Ceannards."

They didn't speak. His anxiety mounted, but Logan struggled to conceal his unease. Enforcers were expected to have near-perfect control over their emotions, and if he didn't, they'd start wondering why. He didn't want to think about the council's response if they learned how close he'd become to Shona.

"It seems, laoch solas," Nessia said at last, "that we have an additional task for you."

The council leader's tone lacked any kind of inflection, but Logan felt some of the constriction ease. His new task could only be telling Shona about the Gineal; nothing else was logical. "Yes, Council Leader?"

"We want you to take the dracontias from Shona Blackwood and bring it to us."

For an instant, Logan didn't comprehend the words. In the next moment they hit with enough force that he physically recoiled. "What?" he choked out.

"You heard us."

"Why?"

"Given the circumstances, it's the best choice."

Fury surged, pushing aside his astonishment. Logan breathed deeply until he had a grip on himself. "With all due respect, it's not the best choice."

"Yes, Logan, it is."

He shook his head. Hadn't they come up with the answer

themselves? It was easy. "The best choice is to tell Shona about the Gineal, to have her do the spell to awaken her magic, and then have her merge her energy with the dracontias. It solves everything. With her possession of the stone complete, it serves no purpose for the Tàireil to go after her, not when they know they can't use it if they take it, and if they kill her, the stone disappears until the next two dragon mages are born."

"Awakening her magic raises other issues."

Logan remembered her art then and that Shona might not want to meld with the stone. He firmed his lips to keep from blurting out the reasons why that wouldn't be a problem. "Yes, Ceannard, I understand that, but we've had one dormant adapt to the responsibility of having power; Shona can as well."

"That wasn't our chief concern."

"Then what the hell is?"

"Laoch solas, you forget your place."

Yeah, he had and Logan figured he was skating atop some very thin ice right now. "Apologies, Council Leader."

Nessia stared at him, her eyes assessing. "The day you were given the job of protecting her, you were told her parents had been stripped of their magic before she was born. That isn't something the council ever does lightly, but in this case there was no other option. Their imprudence risked the safety of our entire society."

He wanted to ask how that had been done, but he suspected he wouldn't receive an answer. "Shona isn't her parents, Ceannard."

"No, she isn't, but all indications are that she's close to her family. Could she keep such a big change in her life a secret from them?" Nessia held up a hand, halting Logan before he could do more than open his mouth. "Shona lives behind their home and this wouldn't be something that would last for a few months or even years, but forever. We don't believe she can do that."

"Taking the stone from her is wrong," he argued, "and it doesn't keep her safe."

"The Tàireil want the dracontias, not Shona. Once they realize she doesn't have it, they'll switch their attention to the problem of breaking into the Gineal stronghold and taking it. That is not an easy proposition as you well know."

It wasn't. There was formidable protection that would have to be breached, and if necessary the council could call on every troubleshooter they had to fight the darksiders. But it was only part of the picture. "If they kill Shona," Logan said with hard-won calm, "the Tàireil take any possibility of her merging with the dracontias out of the equation. That gives them the entire lifetime of their dragon mage to acquire the crystal."

"We'll defeat them long before that happens, but our decision isn't meant to be a long-term solution. Not that it concerns you, but we might yet determine that Shona should assume her powers. However, it isn't something that we will resolve in twenty minutes. We need time to meditate on the ramifications and discuss them among ourselves."

"But—"

"No more, laoch solas."

Her tone brooked no disobedience. "Council Le—"

"Not one more word. Take the dracontias from her and bring it to us. You have your orders."

17
CHAPTER

Sweat drenched his T-shirt and soaked his hair, leaving rivulets running from his temples and forehead, but Logan didn't slow. When he'd returned from his meeting with the council, he'd needed to work off some of his fury and going for a punishing run had seemed like the best option. He'd left Shona sleeping—again—and while that bothered him, he'd decided that her waking up alone was better than watching him climb the walls because he was so angry he couldn't see straight.

The council needed time to think about the ramifications. Logan snorted. Maybe Nessia actually believed that they might return the dracontias later and tell Shona about her powers, but he knew better. Once they had their hands on that stone and the darksiders were no longer an issue, it would be much easier for them to stick with the status quo.

Someone called a greeting from his front yard. Logan waved, but didn't slow down. He'd run this route through the neighborhoods around his house often enough that he was familiar. Sometimes he'd even stop and talk briefly, but not today.

The ceannards had put him in an untenable position.

Shona would be mad that he'd kept secrets because of his magic, but he figured she'd understand after she had time to cool down. She'd be less thrilled about why he'd started hanging around, but Logan was certain he could convince her that why they'd met didn't matter, only what had happened between them afterward. But taking the dracontias from her?

She'd never forgive him for that act and he wouldn't blame her. It was an unconscionable betrayal.

The alternative was just as unpalatable—betray the council and the oath he'd given the day he'd become a troubleshooter. Logan gritted his teeth and picked up the pace.

His vow had been simple—to obey the ceannards unless doing so put the Gineal people in jeopardy. Not *a* Gineal or a dormant, but the society as a whole, and their order to steal the stone didn't come close to giving him grounds to break his word. Maybe if they could use the power of the dracontias themselves, he'd have some wiggle room, but they couldn't; only Shona had that ability. The bottom line was if he opted to ignore the order, he'd be a traitor.

Nausea welled and dread twisted his stomach until Logan thought he'd puke. The punishment for such an act would be severe. He'd for sure lose his territory, likely would have the title of laoch solas taken from him, and it was possible *he* might be stripped of his magic.

That wasn't what made him sick, though—it was the idea of harming the Gineal in any way that did that. He'd been raised to shield them, trained to protect them, and he couldn't forsake his family, his friends, his people—not even for Shona.

Logan turned the corner onto his street. He'd never believed in no-win scenarios. To his mind, there was always a method to come out ahead in any situation, it was just a matter of thinking how to do it. Today, though, despite looking at things in every way possible, he couldn't come up with a single answer. He was caught between a rock and a hard place and there was no room to squirm free. Any choice he made left him screwed.

Pulling even with the mailbox, Logan stopped and leaned over, resting his hands on his thighs as he sucked in oxygen. His legs trembled from exertion, but he ignored that. After a moment, he straightened, got his mail, and, folding the magazines in half over the envelopes, he headed up the drive to his home.

He entered through the side door next to the garage, walked through the mud room and down the hall to the kitchen. Putting down the mail on one of the center islands, he scanned for Shona. Sure enough, she'd gotten up while he was gone.

His T-shirt felt clammy against his skin, but he decided to face the music before showering. Logan went to the back porch and looked out the French doors. He found her sitting on a woven chair facing the lake, with her feet up on a matching wicker ottoman and a can of pop on the table beside her.

When he opened the door, Shona looked up from the magazine she was reading, but she didn't smile. "Hi, hon," he said.

"Where'd you go?" There wasn't any accusation in the question, but Logan knew she wasn't happy with him.

"For a run."

"Why didn't you wake me?"

Logan took a couple of steps nearer to where Shona sat. "Two reasons. One, you didn't have much sleep last night, not with taking care of me, and second, I was mad as hell and didn't want you affected by my mood."

Shona put aside what she was reading. Not one of his car magazines he noted, but some fashion thing one of his sisters must have left behind. "Why were you angry?"

"I had a phone call while you were down—my bosses. They wanted to discuss a project of mine." All true. She didn't need to know the conversation had taken place in Chicago. "They rejected my proposal out of hand—one I really care about—and then refused to listen to any rebuttal on the subject."

"I can see how that would be frustrating."

Logan crossed his arms over his chest and shook his head. "Infuriating, not frustrating. There's a big difference."

Swinging her feet from the ottoman, Shona stood and walked over to him. "You're still mad, aren't you?" she asked, running her fingers lightly over the tight muscles in his jaw.

He nodded. "But better than I was about an hour ago."

"Can you appeal their decision to their bosses?"

Logan captured her hand and held on to it. "I was talking to the board of directors of the Gineal Company—there is no one higher up in the chain of command."

"Oh. Do you always deal with the board?"

The question seemed innocent, but Shona was fishing for more information about his job. It was natural. He'd told her next to nothing and been vague with what he had said. When they'd first met, she'd probably felt no need to press or maybe she'd believed that she didn't have the right to force the subject, but now that they were lovers, she wanted to know more. Too bad he couldn't tell her anything. "Rarely."

He could see how unsatisfied his answer left her, but his hands were tied. Rubbing his thumb over her palm was his way of apologizing, but how long were his non-answers going to be enough for her? At some point—likely sooner rather than later—Shona would try to pin him down. "How long have you been awake?" he asked, changing the subject.

"I don't know. A while." Shona pulled her hand free. "It's comfortable out, but you're soaked. You must have really pushed yourself."

"Like I told you, I was furious. It took some time and exertion to burn off most of it." Logan drew a deep breath, got a whiff, and grimaced. "I need a shower and some fresh clothes."

"Yeah, you do." She smiled as she said that.

"Sorry. I'll be back out in about twenty minutes."

Shona nodded and Logan retreated into the house. He stepped out of his running shoes when he was in the bedroom and shed his clothes in the bathroom, dropping them on the floor. This time he didn't pick them up, but kicked them into a pile next to the hamper.

The shower felt damn good, and after washing his hair and body, Logan stood under the spray with his eyes closed, letting the hot water soothe his muscles. He wasn't sore—exactly—but the heat loosened him up.

The bathroom door opened, but he stayed motionless. There was only one person it could be and he was curious what Shona was going to do. He couldn't help but peek from beneath his eyelids.

She was undressing. His lethargy galloped away, but he didn't open his eyes any farther, afraid that it would stop her. Logan's lips tipped up at the corners. His shy little Shona had been the instigator twice today and he loved the hell out of it. He felt a draft as the shower door opened and he couldn't pretend to be unaware of her any longer.

"You're letting the cold air in," he said, and pulled the door shut behind her. For a moment he stared. She was perfect and she was his. He always forgot how tiny Shona was—maybe because of her height—but she was incredibly delicate. Logan turned and reached for her, tugging her into his embrace.

Desperation nearly overwhelmed him, but he beat it back. Every minute with Shona was borrowed time because of that damn necklace she wore and he could nearly hear the clock ticking down. Logan kept his hold loose, his hands only resting at her waist, and stared at her face, trying to memorize everything about her. She put her right hand over his at her side and laid her left arm over his shoulder, urging his head down to hers.

Logan paused—his nose brushed against hers and his lips were mere inches away from her—but he didn't take her mouth. He wanted to imprint this moment on his brain, too, to be able to recall every sensation years from now when he had nothing except his memory of Shona.

She closed the gap, kissing him gently. Slowly. With more feeling than he expected. More than he deserved.

Shona eased back and stared up at him with a small smile. Her hand went from his wrist, to his chest, her palm flat against his pec. She trailed it downward, her fingers caressing him as she moved. He was hard long before her hand closed around his shaft. "I always wanted to make love in the shower," she said.

He shook his head. "It looks better in the movies than it is in real life. We can fool around, but we'll wait until we're out to go farther."

"Please?" she asked, stroking him.

"No." She kept looking up at him, caressing him. "It's dangerous. We could do it standing up when you were wearing heels, but barefoot? I'd have to lift you and it's slippery in here." He jerked as she gave him a gentle squeeze.

"You're not very adventurous—there are other positions."

The idea of her bent over with both hands against the tile while he took her from behind made his breath catch. Or he could sit down on the bench next to the shower head and she could sit on top of him. Or maybe— "I'm not adventurous?" He couldn't prevent the laugh. "I did you in the restroom at an art gallery while two people were in there with us. If you think that's staid, I can't wait to see what you have in store for me next."

That made his humor fade. After he took the dracontias, the only thing she'd have planned for him was a fist to the gut—if he was lucky.

Shona didn't understand what was going on with Logan. One minute he was laughing, the next he was holding her tightly, as if he were afraid she would run away from him.

Like that was going to happen. She was exactly where she wanted to be.

God, she loved him. Telling herself it was too soon for her feelings to be this deep wasn't working. She couldn't think about the future—not tomorrow, not next week, not next year—without seeing Logan at her side. It scared her how thoroughly he'd entwined himself into her life, but there was no reversing what had happened, no changing how she felt, and she wasn't sure she wanted to even if she could.

His shoulders blocked most of the spray and Shona leaned into Logan hard enough to force him to take a step back. Now the water ran over both of them, making their skin slick. She straddled his leg. "Do you know that every time we've made love, I've had to make the first move?"

"Unfair," he protested. His hands slid from her waist, over her hips, and settled on the cheeks of her bottom. "The first time we were in public. How was I supposed to know you had an exhibitionist streak?"

Shona began to disagree—she was not an exhibitionist—but he raised his leg until she was riding his thigh and her objection became a gasp.

"Our second time was three days after you asked me to slow down. We obviously have different definitions of the word *slow*."

He rocked her into his thigh and she gripped his shoulders tighter to hold her balance. They were arguing about something, but she couldn't remember what it was.

"I will give you this one—although if you consider I was drenched in sweat until a few minutes ago, I'm being generous."

What? Shona shook her head. "It doesn't matter. How much more talking do you plan to do?"

"I think I've made my point."

Logan turned, pressing her back against the tile wall and his mouth came down over hers. There was nothing tentative about this kiss; he demanded she give everything to him and Shona did without question, without hesitation.

He eased away and she saw the apology on his face. Shona didn't want apologies, she wanted this. Clasping him more firmly, she pulled his mouth back to hers and this time she was the one who made demands. Logan was hers and she wasn't quitting until he understood that.

She skated her palms over his shoulders and down his chest, loving the way the light sprinkling of hair tickled her skin. His fingers dug into her hips, keeping the lower halves of their bodies pressed closely together and she wasn't able to stroke the hard muscles of his abs. Shona decided the feel of his erection pushing insistently into her stomach was better anyway and she moved to his back, caressing every inch she could reach.

Logan broke free, and when she tried to drag him back, shook his head. "Huh-uh. My turn."

Shona blinked until she could see clearly, and when she read the fire in his gaze, she relinquished the lead. He reached over, filled his hands with body wash, and soaped up her torso, starting just below her breasts. She wanted him to go up, but instead he went down, kneeling in front of her as he sudsed up her sides and stomach.

"Outie," he rasped, running a finger around her belly button.

"No, it—" But those were the only words she got out before he parted her folds and kissed her between her legs. Shona could feel her eyes roll back as what he was doing at this moment combined with the pleasure she'd remembered him giving her earlier, but after a couple of flicks of his tongue, he stood again, leaving her wanting more.

He cupped her breasts at last, but now Shona was more interested in Logan finishing what he'd started on his original path. Her plea was incoherent—a mixture of moan and an order—and she wasn't surprised that he ignored it.

Her arms came up, but Logan caught them and pressed

her hands back against the wall, palms flat. "Keep them there," he told her.

There was a ferocity in Logan's cobalt eyes that she'd never seen before and every muscle in her body clenched, that's how strongly that gleam aroused her. Shona flexed her fingers against the smooth tiles, but she kept her hands where he'd put them and waited to see what he'd do next.

Logan traced his forefinger over her face with exquisite gentleness. He smoothed her brows, trailed it down the length of her nose, and over her cheekbones. Carefully, making sure he didn't pull, he moved her hair behind her shoulders and kept going, outlining the shell of her ear, her jaw, and chin. There was only one place he skipped and Shona was about to point it out to him when Logan rectified the situation.

He used his tongue to catch her lips.

With a moan, she opened for him, but Logan pulled away. Shona started to reach for him once more, but he made a sound that had her putting her palms back against the shower wall.

It was frustrating beyond anything she'd ever known—and Shona didn't know if she'd ever been this hot before. For the first time in her life, she started thinking about bondage games and what it would be like if he tied her to his bed. She could do it with Logan—she trusted him.

"I like it better," he said, nipping her shoulder, "if you do it without bonds. Like now." He raised his head and grinned.

Shona gasped, but it was with mortification, not arousal. She couldn't believe she'd said the bondage thing out loud. He smoothed his hands down her arms, going slowly and she forgot about her embarrassment. "Maybe I'll tie *you* to the bed."

"Not my kink." Logan ran a finger across her collarbones before tracing the tip down the length of the chain between her breasts.

"What does turn you on then?"

"You." He circled her nipple before lightly pinching it. "Just you."

And that quickly, the games were over. Shona wrapped her arms around his neck and Logan gathered her against him. This kiss managed to be both ferocious and tender at the same time, and she savored it. "Shower sex?" she asked hopefully as he ground his erection against her.

"No."

"Why not?" The water was still warm as it hit her right shoulder.

Logan put her away from him, but before she could protest, he slid his hand between her thighs. "Part your legs a little for me."

As soon as she complied, he slipped a couple of fingers inside her. She was aroused enough that they went in easily, but as he moved them in and out, it started to feel less good until she grabbed his wrist.

"That's why not. I don't want to hurt you."

"The water," she realized.

He nodded and reached behind her for the control to turn off the shower. Logan stepped out first and then held out his hand to help her down. There weren't any towels nearby, and he left a trail of water as he padded over to the linen closet to grab some. Shona bit her lip as he headed back toward her, torn between wanting to stare at his erection and worrying that he might slip on the wet floor. Of course, he was far too graceful to do something like lose his footing and then have to flail around to regain it. That was what would happen to her.

Logan handed her a towel and she started to rub her hair, but instead of using his to dry off, he ran it over her body. Shona watched, bemused, as he took care of her. The man who gave orders in the shower seemed a long way from the one kneeling in front of her, making sure he dabbed every drop of moisture off her stomach, but both sides belonged to Logan.

"Do I get a turn now?" she asked as he finished.

He stood. "If you want."

"I want." She dropped her towel over his head and plucked the one he'd used on her from his hand. As she dried him off every bit as thoroughly as he'd dried her, Logan ran the other one over his hair, then let it fall to the floor.

He took hold of her shoulders, but Shona said, "No." Grasping his hands, she put them down at his sides. "Leave them there. I'll tell you when you can move."

His eyes narrowed, but Logan didn't argue.

Shona didn't plan to spend as long as he had when he'd teased her, but turnabout was fair play. She mimicked what he'd done to her exactly, using her fingers and mouth precisely as he had—until she knelt in front of him. When he'd been in this position, he'd kissed her—and more—but she'd never done this before, and well, she didn't want to do it wrong.

"I dare you."

She tipped her head back to see his face, and while he was as aroused as she'd wanted, there was also a challenge to go along with his words. Something about his expression made her determined to meet it. Wrapping her hand around his shaft, Shona leaned in and kissed the head, taking her time and letting her lips open slightly. His groan came from deep within his chest, but he kept his arms at his sides like she'd told him.

But Logan hadn't just kissed her earlier and if she wanted to match him . . . Locking her eyes on his, Shona leaned forward and ran her tongue over his tip.

That's as far as she got. Logan pulled her to her feet and tugged her into the bedroom. He grabbed a condom off the nightstand and followed her down onto the bed. His hands shook as he rolled it on. "You want to be on top again or should we try missionary for a change?"

"Why don't we be daring?" She laid back, brought her knees up, and let her legs fall open.

He didn't waste any time settling between her thighs and entering her. Shona sighed as he filled her, loving the sense of completeness that only happened when Logan was inside her. For a minute, he stayed still, his gaze on her face, and then he rocked into her.

With all the playing they'd done in the bathroom, Shona knew it wasn't going to take long for either of them to come. She could feel Logan's level of arousal as clearly as her own and knew he was hanging on, waiting for her.

"Harder," she told him breathlessly. "I won't break."

He was going to hesitate, she knew it, and Shona was prepared to roll him onto his back and show him what she wanted. But he didn't pause, and on his next thrust, Logan gave her what she wanted, what she needed. She matched him stroke for stroke, arching up to meet him.

Her orgasm hit her before she expected it. Tightening her hold on Logan, Shona gave herself over to every sensation raging through her.

She liked that Logan called her name as he came and she liked the weight of his body on top of hers. It didn't last long enough before he rolled off her and wordlessly disappeared into the bathroom. He returned quickly.

"Well, hon," he said, pulling her back into his arms and cuddling her close. "You almost flipped me and took charge, but you managed to hold out. I'm proud of you."

Shona growled low in her throat, but before she could reply, her stomach rumbled. She splayed her hand over it, but it was too late—Logan's body was shaking as he laughed.

"Guess I better feed you. Do you want to order in?"

"Not a chance." She propped herself up on his chest and gazed down at him. Shona ran a finger just below his bottom lip, before leaning down to kiss him lightly. "Let's go somewhere nice for dinner. We can swing by my home so I can change and then head out for the restaurant."

"A place where they require a jacket and a tie?"

"Yes. I can wear this sexy, yet incredibly elegant black

dress I have and you can fantasize about getting me out of it."

"If we stay here, we can eat naked in bed." Logan gave her an exaggerated leer.

Shona kissed him again. "Come on—it'll be great!"

It was a good forty-five minutes later before they were on their way to her apartment. She'd hoped for one of his classic cars, but wasn't surprised he'd taken the Jeep. Logan wore his dark suit with a purple tie and she was in the same clothes she'd worn when she'd brought him home that morning. He braked for a traffic signal, his fingers tapping lightly against the steering wheel as they waited. "I feel underdressed."

"I could turn around and change into jeans," he said with a hopeful note in his voice.

"You look hot in a suit." She let her eyes trail over him and licked her upper lip. Before she could continue to tease him, the light turned green and at the same time her phone went off. Shona dug it out of her purse and saw she had a text alert. "Oooh!"

"What? Is something wrong?"

"No, Eleventh Eternity is going to be playing—tonight only."

Logan frowned, but Shona ignored it. He'd been unhappy since he'd put on the tie. "What the hell is eleventh eternity?"

Where did he live? Under a rock? "They're a local band and my absolute favorite, but they broke up last year. I'm on their text message list for updates." She waved her phone, sure he'd see it with his peripheral vision even though his eyes were on the road. "They're playing together again, but just this once. Do you mind if we go?"

"I'm wearing a suit," he grumbled.

Shona leaned over and kissed his cheek, knowing that his answer was the same as a yes. "Thanks, and don't worry, you won't be overdressed. The club requires evening attire, so I still need to change."

His frown became a scowl. "Where are they playing?" he asked and there was a note of suspicion in his voice.

She ignored it. "Club Red."

18
CHAPTER

Logan couldn't believe he was standing in Club Red. He hated this place. It was pretentious, attracted people who were superficial at best, and what they charged for a cover should be criminal. And in the height of hypocrisy, management required that their customers dress up while the bar itself was decorated in some high-end industrial modern style that tried to be classy, but failed. Instead, it was cold and unappealing.

He might be the only one in Seattle who felt this way—it was Tuesday and the place was packed. Worst of all, he couldn't scan with much accuracy because of the crowd. Although, with the Tàireil ability to cloak themselves, it might not make any difference. It had Logan uneasy, but when Shona had asked if they could come here after dinner, he hadn't been able to think up a good reason to say no.

Her hip bumped his and he tightened the hold he had around her waist. Shona looked up at him and smiled before turning her attention back to the band. Only a selfish jerk would refuse to bring her to see Eleventh Eternity, especially after she'd gone to the places he'd picked for their dates without complaint.

Despite that, he'd tried to talk her out of coming here, but it hadn't worked. If he didn't want to go, she'd told him, she'd be perfectly happy to come here by herself.

Like he was going to let that happen.

But there was one important thing he'd forgotten about Club Red—the area in which it was situated. During the day it was bustling with people, but at night it cleared out and became virtually deserted except for the club patrons. The site made it the perfect tactical location to arrange an ambush.

Logan scowled and tried again to scan long range, but he couldn't pick up anything. That wasn't surprising.

Probably there was nothing to worry about. How could there be? Even he and Shona hadn't known they were coming here until the last minute. Did he think the darksiders had somehow known this was Shona's favorite band and had arranged for them to reunite for a one-night-only gig? He'd have to be totally paranoid to believe that and the Tàireil had been scoping out her home only last night. *That* was the most likely location for an attack and the one place they could be sure to find her.

"I'm sorry you're not having a good time," Shona said when the band took a break.

"I'm having fun." And he would have been if he didn't have to worry about protecting her. To his surprise, he'd liked the music, and though he would have preferred not to be distracted, Shona had dragged him closer to the stage a couple of times. He'd had to work them to the back of the throng time and again. The number of people here was bad enough, but to be in the middle of them? No.

She didn't look as if she believed him.

Logan shrugged and said, "I have a problem with crowds, that's all. Remember, the places I chose to take you had a lot less people than this one."

"True."

Shona seemed happier and that made him happy. Damn, he had it bad and he didn't want to change a thing. With his free hand, he reached up and pushed her hair behind her shoulder.

The wild curls appeared effortless, but he knew better. She'd spent time on them and Logan appreciated the sexy look—it went with the dress she wore.

It was simple—sleeveless with a V neck front and back—but on Shona it was incredible. As closely as it fit her, she made the dress. The neck didn't drop too low and it was a fifty-fifty proposition whether or not she was wearing a bra—he was hoping for not. Logan's eyes followed the chain that went around her neck, dipped between her breasts, and kept the dragon stone out of sight behind the dress. It brought him back down to earth. He'd better enjoy what little time he had left with her.

"What do you say we duck out and go home?" he suggested. "We could do a little dancing on the back porch and watch the moonlight shimmer on the water."

"Maybe we could do that later." She sounded apologetic, but firm. "If Eleventh Eternity stays with the way they used to do their shows, there should be one more set and then they'll wrap up for the night."

"Okay." Logan kept his voice easy, but he wanted Shona safe behind the walls of his home.

He'd never been precognitive, but he had a twitchy feeling tonight. Could the Tàireil have a tracker who had located them at the club? The odds were against it, he decided.

Tracking was an ability they hadn't needed to develop in their world, not like the Gineal and the way they used it to find dark-force creatures before they could cause a problem. Without years of honing the skill, there was little chance the darksiders had been able to follow them through town, even if they'd tried to tail them when they'd left Shona's home.

Could their dragon mage have an affinity with the stone, enough to track it around the city? That was a possibility, but Shona could pick out the Tàireil energy even when they were cloaked. If they'd been following the dracontias, she'd be familiar with their signature and wouldn't have called it "strange."

If his instincts were jangling, it was likely because they intended to attack at Shona's house. Logan stroked her hip. He planned on bringing her to his home tonight, though, and keeping her there, so he had nothing to be concerned about—at least not at the moment.

"Cheer up, Logan." She ran her fingers over his cheek. "It's not that bad."

Yeah, sure it wasn't. The Tàireil wanted that stone. They'd been willing to take their time before now because she didn't know what she had and didn't have the spell to meld with it. Logan's presence, though, changed the playing field and they had to believe the Gineal were going to claim their dragon mage soon. And the Tàireil should be spot on about that, damn the council.

He'd avert their attack this evening by not going to Shona's house, but short of holding her prisoner, there was no way he could keep her completely safe. If they didn't have a chance to get at her tonight, then they'd try tomorrow night or the night after that. It was only a matter of time until he'd be fighting the darksiders and somehow he had to defeat them while hiding his magic from Shona and doing it quickly enough that he didn't have a seizure. And oh, yeah, it would be at least two against one. Right. Not that bad.

"Sorry," he apologized. "I'll try not to ruin your evening."

"You're not ruining it." Shona gave his cheek another caress. "I just want you to enjoy yourself as much as I am." She hugged him. "Now that the band's back, why don't we get up closer to the stage?"

He hesitated.

"Please?"

And that easily, he capitulated. Shona smiled, took his hand, and led him through the densely packed crowd. God, she had him wrapped around her finger, but Logan didn't think she realized it.

The music was slow and dreamy, and Shona stood in front of him, pulled his arms around her waist, and swayed against him. He didn't need this. It was another distraction when he was already at overload, but when Shona pressed her bottom against his groin, he drew her even closer. And he found himself trying to memorize this moment, too, to store it away for the cold, lonely days when she was gone.

With a soft sigh, Shona relaxed into him. Everyone and everything else receded until it was only the two of them and the music. She was deliberately trying to arouse him with her wiggling, trying to make him lose control, and he didn't stop her.

Logan couldn't get near enough, couldn't hold her long enough. He ached. And not only with need.

He slipped a hand under the fall of her hair, lifting it and pressing a kiss to her nape, to the skin of her back exposed by the dress. She leaned more firmly into his erection and teased him more. The urge to turn her around and take her mouth nearly overwhelmed him, but he didn't want to embarrass Shona. Logan closed his eyes and tortured himself by concentrating on every brush of her body against his.

If they were home, he'd be able to kiss her. If they were home, he could take her to the bedroom and make love with her. Hell, if they were home, he could make love to her on the porch in the moonlight without worrying about anyone seeing.

He was steeped in her, so lost in Shona that when the music ended, he blinked in confusion. The applause brought the crowd back into his awareness and Logan did turn her then, staring down at her. He wasn't alone—she was as steamed up as he was and just as startled to be jerked back into awareness. "Let's go home."

"Yeah, I'm ready."

So was he, but they were probably talking about two different things. Although as dilated as her pupils were, maybe not. The band was doing an encore and they seemed to be the only two leaving. "Have you ever thought about making love in a car?" he asked as he maneuvered her through the crowd.

Shona's lips curved. "Like maybe in a Jeep?"

"That would be the one. It's a long ride home."

"If you can find somewhere private, I'm willing to consider it."

Logan had to tamp down the heat that flared or he'd have gone up like dry tinder. He moved them through the throng faster, not slowing down until they were outside, and he only did then because Shona said, "You're lucky I'm tall or I wouldn't be able to keep up with you."

"Sorry."

She laughed softly. "Don't be. I'm flattered since it's only been a few hours since the last time we were together."

"More than a few," he corrected.

Shona stopped, pivoted until she was in front of him on the sidewalk, and wrapped her arms around his neck. Before he could say anything, she kissed him. For an instant, he resisted, but he was still running hot and her passion reignited his own. He decided they could chance a minute—or two.

He was thinking with his little head—that was the only excuse he had for the stupidity—but Logan came back to reality in a nanosecond when he felt the presence of a Tàireil. In a heartbeat, he had Shona behind him and tossed a couple of fast fireballs at the woman running toward them.

She was smart enough to have protection in place and his shots lit up the field. Logan started silently chanting his own spells to keep Shona and himself safe.

It was only after he closed his incantations that he realized the woman wasn't returning fire, in fact she was holding both hands up in the universal sign of surrender. What the hell? Tàireil didn't surrender.

He studied her more closely. She was short for a darksider, but a little over average height for a human woman. Her reddish hair was cut in one of those sleek bobs, she was wearing a white shirt, a skirt with blotches of blue and black, and she had on heels. Not exactly attack attire.

He was trying to decide what the game was, when Shona spoke up. "What are you two?"

Damn. She sounded dazed and why wouldn't she be? He'd

just shot fire from his hands and the woman had stopped it with an invisible shield. "Not now, Shona."

"I'm not going to hurt you," the darksider said. "In fact, you should be thanking me. Damn it, Gineal, you're supposed to be watching out for her! I trusted you to do that much."

"Who the hell are you?" he demanded.

"That's Farran," Shona answered softly.

This was Farran? Her best friend forever? "You met her two months ago, didn't you?" he guessed.

Shona made a sound he took to be assent. They'd been plotting to get at the dracontias since shortly after it had been found. "Why should I trust you," he challenged. "You're Tàireil."

"And I've done everything I could to protect Shona until there was nothing left that I was able to do." She took a couple of steps forward. "You're the one assigned to take care of her—why are you standing on the sidewalk kissing her when there are other Tàireil in the vicinity?"

"What?" He scanned, but picked up no one. "Where? They're cloaked from me."

"Three of them," Farran said, "still a number of blocks off, but they won't be for long."

"This was a setup."

"Of course; they wanted her at Club Red." She looked past his shoulder. "I'm the one who told them how much you love Eleventh Eternity and they took it from there, doing what they needed to in order to arrange the one-night reunion. I'm sorry, Shona."

Logan thought she was sincere, but he couldn't trust her—he knew what the Tàireil did to traitors. "And I'm supposed to believe you're risking your life to help Shona out of the goodness of your heart."

Farran shook her head and moved closer. She came to an abrupt halt when Logan raised his arm, ready to fire again. "I'm not risking my life—at least not yet. They need me alive under the present circumstances."

"And those are?"

"I'm the dragon mage." That surprised Logan—he'd assumed it was the arrogant brat he'd fought last night. The woman read it on his face, he was certain of that because she smiled. "They want to rule our dimension and they can only do it through me."

"And you expect me to believe you don't want to be empress?"

"I don't." Farran's lips twisted. "If I had my wish, I would stay out of the politics in my world entirely, but my family has other ideas and since they're stronger . . ." Her voice trailed off. "I tried to steal the stone myself, but Shona never removes it and I had to go to Plan B. That failed, too."

More pieces fell into place. "You're the one who sent the human after Shona."

"Not after Shona, after the dracontias. I didn't want her harmed, but I'm out of the picture now and they've taken over the job of acquiring the stone. They'll kill her without hesitation if that's what it takes." Farran looked over her shoulder. "We don't have much time—get her out of here."

Smart advice—if she was on the up-and-up and not part of a bigger setup. Of course, they didn't need to use the woman. He'd been almost completely oblivious to everything going on around them. If Farran wanted Shona dead, Shona would be dead. "Yeah, you're right. Come on, Shon, let's move, but stay between me and the building, all right?"

"No. I'm not moving until someone tells me what the hell is going on here."

"When we get home," he said through gritted teeth, but Shona simply glared at him. Maybe her friend could talk some sense into her. Logan turned back to Farran, but she was gone.

That wasn't a good omen.

They needed to get out of here ASAP. Shona had already seen too much—what was one more thing? He did the spell to open a transit.

Nothing happened.

They were in big trouble if the Tàireil had put a spell in

place to keep them from escaping. Logan reinforced the protection spell around Shona and then did his own. "Let's get to the Jeep—move, Shona!"

"Logan," she whispered. "There are three of them out there."

Damn, too late. "Where? Give me their positions."

The first shots lit up the night before she could answer. He didn't need the information any longer—the trio had attacked simultaneously. He crowded Shona against the building behind them and returned fire.

Quickly, he assessed their surroundings. The streets around Club Red were deserted except for a scattering of parked cars. He and Shona were away from the street lights and the club protected their backs, but with darksiders at the nine, twelve, and three o'clock positions they were pinned down. No cover, nothing to protect them except his spells.

Forming a cloud of fire, Logan brought it down over the Tàireil directly in front of them. His adversary sent it skyward so quickly he had to be completely unharmed by the flame.

Damn. He couldn't believe they were in this situation. He couldn't believe his stupidity was the reason they were in this situation. Moron. Idiot. Fool. If he hadn't stopped and returned Shona's kiss. If he'd trusted Farran more quickly.

Logan got off two quick bursts of fire. Lightning was his weapon of choice, but if he damaged a structure or vehicle, he wouldn't have the strength left afterward to clean up the mess.

One of the Tàireil let loose with a burst that blackened the building to their left. Too close for comfort. Shona had been awfully damn quiet. "Hon, are you okay?"

"Just fine." She sounded out of it, but whether it was because her shield took some of the hit or she was emotionally stunned, he didn't know.

He did a spell to protect their ears and those of the humans in the area. As soon as it was in place, Logan let loose with a pressurized cannonball of air. It exploded as it hit the shield of the Tàireil on his right, but whether or not the concussion deafened him or the others was anyone's guess.

The council was going to ream him for getting caught in

this mess. Logan followed up with a continuous rope of fire, hoping the darksiders were affected by the noise.

From day one of training, he'd been taught to control his emotions and that included lust. Two darksiders shot back at him and this time it was his shield that glowed. If they had been in a stupor, they weren't any longer. Damn, he'd wasted too much magic for too little reward.

Emotion caused mistakes. Emotion left the troubleshooter open to the dark forces. Emotion had no place in battle. Logan thought he'd learned that lesson, but he'd been wrong—and his lapse had put one of the people who meant the most to him at risk.

There was no place for him to go. Nowhere to hide Shona. He was her bulwark, and if he went down, she faced three Tàireil males without magic. The answer was simple—he couldn't fall.

Gritting his teeth, Logan set off another volley of shots. They weren't trying to close ground, but then they didn't need to. They could outwait him. He couldn't win—not three against one—and they knew it.

Retreat. Find a way to get out of here, get Shona safe, and then fight them on his terms. To block his transit, they had to be combining their magic—it wasn't something a single Tàireil could do. Had they dropped the barrier, thinking he wouldn't try it after it failed once?

He rained fire on them, and as it fell, he tried again to open the gateway. Still closed off.

If he took out one of the three from the magical blockade, then he could get Shona and himself out of here. Logan needed to do it soon. Not only were they vulnerable without cover, but he was burning through magic trying to keep their shields strong.

Then there were the humans in the club. How long till they came streaming out? It was a sure bet the Tàireil hadn't done anything to keep them away and Logan didn't have the power to spare for that.

Leverage. The humans became leverage against him.

Attack the weakest link. Was that hotheaded kid one of the three out there? "Shon, are two of the energy signatures the same as what you sensed last night?" No answer. "Shona!"

"Yes." Her voice shook.

Logan released a stream of fire and reached back to reassure her. He found her hip and rubbed gently. "Which two? Give me their positions." He could nearly sense her confusion. "Think of a clock. Where are they? Noon? Nine? Three?"

"Nine and three," she said.

Okay, that gave him something to use. He was curious about who was dead ahead—that had to be the leader, the man orchestrating the attack—but he couldn't worry about him now.

Logan released Shona. Bringing his hand forward, he raised a dust storm, sending it out to the Tàireil. "Remember when you left your body and followed your attacker to his car? Can you do that again?"

"I don't know. I can try." She sounded less shaky.

"I want you to go to the nine and three o'clock positions and take a look at those men. I need you to tell me which one is the youngest."

The dust storm dissipated rapidly and he was sure the Tàireil had put an end to it. With their protection in place, it wouldn't have done much damage anyway, not even with the added debris it had picked up on the streets.

His shield faltered on the next direct strike and he fought the urge to tell Shona to hurry up. His voice might pull her back if she was starting to leave her body. Or she might not be able to voluntarily do it. The one time she had sent out her consciousness, she hadn't had a clue what was going on.

So pick a darksider, any darksider. It was better than standing here, waiting to run out of magic.

Logan focused on the Tàireil at three o'clock and turned the air around him ice-cold. It was unlikely that their original protection spell had included temperature and the darksider would have to use magic to add that component.

"Does he have light brown hair and smug little smirk on his face?" Shona asked.

"That's him."

"He's at three o'clock."

Logan nodded. He'd picked the right one. Letting loose with another stream of fire, he tried to decide the best way to get under the kid's skin. He didn't think verbal insults were going to work. That Tàireil might be volatile enough to explode if he was alone, but with the leader along, Logan didn't see it happening.

An incantation that worked on emotions? Would the darksiders' protection spell include feelings or would they discount them as unimportant?

A shot came in and hit Shona's shield, illuminating it brightly. Worse, it faltered. Logan quickly sent more magic to the force field, but he was running out of time and power much too fast. He had to try the attack on the emotions.

The incantation was far more complicated than spells normally used during battle and it cost him. This had to work because he didn't have much longer. Logan could feel the seizure off in the distance, but moving closer with every second.

Pushing it from his mind, he concentrated on the youngest darksider, raising inferiority and insignificance within him. Anyone as full of himself as that kid was either had a deep-seated inferiority complex or he was so damn arrogant that realizing his insignificance would—

The roar was pure outrage.

Direct hit.

The boy ran from behind the building he'd been using as cover, flinging fireballs without bothering to aim. He continued to charge toward Logan until he hit an invisible wall and fell to the ground. The leader had brought the kid down himself.

Logan didn't hesitate. He chanted the spell to open a transit. This time it appeared.

Grabbing Shona by the waist, he half lifted, half pushed her through the portal and jumped after her. Without pausing a second, he waved his fingers, closing the glowing gate.

Shona was on her hands and knees on the floor of his bedroom. She'd probably lost her balance when she'd landed. "Are you okay?" he asked. He was almost out of time and he fought to hold off the seizure.

"Oh, just fine." The sarcasm was heavy. "You want to explain to me what the hell you are and what happened tonight?"

No, he didn't. What he wanted to do was erase her memory, but before he could come up with the words to the spell, the tremors hit. Logan fisted his hands, trying to stave it off. Damn it, he couldn't afford this, not now. Sheer willpower, though, wasn't working. The trembling became stronger.

"Hell," he muttered and sat on the floor. If he didn't, he'd fall down. He fought harder, hating the damn visions as much as the loss of control. If he could see them, understand them, maybe it would be different.

The blinding light gained on him. He tried to tell Shona not to leave his house, but Logan didn't know if the words were intelligible or not. He fought one last, desperate skirmish, but the light won and Logan was lost to everything except the images flashing through his mind.

19
CHAPTER

Shona wanted to yell at Logan, to demand answers, and then yell at him some more, but she couldn't shout at a man who was convulsing on the floor.

Damn it, this was the third time in a week that he'd had a seizure. Something was seriously wrong and he needed help whether he'd admit it or not. Shona crawled closer, but stayed out of flailing range. As mad as she was—as scared as she was—his pain still affected her. She noticed a small table was too close to where he lay. Standing, she grabbed hold of the edge and pulled it out of range. There was nothing else that needed to be moved.

She sank to the ground, leaning her back against the side of the bed. Should she try to get closer and remove his tie? Shona didn't want him to choke himself, but he seemed really agitated right now—worse than last time—and she didn't think she could get in there without him inadvertently connecting with her. Maybe she'd wait and see.

After a moment, she pulled her necklace out from beneath her dress and stared at the gem. Shona hadn't understood a lot of what she'd heard Farran and Logan talking about, but she did know one thing—her beautiful thrift store find was the root cause of so many things.

Rubbing the stone with her thumb, she thought about what had happened in her life the last couple of months and this time she juxtaposed the events with the discovery of her necklace.

Around the same time she stumbled across it, she lost her interest in doing her art. It seemed farfetched to claim the stone was responsible for that, but why not put it on the list? It wasn't any stranger than the other things she'd seen tonight.

Within a week of finding it, Farran had appeared out of nowhere and taken a job in the one place Shona stopped at regularly. That wasn't coincidence, she knew it after what she heard tonight. It had been Farran who'd pursued the friendship, Farran who'd invited Shona out for coffee to talk about art, and Farran who'd wormed her way into Shona's life. And it hurt to know that the woman she considered as close as a sister hadn't felt the same kinship. Her only interest had been in getting the stupid stone, not in making a friend.

That pain was nothing compared to what she felt when she thought about Logan, though. Farran had said he was assigned to take care of Shona and he hadn't denied it. She waited for tears to come, but they didn't. This hurt cut too deeply for them.

His moan drew her eyes back to him. Assigned to take care of her, but by whom? For what purpose? And Logan had been so adamant when he'd insisted that he wasn't just looking to nail her. Before she could stop it, her heart leapt, latching on to that small bit of hope. Could she be more to him than a job?

Be fair, the foolish part of her whispered. How could he tell you what he was capable of?

True. Could she expect him to introduce himself and then say, oh, by the way, I'm a mutant who can shoot fire from his hands? "Mom, Dad," she whispered. "I'd like you to meet my boyfriend. What does he do? Why, he's a superhero, of course."

Shona smiled at the thought. What was his code name? Flametron? Super Fireman? Flamethrower? She remembered his family and she wondered if they were all superheroes like in *The Incredibles*. What powers did they have?

Her humor faded abruptly when Logan started thrashing harder and shouting in that strange language. Shona tensed, waiting for the wave to pass, but it didn't. This was worse than it had been last night and that had been scary enough. She clutched her stone tighter and waited some more, but it went on and on. Maybe she should try to get his cell phone or search his house for a phone number for his family. Maybe his brother. If he were here, wouldn't Logan's brother know what to do?

One of those shimmery gates like Logan had pushed her through appeared in the bedroom. What if those men had found them and could travel like Logan did? Shona squeaked and then realized how vulnerable he was. She moved, scrambling to put herself between him and the potential threat.

Shona lowered her fists when she saw the man's face. She'd known they were twins; now she knew they were identical. He glanced from her, to Logan, and back again. "Can you help him?"

"I'll try," Kel said grimly. He made a gesture with two fingers and Logan stopped flailing. It didn't stop the convulsions, but it was as if Logan's arms and legs were locked in place. Only then did Kel move.

Sitting down next to his brother, Kel put one hand on his head and the other on his chest and closed his eyes. After a moment, Kel looked at her, nodded, and then shifted until he was by Logan's head. Reaching out, he rested both hands near Logan's temples. And as she watched, a green glow peeked out from between Kel's fingers. Shona clutched her stone, clinging to it for strength. For courage.

She couldn't have said how, but Shona felt it when Kel

stopped whatever it was that kept Logan from moving. She also felt when the green glow began to lose intensity long before she saw it with her eyes. The weird just never stopped.

Kel stood and came toward her. "How is he?" she asked.

"Fine. He'll be coming around in a bit, but Logan will need to sleep for a good eight or ten hours before he's back to normal."

"Can superheroes be referred to as normal?"

For an instant, Kel stared at her as if she were insane and then he grinned. She waited for the thunk she felt around her heart whenever Logan gave her one of those crooked smiles, but even though this man had Logan's face, nothing happened.

"You saw him throw a few bolts of lightning and now you think Logan's a superhero?" She heard the suppressed amusement.

"Um, he threw fireballs and strings of fire and made it rain fire. He can hurl lightning, too?"

Kel sobered. "I think I better keep my mouth shut and let Logan talk to you. How'd you summon me, anyway?"

"What do you mean, summon you?"

"I heard you in my head clearly and you said—Kel, please come, Logan needs you."

Her hand tightened on the stone. "I didn't do that."

"It was you, Shona. You sounded the same in my head as you do now. Besides," Kel looked down at Logan, then back at her, "do you see anyone else around here who could call me?"

No, she didn't and she had been wishing she could get Kel over here. Deciding she didn't want to think about that right now, she changed the subject. "How do you know who I am?"

One side of Kel's mouth quirked up. "How do you think? Logan's talked about you."

"He has? He told you about me?"

"Yes."

Kel didn't expound on that and she had to stop herself from asking questions. She didn't want to sound pathetic. Shona changed the subject again. "You didn't know Logan had seizures, did you?"

"No."

"So they're not something he's lived with all his life."

"Tell me what you know about them," he ordered.

Good, someone was taking them seriously. Maybe Kel could get Logan to deal with them. "This is the third time in a week that he's had one. Tonight, it started almost as soon as we crossed that shiny gate into his bedroom."

"Transit." She must have looked blank. "We call the shiny gate a transit."

"Okay." Shona waved that off. It wasn't important. "He was fighting with these three men, throwing fire at them and they were throwing fire back, and then he opened a transit, we ended up here, and he almost immediately went down. Yesterday, he sent me into my house and confronted two of the three men he fought tonight. When he came inside, he was shaky, but he was able to talk for a while and he told me not to call anyone."

Kel frowned and dug his hands into his pockets. "Tell me about the third time," he demanded brusquely.

"It was last Wednesday. I only saw the aftermath, but he admitted he'd had a seizure earlier, before I got here."

Pivoting sharply, Kel paced around the room, muttering obscenities. Shona found herself comparing the two men. Logan wore his hair shorter and neater, and she'd never seen him with a few days' worth of stubble on his face. Like Logan, Kel apparently preferred jeans and T-shirts and he moved with the same unconscious grace. The biggest difference to her mind, though, was how she reacted to them. Simply looking at Logan made her heart pound faster—Kel? Nothing.

"If you're done swearing," she said when he paused, "do you want to check on Logan? Shouldn't he be coming around by now?"

"Give it a few more minutes."

Shona bristled at the tone, but took a deep breath and tried to let it go. Kel loved his brother, she had no doubt about that, and he wouldn't be cavalier if there was something to worry about. "Do you have superpowers, too?"

He rounded on her. "Don't ask questions."

After the evening she'd had, the last thing she needed was his rudeness. "You know, I bet no one ever confuses you and Logan. It's not the hair, it's the attitude. He's a lot nicer and kinder and gentler than you are."

"That's the consensus."

"See?" Logan said from his spot on the floor. "Even people who've just met you know that I'm the good twin and you're the evil one." He tried to sit, but didn't get too far. "Help me up, would you, Kel?"

She expected Kel to make some smart-aleck remark, but he wordlessly went over and gave Logan the leverage he needed to get to his feet, and when Logan swayed, Kel slung an arm around his shoulders and steered him to a chair. "Okay, little brother, time to start talking. What the hell is going on with you?"

Logan stayed stubbornly silent.

"I already told him about your other seizures," Shona said. "You might as well come clean."

"Damn it, Shon, I asked you not to say anything."

"Damn it, Logan," she bent down and got in his face, "this one was really bad. You need to see a doctor."

"You're still worried about me? Even after everything you saw and heard tonight?"

Shona straightened and moved away. "We'll fight about that later." When they were alone and she had a chance to get her mind around everything.

"I'm not leaving until you tell me what's going on and if that means I sit here all night, so be it." Kel crossed his arms over his chest and glared at Logan. The stare-down between the brothers lasted for a couple of minutes before Logan caved.

"It's not that big a deal." He shrugged. "About six weeks ago, I went hiking. I fought a bouda and won, but I burned a lot of power. Next thing I knew, something's barreling down on me inside my head. I open the transit, go home, and have my first seizure. It's been happening ever since whenever I use too much magic."

"Describe one of these seizures." Kel looked odd, but Shona didn't understand why.

"It usually starts with a bright light settling over me and then I get these visions flashing through my brain. They go fast, so fast that I can't get a handle on what I'm seeing, and while my brain is lost in that, it's like my body is being electrocuted or jolted by something powerful. Something painful."

Logan's tone had been matter-of-fact, but Shona could imagine how confused and scared he must have been the first time. Probably kind of like she'd felt tonight. She nearly went to him, wanting to reassure him, wanting to offer support, but she couldn't. What she'd heard Farran say about Logan's watching out for her being his job undermined her confidence in his feelings for her.

"Almost like you're having some kind of flashback?" Kel asked.

"I guess." He shrugged again, one shoulder this time. "Only nothing is familiar."

"Yeah." Kel was silent for a long while, and when he spoke, his voice was soft and the words came so fast, that Shona had to strain to hear everything. "You see, about six weeks ago, I altered a spell to get rid of *my* flashbacks and send them to the universe. Only it sounds like you got them instead."

Kel held up a hand, stopping Logan before he could say anything. He started chanting something in another language that sounded similar to what Logan used when he was having a seizure and Shona didn't understand another word until he said, "And so it is."

"What did you do?" Logan asked.

"Reversed the spell. Hey, they're my flashbacks," he said,

trying for a smile and failing. "You should be safe to use your magic again without worrying about the consequences."

"What about you? What about when you use your magic?"

"It doesn't work that way with me." Kel grimaced, shrugged. "It's not related to my powers."

"Kel—"

"I have to go." He opened one of those transit things. "I'll keep quiet about this if you keep quiet, deal?"

Logan nodded and Kel cut out before she could say anything. "Why did he run off so fast?" Shona asked.

"Because of me." Logan studied her for a minute, and then he said quietly, "The flashbacks? They have to be related to his disappearance six months ago. He's probably worried I saw more than I told him and he didn't want to answer any of my questions."

"No one knows anything about it? Really?"

His lips tightened. "No one in the family, but I'm sure the council is aware of exactly what happened."

"Council?"

"I'll explain about them later."

Shona nodded, the motion feeling jerky to her. "You talked about magic with your brother—you're not a superhero like Batman or Superman, then?"

"No, not even close."

"So by magic we're talking *Charmed* or *Bewitched*?"

"Kind of, yeah." He reached up and loosened his tie. "It's along those lines at least."

She took a moment to digest that. The secrecy about what he was made sense. It was easy to imagine the government rounding up Logan, his family, and any others like him and forcing them to use their magic in the name of national defense. Or being herded into a lab to be studied like guinea pigs. Or being hounded by people wanting them to use their powers to grant wishes. The more she thought about it, the more scenarios came to mind and the more she understood why Logan had kept quiet.

He stood, shrugged out of his suit coat, and started toward the closet. "Don't move!" she ordered. "I'm not done yet."

"I know you're not. I just want to get comfortable."

"Answer one question for me first. Did you have sex with me as part of your job?"

Logan tossed his coat toward the bed, missed, but didn't bother to pick it up. Instead he walked over to her and looked into her eyes. He said, "No. Making love with you was not part of my assignment, and in fact, if anyone finds out about it, I'll be in a lot of trouble. What happened between us was real and it meant something. Don't doubt that."

She stared at him, trying to read him, trying to decide whether or not he was telling the truth.

"I'd kill to keep you safe, but that's my job." The intensity in his voice had Shona holding her breath. "There are damn few people, though, that I'd be willing to die for. You're one of them. Think about that while I change."

Logan leaned over, kissed her forehead, and walked away.

Shona sat with her feet propped up against the bed and watched Logan sleep. It was late, after three A.M., but she couldn't relax enough to even think about going to bed. Not yet. He'd told her quite a bit before he crashed and she was still mulling it over.

It seemed so fantastical—Gineal, Tàireil, dormants, dragon mages—but she had to believe it, right? Even if she could discount the way he'd fought with fire, she couldn't write off the fact that he'd transported all her clothes here to give her a choice of what to wear. Right. Like she bought that story. Although as off balance as she was, she might have gone for it if he hadn't suggested moving in with him again.

Her first reaction had been to say no, to tell him she'd be fine in her own home, but Shona wasn't naive enough to believe that. It was obvious to even the biggest idiot that she was no match for men who shot fire as casually as throwing a baseball.

Magic existed. Incredible.

That wasn't what she was spending the most time thinking about, though. Logan had said he was willing to die for her. That was the last thing she wanted, but Shona couldn't help wondering what it meant. Did he love her? He hadn't said that and she'd been too cowardly to ask.

The one thing she did believe after their talk was that their relationship was real—he'd even said that straight out—and once she'd reached that conclusion, she'd been able to listen to Logan as he'd explained. It hadn't taken much thought to figure out that he couldn't go around telling people about what he could do and that included her. If they'd known each other longer, maybe she could be mad, but although her heart felt as if she'd known him forever, it had only been eleven days.

She had a harder time dealing with the fact that they'd met only because he'd been protecting her, but Logan had soothed her hurt and anger on that score, too. Maybe it made her a pushover, but she'd understood his actions and forgiven him. He hadn't been using her, he'd been as out of control with her as she was with him. That had to mean something, right?

She sighed. If she spent any more time wondering about what Logan felt for her, she'd make herself crazy. She reached for her stone—no, the dracontias—and rubbed it lightly with her thumb. He hadn't been able to tell her much about dragon mages, something he'd been apologetic about and a bit sheepish. That's when he'd started making books appear until he'd found one in English. He'd been apologetic about that as well, explaining that it probably wouldn't tell her much more than he had, that the important works were written in Cànan, the old language of the Gineal.

The book had slipped off her lap and was between her hip and the side of the chair, but she'd shifted until she could feel the press of the hard cover against her leg. It helped ground her, remind her everything was real, but Logan had been right—there hadn't been a lot in it beyond what he'd already told her.

She was a dormant with blocked-off magical powers. Her!

But she had to do two spells to really be the dragon mage—one to become a Gineal person, and the other to merge with the stone.

One of the incantations—the dracontias one—was in the book and in English. The temptation to recite it had been there, but Logan had told her that his council believed if she did both spells, the creativity required to do her glass work would be lost to her forever.

She was scared, though, that it wouldn't make any difference whether or not she used the incantations. Two months had already passed and her creative energy might never return, but she wasn't ready to abandon all hope. That's what doing the spell meant—at least to her.

Shona needed to move. She got to her feet and slipped out of the bedroom. The artist in her wanted to take off the necklace and hand it to Farran, tell her *here, it's all yours*. But it wasn't that easy. Somehow, the stone had become part of her. It might sound silly, but it pulsed in rhythm with her heartbeat and she simply couldn't take it off.

She drifted out onto the back porch and came to an abrupt halt. Shona had to choke off her scream. Something was wrong with her vision. "Oh, my God. Oh, my God!"

Get control. Get control. Dropping into the nearest chair, she clutched the dracontias even though she was sure it was responsible for this, closed her eyes, and took deep breaths. This wasn't anything to panic over. It wasn't.

Shona peeked out from beneath her lashes, but she could still see the yard and lake as if it were daylight and not the middle of the night. The next breath she took sounded wheezy, but she kept at it anyway. Being able to see in the dark was an advantage, she told herself. There were people after her and she'd be able to see them coming no matter when they attacked.

But why now? What had changed?

Maybe nothing. Maybe the longer she wore the stone, the more things would manifest themselves. That allowed her to unclench her fingers. Logan had said *she* controlled the dracontias, and if that were true, she should be able to return her eyesight to normal. Somehow.

Before she could try to override the dragon stone, she picked up motion in her periphery—like she had that day in the shop. Almost afraid of what she'd see—or wouldn't see—Shona turned her head. Her whimper was barely audible.

Two tiny dragons were chasing each other.

Oh, my God.

As if sensing her attention, they stopped, looked her directly in the eye, and scampered off.

It was a dream. She'd fallen asleep in the chair next to the bed and this was all some bizarre dream based on what Logan had told her and what she'd read. Any second now, she was going to wake up and everything would be semi-normal again.

"Wake up, wake up, wake up," she whispered.

Instead, things got weirder. The Loch Ness Monster stuck its head out of Logan's lake. Two Loch Ness Monsters. There was laughter in her mind and an image of their full forms appeared in her head even though her eyes were wide open.

"You're dragons. Big dragons."

Water dragons.

The two little dragons popped up between the adults. A family. She was looking at a family of dragons—if she wasn't asleep or out-of-her-head crazy.

We've watched you, weighed your choices, and we're prepared to give our report on your actions.

And to make our recommendation. This voice was feminine.

Without another word, the heads bobbed out of sight—the two adults first, followed by the children. The lake went completely still.

What were they talking about? What recommendation? What report? The stone became inferno hot, but it didn't burn her hand, and instead of dropping it, Shona hung on to it tighter.

Things were happening faster than she could absorb and she wasn't sure if she should curse the day she found the dracontias or celebrate it. One thing was for certain, though: she'd better get used to strange things. As long as she had the stone—and was involved with Logan—they'd keep happening.

20
CHAPTER

Farran hurried along the sidewalk, threading her way through the humans headed for their jobs. She was in trouble and she had nowhere to turn. It hadn't been a lie when she'd told the Gineal troubleshooter that she wouldn't be killed, but they would hurt her—betrayal deserved punishment. The fact that these men were her brothers and father wouldn't matter a whit to them.

She'd known the risk she was taking, but Shona was the first true friend she'd ever had and Farran couldn't stand by and allow any harm to come to her. Once her brothers had been given the task of taking the dracontias, she'd started following Shona, making certain the Gineal was watching out for her the way he should.

It was a good thing she'd done that, too. They'd stood on the sidewalk kissing as if there were no threat, as if Shona weren't being hunted by the cold-hearted bastards Farran called family. What choice was there except to leave her hiding place and warn them?

Farran paused at the light, looked over her shoulder, and chanced darting across traffic. Horns blared, but she ignored them and continued moving.

If it had only been Jal and Lathan last night, she wouldn't be worried. Jal would have been too lost in his bloodlust to notice her presence, and if Lathan hadn't been told specifically to scan for her, he wouldn't bother. He lacked initiative.

But Roderick had been with them, guiding the attack, and Farran had no doubt that even blocks away, he'd been examining the area with every talent he possessed. She also had no doubt that he'd known she was there.

By now, her father had given orders for her to be brought to command central and taught what happens to those who dared defy The Hammer. Daughter or not, dragon mage or not, she'd pay.

She swerved around a couple of slow-moving people. Her only hope of evading capture was to keep moving. It was a long shot. The Tàireil didn't have use of their magic between sunup and sundown, but they did still have their heightened senses and all her brothers had strong tracking skills. She also shared a blood bond with them, making it easier for them to find her.

If only she'd managed to acquire the dracontias on her own.

When her father had discovered the Gineal dragon mage was a dormant and that her own people were unaware of what she had, he'd assigned Farran to get the stone by subterfuge. And—miraculously—he'd been willing to give her adequate time to accomplish her task. She'd wondered why for a while, not daring to ask the question, but she reached the conclusion that he'd been worried the Gineal would sense one of her brothers on the hunt and he wanted to get in and out without anyone being aware they'd ever been in this world. With Farran's weak magic, there was little concern that anyone would discern her presence from a distance.

Somehow, though, the Gineal had found out about Shona anyway. Farran crossed against the light again, not able to stand still for even the few minutes it would take to get the walk signal. It was because of Jal, she was positive of that.

She'd caught her youngest brother stalking Shona and the Gineal must have picked up his excitement.

He'd been waiting for Farran to fail, anticipating it, so that he could grab the stone. It was whatever else he might do to Shona that made Farran feel ice-cold.

But Shona had the troubleshooter now, and despite last night's lapse, Farran had to trust him to protect her friend. There was nothing else she could do now. Nothing.

Farran neared another corner and stopped short when she saw a man turn to confront her. Lathan.

Before she could pivot, Jal and Derril walked up on each side of her and took an arm. "We've been searching for you, sister mine," Jal said, and he smiled.

Logan woke slowly. From the amount of light coming in the room, it had to be close to noon, later than he'd meant to sleep, but Kel had said he needed lots of rest and Logan did feel better. Normal.

No more seizures after using magic. He had a hard time believing that, but his brother should know. Kel could have been a healer if the Gineal hadn't needed troubleshooters more, and since the fits had begun because of Kel's spell-casting, Kel should know whether or not he'd successfully reversed it.

A short puff of air against his shoulder stopped Logan's thoughts and he turned his head.

Shona.

Tension he'd been unaware of disappeared. He'd offered her any bedroom in the house if she didn't want to sleep with him, but she'd shared his bed. That had to be a good sign. After yesterday, he wasn't sure which direction she'd go.

He propped himself up on his elbow and gazed down at her. Damn, she was beautiful. The blankets were tangled around her gorgeous long legs, and because she slept in panties and an abbreviated T-shirt, he had a great view. He took a minute to appreciate the curve of her hips, her waist with her outie belly button—he grinned—and moved to her breasts. It took Logan a while before he noticed the dracontias was outside her shirt.

The sight drove the pleasant, low-key arousal out of him faster than a plunge into the Arctic Ocean.

Her face was relaxed, her full lips slightly parted. She trusted him and not only with her body. In a way, sex was easier than sleeping beside someone. Sex was all about pleasure, about coming, but sleeping next to a woman was about closeness. He'd never spent a full night in anyone's bed, had never invited anyone inside his house, or into his bedroom— until Shona.

Reaching out, he carefully picked up the chain and lifted the stone. The council wanted him to betray her trust and take this from her. He could do it now, just lift the necklace over her head, do a spell to erase her memories of it and of the fight she'd witnessed last night, and send it to the ceannards.

Logan didn't move. He couldn't. His chest was tight, his throat constricted, and simply breathing was hard.

The dracontias glinted. Protecting himself against the vibration, he let his hand slip down until the crystal rested in his palm. For a gem that was only about the size of a large ripe olive, it had caused as much trouble as the Hope Diamond.

He knew what he should do, what he'd been ordered to do, but something inside him balked at the idea. This stone belonged to Shona, but it went beyond that. Taking the dracontias from her while she slept beside him was such an enormous breach of faith, that even without her memories of the stone, she'd carry a vague sense of distrust about him. What they shared would disintegrate bit by bit until it ended with bitterness. His hand fisted around the gem and Logan forced himself to unclench his fingers.

Maybe it wouldn't even get that far. Did he really believe the council would let him have a relationship with any dormant for long before they reined him in? Logan's stomach knotted up tightly enough to make him feel sick. He couldn't lose Shona.

After carefully lowering the stone back to her chest, he ran his fingers over her cheek, stroking her lightly. There was nobody else like her and there never would be. How could he do the one thing that would cost him this woman?

What was the alternative? Defy the council? He'd been nineteen when he'd given his vow to obey their orders and he'd never rebelled, not even when he'd disagreed with them. The fact that they'd always been right in the past made it doubly hard to do it now.

He was standing at a crossroads—that wasn't fanciful, it was truth. Whatever he decided would affect the rest of his life. Shona or the council? The lady or the tiger?

It was tempting to wait, to let the moment slip past until it was too late. That would save him having to choose, but it was a copout and Logan wasn't that big a coward. Did he risk the entire Gineal people because of a woman? His gut clenched again.

But was her knowledge, her possession of the stone, a threat to the Gineal in any way?

The ceannards didn't know Shona, had never spoken with her or spent time with her. She was just a dormant to them and the policy across the board was that dormants were not told about the Gineal. He understood their concerns about her parents, but Shona could keep quiet about her powers, and if she was living with him, their worries about proximity wouldn't be an issue either.

Logan's hand went still. Living with him?

He paused to let the initial stab of panic subside and then considered the idea. It went without saying that he'd enjoy making love with her, so Logan didn't spend a great deal of time on that aspect. Instead, he focused on what it would be like to live his life side by side with this woman—waking up beside her every morning, arguing with her about putting his dirty clothes in the hamper, cooking with her, cleaning up afterward, making sure her car was serviced and running the way it should. And Shona would worry about him. When he came back from an assignment, she'd be here waiting.

It felt right and what scared him was that the idea *wasn't* frightening. Logan returned his hand to his side. What he wanted was easy, but his desires, his needs weren't as important as his people.

Shona shifted and Logan held his breath, but she didn't wake.

Time to make the decision, he couldn't dawdle any longer. The bottom line was, did he believe that Shona would endanger the Gineal either on purpose or inadvertently?

He gave himself a minute to think about it, to let his emotions ease enough to let him look at it logically, rationally. And the answer was no. She already understood the reason for secrecy and she wasn't someone who chatted indiscriminantly. She could be relied upon to keep her silence and the council was flat-out wrong in this case. If Shona decided on her own that she didn't want the stone that would be one thing, but he wasn't taking it from her, the council be damned.

Logan expected anxiety to rear up, but he felt peaceful, and in his mind that meant he'd made the correct decision. The ceannards wouldn't agree, of course, but he'd defend his choice right up until they yanked him out of Seattle and demoted him.

He turned his attention back to Shona. The contentment deepened, wrapping around him like a cocoon, and Logan had to touch her. He ran the backs of his fingers over the exposed skin of her stomach, enjoying her warmth, her softness before tracing a circle around her navel.

"What time is it?" she asked sleepily.

"Noonish. What time did you finally come to bed?"

"I think it was five."

"I'm sorry I woke you."

"You didn't, but what is your fetish with my belly button?" Shona put her hand over his, stopping him from caressing her.

"It's sexy—just like the rest of you."

"You're a pervert."

Damn, she was teasing him and he loved the hell out of it. "Who pulled who into the restroom?"

Her face went red. "You're not going to forget that, are you?"

He grinned and kissed the tip of her nose. "Not a chance, honey, not a chance."

Still blushing, she smiled back at him, and as he gazed into her eyes, the entire universe froze. For a moment, he couldn't breathe, then the world started rotating again. Well, hell. He should have figured it out earlier.

Yeah, he thought. Yeah. "Put some pants on; I want to show you something."

"Don't you mean take my panties off, you want to show me something?" Her cheeks were scarlet, but that didn't stop her from cupping him.

"Who's the perv?" It almost pained him to lift her hand, but he really did want to show her something. "Come on, up and at 'em, hot stuff."

Of course, it wasn't as simple as Shona dragging on a pair of pants. She needed to use the bathroom, brush her teeth, comb her hair, and she was talking about showering when he finally took her hand and tugged her down the hall.

They reached the kitchen. "Breakfast?" She sounded hopeful.

Logan shook his head. "At this time of day, it's called lunch, but no, it's not food related." He put his hand on the knob of the basement door and popped the lock.

"Wow," Shona said when they reached the bottom of the stairs, "your basement is nicer than some people's entire homes." She stopped and pointed. "What's behind that door?"

"The game room. I didn't bring you down here for another tour—if you want, you can explore later. There are two big pieces of my life in this house. I showed you my cars, now I want to show you the other."

She followed him willingly to the door to his magic room. It didn't look like much, he knew that. Unlike the rest of the house, the builder hadn't done anything with this space, leaving it unfinished. He, Kel, and their dad had worked to put up the drywall and Logan had spent weeks painting, putting bookcases together, and setting up everything the way he wanted it. Shona looked up at him and he saw she didn't understand.

"On the shelves are my books—some are for reference and others have incantations—a good library is important to a troubleshooter. Even ones like me who should study more." He walked over to a wooden armoire and opened both doors. "I keep my supplies in here. Some rituals call for candles, crystals, sand, or earth and I like to make sure I have everything on hand."

Shona peered closer. "You must have every shade of candle they make."

"Different rites need different colors."

"Color has power?"

"Yeah. It depends on the spell to a great degree, but generally green is the choice for healing, blue for peace, and I'd grab brown if I needed extra earth energy."

Logan pulled out the drawers, showing her his essential oils and the flower essences he had. His explanation ran a little long, and probably got into more detail than she needed, but Shona didn't look bored.

"You don't have eye of newt and bat wings hidden somewhere?"

He shook his head. "I can't think of a single rite that calls for either item, but if we—the Gineal—did need it, we'd probably find something else other than the actual body part to represent that energy. Pretty much everything involved in spellcasting is to help the one doing the incantation to focus."

Shona walked around as he put the drawers back in place

and closed up the cabinet again. She sounded delighted when she said, "You have a crystal ball!"

"It's a scrying crystal." Okay, so it was a crystal ball; he didn't want Shona equating what he did with any carnival psychic who was more con man than seer. Logan reached up, took it off the top shelf, and brought it over to his table.

"Can I touch?"

With a smile, he nodded, pleased that she'd asked. A lot of gems held on to vibrations and were difficult to clear, but this wasn't just any stone and it was okay for others to handle it. Like Shona was doing now. She had her right hand curved around the side as she peered down into it.

"Do you predict the future?"

"No, I'm not precognitive. I could look into it and see the present."

"What good is that?"

"Sometimes not much," Logan admitted, "but when Kel went missing, all I needed to know was where he was right at that moment."

She raised her gaze. "You didn't find him, did you?"

Logan shook his head. "I almost had something, but instead I burned out my scrying talent." He tucked his hands into the front pockets of his jeans. Its absence gave him some insight into what Shona was going through without her art. It wasn't exactly the same, of course—his skill had never been his life's passion—but it had been important to him. "That crystal used to sit in the center of my table, but it became a symbol of what I'd lost. I had to put it somewhere else, so that I wouldn't see it all the time."

She was quiet for a moment, then said, "Maybe it will come back once it's had time to regenerate."

"Maybe." But maybe not. After the first five weeks or so, he'd stopped attempting to scry. The temptation to try again right this moment was there, but he wasn't ready. If he couldn't use the talent now, he'd have to accept it was gone for good and that would hurt too damn much.

Shona bent over the crystal again and put her other hand around it, lifting it from its stand and cradling it. "I can't see anything," she said sadly.

"You don't have your power, but even if you did, it might not lend itself to scrying. It depends on your talents."

Carefully, she put the crystal back in its base. "Dragons have the gift of prophecy," she said and went over to examine his shelves.

He watched her pull random books and flip through them, but everything was written in Cànan, so she wouldn't be able to read them. *Dragons have the gift of prophecy.* He didn't know if they did or not, but Shona had sounded absolutely certain. What had happened last night after he went down for the count?

"Logan?" she called, turning from the bookcase.

"What, hon?" He walked over to where she stood.

"Why did you bring me down here?"

Smoothing her hair off her cheek, he said, "Because you're important to me and I want to share everything that's significant in my life with you."

He opened his mouth to say more, but chickened out and shut it again. Later. He had time.

Shona hummed under her breath as she worked alongside Logan in the kitchen. Making sandwiches wasn't exactly cooking, but there was something homey about standing close and putting together subs.

She should tell him about the dragons she saw and heard last night. He'd want her to keep him informed. Then there were the questions that she had about the Gineal. He'd only touched on a fraction of what there was to know, but she didn't ask. Not now. Now was a time-out, an oasis to just enjoy being with Logan.

"Want to pass the salami, please?"

Wordlessly, she handed it over.

His stomach growled loudly. "Sorry, I'm starved."

"You can't blame me. You were the one who joined me in the shower."

"Was I complaining?" Logan brushed a fast kiss over her lips and went back to assembling his sandwich.

"It sounded like it."

"Nah, just explaining."

Taking a couple of slices of cheese, she placed them on top of the meat. She was hungry, too, but the delay had been worth it. Not so much the playtime in the shower, or the lovemaking when they got out—although those had been great—it was the visit to his basement that left her with a need to grin. He'd said she was important and that he wanted to share everything that meant something to him. Just remembering that made her warm inside.

"So what's on the agenda today?" Shona put the top piece of bread on her sandwich and took the knife to cut it in half.

"I want to talk to your friend, Farran. She knows a lot more about what the darksiders are up to than she had a chance to tell us last night."

"Yeah and there are a few questions I have for her, too." The hurt was still there. Logan had been able to explain his actions, to reassure her that what they had wasn't a lie, but Farran had run off.

"You're not going," Logan said.

"Of course I am. She'll probably tell me more than she'd tell you anyway."

"Maybe so, but you're staying here. There's magical protection around the house—no one can enter it, the garages, or the back porch without my permission—and as long as you don't step outside the boundaries, you'll be completely safe. Aside from you, my family are the only ones who can come and go as they please, which means the sole risk you face is my sisters showing up and asking a whole bunch of nosy questions." He grinned. "Just start asking nosy questions of your own—they'll back off."

Shona gulped. Had she been making love with Logan with the risk of his family arriving in the middle of it? "Do they often show up out of the blue like that? Without any warning?"

He sobered. "It's okay, no one is going to pop in our bedroom unless it's a situation like last night, when you specifically summoned Kel."

"What about into the living room, where they can wait for us to emerge from the bedroom?" That would be embarrassing, more than embarrassing, mortifying. What would his parents think? And his youngest sister was still in high school; that wasn't exactly setting a good example.

Logan put his arm around her shoulders and hugged her. "The odds of that happening are small."

But not nonexistent. He picked up the plates and took them to the table. Shona trailed along behind him. "Isn't there something you can do, like the magical equivalent of putting a sock on the doorknob."

His lips twitched, but Logan managed to suppress the smile. Mostly. "I could take access to the house away from them." He pulled out a chair for her and held it until she was seated.

"You'd do that for me?"

He took the seat beside her. "I would. I want you to be comfortable here."

Logan picked up his sandwich and started eating, but Shona couldn't get past the fact that he was willing to bar his family for her. For her! She knew how close he was to them, how much they meant to him. "You don't have to do that," she said.

"Have to do what?"

"Lock out your family. I'll be okay."

That got her that crooked grin of his. "Thanks."

They were nearly finished with lunch before Logan started asking her questions about Farran—where she worked, where she lived, what she liked to do. After Shona answered everything, she said, "I wish I was going with you."

"I know." He stood, collected their plates, and brought them over to the dishwasher. Shona grabbed their glasses. "I don't plan to be gone long. I'm going to use the transit to pick up the Jeep, then drive over to her apartment. With a little luck, she'll be there, we'll talk, and I'll come straight home."

Shona rinsed out the cups and handed them to Logan. "Then what happens?"

"It depends on what she tells me, and no, I'm not being evasive." He shut the dishwasher. "If I can get all the darksiders locked down before the sun sets, I'm going to do it."

She didn't like that answer, but she supposed she better get used to this since it was his job. "Why couldn't you have a nice, normal career like a stockbroker?"

"Too boring." Logan moved into an open space between the kitchen and the room they'd watched movies in and patted his back pocket, then his front. With a flick of his fingers, a transit appeared. "Come here and give me a kiss."

"You're going now?" Shona put her arms around his waist.

"Sooner the better." With a hand on her nape, Logan leaned over and kissed her. Slow. Long. Deep. She was half-dazed with arousal by the time he lifted his head. Putting her away from him, he went to the transit. "Shona?" She blinked, trying to clear her thoughts. "Just so you know. I love you."

And he disappeared, the gate closing behind him.

21

CHAPTER

Shona couldn't settle anywhere or focus on anything for long and it was all Logan's fault. How could he tell her he loved her and then run off? He wasn't usually a coward—not that she was in a position to judge him on that score when she hadn't found the courage to say those three words at all—but still.

She started to head out on the patio, remembered seeing the dragons, and opted for the solarium instead. For all his seeming openness, Shona had learned that Logan was reserved and he didn't share himself easily. Looking back to when they met, she could see that his stories about himself and his family were . . . not impersonal, that wasn't the word she wanted . . . superficial, maybe. All surface, no depth.

That had changed over time, though, and Logan had allowed her inside his walls. Shona was willing to bet that most people never noticed how adept he was at keeping them at a distance—she hadn't seen it herself until he'd stopped holding her away. Had he picked up the habit because he could only let someone without magic so close and no closer?

Choosing a chair with an ottoman, she sat and swung her feet up. Because of his reserve, she knew that Logan hadn't said *I love you* until he'd been completely certain and ready for the next step in their relationship—she could take that to the bank.

Shona grabbed her cell out of the phone wallet at her waist and she pressed the preset she had for him. If he could say *I love you* and run, she could say it over the phone. But before the call went through, she stopped it. What if he was in the middle of something dangerous?

She slipped the phone back in the case at her waist. It would be better to tell him face-to-face anyway—when he couldn't bug out on her. That should make him uneasy. Shona's lips curved.

Unable to tolerate sitting still, she wandered into the bedroom. The dragon mage book Logan had given her was on the table where she'd left it. Rereading it hadn't produced any new information, but that didn't matter. What was there was so incredible she'd needed that second run-through to convince herself it wasn't all some fantasy.

The book was open to the spell that would meld her energy to the stone and Shona ran her fingers over the page. It called to her on a level that she hadn't realized existed and she felt as if she stood on the edge of some new world. All she needed to do was take that last step.

Did it matter if she recited the words? It wasn't as if she could do her art anyway and this would end her limbo. She'd have an identity—she'd be Shona Blackwood, dragon mage. But until she did merge with the dracontias there was always the chance that she might give up the gemstone and reclaim her creativity.

Shona pulled the chain out from beneath her top and stared at it. Why her? Why not someone else, someone who'd been born to the world of magic? Why hadn't Farran found it first?

Unable to resist, Shona rubbed her thumb over the stone

and read the first line of the incantation before she realized what she was doing. Pivoting sharply, she practically ran from that damn book. If she did the spell—and that was a great big if—she wasn't going to be drawn into it. She would make the decision with her eyes wide open.

She wandered aimlessly through the house. Logan had been gone for hours—was he having trouble tracking down Farran? He should have brought her along with him. She could have helped, and with him there to protect her, how risky could it be?

A memory of last night and the way they'd ganged up on him three against one lodged itself in her head. With it came the echo of Logan telling her he'd die for her. Shona swallowed hard. No, he'd been right, she should stay inside the house; that improved the chances of *Logan* remaining safe.

Shona made a circle around the center islands in the kitchen, but she'd already wiped down both of them on a previous trip through the house and there was nothing left to clean. She stopped when she saw the basement door. Maybe she should put Logan's scrying crystal back in his workroom. She'd brought it upstairs earlier because she'd wanted to try to use it again and had left it on the kitchen table.

She had her hand on the doorknob and the other wrapped around the crystal ball when her phone rang. Logan! Shona grabbed it from her waist but the screen said *unknown caller.* "Hello?" she said cautiously.

"Hello, Miss Blackwood."

The voice was formal, older, and Shona didn't recognize it. "Who is this?"

"How deeply do you care for your friends?"

Her instincts went on alert. "It depends on the friend," she said cautiously, unwilling to give this man an opening.

"Ah, I see. What are you willing to do to save Farran from being harmed?"

She knew who she had on the line then. She was talking to Farran's father and the man was even more reprehensible than she'd expected. "You won't kill her, you can't. You need her."

"I never said we'd kill her." He was plainly amused. "We can harm her, and quite severely, without killing her."

Shona nearly dropped the crystal ball and she put it on the counter as she fought for calm. She wouldn't let him feed off her emotions. "What kind of monster are you?" she inquired, using the same tone she'd use to ask what he wanted on his pizza. "She's your daughter."

"She's a means to an end."

The man had to be a sociopath, no normal person talked this way. Her next breath was jagged, but she put her hand over the phone to block the sound. Shona thought of Farran and the way she'd pale and become nervous whenever her father called. The question of whether or not Farran had been abused was answered now. "What do you want?"

"You're well aware of what I want. We'll meet tonight, say at 8:40, and come alone. Your Gineal friend is not welcome."

"Where?" she asked. She was trembling when she pulled a pen out of the cup next to the kitchen phone and dragged the pad of paper closer.

The address he gave her sounded like a residence, but she didn't have the opportunity to ask any more questions before he disconnected. Shona looked at the clock on her phone. She had just under an hour until the meeting, but it would take her at least half an hour to drive there—if she didn't get lost.

She needed to call Logan. With shaking hands, she pushed his preset. "Come alone. Yeah, right."

Logan's voice mail picked up. She left a quick message and paced. What did she need to do first? Think.

Directions. She needed directions.

Ripping the sheet of paper with the address off the pad of paper, she ran down the hall to the office and booted up the computer. What else did she need to do after she printed out directions? Her brain was muddled and she couldn't think. Logan would tell her what to do. Shona pressed his number another time, but it still rolled to voice mail. Damn it, damn it, damn it. Where the hell was he?

It only took an instant to pull up the browser and go to one of the map sites. As soon as she had the driving route printed, Shona studied it. It looked pretty straightforward.

With her phone in one hand and the papers with her directions and the address in the other, Shona rushed into the kitchen and stopped. What did she do now? She looked around, but nothing occurred to her. Something. She needed to do something.

Clothing! Shona had to look down to remember what she was wearing—shorts and a spaghetti-strap tank top with flip flops. Great for hanging out at home, not so great for a meeting with a monster.

She loped across the house to the bedroom. After she changed into black jeans and a black T-shirt with tennis shoes, Shona went into the bathroom and braided her hair. Now it wouldn't fall into her face and obstruct her vision.

Another call to Logan and another roll to voice mail.

What was he doing? Logan was never unreachable! He always had his phone on, he said he had to because of his job.

A thought occurred to her. When was the last time he'd recharged it? Shona groaned softly. Not last night or the night before—he'd had seizures.

It was probably dead and she'd bet he was so used to it always being ready to go that it had never dawned on him that it wasn't now. She tried to recall if he'd checked the phone before clipping it at his waist. No, she didn't think so. They'd been touching and teasing each other, swapping kisses and caresses as they'd gotten dressed and he'd been distracted. She'd made sure of that.

Shona left the bathroom and perched on the edge of a chair near the table and gave Logan another try, but she wasn't surprised to get voice mail again.

The dracontias! She'd summoned Logan's brother by holding the stone, maybe she could communicate with Logan the same way. *Logan, I need you. Come home.*

Now all she had to do was wait.

After a minute, she tried again. And again. After five minutes, she had to concede; Logan wasn't receiving her. She tried Kel because she'd connected to him last night, and if he couldn't reach Logan, Kel would probably help her. She alternated psychic pleas with the phone, but she was still only getting Logan's voice mail.

The telepathy didn't work with Kel either, and while it was disappointing, it had been a long shot. Last night had been a fluke and she didn't know how she'd done it.

Okay then, she was on her own and needed to make some decisions. The first was whether or not she was really going to attempt to help Farran, but that was easy to answer. Shona couldn't turn her back on her friend.

Taking a deep breath to clear her head, she moved on to the next problem—Farran's father wasn't making a hostage exchange. It wasn't as if Shona had struck a deal—she handed over the stone and he'd turn Farran loose—the other woman was needed to rule in the Tàireil world. And even if Farran's father didn't harm her this time, what about when they returned to their home? The dragon mage might be stronger, but Farran had been abused her entire life—she'd be too afraid to use that power.

What were the odds she or Farran would make it out of this alive? Logan had said they'd murder her to get the dracontias, but it was the only leverage Shona had. Once she turned it over, there was no reason not to kill her anyway. It didn't matter that they'd have Farran do the spell to meld with the stone immediately; Shona was still a loose end. A thorough man would eliminate any potential threats, and from everything Farran had told Shona about her father, he was very meticulous.

Shona checked the clock; she'd have to leave in a few

minutes, and before then, she needed a plan—of some sort. She was in trouble—she knew nothing about fighting or about battle strategy. Yeah, she'd beaten the guy who'd broken into the shop, but she'd been reacting to what he did. She couldn't simply show up tonight with the idea of winging it.

The other problem was her lack of familiarity with the location. She'd looked at a satellite image of the area on the map site, but it couldn't provide the kind of detail she needed. All she knew was that it was a house on a large parcel of land with a lot of trees.

Maybe she could use the copse as some kind of cover, but what if the property was fenced in? She'd be forced to go up the driveway and they could just pick her off. Moaning softly, Shona reached for the dracontias. Its pulsing soothed her, helped her calm down.

What would happen if she did the spell to meld with the stone?

There was immediate resistance to the thought, but Shona waited until it subsided. She'd lose her art and that was her spark, her passion, but was that worse than losing her life?

The idea had cons. There was no guarantee that doing the incantation would keep her alive. Her magic, after all, was dormant and she didn't have the spell to change that even if she wanted to. And if she did merge with the stone, that meant Farran became expendable. Would her father murder her? Shona didn't know, but on the phone he'd sounded cold enough to do it.

Only one pro came to mind—if Shona did it, there was no point in killing her because the dracontias would disappear on her death. At least with her alive, they'd still have a chance at the stone, right?

Or would that simply encourage Farran's father to drag Shona back to the Tàireil world and use her as the figurehead he needed to rule? Oh, God. Was there any good choice she could make?

With her free hand, she rubbed her forehead. She didn't have much more time left to think before she had to drive—

Drive. Her car was at home. That meant she had to take one of Logan's muscle cars. What were the odds that any of them had an automatic transmission? He'd talked about that kind of stuff when he'd toured her through the garage, but she hadn't been paying attention. Why the hell hadn't she listened?

There went her extra time. She'd have to check all three cars, and if none of them were automatics, she was in trouble—the last time she'd used a stick was in driver's ed more than ten years ago.

Do the spell or not do it? She had to decide now.

Her instincts said do it.

Before she could second guess herself, she grabbed the book. At least she wouldn't be a sitting duck this way. Careful to say each word, Shona read the spell aloud. Nothing happened when she reached the end. It felt incomplete, like there should be something more. Then she remembered last night when Kel had done that reverse incantation. "And so it is," she added.

A whoosh went through her that took her breath. As soon as she recovered, Shona grabbed her directions, the address, and her phone and ran for the garage.

She dialed Logan as she checked the cars. Shona nearly zoomed by before it registered: The Mustang didn't have a clutch!

Her elation was cut short. Voice mail, damn it.

She left a detailed message this time and gave him the address she had. He might not get it early enough to help her, but who else did she call? The police? Like they'd have a chance against men who threw fire.

Putting her phone away, she got into the vehicle and pressed the garage door opener. The keys were in the ignition and it started right up—she didn't even need to adjust the seat. Backing out cautiously, Shona made sure she closed the door, before she turned the car around, and headed down the driveway.

Go the speed limit. Shona eased off of the accelerator. She couldn't risk the police pulling her over for a traffic violation, not when she couldn't hide her panic.

And she was scared. Farran's father was going to be outraged when he discovered Shona had done that spell. Maybe she should have thought about this some more. Sure, she was vulnerable without it, but how much better off was she with it in place?

Maybe she should turn around. What could she do anyway? It wasn't like she had any training—not in magic and not in fighting techniques.

But she couldn't. Torture was an ugly thing, and if Shona chickened out, she'd be as responsible for what happened to Farran as the man who hurt her. Tears started to fill her eyes, but she blinked until they went away. She couldn't drive with her vision impaired and she didn't have time to pull over.

Shona took her phone out again. She didn't like to use it while she was driving, but this was an emergency. Voice mail again. "Logan, in case something happens, I love you, too. Just so *you* know."

Logan was frustrated. He'd spent hours searching for the darksider, but Farran had apparently gone to ground, damn it. Staking out her apartment complex was a long shot and one he wasn't going to pursue indefinitely, not when he wanted to be home with Shona before the sun went down.

He understood Farran's disappearance last night—in her place, he wouldn't have hung around either—but her absence today worried him. She'd either thought better of helping Shona and was trying to avoid Logan or she'd been made last night.

Farran had said they wouldn't kill her because she was the dragon mage, but that didn't mean they wouldn't hurt her. Traitors were dealt with harshly in the Tàireil world.

Of course, the consequences were steep among the Gineal, too. Logan didn't think he had much time left before the council called him in and asked why he hadn't brought them the dracontias, and once they discovered how much Shona knew, he'd probably find out firsthand how punitive they could be.

Thinking of Shona drove thoughts of the council away and made him smile. Logan couldn't help but wonder what kind of reception he'd get when he saw her again. He was pretty sure she felt the same way he did, but telling her and then crossing the transit had been a craven thing to do. That hadn't been his plan. He'd meant to say it quietly before they kissed, or at least while she was in his arms, but he'd chickened out. He shrugged—it would be easier next time and he *had* said it.

Logan tried to stretch his legs in the confines of the Jeep, but didn't have much luck. Maybe he'd go and knock on Farran's door one more time and then leave. That might—

The energy shift he felt was so strong, it sucked the breath right out of him. Logan froze and tried to discern what had just happened, but he didn't have a clue. Extending his senses, he scanned his house. The protective field was still in place. It was impossible to check behind it—that was the way the council had set it up—but the fact that it was still intact should mean everything was okay. He reached for the ignition and started the SUV anyway. His gut told him to get home to Shona now.

It was all he could do not to drive at NASCAR speeds, but Logan held it within ten miles of the speed limit. He cursed as he got stopped at a traffic light. "Come on, come on."

Why the hell did Farran have to live so far away? It was going to take him forever to reach his house. The light went green and Logan punched the accelerator.

Whatever he'd sensed probably had nothing to do with Shona. It was the energy shift itself that had him anxious. For all he knew, it meant the god-demons who were loose had popped in to Seattle for a visit or maybe that the thinned barrier between their dimension and this one had failed completely.

Neither thing would involve him or Shona. The council would send the roving troubleshooters after Horus or Set or any other god-demons that were at large—it was their job to handle the toughest assignments—and if the barrier had failed, well, there was nothing Logan could do about that either.

But no matter what he told himself, he was on edge for every minute of the half hour it took until he turned into his driveway and raced up to his home. Everything was quiet, but it was dark. His uneasiness climbed higher. Maybe Shona was in the solarium or the kitchen—both rooms were at the back of the house.

He was nearly a quarter of the way into the garage when he slammed on the brakes hard enough to jerk the SUV. The Mustang was missing.

He threw the Jeep into park, twisted the key, and ran through the garage to the door into the house, scanning as he went. Empty. Damn it, he'd told her to stay indoors, that his home was protected. He skidded to a halt in the kitchen. What the hell was his scrying crystal doing on the counter near the phone?

Phone. Logan yanked his cell off its clip, flipped it open, and cursed. Dead. He put his finger against the battery, gave it a charge and checked messages. There were a bunch.

His knees buckled when he heard Shona's voice and he had to sit down when he reached the message where she explained what she was doing and why, but it was the last voice mail that damn near killed him. She wanted him to know how she felt in case she didn't make it out alive. God.

He shook it off and looked at the clock; it wasn't 8:40 yet. It was no surprise they'd chosen sundown, but it gave him time to get to Shona.

His legs were weak when he stood, but Logan ignored that and opened the transit. It snapped shut almost immediately.

What the hell? He opened it again and the same thing happened.

Darksider spell. Damn it, they'd put up a barrier and made sure that he couldn't appear at Shona's side. He needed to know the boundaries of their force field.

Logan eyed his scrying crystal. He'd been blank since he'd tried to search for Kel, but he hadn't attempted to use it in months and it would be quicker if he could do it himself. If he had to get someone to scry for him, it would take a lot more time and he'd waste precious minutes on explanations.

He crossed to the stone, and closing his eyes, breathed deeply to center himself. To reach that place of calmness, he had to lock his fear for Shona away and it wasn't easy.

When he thought he had it, Logan opened his eyes and peered into the crystal. For an instant, nothing happened, but before he could give up, a murky scene began to form. He took another breath and tried to bring it into focus. The image remained blurry—not like it used to be—but it did sharpen enough that he could make out what was going on.

The darksiders hadn't found Shona yet. Somehow she'd managed to cloak herself and they were wandering around searching for her. "Good going, honey."

Five, no six, Tàireil. He didn't like those odds, but he'd fight an army if that's what it took to get Shona safely out of there. Logan pulled his vision back enough to look for the wall of energy they'd erected. When he had it, he opened another transit, one outside their shield, but as close to Shona as he could manage. This time it stayed open.

As soon as he crossed, he put a protection spell in place. He couldn't put one around Shona, though, not with the barrier keeping them separated. Taking a deep breath, he locked down the fear again. If he didn't maintain control, he'd be useless.

He went up to the force field, probed, and received a shock. Jerking back, Logan tried coming at it from another direction. No go. He only needed it down long enough to get through it, but the damn maze of energy that went into the wall frustrated him.

His third, fourth, and fifth tries to circumvent their field failed, too. Scowling, he mentally called for Kel.

His brother showed up almost immediately. "What's up?"

Not taking the time for words, Logan telepathically transmitted the situation. With a nod, Kel started working on the barrier. "Whoever put up this one," his brother said, "was damn set on keeping you out."

"I know, but it's coming down. Shona's in there."

"Relax, we'll reach her." Kel worked a little more, then shook his head. "You know who might get us past this barrier."

"No, I don't want her at risk."

"Don't think of Tris as our little sister, think of her as a fellow troubleshooter and a genius when it comes to energy puzzles."

If it was just the field, that would be one thing, but if he called Tris, she'd join the battle, and while he'd fought beside Kel before, he'd never done that with his sister. Logan wouldn't be able to watch out for her against the Tàireil, he couldn't, not when Shona needed him more. He and Kel could get through the barrier on their own, they had to.

The scream stopped his heart.

Time had just run out.

22

CHAPTER

Kel had to restrain him.

"Calm down, damn it. You think you're going to do her any good if you fry yourself trying to run through the barrier?"

Logan took a deep breath, found some control, and shook Kel off. They had to get past this field *now*. He put out the mental call for Tris. Kel was right—she was a troubleshooter and trained for battle—she could take care of herself.

She arrived faster than his brother had.

It was Kel who told Tris what the deal was; Logan was too agitated. Contain it, he told himself. Emotion in battle got people killed and he couldn't put Shona in more danger.

Tris magically probed the shield and let out a soft whistle.

"What?" Logan demanded.

"This is the most complex force field I've seen."

"Can you get us through?"

Tris nodded. "Of course."

While his sister worked on the barrier, Logan worked on compartmentalizing. He had to be ice-cold and clear-headed when they crossed. Kel was already watching, trying to measure how big a risk Logan would be to them. He squeezed the last of his emotions into a box and threw a padlock on it. When he looked back at his brother, Logan was in complete command.

"I have it," Tris said. "But I'm only going to be able to weaken one section of it for a couple of seconds."

"Which section?" Logan asked.

"From where I am over to Kel."

Logan nodded and moved between the two of them. He was just inches away from the barrier and ready to cross. "Let us know when."

Tris straightened. "Go!"

As soon as he was on the other side, Logan reached out mentally for Shona. Still alive. Not hurt that he could tell. With a bead on her location, he scanned for the Tàireil. They weren't too close. Without waiting any longer, he opened a transit and crossed to her. He didn't have to look over his shoulder; he knew Kel and Tris were right behind him.

Shona whirled, but as she recognized him, her expression changed. Logan held his finger to his lips, warning her to stay quiet, and she nodded. She took a couple steps forward, and then she was in his arms. He held her tightly, his face next to hers and that's when he realized what had happened—she'd done the spell to combine with the dragon stone. "Are you okay?" He felt her nod. "I heard you scream."

"Farran. That was Farran. I think they hurt her to try and draw me out, but I didn't know what to do. I'm an artist!"

Logan grinned, mostly in relief. "Not just an artist, you're the Gineal dragon mage."

"An untrained one without access to her power."

"Dragons use magic instinctively, remember?" Reluctantly, Logan put her from him, but he kept hold of her hand. "Since you came here to rescue your friend, I suppose you want us to finish that job?"

Shona nodded. "They might kill her."

Yeah, they probably would since Shona had merged with the stone, but Logan didn't say that. "Send your consciousness out of your body and give me an aerial view, okay? It'll be easier now because you've melded with the stone."

At first, Logan didn't think she was going to do it, but slowly it happened. She transmitted directly to him and he passed it on telepathically to Kel and Tris. This was a mansion sitting on an estate that made his place look about as luxurious as a tent pitched on a vacant lot. The angle wasn't perfect, but from what Shona showed him, the house was surrounded by a thick triangle of trees; there were two swimming pools, a network of paved walkways, and a tennis court; and four other structures in addition to the house.

The view cut off abruptly. "Sorry," Shona said. "I could try again."

"Not necessary." Logan turned to Kel and Tris. "I need to rescue a Tàireil from five other darksiders. You guys in?"

"Hell, yeah," Kel said. "Do you think we'd leave you outnumbered?"

"Tris?"

"Of course. I already alerted the ceannards that we're going into battle."

Logan barely suppressed a grimace, but Tris had done the right thing. The council did need to be aware of what was happening and where, because if anything went wrong, someone else was going to have to come in and fix it. "Shon, I'm going to open a transit so you can go home. As soon as we're done, I'll join you, okay?"

She nodded again. "I left your Mustang parked on the street about a block and a half from here."

"I'll find it." Logan did the spell to open the gate, but it snapped shut just like it had earlier. As a test, he tried opening one that would take them to the pool house and that worked. Damn it, the darksiders had disabled travel into and out of the area surrounded by their force field. He closed the gate.

"Looks like they made sure it wasn't going to be easy for Shona to escape," Kel said at his side.

"I know. We'll have to transport to the edge of their field, have Tris take it down again, and—"

"Too much time. They're monitoring for Shona and they'll zero in before we can get her on the other side and through a transit.

"She's cloaked."

"Not completely, she isn't," Kel said. "It's wavering in and out. If they find us by the wall, we'll be without any cover and have no tactical options. How long do you think our magic is going to hold out in that situation?"

Not long. It hadn't last night when Logan had fought without any cover except his protection spells. "Hell."

"I know, you want her out of here, so do I, but the risk is too great. She's safer with us."

"Yeah." But he didn't like it.

"I'll follow orders," Shona said. "You tell me what to do and I will without questioning you. I won't be a liability."

Logan squeezed her hand, but didn't have the heart to tell her that her presence alone was a liability. It couldn't be anything else because his number one priority wasn't beating the darksiders or rescuing Farran—it was defending Shona. Since she couldn't leave, he started a protection spell for her, but stopped short of closing it. She already had one around her that was stronger than anything he could create. The dracontias?

Tris looked over her shoulder at them and said, "The darksiders just disappeared. I think they cloaked."

Logan checked and was only able to locate two inside an outbuilding. He'd bet that Farran was one of them because from what he'd seen in the aerial view, it was the most defensible of the structures, and because it faced a clearing, there'd be no cover for them to sneak in and attack. The sun might have set, but it was still twilight, and even if they waited for full dark, the Tàireil would be scanning around the building constantly.

"How are we playing it?" Tris asked. "Neutralize the darksiders and then rescue, or rescue first?"

"Rescue," Logan said. "They'll use her as leverage against us, and if they're defending the building where they're holding her, we'll have all the Tàireil in one general location."

"Closest cover is about a hundred and fifty yards from the structure," Kel said.

He brought the overhead view back into his mind. "That small stand of trees?" Kel nodded and Logan was torn. It was the best cover and that kept Shona safer, but it was too far away from where Farran was being held. They'd have to defeat the four darksiders first and then go for the outbuilding, which still left Farran as leverage. "It's not a good position and not just because of the distance. It's low ground."

"There is no other cover close by unless we use the mansion itself, and with all the windows and doors it has, there are too many ways for the darksiders to get in and get behind us. It's not a workable position."

"Make a decision, boys," Tris drawled, "before the Tàireil arrive."

"The back of the outbuilding borders the front yard. There are a couple of big fountains up there and some enormous planters. We'll use them as cover and hit the structure from behind," Logan decided. It wasn't perfect, but Shona had her own strong protection around her and the three of them should be able to hold their own against the darksiders. He hoped.

Kel nodded, but they both knew it was Logan's decision. It was his mission, that meant he called the shots. And took the responsibility if he was wrong.

"Shon, they'll probably try to separate you from the group, but you stay next to me unless I tell you to move."

"Got it."

"They just opened a transit," Tris reported.

"Let's go," Logan said and opened his own transit. He brought Shona across with him and took a position behind the large fountain with a planter to its right. "Stay down," he told her.

Force field around the outbuilding, Tris sent. *It's more complicated than the one surrounding the estate by a long shot.*

Can you—

A rope of flame hit the fountain in front of him, cutting him off. The Tàireil were using the outbuildings and the side of the mansion as cover. Logan returned fire at the pair nearest him while Tris and Kel took on the other two.

He had the kid, Logan knew it, and maybe the one he'd pegged as the leader last night. This time the older one would keep the brat from going off half-cocked.

Fire scorched through, burning the flowers in the planter down to the dirt. Gritting his teeth, Logan took aim and sent a couple of bolts of lighting one on top of the other. He chipped a piece off the side of the mansion, but missed the Tàireil.

There wasn't time to get off another shot before the darksiders let loose with a barrage. He dropped to the ground, covering Shona with his body. He didn't give a damn how strong her shield was, Logan wasn't taking any chances with her.

It went on and on. His protection took hit after hit even with physical cover, and while he continued to fire back, he didn't get off even a fraction of the shots that the enemy was sending his way. When it finally stopped, his defenses were battered.

Logan reinforced them and edged off Shona. "You okay?"

"Yeah, nothing touched me."

Kel, Tris, you guys okay?

Battered, but okay, Tris said.

Kel? Logan prompted when his brother didn't check in.

Dazed, but otherwise fine. What the hell was that?

"They combined their magic," Shona said softly beside him. "It enabled them to increase the power of their shots and synchronize them so that it was hard to respond."

Logan stared at her for a split second, then realized he'd better start returning fire before—

A second bombardment was launched at them and Logan

moved on top of Shona again. The only way they could hope to match the firepower was if he, Kel, and Tris combined their magic, but it was difficult enough for him and Kel to do it and they were twins. They'd never tried it with Tris before at all and it was risky to make their first attempt while they were in the middle of a battle. All they needed was an instant when their shielding was lowered and boom—direct hit.

His protection weakened, and as he tried to reinforce it, a shot connected. Logan's body stiffened, then shuddered.

"Logan!"

He didn't answer Shona, he couldn't. And then he felt her in his mind. She was trying to heal him, and while it helped some, she didn't know enough to do much.

Another lull, but he couldn't take advantage of it this time. He was trying to recover.

We're in trouble over here, little brother. A few more continuous rounds like that one and both Tris and I will probably run out of the magic we need to hold a protective shield.

I'm not any better off. And with the force field in place around the estate, the odds of escaping were slim.

Logan crawled off of Shona. There wasn't any other choice now, he had to ask. He called forward a book written in English. As quickly as he could manage, he flipped to the incantation and handed it to Shona. His arms were still shaking. "Hon, I need you to do the spell to become Gineal. I know how much I'm asking, but if you don't, we probably won't make it out of here."

He'd sugarcoated it for Shona. Qualified it with *probably,* but there was no question about it. If she didn't come into her full dragon powers and use them in the fight, all four of them were going to die.

Shona clutched the book tightly, took a deep breath, and began the spell. Her chest felt heavy and her voice was thick as she said the words, but there was no other choice. None.

It wasn't as if she would have turned her back on the stone anyway. She'd even done the incantation to merge with it to ensure that no one took it from her—Shona knew that now—and her course had been inevitable since then. That didn't make this any easier for her.

The spell went on for pages, much longer than the one to meld with the dracontias. Her new night vision was a blessing. The book was handwritten in spidery cursive and difficult enough to read as it was.

She faltered when she picked up Kel's telepathic shout and Logan's answer to him—things were going badly—but Shona steadied herself and continued. The third round of nonstop firing started and she read faster. Finally, she reached the end, and with another deep breath, she said, "And so it is."

A dam burst inside her and disintegrated further with each passing second. It overwhelmed her, made her head swim, and Shona grew faint. She focused on slowly inhaling and exhaling until she fought back the sensation. Another took its place, filling all her cells with an incredible buzz. She'd expected to feel nothing except pain over the permanent loss of her glass work, but instead, Shona felt alive.

She sensed more strategy being communicated telepathically, and it brought her back to earth with a bang. She didn't have time to enjoy the froth, she had to fight beside the man she loved.

But how?

Instinctual, Logan had said, but apparently when it came to magic, her intuition wasn't very good. She had no clue what to do. Did she just move her arm as if she were throwing a ball and fire would come out instead? Or did she have to do more?

Before she could ask, Logan took a hit that sent him sailing backward. Oh, my God! Shona tried to crawl to him. *I've got him,* Kel sent as he scuttled over to where Logan was laying prone. *Stay out of the way and don't make yourself a target.*

How bad is he hurt?

I've got him.

The repetition told Shona it was bad. Something snapped. Mad as hell that they'd hurt Logan, she stood and roared her outrage. Fire shot out of her mouth, going farther and burning hotter than anything either side had thrown yet tonight.

It shocked her. She closed her mouth and the fire stopped.

"Get down," Tris ordered.

Shona let her knees go weak and dropped to the ground. She'd just shot freaking fire out of her mouth!

Nobody seemed all that impressed.

"There's a war going on," Logan told her. "I'll be impressed later."

"Logan! Are you okay?"

"Yeah." The next words came along their private wavelength, meant only for her, though she wasn't sure how she knew that. *Kel used a lot of energy to heal me. He's not going to be able to hold his own shields much longer. We need to end this now.*

I don't know what to do. It's not instinctive for me.

"Magic is about intent," he said, firing while he spoke. "You visualize the outcome as you channel the energy through yourself."

A Tàireil screamed and Logan grunted, looking satisfied.

"So I picture fire coming out of my hand and it does?"

"Do you feel the energy dancing around inside you?"

"Yes."

Logan's next shot fizzled and Shona looked at him, really looked and with more than her eyes. He was low on magic, too, she realized. Reaching out, she rested her hand on his back and visualized sending some of her power over to him. It seeped at first, but as the image grew steadier in her mind, the speed increased. The amazing thing was that it didn't matter how much she gave, the well seemed infinitely deep.

"Whoa! Thanks." Logan grinned, but it lacked his usual spark. "And you just used your magic, that's how you do it."

She hadn't done anything, that's what she wanted to tell

him, but Logan was busy shooting lightning at the darksiders again. Maybe she was thinking too much.

The planter on the left, the one Kel was using as cover, exploded, sending shards and dirt flying everywhere. He moved, trying to reach the fountain she and Logan were hiding behind. Shona drew her hand back, and closing her eyes, imagined fire spewing forth, protecting Logan's brother.

It didn't happen.

Why couldn't she do it? Instincts. She had instincts. Shona detected motion off to the side and looked. Farran? Had she gotten free? Now she had two people to protect—her friend and Kel. Maybe she should stand and roar again.

Shona got to her feet, but her legs were trembling. One of the shots from the Tàireil nearly hit her and she flinched. Okay, here goes nothing. She roared. Not one spark of fire.

"No!" Farran ran and dived at her.

It happened in slow motion, as if time itself had been stretched. Altered. Shona could see everything, but couldn't react quickly enough. The Tàireil fired. One shot caught Farran in the face, the other three on the torso. They spun her around, sent her flying. She hit the ground and didn't move.

Stifling a scream, Shona ran for Farran, and was pulled up short by Logan. "There's nothing you can do for her now. All you'll do is make yourself a target."

"But—"

"No buts. They were trying to kill you. If she hadn't put herself in front of you, who knows what might have happened. Do you want her sacrifice to be for nothing?"

"No."

"Then stay behind cover, damn it."

Shona nodded. She'd promised she'd listen and not endanger anyone, but it hurt to leave Farran laying like that.

"They're gearing up for another nonstop shooting spree," Shona told Logan quietly. He looked at her oddly. "I can feel them melding their energies."

"You were in my mind earlier, can you do that again?"

"Yes."

"I'm going to shoot at the Tàireil. Monitor how I use my magic, okay?"

She nodded and let herself flow into Logan once more. As he shot a few lightning bolts at the darksiders, something clicked. She got it. She got it!

But why waste time with fire and lightning? Those were puny weapons in battle. She slashed with magical talons at the auric fields of her enemy, slicing through their energy and ripping it away from them.

She didn't need cover, she realized. No weak Tàireil was going to penetrate her armor, only another dragon had the power to do that and her kind had long abandoned this dimension.

Bringing in a storm in less than a heartbeat, she crashed real lightning down on them and continued to claw at their energy. Logan tried to shield her with his body, but she moved in front of him. He's the one who needed protection. "I've got dragon armor—they can't breach it."

And she strolled toward the darksiders.

"We're in this together, honey. I don't care if you are the flipping dragon mage, I'm not letting you go into battle alone."

Shona felt warm inside at his words. Reaching out, she put a hand on his arm, wanting to touch him one last time— just in case—but something happened. Her dragon armor expanded, snapping shut around him.

"Holy— Let's go wrap this up," he said with a grin, "so we can tend to the wounded."

The one in the house left this dimension, she told Logan. That disappointed her. She'd wanted Farran's father. To make sure the others didn't get away, she blocked the use of a transit.

We'll take care of the minions, then.

She nodded. The three remaining Tàireil tried to combine the last of their magic, tried to create an incantation that would stop her. Didn't they know dragons were resistant to the spells of others?

"Where's the fourth one?" Logan asked.

She looked at him.

"There were four, Shon."

Shona keyed in on the energy of the men who'd been firing at them, traced it and their movements. She saw the trail of one, the oldest of the four, break off from the group before she'd started tearing into the auric fields of the Tàireil. She showed Logan this, and his path into the outbuilding where Farran's father had been. It ended at the transit.

"They bugged out together. Hell."

The darksiders tried to run and Shona called up an illusion, an army of earth dragons to block their way. The enemy stopped short.

As one, the three men turned to face her and let loose with all the power they had left. She thought of Farran, maybe dead where she'd fallen. She thought of Tris and Kel, both battered and their magic drained. She thought of Logan, how she could have lost him, might have lost him if Kel hadn't healed him.

No mercy.

She tore at their fields again, but now she had access to their life force energy and she ripped it away from them. Shona slashed her etheric dragon claws through their energies again and again until they were utterly shredded.

Until all three men were dead.

She dissipated the electrical storm and let the imaginary dragons fade away to nothingness. Only then did she look at Logan. He was watching her closely, maybe waiting for her to fall apart. "I should feel bad about killing them, shouldn't I?"

"I wouldn't, but you're not me and you've never really hurt anyone before."

"I don't. Feel bad, I mean."

"Maybe you're in shock."

"No. Well, maybe, but that's because I really did magic. About them being dead," Shona shrugged, "I just feel satisfaction. Is that wrong?"

Logan wrapped his arms around her and gathered her close. "This is how I see it. There really are monsters in this world—some are demons, or darksiders, or dark-force creatures or whatever. They think of nothing but their own selfish aims and don't care who they hurt to achieve them. Monsters deserve to die and no one should waste time mourning them."

"Or feeling guilty for being the one to administer justice."

"Exactly."

Shona considered that. He didn't think *she* was a monster for not feeling compassion or guilty or sorry for the men she'd killed. "No mercy," she said.

"Absolutely, no mercy," he told her, voice hard.

Their gazes stayed locked in silent communion and Shona's lips curved. Logan understood her—on all levels. "So what exactly does the Gineal dragon mage do, anyway? Slay demons?"

"Remember that part where I mentioned I don't do the kind of studying I should? Well, this would fall into that category." He actually had a light tint of red on his cheeks. "I don't know what the hell the dragon mage does. We haven't had one in something like two hundred and twenty years or so."

Talk of the dragon mage brought her back to reality in a flash. "Farran! We have to check on her." Shona didn't wait for a response, she hurried to where she'd seen her friend go down. There were tons of people here now, but they were Gineal—she could read their energy—and not a threat.

A woman stepped in front of her, blocking her way. Shona shifted to get around her, but the other woman moved, too. She brought her hand back, but Logan put his arms around her from behind and pinned her own to her sides.

"Whoa, tiger. This is the right-hand woman to the Gineal council." *Definitely not a good idea to take her out.*

Shona felt her cheeks burn. She'd been lost in her power. Maybe she would become a monster.

No, you won't. I'll help you learn where the line is and

how to control the adrenaline that comes with battle. That's all this is, you know, an adrenaline surge.

"Laoch solas, the council wants your presence at once. Yours as well, Dragon Mage."

"We'll transit over as soon as we check on Shona's friend." The woman didn't look as if she liked Logan's answer. "Come on, Jess, have a heart. The friend threw herself in front of Shona and took the hits meant for her. You're not cold enough to deny her a few minutes to find out how she's doing, are you?"

"Five minutes, laoch solas."

"We'll be there."

Logan released her and took her hand instead. They found Kel standing where Farran should be. "Where is she?" Shona asked. "Where's Farran?"

"I don't know. I was healing her—I'd nearly finished, too, the only thing I had left was her face—when Tris called me over. We've been ordered to report to the council chambers."

"About Farran," Shona prompted, not caring about his trip to the council.

"Yeah, so after I said fine, let me just finish this healing, I went back to do that and she was gone. I don't know where the hell she disappeared to or how she felt like moving again that quickly after being hurt as badly as she was."

"Could someone have taken her?"

"I doubt it. All the Gineal were in front of me and the Tàireil were either dead or gone."

"Logan?"

"Do your tracking again, you'll get your answer."

Shona did. There was no energy around Farran except for Kel's and then she saw Kel leave and Farran's energy began to form a trail until it disappeared at the corner of the house. "I think she might have opened a transit, but it's a different kind of gate than what the others used or what you use."

"Then she must be okay," Logan said. "Kel, was the damage you still needed to heal on Farran serious?"

"Like medical serious? No. I healed everything life-threatening and I'd already repaired all the nerve damage to her face. All that was left was closing the skin and making sure there wasn't any scarring."

"I hate to cut this short," Logan said, putting his arm around her, "but since Farran isn't here, we need to get to headquarters and the council."

"Let them wait," Kel said. "It's not that big a deal."

"Yeah, it is. I'm pretty much up to my neck in trouble. Letting them wait so they can really work up a good head of steam isn't in my best interest."

"Why are you in trouble?" Shona asked. Logan had done nothing wrong that she could see and they'd defeated the darksiders.

He turned her so that he could meet her eyes. "You weren't supposed to know anything about the Gineal or magic—that was a direct order." Logan squared his shoulders and Shona held her breath. "And they ordered me to take your stone. Shon, you were never supposed to become the dragon mage."

23
CHAPTER

Logan held Shona's hand as they waited to see the council. He'd decided it was unlikely they'd strip his powers. While his offense was serious, it shouldn't be enough to warrant extreme measures, not when the Gineal needed more troubleshooters as it was. Losing Seattle, though, and being demoted to guarding the library was a real possibility.

That wasn't his chief concern, however. He was worried about what they'd do to Shona. She was incredibly powerful, but the nine ceannards routinely combined their magic to work spells and they might be able to overcome her and take away the dracontias—and her memories.

He was having a hell of a time keeping his worries hidden from Shona. Something had happened when her protection had expanded to surround him tonight. Not only was it still in place and showing no signs of weakening, but one of the side effects was that they were able to read each other's thoughts and emotions with no effort. The Gineal were telepathic, but with their mind shields in place, they had to send thoughts. He and Shona didn't have to send anything—it was all right there. Kind of scary, but in a way, it was cool.

Jess came into the antechamber. "Laoch solas, the ceannards will see you now."

Logan couldn't stop the stab of concern. They were going to talk to him and Shona separately and he didn't want her to face them alone. Reluctantly, he released her and got to his feet, but Shona stood as well and reclaimed his hand.

What the hell, he couldn't get in any more trouble, right?

They walked toward the council chambers and Jess opened her mouth. Logan waited for her to insist Shona remain behind, but instead, she stepped aside.

All nine councilors were arrayed behind their V-shaped table when they entered and none of them looked even remotely happy. Logan took a deep breath and approached. "Ceannards," he said and inclined his head when he reached a respectful distance.

"We only asked for you, laoch solas," Nessia said, giving him a hard stare. "The girl must go."

"No," Shona said, voice flat.

"No? Who are you to defy the council?"

"Who are you to give me orders?"

Er, hon, she's the council leader.

I didn't vote for her.

Logan had to choke back a laugh. Neither Shona nor the council would appreciate his sense of humor right now, but she was just too cute. Vote for the ceannards? Yeah, sure.

"You're disrespectful," Nessia said. "I lead the council and the Gineal."

"You're disrespectful, too. I'm twenty-six, not a girl, and I'm the dragon mage."

The two women continued to stare each other down and Logan nearly sent Shona a message to watch what the adrenaline was pushing her to say, but he decided to wait.

It was Nessia who gave the tiniest inclination of her head and said, "Very well, you may stay."

"Thank you."

Nessia turned her gaze on him and Logan stiffened. "Well, laoch solas, not only have you disregarded the council's orders in nearly everything, you've saddled us with an impertinent dragon mage as well. What have you to say for yourself?"

"At least she's never boring."

"You think this is the time for levity?"

Logan tightened his hold on Shona. "No, Ceannard."

"You were told to keep the existence of the Gineal and of magic from her, yet you not only didn't erase her memories after fighting the Tàireil in her presence last night, you also apparently decided to tell her even more."

He fought the need to scowl. The council had involved a monitor with retrocognitive skills to review his actions. At least no one could see inside his home and know that— Oh, hell, the gallery bathroom. Logan felt his cheeks heat.

You mean they watched us in the restroom? Shona sounded appalled and he didn't blame her.

Probably, but relax, they couldn't have seen much given our positions and how little clothing was actually shifted. Logan hoped he'd hidden the fact that he was lying.

"But tonight, laoch solas, takes the prize. You gave her the spell necessary to meld with the dragon stone and she used it. You gave her the spell to end her dormancy and become Gineal and she used it. You—"

"Council Leader, there was no choice about Shona becoming Gineal. If we didn't have her powers fighting with us, we would have lost. The Tàireil were strong, they'd combined their magic, and were overwhelming the three of us."

"Yes, we are aware of that, but do you think that the events of this day would have transpired at all if you had taken the dracontias as we ordered?"

"Probably not."

"Definitely not," Nessia corrected him. "If you had brought the stone to us, there would have been no point in calling Ms. Blackwood and demanding her presence on the estate tonight. The Tàireil instead would have turned their attention to breaching the walls of the Gineal stronghold and she would have been safe. By disobeying your orders, you not only risked the life of the dragon mage, you also risked your own life and that of two other troubleshooters. What have you to say for yourself now?"

Logan swallowed hard. "I couldn't take the dracontias from Shona—that stone belongs to her and my stealing it or erasing her memories of it and of the magic she'd seen would be a violation of her trust."

"So you decided to violate our trust instead."

"The council made no effort to talk to Shona, to get to know her before opting to take the stone from her. The decision was unilateral and based solely on the fact that she was a dormant, not on who Shona is as an individual."

"Our decision was made because she isn't simply an ordinary dormant, generations removed from Gineal who willingly gave up their magic. Her parents had their powers and their memories of the Gineal stripped from them because of their actions and that makes her knowledge of us dangerous."

Shona gasped. "What do you mean, my parents had their magic stripped from them? Why did you do that?"

"I hadn't told her about her parents."

Why the hell not? Shona demanded.

There wasn't time, that's why. I only shared a small fraction about anything Gineal. He sensed her doubt. *I would have told you, Shon, and that's the truth.*

There was a second's space of time while she read his sincerity, and then she sent, *I'm sorry I doubted you.*

Not a problem. But could you do me a favor? Watch yourself. I know the adrenaline is still surging and you still feel combative, but try to be respectful to the council. They're my bosses and you might think they don't rule you, but the instant you did the spell, you fell under their jurisdiction.

But—

Nessia cleared her throat to regain their attention. "We did nothing," she said about Shona's parents. "It was the council thirty years ago that made that decision and carried out the punishment. Before you become indignant, let me tell you that I've reviewed the files and they were left with no choice. The Gineal survive by remaining unseen by humans, but your parents made little, even no effort to conceal their use of power. They were warned. Repeatedly. The council sent others to clean up the messes they left behind. Repeatedly. Their actions endangered their son and the entire Gineal people and the council did what they had to do."

Logan felt Shona's shock and he released her hand to put his arm around her and pull her close against his side. "With all due respect, Council Leader, that wasn't the nicest way to tell Shona she has family she knows nothing about."

Nessia, to Logan's surprise, actually appeared chagrined. "In that you are correct, laoch solas. My apologies for springing that on you so abruptly."

"Son? You mean I have a brother?"

He looked to the council, but no one there said a word. "Yes, you have a brother. His name is Creed Blackwood and he's a roving troubleshooter, which means he's the elite of the elite."

"Do you know him?" Shona asked.

"Only by reputation. He's older than I am and was already a rover when I first started training."

"Is there anything else I'm going to be surprised with?" she asked, looking first at him, then around the council table.

"There's probably a million other surprises waiting for you," Logan said quietly, "but as far as I know, this is the last of the personal shocks. Everything else should simply be related to the Gineal and magic in general."

"You're assuming that she's keeping her powers," Nessia broke in.

"I know the council has already made that decision, Ceannard. You gave it away when you mentioned something about being saddled with an impertinent dragon mage."

"So I did." For a minute, Logan thought Nessia might

smile, but she successfully squelched the urge. "What do we do with you, laoch solas?"

"I'm sure the council has decided my punishment as well."

Shona's muscles went rigid and she moved in front him. Logan tugged her back to his side and reminded her to back off.

Nessia inclined her head. "The favorite option was assigning you to the tasglann with the newly trained troubleshooters."

Logan scowled, then quickly smoothed out his expression. He'd known he'd probably end up guarding the library.

"However," Nessia continued, "after further discussion we chose another option. It will be your job to train the dragon mage in Gineal magic, history, and knowledge. You will also teach her how to fight as you were taught by your mentor."

For a moment, Logan could only stare. It was probably stupid to speak up, but . . . "Ceannard, I would have willingly done all these things. Teaching Shona isn't a punishment."

There was a moment of silence and Logan suspected they were communicating privately again. He knew he was right when Nessia nodded. He tensed, wondering if they'd reconsidered the library.

"You didn't have time to read any of the books we sent to your house, but had you gone through them, you would have discovered an interesting bit of information," Nessia spoke quietly, her hands folded in front of her. "We didn't realize what was occurring, mind you, until tonight. So, Dragon Mage, do not accuse us of deliberately keeping secrets."

Shona nodded and stepped back until she pressed against him. Logan put his arms around her without thought, but no one on the council looked angry, so he kept her in his embrace.

"You, laoch solas, share her armor. That's only possible between a dragon mage and his or her mate. It also explains why your first loyalty was to Shona and not the council. The books perhaps say the whys more clearly, but the gist of it is that once you met, the bonds began to form and strengthen—not just of the mind and body, but of the heart and soul as well."

Nessia paused and Logan had a sense she was trying to find the right words. "Tonight, everything reached the tipping point and locked into place. The armor will remain around you permanently, leaving you with no need of protection spells any longer. You've probably already noticed that no mind shield keeps her out of your head or keeps you from knowing her thoughts; that, too will remain and grow stronger. No power sharing, unfortunately, but you'll learn things from her that she does instinctively, so your own arsenal will expand over time."

It took him a minute to read between the lines and then Logan grinned. "You mean she's stuck with me."

"As you are stuck with her, laoch solas, but her audacity seems to please you. Heaven knows why."

Shona snuggled close to Logan on the chaise longue made for two. She'd wanted to sit out on the porch to enjoy the night, and though it was close to midnight now, she wasn't ready to move. "I think I like Nessia, although at first it looked as if we were going to have a showdown. Pistols at high noon."

"More likely magic at high noon—you and me against the nine ceannards."

"Me and Nessia," Shona corrected. Her cheeks heated as she remembered her behavior in front of the council. She'd been raised better than that. Logan had excused it by saying it was the adrenaline she was dealing with, but that wasn't a good enough reason.

"Nope, your enemy is my enemy so it'll always be you and me. Nessia and the council come as a unit, too. It would definitely be an interesting measure of just how strong the dragon mage is, but I'd just as soon let some other mage run that test."

It'll always be you and me. Shona felt her throat constrict. "I don't like that you had no choice," she said quietly. "Now you're *stuck* with me whether you like it or not."

"I had a choice," Logan said, following her thoughts easily.

"That's not what the council implied. Isn't that why they didn't punish you for disobeying orders, because you had no choice about me or your actions concerning me?"

"I had a choice, Shona." She started to argue, but he hugged her and she subsided. "I had the dracontias in my hand, all I had to do was lift it over your head and do the spell to erase your memories of it."

She turned so she could see his eyes, his face.

"I didn't just spend two seconds thinking about it or go only on my heart. I debated, let my emotions cool, so that I was logical, rational and I looked at my options from all directions. I knew then that I was facing probably the biggest crossroads I ever would and that whichever direction I went would affect the rest of my life. And after all that, I chose you. I chose us."

She could feel the truth and that relieved her worry. With a smile, Shona settled back against his side and said, "I'm glad. I wanted you to want me, not be trapped by me."

His hand stroked down her arm. "If anyone didn't have a choice, it was you."

"Now you're the one who's wrong. I chose to call you after you left your jacket with me, I chose to meet you instead of mailing that jacket back, and I chose to say yes every time you asked me to do something with you. I was choosing all along."

"And against your friend's advice."

"Yeah." Her contentment was replaced by worry. "Do you think they'll find Farran?"

"I don't know; the council promised to keep looking for her, but if she doesn't want to be found, the monitors are going to have a hard time picking her up. After she's had time to calm down, she'll probably call, you know. You're her best friend."

"Does she realize we're still friends, though? I was mad when the two of you did your magic thing and she might believe that I don't care about her any more, that her secrecy ended our friendship. Farran grew up differently than we did, you know, and her father is a completely amoral sociopath."

"Her father is a darksider. In our world we might consider him a sociopath, but remember, different dimensions have different standards of behavior, of right and wrong."

"Lesson one from my teacher?"

She felt his amusement. "I believe lesson one took place in the restroom at the Covington Gallery. I'm not sure what lesson we're on now. I'll think about it and get back to you."

"Smart aleck."

Logan was quiet for a minute, then he said, "You know when Kel finds out that I have to help you learn about the Gineal and everything else, he's going to laugh his head off. He's been giving me a hard time about not studying enough." He pressed a kiss into the top of her hair. "I guess we better start by you learning Cànan, otherwise I'll have to translate most of the books for you."

"I can already read it, but you can help me learn to speak it."

He sat up, dislodging her from her comfortable position. "What do you mean, you can read it? That isn't possible."

"Yes, it is. I've got access to your mind, remember? And dragons have a natural talent for languages. I haven't heard you speak enough of it, though, to learn the pronunciation, but after a couple of days of listening, I should have that, too."

Logan looked at her for a minute, shrugged, and settled back down. Gathering her against him, he said, "Good, that'll make everything easier."

Her mind hopped back to an earlier subject. "Farran's father and one of the others got away. Do you think they'll return? Do you think they'll go looking for Farran to hurt her? Or come after us again?"

"I don't know." Logan wrapped his arms more firmly around her. "After what happened tonight, they'd have to be pretty stupid to go after you, but attacking once they knew you'd merged with the stone was moronic anyway. It had to be revenge or spite or something. As for Farran, she betrayed them and the Tàireil don't take that lightly. That might be why she ran off."

Another reason why they needed to find her first, Shona decided. She'd keep at the council—politely and respectfully. They had promised, after all.

Neither of them said anything for a while, but simply being quiet with Logan was nice. It seemed as if there hadn't been much of that since they'd met.

"There are dragons in the lake," he said against her ear.

"They're back!"

"Back?"

Shona started to explain, realized it would take too long and just sent him the information mentally. It was a strange way to communicate, but it also came in handy.

"No, humans can't see them," Logan said, picking up on a concern she hadn't meant to share. "At least most humans can't."

"They have children."

"Don't worry, they'll be safe. Dragons have been traveling between their dimension and this one practically since they left. Believe me, they know how dangerous humans are."

"Since they left?"

"Another lesson for later."

"Yeah. I wonder why they're here now?"

Logan shrugged. "Maybe they just wanted to go for a swim. Who knows? Dragons do what they like. They always have."

Shona watched the water until the dragons submerged from sight. "They never stay long," she said wistfully.

"The energy here's hard for them."

"Why?"

"Another lesson—"

"—for later," she finished in unison with him. "Why not now?"

"Because now, I just want to hold you, think about the fact that we've got forever, and to work up enough courage to tell you that I love you without a handy escape route."

Shona froze, then propped herself up on his chest so she could see his face. "I know. I can feel it as plainly as I do my love for you."

"I know that, but it still needs to be said out loud. Words carry power." He took a long, deep breath. "I love you, Shona."

And when she felt the kick around her heart, she knew he'd been exactly right—words did hold power even if they were blurted out. "I love you, too, Logan."

"There. We both did it and survived." He grinned. "Barely."

Shona couldn't help but return the smile. The fear that had risen with saying how she felt had been surprising, but the more she did it, the easier it would get. Right?

"That's my theory." He kissed her briefly. "So, will you marry me?"

The question thrilled her. Of course she wanted to marry him, but did that mean the mating thing the council leader talked about didn't count? "But we're already mated for life, aren't we?"

"I know that, you know that, the council knows that, but your parents don't, or my family, or the rest of the Gineal for that matter, and humans? Not a chance. And since I want the whole world to know you're mine, we'll have to get married."

That made Shona smile. "I like that idea. I want it known that you belong to me, too."

"Then you're saying yes?"

"Not just yes, hell yes!"

Logan looked relieved. Had he really thought that she might turn him down? Shona leaned forward to kiss him. "My parents are going to want to meet you and they're not going to like that we're getting married after knowing each other such a short time."

"Long engagement? You'll be living here anyway, right?"

"That might work to ease their worries. And I kind of figured I'd been moved in when you transported all my clothes and everything out of my bathroom here. There's just one thing."

"Yeah?" he sounded anxious.

"I want to redecorate. This house doesn't fit either one of us like it is now."

She got another one of his grins. "Do whatever you want to it, it's fine with me." Logan sobered. "And we'll build you a studio next to my garage so that when your desire to work on your art comes back, you'll have your own space."

Shona tried to pull away, but Logan tightened his hold. "It's not coming back," she told him. "Your council said so."

"They don't know everything. Just think, you can make your glass and I'll work on my cars, and we'll meet out here for sex."

She glared at him.

"Or lunch. We can save sex for the bedroom." He winked at her, then became dead serious. "I know your creativity's going to come back. I feel it here." He put a hand over his heart. "The dracontias is part of you, but it's not everything. You still have room for me and you'll find out one day that there's room for your glass, too."

She wanted to believe, but. . . .

"The first piece you make after you start working again is going in our house," Logan said. "Right where you can see it every day and know that your mate is never wrong."

Shona sputtered, then laughed. "Damn, I love you—even if you are going to be a pain."

But he believed in her even when she didn't believe in herself. A man like that was worth hanging on to.

Epilogue

FIVE WEEKS LATER

Shona stepped out on the back patio, a plate full of sliced buns in her hand. She paused for a moment, enjoying the scene in front of her—she was part of a big family now. Logan's dad was manning the grill with Keavy beside him, but she wasn't helping. When they'd arrived, she'd run to Logan asking him to talk their dad into buying her a new car. She hadn't liked Logan's answer and Shona would bet that Keavy was still pleading her case.

Tris and Kel were playing badminton, Iona was at the table, studying, and Logan had been sent to the store on a last-minute grocery mission. Shona walked over and put the plate down in the center of the picnic table.

"Does Mom need help in the kitchen?" Io asked.

"I don't think so. I just got shooed out of there."

"She's about done then. Mom never dismisses anyone from kitchen duty early." Io bent her head to her book again, but raised her gaze back to Shona. "Sorry. I have a test tomorrow."

"You don't have to entertain me."

"Thanks." Iona went back to her textbook.

Shona walked over to watch the game. This Labor Day cookout was the third Andrews family event she'd taken part in and she'd quickly learned to keep a safe distance when Tris took on one of her older brothers—especially Kel. Logan would let her win when he'd had enough, but Kel never gave in and neither did Tris.

"Hey, hon," Logan said, coming up beside her and putting his arm around her waist. "Miss me?"

"You were only gone fifteen minutes." But she had missed him and turned toward him to get a proper hello.

"I missed you. Why don't we sneak off behind the gazebo, so I can kiss you the way I want."

"This isn't going to be like the gallery restroom incident, is it?" she teased, willingly walking with him across the lawn.

Logan laughed. "Of course not. If you get desperate for me, my parents have bathrooms, too, you know."

He could still make her blush, darn it, but that didn't stop her from giving it right back to him. "If I get desperate, we can use a transit, pop home, have a quickie, and return. How fast can you come?"

"The correct question is how fast can I make *you* come." Logan winked at her and Shona felt her cheeks burn. She conceded the round to him.

Reaching down with her thumb, she touched the back of her ring. It had become a habit, a way to make sure it was all real. The long engagement had calmed both families and besides, her parents weren't scheduled to return from London for another eight months. Shona wanted her mom's help in planning the wedding every step of the way.

"Alone at last," he said and drew her against him.

Shona put her arms around his waist. "We don't have long; the food should be off the grill soon."

"We have a little while. Keavy is distracting Dad."

Logan lowered his head to hers, his lips brushing over her mouth softly before he came back for another, longer kiss.

With a sigh of contentment, Shona leaned into him and invited him to deepen the embrace before they ran out of time. She was completely immersed in him when someone cleared their throat.

"Get lost, Kel," Logan said, his lips still against hers.

"It's not Kel."

Logan jerked his head up and she heard him groan. It wasn't a sound of arousal. "Oh, hell," he muttered.

Shona turned to see who was standing there, but the man was a stranger. Something about him, though, made her uneasy and she moved closer to Logan before she remembered that she was the dragon mage and could kick butt on her own.

The man was a couple of inches taller than Logan with shoulder-length, wavy black hair and dark brown eyes. She pegged his age in his mid thirties and there was no missing the challenge in his gaze. Shona lifted her chin. If he planned to take on Logan, he was taking on her, too. She'd defend her mate against anyone and anything.

"Er, hon, before you decide to zap him, let me introduce you. This is Creed Blackwood, your older brother. Creed—sir," he corrected when the man stared at him even more coldly, "this is Shona. The woman I'm going to marry."

Shona had to bite her lower lip to keep from laughing. Logan couldn't really be nervous about this guy, could he? Okay, so meeting her brother in the middle of a passionate kiss wasn't ideal, but it could be worse. Somehow.

"You look like my dad—a little," she said grudgingly.

"A lot," Creed corrected her. "I saw you once before, you know. You were like nine and riding around on your bike."

She nodded and turned to Logan. "Did you know he was going to be here today?" she asked.

"No, I didn't. I'd never let you be ambushed like this."

"It was my idea; no one was alerted beforehand," Creed said. "You've been avoiding me."

"Maybe I wasn't ready to meet you yet." Glaring, she took a step closer to him.

"Maybe some things are easier if you do them fast instead of thinking about them forever." He stepped closer, too, and glared back at her.

"Maybe you're right. Am I going to like you?"

"With my charm, you won't be able to help yourself."

Logan's snort changed to a cough when Creed looked past her. "Why don't you join us for dinner?" Logan asked.

Shona threw him a thank-you glance. This was weird and she didn't know how to react, didn't know what to say to this man who was her brother yet ultimately a stranger. Having him come to dinner would give her time to calm down, time to get her nerves under control. "Yes, please join us for dinner."

And something in Creed's face seemed to soften, although it was hard to tell. He offered her his arm and Shona took it, then reached her free hand out for Logan. They returned to the patio at an easy pace, Shona tucked between the two men.

"You should have bought her a diamond ring," Creed said over the top of her head.

"I tried. She wanted the sapphire."

Creed grunted. "The least you could have done was spring for a few more carats."

"I tried. She said she didn't want something that weighed more than a boat anchor." Logan sounded aggrieved.

"So she's stubborn then?" Creed asked.

"You have no idea how—"

"Hey," Shona interrupted. "I'm right here you know."

"Believe me," Logan said, "I always know exactly where you're at." It was that protective streak of his, but Shona wasn't about to complain.

"If we invite him to the wedding," she asked Logan, "is it going to be a problem with my parents?" Creed Blackwood might be a pain in the butt, but he was family.

"It won't be," Creed answered. "I won't let it be."

"Logan?"

"You can trust his word."

"Okay then." She looked up at Creed. "You're invited."

"Thanks."

Shona pulled to a halt as she noticed another stranger on the patio. "Who's that?"

"My wife," Creed said, his tone warm. "I'll introduce you."

It was dark and she and Logan were the only two left outside, but she wasn't ready to leave yet or go indoors. Lanterns cast a dim glow over the yard and magic kept the bugs at bay. Shona ran her fingers up and down the inside of his thigh, but she restricted her touch to down around his knee.

"Creed's abrasive," she said.

"He has that rep."

"I think I like him anyway. And his wife."

"I'm glad." Logan put his arm around her shoulders and tucked her closer to his side.

"It's going to get complicated, you know, trying to remember what I can and can't say to my parents."

"That's what the council was concerned about." Logan paused. "Do you wish I'd done what they told me to do? If I'd taken the dracontias, you could have had a normal life."

"Normal's overrated. I'd rather have you."

"Thanks. I think."

Shona turned toward him and with her free hand caressed his cheek. "I love you, Logan. I wouldn't trade my life now for anything—not even my glass work."

"I love you, too, Shon, and I still think you'll get your creative ability back."

"I know you do." He'd actually hired an architect to design a studio for her just like he'd said, but Shona didn't share his optimism. "But the stone is all-consuming. I feel it."

"We'll see."

It was his standard answer and one she couldn't argue with. They would, indeed, see. She kissed him softly. "Let's dance."

"There's no music."

"Sure there is. Hear the crickets? Nature's playing our song."

They barely moved, but Shona was in Logan's arms, right where she wanted to be. The dracontias was pressed between them, pulsing in time with her heart and the breeze was warm, although she could feel a taste of fall beneath the balminess.

Logan sent her a vision, the two of them dancing like this when they were old and gray. What they had would last forever. She knew it. Logan knew it.

Dragons mated for life.